Twenty years ago Kylie Chan married a Hong Kong national in a traditional Chinese wedding ceremony in Eastern China. She and her husband lived in Australia for eight years, then in Hong Kong for ten years. She has seen a great deal of Chinese culture and come to appreciate the customs and way of life.

Two years ago she closed down her successful IT consultancy company in Hong Kong and moved back to Australia. She decided to use her knowledge of Chinese mythology, culture, and martial arts to weave a story that would appeal to a wide audience.

Since returning to Australia, Kylie has studied kung fu (Wing Chun and Southern Chow Clan styles) as well as tai chi and is now a senior belt in both forms. She has also made an intensive study of Buddhist and Taoist philosophy and has brought all of these together into her storytelling.

Kylie is a mother of two who lives in Brisbane.

Books by Kylie Chan

Dark Heavens

White Tiger (1)
Red Phoenix (2)
Blue Dragon (3)

BLUE DRAGON

DARK HEAVENS: BOOK THREE

青
龍

KYLIE CHAN

HARPER
Voyager

HarperVoyager
An imprint of HarperCollinsPublishers
77–85 Fulham Palace Road,
Hammersmith, London W6 8JB

www.harpercollins.co.uk

This paperback edition 2011
1

First published in Australia by
Voyager 2007

A catalogue record for this book is
available from the British Library

ISBN: 978 0 00 734981 4

Set in Sabon 9.5/12 by Helen Beard, ECJ Australia Pty Ltd

Printed and bound in Great Britain by
Clays Ltd, St Ives plc

MIX
Paper from
responsible sources
FSC® C007454

*The water brightened. The Serpent drifted upwards.
The sunlight made streaks of vivid blue in the water.
The Serpent reached the surface and lay, unmoving,
just beneath.
It raised its head slightly above the water, then
dipped it below again.
It cried.
There was no answer.*

CHAPTER ONE

I tapped gently on the door. 'Mum? Dad?'
'Come in, sweetheart.'

I opened the door and sidled in. My father was rummaging through his suitcase on the desk. My mother was further inside, folding clothes on the bed.

'You okay, guys?' I said.

Both of them smiled weakly at me.

'You don't need to worry now,' I said. 'That attack's been coming for a while. I think he threw everything he had at us. It's finished. It'll be quiet for a long time.'

My mother came into the little sitting room and gestured for me to sit next to her on the couch. Her bright blue eyes were serious under her short greying brown hair, and her long, kind face seemed more lined than usual. 'Does that sort of thing happen often?'

'Small attacks, all the time. Big ones like that, no. That's only the second or third time we've had so many demons thrown at us at once.' I paused and thought about it. 'No, actually more than that.' I smiled an apology. 'We had about five demons come into the apartment when the Mountain was attacked last January. Then a couple of dozen came at us in China last April. The King of the Demons himself threw about

3

fifty small ones and a dozen big ones at us in London, August of this year, and then straight after that the little bastard who came after us last night had a go at us with a big group at Jennifer's house.' I counted them up. 'Four, not counting last night.'

'Jennifer's house? You mean your sister Jennifer?' my mother said. 'Oh, that's right, Leonard works for Mr Chen. *Jennifer* was attacked? So she knows all about this?'

'Yes. But Jennifer wasn't attacked. They attacked us, at her house. Her family weren't threatened at all, from what I could see.'

'She never mentioned it,' my father said.

'I don't think she wants to dwell on it,' I said. 'It was a very frightening experience for all of them. We've posted guards at their house, but no more demons have gone anywhere near them. The demons are after us. Wong wants to take John's head to the King.'

'They have a King?' my father said, coming to sit next to me. Close up, the deep lines around his blue eyes made his tanned, leathery face look older. He studied me with concern.

'Yeah. Big red-headed bastard. The little creep who came after us last night is his son. The King's said that anyone who can bring him John's head will be promoted to Number One son.'

'They want his head?' my mother said.

'John — Xuan Wu — is the mightiest demon killer ever to exist. He ran them all off the face of the Earth a long time ago and they hate him. While he's weak like this, they'll keep attacking him. If they get his head, he'll be gone for a very long time.'

'What do you mean "gone"?' my father said. 'Dead?'

'No. If they take his head, he'll revert to True Form. He'll change into a turtle, combined with a snake, and have to go away for a long time to recover from the

4

exertion of maintaining his human form to stay with Simone and me.'

'He'd change into a *what*?' my mother said.

I sighed. 'Yeah, I know it's weird. Even the other Shen say he's strange, and they're all completely unbelievable themselves.' I explained before she could ask. 'They're called Shen . Spirits. Not really gods, but that's the closest word in English we have for it.'

'So this guy you're engaged to isn't a human being at all,' my father said. 'He's some sort of animal spirit.'

'Got it in one. He's the Spirit of the North, Emperor of the Dark Northern Heavens, a combination of a serpent and a turtle.' They both opened their mouths and I answered before they could ask. 'Yep. That's right. He's *two* animals. And it gets weirder. The Serpent is missing. Gone. Right now he's just the Turtle.' I spoke more softly. 'It's killing him to be divided like this. The Serpent is out there somewhere, looking for him, and he misses it terribly.'

'Christ. Then that Tiger guy . . .' my father began.

'Yep. He's really a white tiger.'

My mother's mouth flopped open. 'We had dinner the other night with a *tiger*?'

'Remember what Leo told you — that he's about the only normal human member of the household? He's right,' I said. 'John is a turtle. The Tiger, Bai Hu, is a white tiger. Gold is a rock, Jade is a dragon — you saw her. Simone is half Shen; she may take some sort of animal form when she grows up but she's the first human child John's ever had so it'll be interesting to see what she grows into. Michael is half Shen too, half tiger, being the Tiger's son. He may be able to transform too.'

'All right. So why were you a snake, love? You're one of us,' my father said.

I ran my hands through my hair. 'I honestly don't know. The whole thing has me really worried.'

5

'The lady last night,' my father said. 'What was her name?'

'Kwan Yin. Goddess of Mercy.'

'She said that being with him has changed you,' my father said.

'Has it?'

'Frankly?' my mother said. 'Yes.'

'In what way?'

My parents shared a look. My father shrugged. They both smiled slightly at me.

'You have no idea at all,' I said.

Neither of them said anything.

'Would you say that I'm more cold-blooded?'

My mother shifted. 'I wouldn't say that you're *cold-blooded*, dear —'

'Yes,' my father said. 'You always were a bit of a heartless bitch, but now you seem even more heartless.'

My mother was horrified. 'Brendan!'

'Last night, when we were threatened by those things. She was only worried about Simone; she didn't even seem to notice us. When that black guy, Leo, said he wanted to die for them, what did she say? "Fight well."' He turned to me. 'You were quite happy to let him go in front of you and die, Emma.'

'So was John.'

'Yeah. He's unbelievably cold-blooded too.'

'You don't know everything about Leo, Dad. He's terminally ill, he has AIDS. For him, to die on the battlefield protecting us would be the greatest thing in the world. I sincerely hope he doesn't die in a hospital bed. He deserves much better.'

'Oh my God,' my mother said softly, her eyes wide.

'Are you worried about catching it?' I said. 'I thought I knew you better than that.'

My mother snapped out of it and focused on me. 'You just said that you hope he doesn't live as long as he can, that you hope he can die sooner, in a fight. You really *are* cold-blooded.'

'She is learning our ways and attaining the Tao,' the stone in my ring said. 'She is becoming detached and part of the *One*.'

My parents cast around, bewildered.

'Who spoke?' my father said. 'Sounded like an Englishman.'

I showed them the ring. 'The stone talks. And I wish it would *shut up* sometimes.'

'My Lady, your mother has a headache and needs her morning caffeine hit, and your father is starving,' the stone said. 'Stop talking their ears off and take them to have some breakfast.'

'He's right,' my father said ruefully.

'Do not refer to me as *he*!' the stone snapped. 'Gender is reserved for you animals. We stones are above that sort of weakness. I don't know why I give you the benefit of my wisdom when you insult me so casually.'

'Come on, guys,' I said, rising from the couch and opening the door to lead them out.

'Why do you put up with that, Emma?' my father said. 'I'd be throwing that bloody thing down the toilet.'

I sat my parents down at the kitchen table. 'Where's Simone?' I asked Ah Yat.

Ah Yat concentrated a moment. 'Miss Simone and Master Leo are in the training room together.'

'And Lord Xuan?'

'Right here,' John said from the doorway. He came in and sat at the table across from my mother. 'Morning, Brendan, Barbara. Tea, *tikuanyin*,' he ordered without looking at Ah Yat. Ah Yat busied herself with the teapot while my mother's coffee infused.

7

I glared at him. 'Stand up.'

His face went rigid and he didn't move.

'Celestial Highness Emperor Xuan Wu of the Dark Northern Heavens, you stand up right now,' I said.

His face went wry and he rose, pushing his chair back.

I moved as close as I could to him while still remaining safe. He towered over me, a good head taller. His long hair was already coming out from its tie. It was more than four months since his last energy session with Ms Kwan and he was running low. He looked in his late forties; his hair had turned grey at the temples. He smiled slightly at me and his eyes wrinkled up.

I pointed at his black cotton pants. 'They were new. Leo bought them only a couple of weeks ago.'

He glanced down. They already had a hole in the left knee.

'You did that deliberately to annoy me, didn't you?' I said fiercely. 'To get me back for throwing those old ones away. I *told* you not to wear them for Short Weapons.'

He threw himself down again and pulled his chair closer to the table. Ah Yat presented him with the tea and he poured for himself. 'I am a creature of my word, and it was an accident,' he said. He turned to my parents. 'Has she always been this impossible?'

'You are absolutely the scruffiest Immortal I have ever met,' I huffed. 'I'm surprised your Celestial Form is so tidy. Your armour doesn't have any holes in it. Why do your clothes?'

'That is extremely good coming from you,' John said mildly. 'Look at your jeans.'

I glanced down at my jeans and felt my face redden. I pulled a chair out and sat next to my father. 'I didn't know that was there.'

8

'My Lord Mr Donahoe, my Lady Mrs Donahoe, what may I prepare for you?' Ah Yat said.

'Just Brendan, and if you have any cornflakes that'd be great. Otherwise, whatever's going,' my father said.

'Just some fruit and toast, please,' my mother said.

Ah Yat nodded, smiled, and disappeared. Both my parents jumped.

'No cornflakes,' I said. 'She's gone to buy you some.'

'Speaking of armour, I must have some made for you,' John said.

'Don't worry about it. Right now, every attack's an ambush so there's no point,' I said. 'And how come I came back with clothes on last night? I shouldn't have been able to conjure them.'

'What are you talking about?' my father said.

'When we transform, we lose the clothes. Of course,' John said.

'The Tiger loves it,' I cut in. 'Shocking exhibitionist.'

'*Anyway*,' John said, glaring at me, 'we conjure the clothes when we return to human form.'

'But I shouldn't have been able to do that,' I said.

'Obviously the Serpent in you could,' John said. 'The stone was right: we must start some more advanced training with you. Who knows what you'll be able to do? Try something now,' he said, sitting straighter. 'Try calling me.'

I thought hard at him.

'Nothing,' he said, sounding disappointed.

I shrugged. 'Not surprising. The snake's probably hiding right now.'

Ah Yat appeared with the cornflakes and placed the breakfast things on the table in front of my parents.

'Thanks,' my father said and poured the cereal. 'How old are you, John?'

'I have no idea,' John said.

'You look about forty or forty-five,' my mother said.

'Yeah,' I said. 'Far too old for me.'

'I'm probably in the region of four to four and a half thousand years old,' John said amiably. 'I have no recollection of being born. I don't know exactly when I gained consciousness. I joined with the Serpent about three and a half thousand years ago.'

My parents stared at him, speechless.

'About three thousand years ago the human form was Raised and I was promoted to Dark Emperor,' John said, almost to himself. 'Celestial General. That sort of thing.'

'And you still haven't grown up,' I said. 'Tea, Ceylon. Toast with peanut butter, please, Ah Yat.'

Ah Yat disappeared again.

'Must have run out of peanut butter,' I said. 'Don't know why all the demons like it so much. Remind me later to ask her for a shopping list — we can order in bulk on the internet, have it delivered, and she can stop flitting around like that. People at the supermarket will notice.'

'She probably changes her form if she has to go twice in a row,' John said.

'Eat,' I said, gesturing towards my parents. 'You'll get used to it.'

'Why black?' my mother said. 'You only wear black. Everything. And Tiger the other night — he called you a Black Turtle. What was that about?'

'You know the Suzy Wong reference?' I said, and she nodded. 'Well, Black Turtle is Cantonese street slang for pimp. The turtle in general is renowned for its …' I grinned at John, '*behaviour*, and there are a lot of nasty insults surrounding it. It's not a good idea to say the word anywhere near anybody.'

Ah Yat appeared with a jar of peanut butter in her hand. She put it on the table in front of me.

'Did you pay for that?' I said.

Ah Yat didn't reply; she just turned and busied herself at the sink.

'You dishonour us, Ah Yat,' I said. 'Later, you will go back there, pick up one of these, pay for it and put it back on the shelf, and that is an order.'

'I'm a turtle egg,' John said.

Ah Yat silently collapsed over the sink.

'See?' I said. 'He just called himself a motherless bastard.'

'Well, I am,' John said mildly. 'I have no idea as to my origins or heritage. I just *am*.'

Ah Yat disappeared.

'Damn. I wish you'd stop doing that,' I said. 'It'll take ages for her to pull herself together and come back.' I turned to my parents. 'What would you like to do today? Would you like to see the Academy? Some kung fu? The students would love to show you.'

'Anything you like will be fine with us, Emma,' my mother said weakly.

'Sunday, Emma,' John said.

'Oh yeah, I forgot,' I said. 'I'll find Simone and let Leo go. He should have said something.'

'Go,' John said.

Leo and Simone were working with the sword together. Simone was using my weapon.

'Can you make it sing, Simone?' I said.

'Watch this.' Simone put the sword out in front of her and stilled. The sword made a pure resounding note of indescribable beauty. Simone ran it through a gentle scale, each note making the air vibrate in harmony. The sound stopped and she relaxed.

Leo and I stared at her with awe.

'That was wonderful,' I said. 'How come it sounds so splendid for you?'

'I used shen,' Simone said, 'not chi.'

'Does Mr Chen know you can do that?' Leo said.

Simone smiled and shook her head.

'We need to let Leo have his day off, Simone,' I said. 'I'm still having breakfast with my mum and dad. Want to sit with us?'

'Sure,' Simone said. 'I forgot, Leo, sorry. You go.'

Leo saluted us both and went out without saying a word.

'Can you do shen work apart from that, Simone?' I said as we went down the hall together.

'No. Just that. I did it by accident the first time. It sounds really pretty.'

We went into the kitchen together.

'Hello, Mrs Donahoe, Mr Donahoe,' Simone said.

'Hello, dear,' my mother said. 'Are you okay after last night? You weren't too scared?'

John grabbed his teapot and cup, nodded to my parents, and rose.

'Wait!' I said quickly, and he stopped in the doorway. 'Did you know that Simone can make the sword sing with shen?'

John glanced sharply at Simone, then returned to the table and put down the pot and cup. He pulled Simone to sit in his lap.

'You put shen into Emma's sword?' he said.

'It sounds really pretty when you use shen, Daddy,' Simone said. 'Much nicer than when you use chi.'

'Don't try to use ching, you're too little,' John said sternly.

'Don't be silly, Daddy,' Simone said. 'Of course not.'

My parents silently watched the exchange, bewildered.

'Good,' he said gently. 'Can you hold out your hands for me and put some shen into them?'

'Is that okay to do?'

'It should be all right while I'm holding you.'

Simone held her hands out and concentrated. A ball of pure silvery-white shen energy appeared above her outstretched palms.

My mother gasped quietly.

'How much do you have, do you think?' he said.

'I don't know. There's still a lot inside me.'

'Put it back, sweetheart.'

The shen disappeared.

'Is she already Immortal, John?' I said. 'You said only Immortals can work with shen.'

John put his hand on Simone's forehead and concentrated. 'No.'

'Well then, why can she do that?'

He smiled gently. 'Because she is who she is. Same as you.' He rested his chin on the top of her head. 'Don't do that too much, sweetheart, it can be dangerous. Don't do it unless I'm watching you.'

'Okay, Daddy,' Simone said. 'Where's Ah Yat? I'm *hungry*.'

'You're always hungry when you're working with energy,' I said.

Ah Yat appeared. 'Yes, my Princess?'

'Can I have some ramen, please, Ah Yat?'

Ah Yat bowed slightly. 'My Lady.'

'I have work to do. I'll leave you to it,' John said. 'When you want to go out, call me. I'll take you. There may be strays.' He nodded to my parents. 'Brendan, Barbara.' He rose and gently slid Simone onto the chair. 'Don't do shen work unless I'm with you.'

'What about the sword?'

'That too.'

'Okay, Daddy.' Simone hopped off the chair and went to the fridge to find some apple juice.

Emma, I need to talk to you, John said silently. *Come with me into my office.*

13

'I'll be right back,' I said to my parents. I glanced at my tea. 'I'll never finish this.'

Bring it with you.

'Good idea.'

My parents stared at me as if I was completely crazy.

'I *am* completely crazy,' I said. 'I'd have to be to put up with this.'

Too true.

'Enough!' I picked up my teacup and went out with John. Simone watched us go, her eyes sparkling with amusement.

Daddy just likes annoying you sometimes, she said silently.

'I will make a rule about this if you two don't stop it,' I said fiercely.

'What's going on?' my father said.

'You explain to them, Simone,' I said. 'Since you're so clever.'

I stopped at the doorway and watched. Simone concentrated on my parents over the top of her apple juice. They both jumped as if stung.

John sat behind his desk and I took one of the visitor's chairs. The desk was in an even worse mess than usual, probably a result of the end-of-year budgeting and the recruitment of the new novices.

'I wish I had time to go through this room properly,' I said. 'When my parents have left, I'll spend a whole day in here sorting this lot out. Even the Sanskrit.'

'Go right ahead.' He leaned forward over the desk. 'What Simone just did is exceptional.'

'I thought so,' I said. 'She's not even on the Celestial Plane.'

'Only the very few of the very largest of us can do that.' He leaned back and retied his hair. 'And she's not even Immortal yet.'

'You mean she may end up more powerful than you? I find that difficult to believe.'

'I don't think so. But she will certainly outshine many on the Plane. Emma, listen carefully.'

'I'm listening.'

'Stone.'

'My Lord,' the stone in my ring said.

'Record this.'

'Very good, my Lord.'

'Emma, I'm just having the stone record this so that you don't need to remember all of it. You and the stone can pass the instructions on to the Masters. Here goes.' He leaned his elbows on the desk. 'After I'm gone, I want Simone to learn travel, advanced energy weapons, summoning, and yin.'

'Yin?' the stone said.

'Record. Do not comment,' John said. 'I want her to learn level three binding. Up to level ninety taming. Shen; all aspects of shen work. If I have not returned by the time she is twenty years old, then ching as well. I want her to have Dark Heavens immediately both myself and Leo are gone. And when she is fourteen years old, Gold is to bring down Seven Stars for her.'

'When she's only fourteen?' I said softly.

'Yes. Unfortunately, nobody else besides me knows how to make it shine, so I'll tell you now, just in case.'

'I've never seen it shine,' I said.

'I wish you could,' John said, looking me straight in the eye. 'Right now I can't do it; I need to be near full strength and in Celestial Form. It is a sight to see. Hopefully you can pass the information on to Simone, and she will be able to make the sword resonate.' He glanced at the stone. 'Record this carefully.'

'I really am most profoundly honoured, my Lord,' the stone said softly. 'Are you sure you want to tell me this?'

'I think when Simone is about fourteen she will take some sort of Celestial Form,' John said. 'Based on what she did this morning, it is quite possible.' He dropped his head and grimaced. 'I won't see it.'

'What about a True Form?' I said.

He smiled and shrugged. 'No idea. I like to think she will be a Serpent, as you are.' He obviously had a sudden thought. 'Stop recording, stone.'

'My Lord,' the stone said.

'Emma,' he said, studying me intensely, 'you never named your own sword. Why not?'

'I just felt it was too pretentious.'

'It's easier to refer to the weapon by name, you know. Immortals can call weapons to them when the weapons have names.'

I sighed. 'I know. I just didn't feel right about it. It's just my weapon, nothing special. Same as me, nothing special.'

He made a soft sound of amusement but didn't rise to it. 'Did it occur to you that the blade may already have a name?'

'No, not at all,' I said. 'I never really thought about it too much, it was just my weapon. But I think I should give it to Simone now. It sings much more sweetly for her.'

'It is the Silver Serpent.'

'You're joking. The sword's name is the *Serpent*?'

'That is the Serpent?' the stone said.

'Yes,' he said to both of us. 'Begin recording again.'

'My Lord,' the stone said.

John looked down at his hands. 'To make Seven Stars resonate, Simone must be able to take a Celestial Form. Then she needs to light all the cauldrons and open all the gates. Do you know what a chakra is, Emma?'

'I know. But that's an Indian thing, not Chinese at

all. You have dan tian, cauldrons and gates, not chakras.'

'Same thing,' John said. 'Three cauldrons, the three dan tian. Three gates. One Inner Eye. Each corresponds to a chakra, there are seven altogether. There are seven cavities on the sword. One for each star, one for each chakra. She will need to load the sword with her own chakras for it to shine.'

'That will be an incredibly difficult process to master,' the stone said with awe. 'One wrong step and she could destroy herself.'

'I am well aware of that,' John said. 'I think she will be able to do it.'

'She'll be projecting her own dan tian into the sword?' I said softly.

'Yes. The sword will become perfectly aligned with her. She and the sword will protect each other. Part of her consciousness will enter the sword.' His eyes turned inwards and he smiled. 'The experience is incredibly euphoric when you do it right. The destructive power of the loaded weapon is immeasurable.'

'Under what circumstances would she need to use it, though? There probably won't be any demons that she'll need to fear anyway, once she's all the way there.'

'You are quite right, Emma,' John said. 'She will only need to use it if faced by an overwhelming force.' He leaned back. 'Now, go and talk to your parents.'

'How long do we have, Xuan Wu?'

His face went rigid. 'Not long.'

CHAPTER TWO

I went back with my tea and sat at the kitchen table. Simone was amusing my parents with stories of Zhu Que's chicks.

'The birds talk?' my mother said.

'They're not really birds —' I began.

'Yes, they are, silly Emma,' Simone said. 'They're really *birds*. Not really children at all.'

'They look like baby emus,' I said.

'What's an emu?' Simone said.

'I should take you to Australia again.'

'That would be fun,' Simone said. 'Maybe after Daddy has gone, and we don't have to worry about the demons so much. After he's killed One Two Two.'

My mother made a small sound and I glanced at her. Her face was unreadable.

I turned back to Simone. 'It's a deal. Maybe next Christmas. Even if he's still here, we'll go and take him for a swim in the sea.'

'What would you like to do today, Mrs Donahoe?' Simone said. 'Where would you like us to take you?'

'Any suggestions, Emma?' my father said through his cornflakes.

'It's difficult on a Sunday,' I said.

'Why, nothing open?' my mother said.

Simone giggled at that. My mother looked at her with bewilderment.

'Everything'll be open, Mum, that's not the problem,' I said. 'Hong Kong is very densely populated, and for many people Sunday is the only day off. So the shopping centres, the streets, everywhere, will be packed.'

'You can't move in the middle of Causeway Bay,' Simone said, still delighted. 'The ground floor of Sogo is packed. You can't even get in.'

'Sogo is a big Japanese department store in Causeway Bay,' I said. 'I don't know why, but everyone agrees to meet at the entrance on a Sunday. It's absolutely packed to the rafters with people.'

'Want to go *yum cha*?' Simone said. 'There's a couple of places that know Daddy, and we don't have to take a number.'

'Oh no, *please*, Simone,' I moaned, 'you know I can't eat anything there. Hardly any of it's vegetarian.'

'What?' my father said, still through the cornflakes.

I ran my hands through my hair. 'I'm mostly vegetarian now, guys. Sorry.'

'It's because Emma's becoming Immortal,' Simone said with relish. 'Human Immortals are vegetarian. Like Kwan Yin.'

The phone rang. I rose to get it, but John answered it in the study.

'Tell us about this Immortal stuff, Emma,' my mother said as I sat back down.

I was silent. I didn't want to go into detail about it.

'If a human being attains the Tao, then they become Immortal,' Simone said, her eyes sparkling. 'That's what Emma's doing.'

'Tao?' my father said.

'The Way,' I said. 'It's complicated. I'd prefer not to talk about it.'

'You are no fun at all sometimes, Emma,' Simone said, sounding much more mature than her six years.

John appeared in the doorway and leaned in to speak to us, one hand on either side of the frame. 'Emma, we have problems.'

My heart sank. 'Already?'

'Leo called from the dojo he teaches at on Sundays. It's in Causeway Bay. Michael's there. About fifty low-level demons have turned up at the front door seeking sanctuary.'

He stopped and went rigid, his eyes unfocused. Then he snapped back and smiled gently. 'More have turned up at Turtle's Folly. And about a hundred appeared outside the car park of Hennessy Road. Altogether, about two hundred demons, all over Hong Kong, all pleading for protection.'

The intercom next to the front door buzzed.

'Oh my God, no,' I said.

John answered it.

'Yes, Barnabas?' he said. 'How many? Okay. I'll be right down.'

He came back to the doorway, leaned in and smiled. 'About twenty downstairs. We have a busy day ahead of us.'

'What's going on, Emma?' my mother said weakly.

'What are we going to do?' I said. 'I wanted to show my parents around.'

'We can do that at the same time,' he said. 'You finish your breakfast; I'll go downstairs and sort out the demons here. Then we'll go to the Folly, then the dojo, then to Hennessy Road.'

'Do the dojo first,' I said. 'It doesn't belong to us. The owner will be upset if the demons don't disappear in a hurry. Does he know who you are?'

'No, you're quite right. He has no idea who I am, only that I'm one of the best there is. He knows I taught

Li. I'll do downstairs first, and then we can go to Causeway Bay.'

'Damn,' I said. 'What the hell will we do with two hundred demons?'

'I have no idea,' John said. 'All suggestions welcome.'

'What is this all about, Emma?' my father demanded.

'Explain while I go downstairs and sort them out,' John said.

'Can't a Master do this?' I wailed.

'Nope. Only a Celestial, and I'm the only one around today. Oh,' his face cleared, 'what a good idea. Simone.'

'Yes, Daddy?' Simone said through her noodles without turning around.

'Want to come and have a lesson in demon taming?'

'*Cool*!' Simone squealed. She jumped up and threw her chopsticks onto the table.

'I wonder if you can do it too,' John said, eyeing me appraisingly. 'Considering what you are. Stone.'

The stone didn't reply and I tapped it.

'Yes, my Lady?'

'Have a look at Emma. Do you think she can tame demons directly now?'

The stone was silent for a moment. 'Not right now. On the inside she appears to be a perfectly normal human being.'

'What about the Serpent?'

'Damn,' I said softly.

'Probably,' the stone said. 'But right now it's not there.'

'Okay,' John said. 'Just me and Simone then. Emma, you stay up here and keep your parents company. This will take about half an hour, then we'll all go down to Causeway Bay. Come on, Simone.'

Simone bounced to her father and grabbed his hand. 'I want a demon servant for myself!'

'No way!' I shouted at their backs. 'You do your own cleaning up!'

I heard the door open. 'You are no fun at all, Emma,' Simone said faintly just as the door closed.

'I do not appreciate being ignored like this,' my father growled.

'Sorry. We just had to organise what to do,' I said.

'What's the big problem?' my mother said.

'Demons have turned up on our doorstep looking for sanctuary — hundreds of them.' I ran my hands through my hair. 'There are different levels of demons, and the low-level ones are usually servants — except more like possessions — of the larger ones. When a really big demon gets annoyed, it usually takes it out on the small ones. The demon we saw last night is a really big one, a Prince, and he's particularly cruel to his thralls. Looks like just about every single one of them has tried to escape him and turned to us.'

'What is John going to do?' my mother said.

'First he has to check that they've really turned. Then he'll send them somewhere to work for him — although God knows what we'll do with two hundred demons. We really don't have the room for them.'

'I'm really beginning to wish that I'd never come to this awful place, Emma,' my mother said softly. 'And that you'd never come here either.'

'You'll be fine.' I tried to reassure her. 'When John and Simone come back up, we'll all go down to Causeway Bay and have a look at the shops while he sorts out the demons at the dojo. Don't worry, we'll be safe.'

'I don't know how you can live like this,' my father said. 'You act as if you're totally unafraid. As if it's the most natural thing in the world.'

'I hardly recognise you,' my mother whispered. 'You

22

aren't the girl that left Queensland six years ago to work in Hong Kong for a couple of years.'

'I'm still the same person.'

'You're a bloody *snake*!' my father cried. 'If that lady hadn't shown us inside you, I would swear you were a different person. That you aren't Emma at all.'

I didn't know what to say.

'Are you *sure* we'll be safe?' my mother said.

'Absolutely positive.' I tried to smile. 'Come on, you might enjoy yourselves. The shops around Causeway Bay are great fun.'

'Simone said something about Leo's mother hurting his mouth and that's why he has a speech impediment,' my father said from the front of the car as John drove us all down to the dojo. 'What happened?'

'Not *Leo's* mother, a *Snake Mother*,' Simone said patiently. She was sitting between my mother and me in the back seat. 'Snake Mothers are big demons.'

My parents glanced at me, questioning. I looked out the car window and didn't say anything.

'What did the demons do to him, Emma?' my mother said.

'They cut his tongue in half,' John said, without looking away from the road. 'Right down the middle. We were able to heal it, but he'll never speak clearly again.'

My parents were silent. I could picture their faces, but I still didn't look.

John made himself appear very old as we neared the Causeway Bay dojo.

'Have you been here before, Emma?' he said.

'Yeah,' I said. 'A couple of times, to pick up Leo.'

John eased the car up into the car park and parked it not far from the smaller Mercedes.

'Do you need a cover story?' I said before we stepped out of the car.

'No. I'll just be me, John Chen Wu. The owner of the dojo just knows my name and that I'm Leo's employer.' He grinned at me. 'Do I look about ninety?'

'At least.' I grinned back. 'Very cute.'

'He doesn't look cute, he looks *stupid*,' Simone said.

'Respect your elders,' John said sharply in a thin elderly voice.

Simone screamed with laughter.

'You okay to get around like that?' I said. 'You don't need help?'

'Nope,' he said in his usual voice, his dark eyes sparkling under his bushy white eyebrows. 'It's only the outside. The Dark Lord is inside, still as drained as ever.' He glanced at the car park lift. 'I hope Roland has a spare room where we can do this.'

'Come on, guys,' I said to my parents, who were watching us like frightened deer. 'Everything'll be fine. Let's sort out these demons, then we'll go to the shops.'

The dojo was on the eighth floor of a nondescript commercial building in the least glamorous part of Causeway Bay. The lift was tiny, old and filthy. My parents were not impressed.

The eighth-floor lobby was tiled with ghastly dark green tiles, and the walls were bare concrete stained black with smoke from the incense in the altars to the door gods.

Mr Pak had the whole floor of the building, his family had owned it for many years. The dojo's single door had a red demon-warding light above it, a small altar to the door god next to it, and a number of good-luck calligraphy papers stuck all around it. There was a huge metal gate in front of it, but that was left open during the day.

John banged on the door. Nothing happened. He stopped and concentrated.

Leo opened the door and poked his head around. 'My Lord. My Lady. Come on in, we have a lot of explaining to do.'

The whole dojo was a hubbub of voices. There must have been dozens of demons in the training rooms, but the hallway was deserted.

John stilled. The noise hushed immediately. There was complete silence.

'John, your hair's going black,' I whispered urgently. 'Try to hold the shape.'

John concentrated again and gained a few years.

'I do not believe this,' my father growled quietly.

'Maybe take your parents shopping while I sort this out,' John said to me.

'How many are there?'

'About seventy-five, but more are turning up all the time.'

Roland Pak charged down the hall towards us and shouldered Leo aside. 'What the hell is going on?' he shouted in Cantonese. 'Are these refugees from the mainland or something? Illegals? If you don't give me a good reason why I shouldn't call the police, I'll be hitting the phone soon and hitting it *hard*.'

'So sorry about this, Roland,' John said calmly in English. 'New students from the Mainland, came to the wrong address. Should have come to me.'

'Like I said, I gave the bus driver the wrong address, Roland,' Leo said, taking the blame. 'I should have given the bus driver the address of Mr Chen's place in Wan Chai, but I gave him the wrong card.'

'Hair, John,' I whispered under my breath.

'Just let me round them up and get them fixed,' John said amiably. 'I'll check their IDs and then send them over to my building.'

Roland studied John carefully.

I shot a glance at John. He was losing it.

John concentrated on Leo.

'Come with me, Roland,' Leo said, taking Roland's shoulder and turning him away. 'Let's go and have some coffee or tea or something while Mr Chen makes these students disappear.'

Roland shrugged Leo off and faced John. He studied him intensely.

I'm very drained, Emma, John said into my ear. *The last couple of days have taken a lot out of me. I don't think I can hold it.*

'Come on, Roland,' Leo said, trying to turn him around.

'Get your hands off me before I hit you,' Roland hissed. 'What the hell is going on here?'

He stared at John, who had reverted. He didn't look ninety any more, he looked about fifty, and his hair was almost completely black.

Roland's face became a mask of horror. '*Demon!*' he shouted and moved into a guard stance. '*What are you?*'

John completely lost it. He roared with laughter, then straightened and changed back to his normal middle-aged self. He grinned at Roland with delight. 'You think *I'm* a demon? You have seventy-five of them in here already and you think *I'm* a *demon?*'

Roland didn't shift.

'Sorry about this, Leo,' John said. 'Couldn't be helped.'

'Not your fault, my Lord,' Leo said. 'It'll be fun to tell him anyway. Can't wait to see the look on his face.'

'I want to be there too.' Michael came down the hallway and stopped behind Leo. 'I want to see his face when he finds out. I've been looking forward to this for a long time.'

'You three go and tell him everything,' I said. 'I'm taking Mum and Dad shopping.'

'I want to come too,' Simone said. 'I brought my wallet.'

'Go,' John said. 'If any demons approach you, send them up here.'

Roland stiffened when John said 'demons' but didn't move otherwise.

'Hi, Roland,' I said.

Roland didn't move or shift his gaze from John.

'Look behind you, at the end of the hallway.'

Roland still didn't move.

'See the altar at the end of the hallway there?'

'I know it's there,' Roland said.

'Who put it there?'

'Leo.'

'Yeah,' I said with a broad grin. 'Which god is it for?'

'Pak Tai.'

'Yeah, Pak Tai. Chen Wu,' I said. 'Leo put it there 'cause Leo works for *Chen Wu*.' I gestured towards John. 'This guy.'

Roland dropped his arms and his face went slack. 'No.'

'Come on, guys,' I said to my parents. 'Let the boys have their fun.'

'I think you spoiled their fun already, Emma,' Simone said with delight. 'That was great.'

'Call me when you have them all tamed,' I said as we left.

My parents' faces were white as we took the lift down to street level. I didn't know what to say.

'Can we go to Toys R Us, Emma?' Simone said. 'I have some money to spend.'

'How about we show my mum and dad some grown-up stuff?' I said. 'You can go to Toys R Us any day.'

'Oh, okay,' she said. 'Of course.' She looked up at my mother. 'What sort of things would you like to buy?'

My mother stared at Simone as if she were a creature from another planet.

'She's just a little girl, Mum,' I said.

'Yeah,' Simone said with a grin. 'Emma's the one that's the *snake*.'

Both my parents stiffened.

'Damn,' I said softly. I raised my voice and tried to sound cheerful. 'Let's go to the China Products store. There's a lot of great stuff there from the Mainland — Chinese handicrafts. You said you wanted to see that, right, Mum?'

My mother watched me, silent.

'Are you okay?' Simone said.

Neither of my parents spoke.

What's the matter with them, Emma? Simone said into my ear.

'Come on, guys,' I said. 'Let's go and be tourists. Perfectly ordinary, normal tourists.'

CHAPTER THREE

*F**inished, Emma, come on back.*

'John's finished with the demons at the dojo,' I said. 'We'll go back and move on to Bright Mansions.'

When we reached the dojo, Roland Pak was in his office with John, beaming with delight.

'Where's Leo and Michael?' I said.

'In one of the training rooms,' John said. 'Leo's teaching a group of youngsters. Michael's assisting.'

'Come in, come in,' Roland said to my parents. 'Come. Sit.'

He rose and gave his seat to my mother, and gestured towards an empty chair for my father. The tiny office was a squeeze with all of us in there. Simone climbed into her father's lap.

'You can throw chi too, Emma?' Roland said, leaning one hip on the desk.

'Yep,' I said, standing behind my father and resting my hands on his shoulders. 'I'm about ten times as good as Michael.'

'And that's just in human form,' John said. 'In Serpent form she's another ten times better than that.'

My parents stiffened and I glared at John, but Roland's grin didn't shift.

'Where did you put them all?' I said.

'I sent them up to the Mountain. Construction will move three times more quickly with so many extra hands, even if they are unskilled. I may have some of them taught to use heavy equipment; we're short on bulldozer operators to clear the rubble.'

'One Two Two's really done us a huge favour then,' I said. 'On to Happy Valley.'

'How about I drop you at the Jockey Club clubhouse in the Valley on the way?' John said. 'You can have lunch there while I sort the demons out.'

'Uh,' Roland began. 'Before you go . . .'

'Yes, Roland?' John said.

'You want me to show you some stuff, don't you,' I said.

Roland nodded.

'Oh, of course,' John said, leaning back. 'Least we can do for you, Roland, after putting you through all of this. Imagine having a hundred demons turn up at your front door like that. I'll get someone to set seals on the studio early next week.' John rose and slid Simone off his lap. 'Do you have a free room we can use?'

'Come this way,' Roland said, his grin even wider.

'You guys can stay here and wait for me, if you like,' I said to my parents.

'I'd like to see, Emma,' my father said. 'Barbie?'

My mother nodded, silent.

Your mother's not talking much, Simone said into my ear. *Is she okay?*

'If it's all too much for you, just say so, Mum,' I said, linking my arm into my mother's and giving her a squeeze as I led her out into the hall. 'I'll take you home and let you rest.'

'I'm okay,' my mother said softly. 'I want to see.'

Roland took us down the hall, past the room where Leo had resumed his lesson, to another training room.

It was only about three metres square and didn't have any mirrors. One wall was windows overlooking the busy Causeway Bay street. I jammed my foot into the mats on the floor to test them: not as good as the ones up on the Peak, just cotton wadding. But they would do.

'What would you like to see, Roland?' I said.

'Siu Lim Tao,' Roland said.

'You're joking. The basic Wing Chun set?'

'I'm impressed, Roland,' John said. 'Good thing to ask for. If Emma performs the set for you, you will see it done by a true Grand Master, in perfection. You should take a video.'

'I can't do it perfectly,' I said, annoyed. 'Nobody can.'

'Not even me?' John said with a grin.

I glared at him. He could see that I wanted to thump him and his grin widened. 'Do it, Emma. If Roland can find any imperfection in your performance of the set, I will be very impressed indeed.'

'I'm going to do the basic set of moves for one of the more lethal types of Chinese kung fu,' I said to my parents. 'But the most effective styles are the least impressive to look at. Don't expect too much, okay? After I've done this for Roland I'll do some pretty stuff for you. And I'm not a Grand Master, Roland. Call me *sigung* and I'll be very cross indeed.'

'*Sigung*,' John said loudly. He dropped to the floor to sit cross-legged and pulled Simone into his lap, holding her around the waist.

'When I am able to touch you again,' I said, moving into position, 'old man,' I flipped my fists and moved into Wing Chun stance, 'I really am going to beat,' I punched with my left fist and then my right, 'the living crap out of you.'

'Stop,' Roland said, and I froze. 'Sorry. Apologies. But you didn't do a signature.'

'A signature?' my mother said.

I nodded, still with my right fist out. 'That's right. Each Master adds a small move to the start of the set. All of their students do that move first, to acknowledge the Master who taught them. It's like the Master's signature.'

'But you didn't do one,' Roland said.

'No. She was taught by me,' John said.

'Oh,' Roland said softly.

I worked through the rest of the set, finished and saluted. I was greeted with complete silence.

I looked at my parents; their faces were frozen in masks of restraint. They weren't impressed at all.

John and Simone smiled indulgently.

Roland grinned like an idiot.

'Emma,' John said, 'show it to Roland at full speed.'

'Some of it's meant to be done slow.'

'Show him the fast bits at full speed.'

'Okay.'

That didn't take much time at all; at full speed I moved through the set very quickly. My hands were a blur.

I stopped and saluted again. Once again there was complete silence.

Then, 'I couldn't see your hands,' my mother whispered.

Roland had a huge smile on his face and tears ran down his cheeks. He spun and went out. 'Don't go anywhere,' he called from the hallway. 'I'll be right back.'

'Roland's seen Michael do energy work. Do some for your parents,' John said.

'Okay,' I said. 'Do you want to see me throw energy?'

'What does it involve?' my father said.

'I take some of my personal energy and push it outside my body. It's difficult to explain. Might be

32

better if I just showed you. Don't be scared, I won't hurt you. If it bothers you, just say so and I'll stop.'

Both my parents stiffened but remained silent.

'You sure you want to see?' I said.

'Show us,' my father said, and my mother nodded.

I generated a small ball of chi, only about the size of a tennis ball. I held it on my hands and waited as they became accustomed to it.

'Okay?' I said.

My mother nodded. My father didn't move.

I lifted the chi and floated it around the room. I didn't move it close to them.

'Generate another the same size,' John said.

I hesitated. I'd never tried that before. I put the chi into the centre of the room and left it there, hovering. I held my hands still and concentrated and, to my surprise, managed another one. I moved it off my hands and put it near the first one. Now there were two balls of energy hovering in the centre of the room.

'Do you think you could produce a third?' he said.

'Let me try.'

'If it gets away from you then drop it,' John said quickly.

I nodded and concentrated, and produced a third ball. I moved it next to the other two. I tried something; I made them spin vertically around a common axis, like a little Ferris wheel.

'Cool,' Simone said softly.

'Merge them,' John said without moving.

I pulled them closer together and they joined to form a larger ball of chi.

'Now separate them again.'

I concentrated and the ball of chi split into three smaller balls again, still spinning. I didn't have it perfect, each ball of chi was a slightly different size.

Roland came in and stopped dead. '*Wah*!'

33

'Make them blue,' John said.

I concentrated. They went from gold to green, then greenish-blue. I lost it completely: the chi snapped back and hit me in the middle of the stomach, knocking me flat.

Simone burst out laughing, but my parents rushed to me, concerned.

'Are you okay, sweetheart?' my mother said as my father lifted me.

'Yeah, I'm fine,' I said. 'Happens all the time when I'm working with energy. It's on an invisible rubber band. If I lose control, it snaps back and knocks me flat.' I gestured towards John and Simone who were clutching each other with delight. 'They think it's really hilarious.'

'Well it *is*, silly Emma,' Simone said, still giggling.

'She's right, you know, Emma,' John said. He sobered. 'Oh. You should know — only Immortals can do that. Humans can't work with more than one chi ball at the same time. Or change the colour. Well done.'

'Damn,' I said softly.

Roland saluted me, falling to one knee. 'Lady.'

'Oh, for God's sake, *cut it out*, Roland,' I said. 'I'm not any sort of Immortal.'

'You certainly look like one to me, Lady,' Roland said with a huge grin. 'If you were Chinese I would swear that you were the Lady Yim Wing Chun herself. Or more likely her teacher Ng Mui.'

'Oh, thank you *very much*,' I said. 'What next?'

'Me,' Leo said, coming through the door with two staves. He threw the smaller one to me.

'Now this is more like it,' I said. 'I haven't beaten Leo up in quite a while.'

'I've been learning, Emma,' Leo said, readying himself. 'Bet you a day's guard duty I can take you.'

'You are *on*!' I said with delight. 'I haven't had a proper day off since I finished my thesis.'

'Whoa, whoa, wait a minute there,' my father said loudly. 'Leo's much taller than Emma and must weigh three times what she does. This is hardly fair!'

'You are quite right, Brendan,' John said. 'Not a fair match at all.' He concentrated.

Michael appeared in the doorway, holding a staff.

'This is more like it,' John said with satisfaction.

'All bets are off if I'm facing both of them,' I said. 'Michael's half Shen.'

'Double or nothing,' Leo said.

'Come on, Emma, give it a try,' John said. 'We might even be able to bring the snake out.'

I gestured towards Michael. 'He's half goddamn Shen!'

Michael grinned and saluted me, holding the staff.

'She'll fight *both* of them?' my mother said softly.

'Yes!' Roland said. 'I have a video camera in my office. Wait! Please!'

'There are a hundred and fifty demons out there waiting for you,' I said.

'Let them wait,' he said. 'I don't think this will take long.'

Roland came back with a video camera. 'Move into the big room.'

'But there are students in there!' I protested.

'Tell them you taught her,' John said to Roland.

'They wouldn't believe me, Your Highness,' Roland said. 'I'd have to tell them that *she* taught *me*.'

'That would work,' John said. He pulled himself up off the floor and took Simone's hand. 'Let's go.'

'You know Emma's only been learning off the Dark Lord for less than a year and a half?' Leo said to Roland as we went out.

'*Wah*!' Roland said. 'Amazing! Such talent!'

'Damn,' I said softly.

'She turns into a snake, you said. Why is that? Is she a Shen?'

'Nobody's quite sure what she is,' John said amiably. 'She's not a demon, that's for sure. We'll just have to wait and see.'

'Maybe she's the White Snake,' Roland said.

John stopped and his face froze. 'Not possible.'

'I'm black in Serpent form,' I said.

'If the Pagoda has fallen then she may be the White Snake,' Roland said.

'If I'm the White Snake then where's the Red Snake?' I said.

'Ah. You know the legend,' Roland said.

'Of course I do,' I said as I entered the larger room. 'I've been doing an enormous amount of research on the nature of Serpent Shen, for obvious reasons.'

'She is not the White Snake,' John said, moving to catch up with us. 'Not possible.'

The students lounged against the long wall, waiting quietly for Leo to return. Roland directed them loudly in Cantonese. 'All of you, back to the far short wall, stand still, stand quiet. You are about to be extremely privileged. Silence!'

The students moved back, quiet and cowed.

Roland gestured. 'Whenever you are ready, my Lady.'

'Mum, Dad, you okay?' I said. My parents nodded. 'Go stand with John.'

My parents moved over to John and Simone in front of the mirrors. This room was larger, about six by four metres. Simone took my mother's hand and smiled up at her.

'Wait,' Roland said. He pulled the video camera out and turned it on. 'Okay, go.'

I nodded to both Leo and Michael. They saluted back. We moved into position. Both of them faced me, side by side.

I held my staff out in front, guarding. Leo I could take easily, but Michael was an unknown quantity: not just half Shen, but half tiger as well. He had been learning from John for months now, and had probably come a long way since I had easily bested him when I trialled him for the job as trainee bodyguard to replace Leo.

Leo came at me first. He swung at my head. I blocked it with my own staff, swung it down, twisted it, and tried to take his feet out from under him with the other end.

Michael came at me at the same time. As Leo's staff went down, Michael went for my head. I flipped my staff under Leo's and guided it into Michael's. Their staves clashed together hard and both of them winced.

Leo dropped one hand from his staff and shook it, grimacing.

I jumped back and waited for them.

'Don't hurt them too much, Emma,' John said with delight.

Michael went for my feet, trying to sweep them out from under me.

I leaped over his staff, somersaulted, and planted both feet into Leo's chest, hard enough to knock him over without hurting him. I bounced off him and somersaulted backwards. I jammed the end of my staff into the floor before my feet hit, spun around it and hit Michael in the chest with my left foot. He staggered back but didn't fall.

I landed lightly on my feet in front of Michael, jumped right over the top of his head, and spun my staff behind me to take his feet out from under him before he had a chance to turn around.

I rolled and spun to face them, snapping my staff under my left arm and my right hand out into a guard. They were both on the floor, Leo on his back, Michael on his stomach.

'Come on, guys, up you get,' I said. 'I didn't hit you that hard.'

'No,' Leo said without moving. 'It's comfy here. These mats are nice and soft, and your feet are damn hard.'

'What he said,' Michael said, gasping.

'Said it wouldn't take very long,' John said.

The students suddenly cheered and clapped as one. Some of them whistled. I could swear a couple of them were jumping up and down with delight.

Michael pulled himself to his feet. 'Can you reverse the Five Point Push?'

'Uh, yeah,' I said. 'Why?'

'Five Point Push?' Roland cried with glee.

'Oh no! I am *not* a circus act!'

'Who'd like to feel a Five Point Push?' Roland called in Cantonese. 'Step forward!'

Just about every goddamn student in the room stepped forward with a huge grin.

'Good,' John said. 'I'll time you. Twelve students. See how long it takes.' He fiddled with his watch. 'Wait.' He pressed the buttons. 'Forgotten how to use the stopwatch on this thing. There. Got it.'

'Line up,' Roland said in Cantonese.

The students lined up side by side, and I moved to the end of the line.

'Ready?' John said. 'Go.'

I didn't bother with all five points on the students. I just hit each of them with a focused band of chi into the central dan tian, one after the other. I had to stop and gather my chi after the fifth student but I made it to the end of the line. 'Done.'

'Twelve and a half seconds,' John said. 'Pathetic.'

Roland went up to one of the students and studied him closely. 'And they're all completely paralysed?'

I picked up one of the students, then laid him carefully on his back on the floor. He was completely rigid.

My mother was astonished. 'Emma!'

'What?'

'How much can you lift?' my father said. 'You picked up that kid like he didn't weigh anything.'

I looked down at the student. His eyes were amused but his face was rigid. 'I have no idea.'

'Oh, good idea,' John said. 'Lifting from a distance. Must try that later.'

'PK?'

'What?' John said, bewildered.

'Later.'

I reached down and tapped the student's stomach, undoing the Push. I held my hand out and helped him up off the floor. He stood and saluted, grinning like an idiot.

'Take it easy,' I said. 'If you feel dizzy then sit.'

I went down the line and undid the rest of the students. A couple of them flopped to sit on the floor, but most of them just shook themselves out.

'Dismissed,' Leo said, and the students carefully saluted us and filed out with huge grins on their faces. The minute they were in the hallway they started loudly discussing in Cantonese what they had just seen.

Roland turned off the camera and came to me. 'Do you think you could come in sometimes and teach?'

'Oh, *no*, Roland,' I said, exasperated. 'It's bad enough teaching at the Academy as it is. No more. You have Leo and Michael, and that should be enough for you.'

'Could you teach me?' Roland said softly.

'Tell you what, my friend,' I said, patting him on the shoulder, 'how about you come over to Wan Chai and learn from the Dark Lord himself? You are welcome to join an occasional class in the Wudang Academy. If you don't mind being put in with a bunch of young people.'

'Wudang?' Roland breathed. 'Wudangshan? Really?'

'Yes. His Mountain,' I said. 'We moved it down here. It's in Wan Chai until we repair the damage.'

'Very good, Emma,' John said. 'Anyone got a card?'

'Gamma can call Roland later and organise it,' I said.

Roland fell to his knees and saluted me, then John. 'I can't tell you what this means to me.'

'Get up off the floor or the deal is off,' I growled. 'And if you do that to me again, the deal is off anyway. I'm starving, John. Let's have something to eat here before we go to the Valley. The demons can wait.'

John bowed slightly to me. 'My Lady.'

I went to my parents. 'You guys okay?'

'That was amazing, Emma,' my mother said. 'You beat both of those huge men with no trouble at all. I was sure you'd get hurt. But you made it look easy. Some of the stuff you did was astonishing.'

'Thanks,' I said. 'Let's go and eat. Leo, Michael, want to come with us?'

'Maybe next time,' Leo said.

'Say hello to Rob for me,' I said, and Leo grinned.

'I'm meeting somebody,' Michael said.

'Cynthia?'

Michael's grin matched Leo's. 'Maybe.'

'Okay, see you guys later.' I turned to Roland. 'Want to join us?'

'Yes! Sure!' Roland said, delighted. 'But only if you let me buy.'

John opened his mouth to do the polite Chinese thing of arguing backwards and forwards about who would pay but I was too hungry to mess around. 'Shut up. Roland can pay. Let's go.'

Roland stiffened, then grinned broadly.

John slapped Roland on the back and guided him out. 'You see what I have to put up with? Typical barbarian Foreign Devil. Manners of a peasant.'

'At least I'll get fed some time today,' I said loudly as I linked my arm in my mother's and held my hand out for Simone. 'Come on, guys, let's go find something to eat.'

We went to a noodle bar not far from Roland's building. It was a typical small Hong Kong restaurant, about five metres wide, with a glassed-in area at the front where the noodles were prepared and a small kitchen at the back for the rest of the dishes. It was nearly full; usual lunchtime crowd, mostly people sitting in the booths at the side, but some larger groups at the round tables in the middle.

A waiter guided us to a large round table that seated six, its plain green laminate top worn through with use. A few menus and cards with daily specials were jammed into a plastic stand next to the bottles of soy and chilli sauce and the big steel chopstick holder.

The walls on both sides were covered with cracked and tarnished mirrors, an attempt to make the restaurant appear larger. Large sheets of cardboard with specials were stuck to the mirrors, the dishes written vertically in black marker with the prices underneath. The floor was well-worn green mosaic tiles, slippery with oil; the walls were matching pale green bathroom tiles. The ceiling was black with grease and a huge, ancient air conditioner throbbed painfully in the centre.

The owner of the restaurant greeted Roland in Cantonese, and plonked glasses of black tea in front of each of us.

'Are you sure this place is healthy? It's awfully ...' My mother searched for the right word.

'Don't worry, you can't get sick while you're with him,' I said, gesturing towards John. 'Besides, being old and tatty doesn't mean anything. The food is still good.'

'Old and tatty?' John said, eyeing me with amusement.

'Exactly,' I said. 'But still good.'

Roland was speechless.

'Can I have some beef brisket *ho fan*?' Simone said.

'Do you want tendon in it?' I said.

'Tendon?' my mother said.

'Yes, please,' Simone said. 'Tendon's good.'

'Tendon?' my mother said. 'Like, gristle tendon?'

'When it's been boiled for a few hours it turns to jelly,' I said. 'It's actually very good. You should try some.'

'Could you choose something suitable for us, Emma?' my father said. 'You know what we like. Something ... something *normal*.'

'Beef stir fry *ho fan*,' John said. '*Gwang chau ngau ho*.'

'Good idea,' I said. 'Vegetarian for us?'

'Of course. Roland?'

'Fishing boat congee,' Roland said. He pulled out the video camera and turned it on with a musical ping. 'I have to see this again.'

'Don't show it to anybody, please, Roland,' I said.

He nodded as he flipped open the LCD screen to view the video. The sound of us talking came through the speakers on the camera as he played it back. Then he went completely rigid and his mouth dropped open. '*Wah!*'

I bent around to see, then quickly put my hand over the screen to hide it from the people at the next table. 'Turn it off! For God's sake, Roland, turn it off!' I grabbed the camera and pressed the button to turn off the playback. '*Really* don't let anybody see that!'

Roland stared at John with his mouth still open.

I placed the camera on the table.

'Was it me?' John said.

I nodded silently.

'What?' my father said.

'It was him,' I said. 'Really him. What he really looks like. I thought you were taping *us*, Roland.'

'You should show your parents,' John said. 'I think they should see.'

I leaned over the table to speak softly to him. 'Yeah, let's just rub it in for the poor people that their daughter is engaged to a goddamn *animal*.'

'Shen,' John said.

'I want to see. Can I see?' Simone said. 'I want to see, Daddy.'

I looked around. Nobody else in the restaurant had noticed, and if Simone was next to me I could hide the screen. Roland picked up the camera and handed it back to me. 'Show her.'

'Okay,' I said. 'Just don't say anything too loud, okay?' I gestured. 'Next to me.'

Simone moved next to me, leaning over my shoulder. My mother bent around to see as well. I turned on the video camera and pressed the playback button.

There we were. Leo and Michael readied themselves. I had my back to the camera, preparing as well. The camera panned to the side wall and my parents appeared. Next to them was the Turtle. It appeared about a metre and a half long, with a massive, gleaming black shell. Its face had the wise expression of a natural turtle, but its eyes were John's and full of amusement as it watched us. John's human form was there as well, a transparent image over the top of the Turtle, holding Simone in his lap.

I froze the image so that Simone could look properly.

'I look really weird like that,' she said.

'What do you see?' John said.

'Both of you,' I said. 'Haven't you seen it before?'

'Nope,' John said. 'Never played it back to watch it.'

We shared a look. He'd made tapes for me, and I'd done the same for him, but we never looked at ourselves, we only watched each other.

His eyes crinkled up when he saw my face. 'Often wondered what I'd look like. In still photos you only see the human form, and I thought it'd be the same in videos as well. I was wrong.'

'It depends how drained you are,' I said. 'You must be running on empty right now. Usually it's just a very faint shadow, almost invisible. This is the clearest I've ever seen it.' He didn't make tapes for me when he was very drained, as well, but neither of us mentioned it. 'How long before you need to see the Lady again?'

'I still have a while. Let me see,' he said.

I passed the video camera to him and he studied it with the same amusement that was visible in the Turtle's eyes. 'Damn, but I'm ugly.' He passed the camera to my father who viewed the image, his face rigid with control.

'The Turtle's not pretty either,' I said, and Simone giggled.

'You really are a turtle,' Roland said with awe.

My father passed the camera to my mother. She stared at it with her eyes wide. She glanced up at John, then back at the image. She didn't say anything.

I took the camera from her and passed it back to Roland. 'Could you do me a favour, Roland?'

'Of course, anything, Lady Emma,' he said, without looking away from the image on the camera.

'Could you make a copy of this for me, my friend?'

Roland glanced up at me, then at John. 'Of course.'

CHAPTER FOUR

Oh, good, you're out. After breakfast, come into my office.

I didn't wait; I made myself a cup of tea and went straight into the study. Gold and John sat on either side of the desk.

'Your parents are still asleep,' John said.

'Probably the time difference screwing them up,' I said. 'They've never been overseas before.'

'It's only two hours,' Gold said.

'They're worn out,' John said. 'You've been dragging them around too much. Take them for a drive today, rest their feet.'

'Okay,' I said. 'I'll take them out to the New Territories, away from the concrete and pollution for a day. We might go to the riding stables — the Country Club's gardens would probably be a nice change for them.'

'Good idea,' John said. 'I thought you should know about this — Gold just told me. He's been cultivating a senior police officer and heard some interesting information about the investigation into Kitty Kwok.'

'That's not a very honourable thing to do,' I said. 'I'm surprised at both of you.'

45

'I didn't know he was involved in the investigation until we'd been going out for a while,' Gold said. 'Purely a happy coincidence.'

'Yeah, right, a coincidence,' I said. 'Wait a second, *he*? Oh for God's sake, John, are *any* of your staff straight?'

Gold chuckled. 'I thought you knew.'

'Gold's a stone,' John said. 'Gender neutral.'

'I think the term is bi, but it doesn't really apply to us,' Gold said. 'We can take either gender, but in essence we are neutral. If we like someone, we mould ourselves to fit their preference.'

'And you're my staff too, technically, Emma,' John said. He grinned broadly. 'I *thought* you and Louise were very close.'

'Oh my God, you are such a *guy* sometimes,' I said. 'Louise and I were *friends*.' I leaned over the desk and looked him right in the eye. 'Is the Turtle female? It's yin.'

He avoided the question and gestured towards Gold, his grin not shifting. 'Kitty Kwok investigation.'

'I do not understand the animal preoccupation with gender,' the stone in my ring said. 'It's more of a nuisance than anything else. And Gold, I am extremely disappointed that you would become involved with one of these ...' It hesitated, then said with emphasis, '*Fleshies*.'

Gold's eyes widened.

'Ignore it,' John said. 'It is being offensive because it craves attention.'

'Yeah, it's a troll,' I said.

Gold's mouth flopped open. John grinned broadly. The stone made a weird squeaking sound, like someone rubbing glass with a damp cloth, but didn't say anything.

Gold shook himself out of it. 'The police are bewildered by the nature of the laboratories producing the hybrids. Police in Europe, Australia and the US are investigating the other business interests, but at this stage it's just the kindergartens that seem to be involved in the underworld activity. Tautech, the biotech company, hasn't been doing anything that they can nail it on. Only the kindergartens have been used to generate funds and launder money for One Two Two's network.'

'So they won't stop the biotech labs,' I said.

'No,' John said. 'And it appears that the Demon King is letting it go too.'

'Damn,' I said. 'What about the thefts from the stone circles in Europe? Have they put that together?'

'No,' Gold said, his face rigid. 'But every single stone Shen, both Eastern and Western, is out for demon blood on this.'

'The Grandmother of All the Rocks herself has put a price on One Two Two's head,' the stone in my ring said. 'That demon will pay.'

'Do you think Wong has more stone elementals than those he threw at us the other night?' I said.

'Hard to tell, my Lady,' Gold said.

'He probably threw everything he had at us,' John said. 'That was his big final thrust. And he failed.'

'One thing I forgot to mention,' Gold said. 'The police are keeping this very quiet — if it gets out there will be mass panic.'

'What?' I said.

'They found large refrigerators full of blood and tissue samples,' Gold said. 'In the kindergartens.'

'Oh my God,' I whispered. 'She was harvesting from the *kids*.'

'I cannot conceive of the sort of creature that would carry out such atrocities,' John said.

'You sure she's not a demon?' I said.

'Only a human would be capable of something like this, Emma,' John said. 'Demons do not possess that sort of depth.'

'Wouldn't the kids go home and tell their parents or the domestic helpers?' I said.

'Not if they've had their memories wiped,' John said grimly. 'Quite common for children to come home from kindergarten with a small wound, plastered over, treated with disinfectant, and say that they fell in the playground. The staff apologise and claim that it is a minor scrape. Perfectly normal.'

'You're right,' I whispered. 'I cannot believe this.' I had a sudden horrible thought. 'You knew Kitty well, John. Did Simone ever go to the kindergarten here on the Peak?'

'Yes, for a while,' John said. 'Leo posted himself inside, guarding. I had to make a special arrangement with Kitty, but provided I paid her extra she would let me do anything. Simone didn't like the regimentation and Leo was a nervous wreck, so after two weeks I gave up and took her out. That was about six months before you arrived.'

'So Leo was guarding her,' I said. 'She never sustained any minor injuries. They never took a sample off her.'

John's face said it all.

I put my head in my hands. 'No.' I looked back up at John. 'Did she remember?'

'No,' he said, his face rigid. His eyes unfocused. 'Your parents are outside the door. They've gone into the kitchen.'

'Anything else?' I said.

'We need to discuss the new Disciples,' Gold said.

'Let me go and say good morning and I'll be right back.'

'I can handle it. Go with your parents,' John said.

'No. I need to know what's happening. Don't do anything without me.' I rose to leave.

'You know?' Gold said.

I stopped dead, halfway out of my chair. I sat back down. They saw my face.

'Sorry, my Lord,' Gold said.

'For a creature with no mouth, Gold, you have an extremely big one,' John said, then he sighed and his shoulders sagged. 'While you were out with your parents yesterday, I had a visit from the Lady. She confirmed what I already knew.'

'What?'

'Two more.'

'The Dark Lord is rather like a rechargeable battery,' Gold said.

'Winding down,' I said. 'Won't hold the charge.'

Neither of them said anything.

'I'll get the school calendar and we'll work something out,' I said.

'Not now,' John said. 'We need to discuss the new Disciples, and you need to spend time with your parents. We'll organise something later.'

'Okay,' I said. 'But I need to be involved in every single meeting from now on.'

'Especially the ones with the Generals,' John said.

'Oh, *damn*.'

'Can't avoid them any longer, my Lady,' Gold said with grim humour. 'You don't have any excuses left. Your thesis is finished, you attained your degree. Time to start taking part in the running of the Northern Heavens.'

I ran my hands through my hair. '*Damn!*'

'Go and have something to eat,' John said. 'Then come back and we'll talk about the Disciples. We won't get very far without you anyway.'

I threw myself out of my chair and left the office without saying a word. Halfway down the hallway I stopped still. Then I turned and went back into the office without knocking.

John and Gold watched silently as I sat down.

They waited for me. I didn't say anything.

Eventually Gold said, 'You too?'

I nodded.

'Do you remember how many times they took samples from you?' John said.

'I worked at her kindergarten for about a year. I must have used two boxes of Band-Aids,' I said. 'At the time I never remembered using a single one of them. I wasn't even worried about not remembering using them.'

'Sore arms?' John said.

I nodded. 'I went to the doctor for iron tablets because I was slightly anaemic. I wondered why he looked at my arms so strangely, but he didn't say anything. Probably thought I was an addict.' I ran my hands through my hair again. 'I had *needle tracks*! I *saw* them! But I just didn't worry about it. That bitch messed with my head!'

'You noticed very few of the unusual things here for the first few months you worked full-time,' John said. 'While you were here part-time you didn't seem to notice anything. You had an astonishing lack of curiosity.'

'I never even saw your sword on the wall. It took me months to notice Dark Heavens in its clips, and even then only when Simone pointed it out to me,' I said. 'Oh *God*. How much did I miss when I was working at the kindergarten?'

'The samples are in the hands of the police now,' Gold said.

'It's too late to be concerned,' John said. 'Go and talk to your parents.'

'What if they used me the other way around?' I said. 'Put the demon stuff into me, instead of just taking the samples out?'

'Then they failed, because they have given me a powerful ally,' John said. 'Go and talk to your parents.'

'If the demons know about this then the odds on me being a hybrid have just become much shorter,' I said.

'Probably not worth putting money on,' Gold said.

'Go,' John said.

'And talk to my parents. Yes, I know.' I rose and went.

The scrabbling of one of the eggs woke me and I pulled myself up on my black coils. Yep; one of the eggs had cracked. It was the oldest nestling, the first one I'd laid.

I put my skinless hands on the shell and felt the vibration, a tingle of anticipation moving through me.

I had a sudden horrible thought. I wouldn't eat it when it hatched, would I?

No. Of course not.

The egg cracked open and I pulled the pieces of shell away, but the nestling would have to climb out itself. Its little hands appeared at the edge of the opening, then it pulled itself up and tumbled out onto the floor of the nest. It lay panting, its little pale sides heaving.

I lifted it carefully and put it into the centre of my coils. It was exhausted, poor little thing. Its tawny hair was plastered to its head with the liquid from the egg, but it would dry quickly. I held it as it rested, a little human child of about four years old.

A while later it stirred and touched my face. 'Hello, Mummy.'

'Hello, my beautiful,' I whispered. 'You feel okay?'

'I'm fine.' The nestling pulled itself upright in the centre of my black coils and stroked my scales. I shivered with pleasure.

The nestling looked around, its little blue eyes focusing for the first time. It saw the other two eggs. 'What are they?'

'They are your little friends. Their names are Simone and Michael. They will be hatching soon too, and then the three of you can play.'

But only *good* games. Not grown-up games.

'Oh, okay.' The nestling curled up in the centre of my coils and nuzzled into me. 'I love you, Mummy.'

I held it close. 'I love you too, Emma.'

I shot upright, gasping. The air conditioner whispered high on the wall. The lights of the city glowed through my curtains.

Just a dream. Just a dream. I banged my head on the pillow and rolled over. *Just a dream*!

CHAPTER FIVE

After a few days of tourist activities, my parents were tired but more relaxed about the whole thing. They seemed to be unwinding and enjoying themselves. Both John and Simone worked hard to win them over. My mother, particularly, was becoming very fond of Simone.

December weather was usually fine and clear, despite the cold, so we took them along the Lugard Road walk. The road was more like a pedestrian path, and wound all the way around the top of the Peak, giving a spectacular view of both sides of Hong Kong Island, Kowloon and the Outlying Islands.

My mother was hesitant about the height, but was okay when I held her hand. Simone and John came with us and the five of us enjoyed each other's company. Simone held my mother's other hand.

My father and John seemed to have hit it off; John liked my father's gruff honesty and my father enjoyed John's relaxed easy-going nature.

'And this trail goes all the way around the top of the island?' my mother said.

'Yep,' I said. 'About an hour's walk all the way.'

'If your artificial hip worries you, let me know. I can arrange for you to be transported back,' John said.

My mother stared at him, her face expressionless.

'He can see inside you,' I said.

'That's very rude, Daddy, you shouldn't have done that,' Simone scolded.

'She's quite right,' I said. 'Do it again and you are in big trouble.'

'This is the Western part of the island,' John said, ignoring us. He stopped at the railing and showed my parents. 'Below us, all those tall buildings, is Kennedy Town. One of the oldest parts of Hong Kong. Then across the harbour you can see West Kowloon. It's a good clear day today, you can see the Tsing Ma Bridge — that's the bridge you came across when Emma brought you back from the airport. And over there,' he gestured towards the left, 'is Lantau Island. The airport is off the north side of that. Lantau is actually bigger than Hong Kong Island, but mostly uninhabited; people like to live near the centre of things.'

'It's incredible,' my father said. 'All the buildings are tall buildings. Everywhere. Where are the suburbs?'

'Suburbs?' Simone said.

'There aren't any,' I said. 'It's like this from one end of the Territory to the other. Even out in the New Territories, people live in packed high rises in "New Towns". There are villages of village houses all crammed together as well, but the vast majority of the population live in tiny high-rise apartments.'

'I should arrange for someone to take you to see a government housing estate,' John said, almost to himself.

'Good idea,' I said, and then saw the look on my mother's face. 'You okay, Mum?'

My mother was staring at the path in front of us, her face ashen. I turned away from the railing and froze.

'Don't anybody move,' John said.

An enormous Chinese cobra lay motionless on the

path. It was shining black and more than two metres long, a really big one.

'Is it dead?' I said.

'No,' John said. 'It's watching us.'

'Is it a demon?' I whispered.

'No,' Simone said.

'Natural snake,' John said.

The snake raised its head. About a third of its body came off the ground. It was nearly as tall as me.

'Don't move,' John said, very quietly. 'Stay very still.'

My mother made a soft sobbing sound of terror.

'Don't worry, I don't think it will hurt us,' John said. 'Everybody, stay very still. I may be able to talk to it.'

John carefully moved around us and eased himself towards the snake. It followed his movements with its head, watching him. When he was about a metre away he stopped to crouch and study it. He was slightly side on to us and his face went rigid with concentration.

The snake glanced at me, then turned back to John.

Then everything suddenly happened at once.

John's eyes went black and he reached out to touch the snake.

Simone screamed, '*No, Daddy*!' and flew around me to tackle her father before he could touch it. She took him completely by surprise and knocked him to the ground.

The snake snapped back, lowered its head, and quickly disappeared into the undergrowth at the side of the path.

Simone beat her father on the chest with her tiny fists and screamed, 'You *don't* leave me. I *need* you!' She shouted at the bushes where the snake had gone. 'You *go away* and leave my Daddy *alone*!' Then she threw herself on him and sobbed.

John sat up and put her head on his shoulder. He squeezed his eyes shut and buried his face in her hair.

'Go *away*, go *away*, go *away*!' Simone sobbed into his shoulder.

'I'm here,' he said gently. 'I'm not going.'

'Don't you *ever* do that again!' she gasped.

'I'll do it eventually, sweetheart,' he said. 'I won't be able to stop it.'

I went to them. John's face was full of misery. I held my hand out and he took it.

'That was it, wasn't it?' I said.

He nodded into Simone's hair.

'Tell it to go *away*,' Simone said into his shoulder.

John used my hand as a lever and pulled himself to his feet, still holding Simone. He released my hand and gently lowered Simone. She held his hand and both of them watched the bushes where the snake had gone.

'What was all that about?' my mother said softly behind me.

'That was his Serpent,' I said without turning. 'The other half of him. If he rejoins with it then he'll be gone for a very long time.'

Simone sobbed again loudly. I reached into my bag, pulled out a packet of tissues and passed it to her. She took one out and sniffled into it.

'It's gone,' John said. 'It's still very weak. It hardly knows what it is. It won't be back for a long time —'

'Good,' Simone said.

'I wonder what happened to it,' John said. 'It's nearly as weak, nearly as drained as I am.'

'Do you remember what happened when you lost it? At all?' I said.

'Not a bit,' John said without emotion. 'I have absolutely no recollection of being divided.' His tone didn't change, his voice was still very mild. 'If somebody has done this to me then they will pay very dearly.'

He turned and spoke to my parents as if nothing had happened. 'Let's go further around and look at Pokfulam. You can see Cheung Chau from there. Would you like to see the temple dedicated to me on Cheung Chau? It's not very exciting, but you may be interested to see some of the stories and rituals that surround me.'

My parents just watched him silently.

'Would you like us to take you home, guys?' I said gently.

My father nodded. My mother didn't move.

'I'll call Jade and Gold to carry you,' John said.

My mother flinched.

'No, thanks,' my father said weakly. 'We'd just like to walk back, if you don't mind.'

'You are perfectly safe as long as you are with me,' John said.

My parents turned and walked back along the path without seeming to notice whether we followed them.

They are not taking this very well, Emma.

'You can't blame them, John.'

Back at the apartment we all sat at the dining table. My parents had glasses of scotch in front of them. The Serpent had pushed them over the edge. They'd had enough. Neither of them had shouted at us, they'd just gone very quiet. I didn't blame them.

'I can give you a choice,' John said. 'You can either go to the Western Palace, where you will be absolutely safe, or you can go back to your own home and I will post guards there for you.'

'Where's the Western Palace?' my mother said.

'It's the Tiger's palace,' I said. 'It's on the Celestial Plane. It's a beautiful place with gardens and fountains in the Western Desert.'

'Heaven?' my mother said.

'Sometimes called that,' John said. 'But not really. More like a higher level of reality. If you go there, you will be perfectly safe. But it will be quite boring for you. You won't be able to continue with your normal lives.'

'How long before we can go back home and be safe?' my father said miserably. 'Before all of this blows over?'

'Probably between one and two years,' John said. 'Depending upon how quickly I can take the head off that little bastard One Two Two.'

'One Two Two?' my mother said.

'The demon that came after us at the graduation,' I said. 'No other demon is dishonourable enough to go after people who aren't directly involved. He's the only one who's that much of a scumbag.'

'What do you want to do, Barbie?' my father said, turning to my mother. 'I think it might be better to go with this Tiger guy.'

'What would you do, Emma?' my mother said.

'Frankly,' I said, leaning back, 'I'd like to send you all to the Western Desert until this blows over. You guys, Jen and her family, Amanda and her family, everybody. Think of it as a family vacation. The palace is really nice, you'll like it. And Jade or Gold can take me there, so I can visit you. Or you can come down here with guards, you'll be fine. John?'

'If that is your wish, and their wish, I have no objection,' John said. 'I will not let this situation continue for much longer.'

'We have to get Simone up to speed.'

'Yes we do. Brendan, Barbara,' John said. 'Would you call Amanda for us and explain? Then we can begin the arrangements. I will call Leonard and see what he wants to do.'

'I just want to get out of here,' my mother whispered.

58

The next afternoon we all waited in the living room: me, John and my parents.

The other three Winds materialised with Amanda's family. They were all unconscious. John and I rushed to help with Amanda and Alan. Zhu Que gently lowered the boys onto the couch, one on each arm.

'Are they okay?' my father said urgently. 'It *is* only temporary?'

'They're fine,' the Tiger said as he placed Amanda onto the couch next to the boys. 'It was quite a long way and it is a very stressful experience for humans to travel like this.'

'It'll be similar for you when you're taken to the palace,' I said to my mother. 'But don't worry, it doesn't hurt.'

My parents hovered, concerned.

'They will be fine,' the Dragon said. 'Phoenix, let's go and get the others.' He disappeared.

'My Lord, my Lady,' Zhu Que said, bowing slightly and saluting. 'By your leave.'

'Go,' I said, nodding to her. She disappeared as well.

Alan came around first. He sat up and rubbed his hands over his face. Then he saw Amanda and the boys, still unconscious, and staggered to them.

'Don't worry, they're okay,' I said, putting my hand on his shoulder to reassure him. 'They'll wake up soon.'

Alan glanced up at me. Then he saw John and the Tiger. He looked around carefully. 'We're really in Hong Kong?'

'Really,' I said. 'It's all true.'

Amanda stirred and moaned. Alan, my parents and myself all crouched around her. John and the Tiger stood behind us.

Amanda opened her eyes and saw us. She cast around, confused, then saw the boys and with a small cry of pain struggled to sit up to check on them.

'They're fine, Amanda,' I said softly. 'They're really okay. You're all okay.'

'Something was chasing us,' Alan said. 'The young man defended us, and then the people carrying us brought us here.'

Gold appeared in True Form at the other side of the room with the bags. He didn't take human form; his stone fell out of the air and landed on the carpet.

'He's injured,' the stone in my ring said. 'Quickly.'

I raced to Gold. 'Can I pick him up?'

'Yes,' the stone said. 'Pick him up with both hands. Let's see.'

I gently lifted Gold and examined him, but couldn't see anything inside him. I didn't risk turning my Internal Eye on him, but his energy level felt like that of an ordinary stone. He didn't feel special at all.

'He's okay,' the stone said. 'Just exhausted. Put him on one of the beds. He'll take human form when he's strong enough, and he can rest.'

'Stay here, everybody,' I said. 'I'll pop him on my bed, he'll be fine.'

'Is that Gold?' my mother said. 'You said he was a stone.'

'Yes, it's Gold,' I said.

'Wait.' John came to put his hand on Gold.

'Is he okay?' my mother said.

'Emma's correct,' John said. 'Drained. He'll be okay. He must have used energy to defend himself. Lay him down, he'll be fine in about four hours.'

'Can you feed him energy?' I asked the Tiger.

'Nope,' the Tiger said. 'He's a stone. Completely different type of Shen. The chi is the same, but our natures are incompatible.'

'Can I feed him?' I said.

Both John and the Tiger snorted with amusement.

'Not a good idea, I think,' John said. 'He'd find that more embarrassing than coming around in your bed.'

'Hop in with him,' the Tiger suggested. 'Freak him out when he wakes up.'

'You're worse than Leo,' I said, and turned away to take Gold to my room.

'Emma,' John said, and I turned back. 'Gold will be very weak when he comes around and probably won't be able to conjure the clothes. Cover the stone.'

I shrugged. 'Okay.'

When I was in the spare room where I was staying I laid Gold gently on the bed, roughly where his chest would be, and pulled a light sheet over him.

'Is he all right like that?' I said.

'Yes,' the stone in my ring said.

I hesitated, watching him. He had nearly given his life for my family.

'I'll really miss him when he's freed,' I said.

Gold transformed into his human form, lying on his side under the sheet. He turned onto his back and looked at the ceiling, puzzled.

'Why?' the stone said.

I knelt next to Gold and took his hand. He smiled at me, heaved a huge sigh, turned his head away and closed his eyes.

'Because I really like having him around,' I said.

Gold shot upright to sit and cast around the room.

'Rest,' the stone said. 'I'll handle it.'

'What?' I said.

'I am in big trouble,' Gold said softly, and fell back onto the pillow.

'You'll be fine,' the stone said. 'Rest.'

'Am I in Lady Emma's bed?' Gold said.

'Yep, quite a coup,' I said. 'Something to tell your friends. Rest now. Whatever the problem is, we can handle it.'

'Go quietly into the living room, Emma,' the stone said, very softly. 'Let's not wake it up just yet.'

As I entered the living room, John was kneeling in front of Amanda and smiling kindly at her.

'Hello, Amanda,' he said, very gently. 'My name is John Chen and I'm the one that's promised to marry Emma. I'm a Shen, a spirit. The closest word you have in English is "god". Please stay very still. It is vitally important that you don't move or speak.'

Amanda's eyes went wide, but she didn't move. Little David sat quietly on her lap.

'Is Amanda a Shen? Or something like me?' I whispered as I approached them.

'No,' John said, without turning away from Amanda. 'Where did she get her pendant, Alan?'

'I gave it to her,' Alan said. 'I found it in an antique shop. It was ridiculously cheap for such a large opal, so I thought it must be a fake or something. But it looked good so I bought it for her anyway.'

'Her opal is a Shen?' I whispered.

John nodded without turning away from Amanda. 'Southern Shen.'

'It will be beyond pissed when it wakes up and finds that we've moved it so far from its Centre,' the stone in my ring said softly.

'Can you take it back without waking it?' I said.

'Nope,' the stone said. 'And I know this one too. It has a temper to rival yours, my Lady.'

John concentrated and Leo came out from the hallway.

'Don't move, Amanda,' John said quickly when he saw her reaction. 'This is Leo, our guard. He can take your boys and care for them while we sort this out.'

Amanda shook her head without speaking.

'Let him, Mandy,' I whispered. 'He's great with kids, he looks after John's daughter, Simone. They'll be safe with him.'

'Alan, I think it would be a good idea if you were to go too,' John said.

Alan hesitated. 'Will the boys be safe with him?'

'Perfectly,' Leo lisped. 'I swear I will guard them with my life. They can come into Simone's room, she has a lot of toys. They'll be fine.'

'He's right, Alan,' I said.

'Brendan?' Alan said.

'Leo's good,' my father said. My mother nodded.

'If the boys will be safe with him, then I'm staying here with Amanda,' Alan said firmly. 'Is it okay with you if he takes the boys, Mandy?'

Okay, Amanda mouthed silently.

'Boys, go with the big man, he'll look after you,' Alan said.

David looked as if he was about to cry and Mark's little face screwed up with terror.

The Tiger concentrated and their faces went blank. They both rose and placidly took Leo's hands, allowing him to lead them down the hall towards Simone's room.

'All suggestions welcome, stone,' John said, still crouched in front of Amanda.

'We don't have a choice, we'll have to wake the damn thing,' the stone said. 'Everybody move back, I'll do it. Don't move, Miss Amanda, I'll handle this.'

The ring drifted off my finger and floated in front of Amanda. She watched it with wonder.

'Lord Xuan, Lady Emma, back you go,' the stone said.

'Brendan, Barbara, you'd be safer with the children and Leo,' John said as both he and I rose and moved back.

'We're staying here with Amanda,' my father said. My mother nodded silently.

'I'm waking it up,' the stone said.

Nothing happened.

'Hi, Opal,' the stone said softly. 'Sorry about this. Didn't know you were there.'

Complete silence.

'Please permit us to return you immediately,' the stone said.

Again, nothing.

'This was entirely unintentional,' the stone whispered.

'Dickhead,' the opal said loudly with a very strong Australian accent. It sounded like a middle-aged Australian man. 'Where the hell am I?'

'Sorry,' the stone said ruefully. 'Hong Kong.'

'That's a bloody enormous Dark Spirit over there. What is it?' the opal said.

'I'm the North Wind,' John said. 'Good day to you, Opal. Thanks for not hurting the lady.'

'I'd never hurt my lovely Amanda in a million years,' the opal said, and everybody breathed a sigh of relief. 'But this ugly green bastard floating in front of me, and that pretentious little prick who thinks he's made of gold, are both in serious trouble.'

'I've been wearing a stone that can talk for more than ten years?' Amanda said with disbelief.

'Remember when your car suddenly swerved out of the way of that runaway truck?' the opal said. 'And the time you fell off the ladder but weren't hurt at all? And the car accident in Adelaide, where the car was a wreck but nobody was injured?'

'I thought I was just lucky,' Amanda said.

'Lucky my arse,' the opal said. 'You and your lovely little family wouldn't be around right now if it weren't for me.'

'Can I say thank you now?' Alan said.

'You are more than welcome, mate,' the opal said. 'You lot are the most delightful family it has ever been my pleasure to adorn. But why the hell are you in Hong Kong? And how come you know about these spirits? You're just ordinary humans. How come you're mixed up in this? That's an enormous tiger over there behind the North Wind, you know that? And what the hell is *this*?'

'What?' Amanda said.

'This snake thing. No, wait, it's an ordinary human. Is that your sister, Mandy? Why the hell is she ... Good God, but she's a bloody great black snake, you know that? A human and a big snake at the same time. Never seen her like before. Hey, Emma, is that you?'

'Yes,' I said.

'Geez, have *you* changed. What have you been doing to yourself?' the opal said. 'Come and pay a visit to the Grandmother with me one day, pet. I'm sure she'd love to have a look at you.'

I took the opportunity. 'Am I a Rainbow Serpent?'

'Mandy, dear,' the opal said. 'Do me a favour, love? Take me off and hand me to your little sister?'

Mandy removed the chain from her neck and passed it to me, the opal dangling from its links.

'Hold me in your hand, I want to look at you,' the opal said.

I dropped the stone into my hand and held it. It was warm and seemed to be pulsing with energy.

'Nope,' it said.

'Damn,' I said under my breath. 'Any idea what I am? None of us knows,' I said more loudly.

'No idea,' the opal said. 'Pass me back. I feel lost without my little Mandy.'

I opened my hand to see the stone. It was quite large, about three centimetres long and two wide, a rough rectangular shape. It was almost jet black with flashes of midnight blue and fiery red through it.

'You are absolutely spectacular, you know that?' I said.

'Yep,' the stone said. 'Pass me back, and then this geological mistake can tell me how I got here and what the story is.'

'Humph,' the stone in my ring said. 'You always were a rude bastard.'

'Shut the hell up and tell me what's going on,' the opal said.

The stone in the ring returned to my finger. Amanda put the opal back around her neck.

'You can talk, I'll just tell the opal what's happening,' the stone said. 'Don't mind us, we'll have a little stone-to-stone talk.'

'Dickhead,' the opal said, and went quiet.

CHAPTER SIX

I burst into John's office without knocking. 'We need some more pillows. Can I send —' I stopped dead. A young Chinese woman I'd never seen before was sitting across the desk from John.

'Whoops, sorry,' I said, and moved to go out.

'Wait,' John said. 'Obsidian here would like to apologise. This is Emma.'

Obsidian fell to her knees and saluted. 'My profoundest apologies, my Lady. I have failed both you and the Dark Lord.'

'She was your sister's guard stone,' John said. 'She never told us that the opal was sentient.'

'Why not?' the stone in my ring snapped.

Obsidian didn't move from her knees on the floor. She didn't look up.

'I do not believe this,' the stone said softly. 'A daughter of mine sleeping with one of *them*.'

'It is the most spectacularly beautiful stone I have ever laid eyes on,' Obsidian said, then she glared at my ring. 'And it's an absolutely *fantastic* lover,' she added defiantly, 'both stone and human. If you knew it was already protecting them, I wouldn't be needed, and you'd assign me somewhere else. I wanted to be with it.'

'Why didn't you tell the Shen when they went to pick up my family, Obsidian?' I said. 'You should have warned them about the opal.'

Obsidian looked down, still on her knees. 'I was at the post-Christmas sales in Brisbane,' she said miserably. 'Opal was looking after them, he said I could go. Obviously he —'

'Fell asleep on the job,' the stone said cuttingly. 'Fine pair of guards *you* are. I've half a mind to reassign you anyway. This is the family of the *Dark Lady* we're talking about here.'

'Obsidian is reassigned regardless,' John said severely. 'And the punishment will be appropriate.'

Obsidian collapsed over her knees.

'Good,' the stone snapped. 'Give her to the Dragon.'

'No,' Obsidian whispered.

I stayed quiet.

'Report to Lord Qing Long,' John said.

'My Lord,' Obsidian choked, saluted without looking up, and disappeared.

'No attempt to defend her?' John said softly.

'She deserved it,' I said. 'Both of them should be sent to the Dragon. I take it you've sent her there because he's Wood and Stone is weak against Wood.'

'Yes. But mostly I sent her to the Dragon because he's a complete bastard to all his staff,' John said. He smiled slightly. 'You are more and more cold-blooded all the time.'

'You're right,' I said, miserable. 'I can't believe I just stood by and let you do that to her.'

'You will make an exceptional Regent, Emma,' John said. 'And I am sincerely looking forward to taking up my Celestial duties again with you by my side. Together we will be the greatest team the Celestial has ever seen.'

I turned to open the door. 'I'm sure they'll be glad to have your warm heart to counter my cold blood.'

'We will,' the stone in my ring said softly.

'I still can't believe this stuff was all around us and we never even knew,' Alan said as we sat at the dinner table. Simone, Mark and David sat with Leo and giggled together.

'Some of the Celestials here in China have never been to the Earthly Plane since they were Raised,' John said. 'I don't think the Celestial himself has been more than two or three times.'

'Who?' Amanda said.

'Their Jade Emperor,' the opal said. 'Their biggest boss.'

Simone piped up. 'Can you give us rides after dinner, Uncle Bai?'

The Tiger glowered at her, then grinned. 'Sure. You eat your vegetables like good children, and you can all have rides.'

David and Simone put their heads together and whispered with excitement. Mark didn't seem so sure.

'You don't have to if you don't want to, Mark,' I said.

He nodded, serious.

'Why are you vegetarian, John?' my mother said.

'It's a long story,' John said. 'All human Immortals are vegetarian.'

'But you're a Shen, Daddy, not a human Immortal,' Simone said. 'So why? Uncle Bai isn't vegetarian.'

I made my voice very deep. 'That is not for one such as you to know.'

Leo did an excellent imitation of John, Cantonese accent and all. 'That information is not for mortal ears.'

The Tiger's mouth opened with astonishment, then he banged his palm on the table and roared with laughter.

'Directly after dinner, twenty-five level one sword katas, both of you,' John snapped, but his eyes sparkled.

'Yes, my Lord!' Leo and I both shot back, saluting.

'You're a fool to have human staff, Ah Wu,' the Tiger said, still chuckling.

'Neither of them are staff, they are family,' John said. 'I love both of them dearly, and they know it.'

A swift expression of pain swept across Leo's face, so quick that it was almost unnoticeable. Neither John nor I missed it though, and we both decided to change the subject.

'The Dragon says they will be here with your sister's family in about an hour,' John said. 'Jade is bringing the bags.'

'Will she be okay? Gold was followed and attacked,' I said.

'With the Dragon and Phoenix carrying them, your family will be protected, Emma,' the Tiger said. 'Jade can outrun just about anything; dragons are much faster than stones. Don't worry about her.'

'Was Jennifer okay about coming?' I said.

John didn't reply.

'Damn,' I said quietly.

'What's a sword kata?' Amanda said.

'You've already seen me do it,' I said. 'A sword set. What I did for you in the yard back home.'

'Wanna see some real stuff?' Leo said.

'Show Amanda how you can take Leo down,' my father said to me.

I glanced at my father. His face was full of pride. I grinned with delight; my father was *proud* of me.

'Let's just rub it in,' Leo growled, but his small brown eyes sparkled as well.

'You want to see?' I asked Amanda and Alan.

'We're here, we might as well have a look,' Alan said.

'Yes, I want to see,' Amanda said. 'Mum's been

telling me some of the stuff you can do, and I find it difficult to believe.'

'Okay,' I said. 'After Jennifer's here and settled in, Leo and I will give you a small demonstration. The sword katas can wait.'

'I ordered you to do them directly after dinner,' John said.

'Yes, my Lord,' I shot back, saluting again. 'Like I said, the sword katas can wait.'

The Tiger roared with laughter again.

The Tiger was giving both Mark and David a ride in the living room when the Phoenix and the Dragon turned up with Jennifer and her kids. Leonard had legal business to tidy up in London and would follow in a week.

The Dragon placed Jennifer gently on the couch, and the Phoenix lowered her boys next to her.

The Tiger quickly dropped to his belly and guided Mark and David off, then changed back to human form.

'I still want to ride,' David whined.

'If I'm a tiger when your cousins wake up they'll be scared to death,' the Tiger said.

John and I went to Jennifer. Amanda pushed John out of the way and she and I hovered above Jennifer, waiting for her to wake.

She came around slowly, rubbing her hand over her face. She saw us, her sisters, then cast around for the boys. She reached out to hold both of them and glared at John. 'Stay away from us,' she hissed.

John and I shared a look and he silently moved away.

Amanda dropped to crouch in front of Jennifer. 'Hi, Jen.'

Jennifer didn't say anything. She hugged Colin, still unconscious, to her and pulled Andrew closer on the sofa.

'What's her problem?' the opal said.

'Stop it!' Jennifer whispered ferociously. 'Go away!'

The boys began to come around. Colin whimpered and Jennifer held him tighter. Andrew's eyes opened and he looked around, then buried his face in his mother's sweater.

'I think it would be a good idea if you people were to leave us alone for a while,' my father said grimly, moving around the couch to sit next to Jennifer.

John nodded without saying a word, and all the Shen disappeared. John turned and went down the hall to his study. Leo took Simone's hand and led her out as well.

'Well, here we are, all three sisters in one place — first time in years,' I said with forced cheerfulness.

Everybody ignored me.

'I'm in Hong Kong?' Jennifer said.

Everybody nodded.

'The Tiger will take you to the Western Palace tomorrow,' I said. 'You'll need some time to rest from this trip before he does. How do you feel?'

Jennifer stared at me and didn't say anything.

'Okay,' I whispered.

'This is all your fault,' she finally said, glaring at me.

'I know,' I said, running my hands through my hair. 'I'm so sorry, guys. I've completely screwed up your lives.'

'Stupid bitch,' Jennifer said and turned away.

I didn't know what to say.

Amanda's son Mark threw himself at me. 'Teach me some kung fu! I wanna learn!'

Everybody was completely silent.

'I don't think that's a good idea right now, sweetheart,' I whispered.

Jade appeared in True Form on the other side of the room with the bags, and collapsed. I ran to her, ignoring the shrieks of fear from my nephews; she was bleeding, her scales ripped in many places. One of her front legs was obviously broken.

She attempted to rise, looking around. 'I *did* make it,'

she said. 'I thought I'd made it. They were so fast ...' Her voice trailed off and she fell heavily.

'John!' I screamed.

John and Leo raced into the room, Simone hurrying behind them. John crouched to examine Jade. My parents hovered behind him.

'Is this Jade? The girl?' my mother said.

'Yes,' John said, placing his hand on Jade's head. He concentrated, and the Blue Dragon appeared next to him in his usual human form.

'Out of the way,' the Dragon said, quickly moving to Jade's side and putting both hands on her head. Everybody retreated to give him room.

The Dragon concentrated, and his long turquoise hair floated around his head. 'I'm taking her home,' he said softly. 'She needs to be under the water. This will take a while. My Lord?'

'How long?' John said.

'I'll still be able to return tomorrow to take the Lady's family West,' the Dragon said. 'Jade will need to recuperate for a few weeks. She has massive internal injuries, far too much for any energy worker to handle. Leave her with me.'

'Go,' John said, and both Jade and the Dragon disappeared.

I flopped to sit next to the bloodstains on the carpet. I lowered my head and shook it. 'Damn.'

'This is all your fault,' Jennifer said loudly from the couch.

I jumped up and stormed to the spare room where I was staying. Gold was still in the bed, his boyish face peaceful as he slept. I sat on the floor next to his head with my back against the wall and buried my face in my knees.

About five minutes later, John came in and sat cross-legged on the floor on the other side of the room. He rubbed his hand over his face, sighed, and tied his hair back.

'No one should be suffering like this for me,' I said into my knees. 'I'm dragging my entire family away from their homes. Gold and Jade nearly died. I can't do this to them any more.'

'Gold, you are released,' John said loudly. 'You have your freedom. Go.'

'You can't release him,' I said. 'He told me only the Jade Emperor can release him.'

'I am the First Officer, Highest Celestial General,' John said. 'In precedence I am second only to the Celestial himself. If I say Gold is free, then he's free.'

Right Hand of the Jade Emperor. I inhaled sharply as I understood. 'But you said that as your chosen, after you've gone I'll be accepted as ...'

'Precisely,' John said. 'As my equal. Over everybody.' He spoke firmly. 'You're free, Gold. Go.'

Gold didn't move. 'No.'

'Why not,' John said, and it wasn't a question.

'Because I love serving you,' Gold whispered. 'I will go if you order me, but I beg you, please, let me stay.'

My father came in and closed the door softly behind him. He hesitated.

'Brendan,' John said, still seated on the floor, 'do you blame Emma for all of the troubles we are having right now?'

'No,' my father said. 'I blame you.'

'Good,' John said. 'You've laid the blame in the right place. Does it make any difference, now that the blame has been laid?'

'Not a bit,' my father said. 'We're still in the same situation, and we'll all make it through somehow.' He leaned on the wall. 'Don't mind Jen, Emma, she'll survive. Right now her kids are fighting with Amanda's for rides on the Tiger. They're having a great time. Don't worry about them.'

'Jade nearly died,' I whispered.

'And if I attempted to free her, she would stay as well,' John said.

'We all love you, my Lady,' Gold said, still without moving. 'We are profoundly honoured to serve you and the Dark Lord. I would rather be here with you than anywhere else in the world, and so would Jade.'

'We do what we have to,' my father said. 'And we survive.'

'Your father is a very wise man, and I can see where you gained much of your own wisdom.' John looked up at my father. 'No snake spirits in the family tree?'

My father shrugged. 'How would I know? Until a couple of weeks ago, I didn't even know that snake spirits existed. What does that have to do with it?'

'Snake spirits are renowned for their wisdom,' I said into my knees.

'Are they renowned for falling in love with the wrong guy?' my father said.

'Nope,' I said, smiling despite myself, 'that's definitely a female thing. All women are renowned for falling in love with the wrong guy.'

'Your mother didn't,' John said.

'I don't think you did either, pet,' my father said. 'This man is about as good as you can get. It's just the situation that's difficult.'

'Thanks,' John said softly.

'Come and help with the kids,' my father said. 'Are all the sleeping arrangements organised?'

'You should take my room,' John said to me.

'We've had that discussion, and you need your rest,' I said, looking up from my knees. 'And the boys *want* to share the same room. They'll have a ball.'

'Where will you sleep?' John said, gesturing towards Gold.

'I'll move,' Gold said.

'You'll stay right there,' I said quickly. 'That's an order. I'll find somewhere to sleep, don't worry about me. I can share with Leo, sleep on the floor in the student room he's using. Or on the floor here.'

'Leo won't let you sleep on the floor; he'll give you his bed and you won't be able to stop him,' Gold said with amusement, without moving.

'Now go and do those sword katas,' John said. 'Round Leo up, he can do them too.'

'You really have to do that?' my father said.

'Oh yeah,' I said, rising. 'Absolutely. When it comes to the kung fu, he's the Master and I'm just the student. If he tells me to do a hundred push-ups, then I have to do it.'

'You still owe me a hundred push-ups from last week,' John said. 'You are extremely disobedient sometimes, Emma.'

'Oh, shut up, old man,' I said as I took my father's arm in mine and opened the door.

Gold made a strangling sound behind us as we went out.

While Jennifer settled herself in the room she would share with my parents, the rest of us went into the training room for the demonstration. Jennifer didn't want to see it, and the children were too little to stay still in such a small space.

'Did you do those katas yet?' John said from the doorway as my parents, Amanda and Alan lined up against the long wall.

'After we've done this,' I said.

John nodded and went out. 'I'll call the carriers for tomorrow.'

'What would you like to see?' I said.

'I'd love Alan to see you take down Leo,' my father said with a grin.

Alan gestured towards Leo. 'He's huge, Brendan, no way could Emma do anything like that.'

'I saw her knock him down with a staff,' my father said proudly.

'She can take me down hand-to-hand, without a weapon, as well,' Leo said. He sounded as proud as my father did. 'And she's one of the finest energy workers that Lord Xuan has ever seen.'

'Lord Xuan?' Amanda said.

'John's real name is Xuan Wu,' I said. 'It means "Dark Martial Arts".'

They all went silent.

'It doesn't mean he's bad,' I said. 'It just means that he's dark and he's the God of Martial Arts.'

'Dark?' Amanda said.

John poked his head in the door. 'Yin. Dark, cold, water, winter, death. That's me.' He grinned. 'I rounded up enough carriers for tomorrow. About 10 a.m. Is that okay with everybody?'

'Death?' my mother whispered.

'He's Death?' my father said.

'No, that's Yanluo Wang,' John said. 'Lord of the Underworld. Great guy. Haven't seen him for ages, haven't been killed in years. I'm just yin.' He pulled his head back into the corridor and disappeared.

'Ten is okay,' I called.

'Good,' he said from halfway down the hall.

'He doesn't seem like a god,' Amanda said. 'He's more like just an ordinary sweet guy.'

Leo and I shared a smile. I turned back to my family and shrugged. 'That's because he is.'

'What did he mean, he hasn't been killed in years?' my father said.

I was silent.

'Tell us, Emma,' my mother said.

'When Immortals are killed, they go away for a while, then return. Every time John's mortal body is killed, he pays a visit to Yanluo Wang, in the Underworld,' I said.

'Don't mince words, Emma,' Leo said.

I sighed. 'Hell.'

There was complete silence.

'They won't talk about it,' I added. 'So don't bother asking him.'

'Hand-to-hand, Emma?' Leo said, moving to the other end of the room, ignoring the looks on my relatives' faces. 'How long has it been?'

'I don't know,' I said, moving into a fighting stance. 'A couple of weeks?'

'Everybody stay still,' Leo said, moving into a guard stance as well. 'We won't touch you, but if you move you could be moving into the line of fire. So stay exactly where you are; we know you're there.'

'Don't worry, as long as you don't move we won't touch you,' I said. 'But if you're freaked out by any of it, just say something and we'll stop.'

Leo grinned and waved a come-on.

'Oh no,' I said, shaking my head. 'You first, Lion.'

'He's a *lion*?' my father said with disbelief.

'Yes,' I said.

'No,' Leo said, and performed a magnificent jumping high kick right at my head.

I ducked and rolled underneath him. 'Oh, come *on*, Leo,' I said, exasperated, as I spun to face him, 'don't treat me like a first year.'

Leo moved forward until he was just out of reach. Then he attacked me. He swung at my face with the blades of his hands, left and right, and I blocked both. I ducked and spun, throwing my leg out with the movement, trying to take his feet out from underneath him, but he easily jumped over my foot and performed a backward somersault, landing in a long defensive position.

'Whoa,' Alan said softly.

I threw a spinning high kick at his head and he grabbed my foot. I used the energy centres and twisted my body, knocking him sideways. He released my foot, rolled and spun upright next to Amanda, who flinched away.

'Don't move,' he said, and raced forward to throw punches at my head and chest, again left and right.

I blocked each fist, but I didn't release them; I held them. I crossed his arms in front of him and arm-locked him with one hand. I readied myself to quickly take his feet out from under him before he could free himself.

Leo grimaced, the muscles of his arms bulged and he moved to throw me off before I could complete the spin. I held him, then hesitated, still holding him.

He tried again and I still held him.

It became a test of strength. He couldn't move his arms; I had them. With one hand.

Holy shit, I'd never done this before, and I was *stronger than Leo*.

Leo fought me, but he couldn't move his arms at all. His face filled with bewilderment. 'Damn, Emma,' he said quietly, and I released him. He stepped back and studied me with awe.

I tapped the stone.

'No need to hit me, I saw it,' it said. 'Why are you acting so surprised?'

'What is it, Emma?' my mother whispered.

'I'm stronger than Leo,' I said.

'What?' my father said sharply. 'How is that possible?'

'The stone told me,' John said from the doorway. 'Emma, see if you can lift Leo.'

'No,' I said.

John came to me. 'Hold out your hand.'

I held my hand out. John gestured to Leo without turning. 'Put your hand on top of hers.'

Leo moved forward and put his dark hand on top of mine.

'Up,' John said.

Leo didn't hesitate. He readied himself, then did a handstand on my hand. I shifted my weight, pushed my elbow into my side, and I could hold him. He held his other arm out, steadying himself, but his balance was perfect. I raised my left arm to help me balance as well. The tips of Leo's toes in his soft leather martial arts shoes brushed the high ceiling of the training room.

'Holy shit,' my father said.

'I'm inclined to agree with you,' John said, watching Leo as he balanced on my hand. He glanced at me. 'Can we put Michael on the other hand?'

'No,' I said. 'I couldn't hold him as well. Leo is about as much as I can handle.'

'How much do you weigh, Leo?' John said.

'Two hundred and ninety-five pounds,' Leo said, still hovering above me.

'Holy *shit*,' my father said again.

'Down,' John said.

Leo effortlessly lowered himself. He hesitated, watching me. There was complete silence as everybody stared at me with awe. Then Leo fell to one knee and saluted me, bowing his head.

'What are you, Emma?' my father whispered.

'I wish the hell I knew, Dad,' I said. I ran my hands through my hair and went out. The silence followed me down the hall.

After breakfast the next morning the entire Donahoe clan was sitting around the dining table when John poked his head in the door. 'They're here.'

I sighed and rose, the rest of the family following me. We went into the living room. The Dragon, the Phoenix and the Tiger were there, as well as a couple of the Academy dragons, and Gold. The Celestial Masters Meredith and Liu had also come to help out.

'Step forward,' the Dragon ordered brusquely. 'I want to re-evaluate you, to see who would be the best to carry you.'

My family stepped forward without saying a word.

'Okay, say goodbye now,' the Dragon said, gesturing impatiently.

I hugged my father and kissed my mother. 'Goodbye,' I choked. 'I'll see you soon. I'll come and visit you in the Western Palace.'

My mother held me close and stroked my hair. 'Come and see us soon, love.'

I went to Amanda and Alan. 'I am so sorry about this, guys.'

'We'll live,' Alan said. 'As long as the boys are safe.'

We hugged and kissed goodbye. Simone raced to Mark and David and kissed them both on the cheek, embarrassing them horribly.

I went to Jennifer and stood in front of her, silently, for a while.

'I'm sorry, Jen,' I whispered without looking up.

'Emma,' she said, and I looked at her. She held her arms out and I fell into them and held her tight.

'You know I can't stay mad at you,' she said.

'I don't deserve a family as wonderful as you,' I said into her shoulder.

John came into the living room. He paused in the doorway, looked down and put his hands behind his back.

'You don't need to say anything, John,' my father said. He gestured with his head. 'Come on.'

John looked up at my father, his face rigid, then strode to stand in front of him.

My father put his hand out. 'Will we see you again?'

John shook his hand. 'I don't know. If you come down from the palace I can see you, but I can't travel there. And it might be best if you stayed in the palace until the demon is destroyed. Destroying it will probably kill me as well.'

'But you'll come back?' my mother said. 'Emma said you'll come back.'

John released my father's hand. 'Yes. I've promised Emma that I'll come back.'

'How long will it take?' Alan said.

John was silent.

'Anything from ten to a hundred years,' I said without looking up. 'Probably something in the region of twenty to twenty-five years is the best bet.'

'Oh God, Emma,' Jennifer said.

'A hundred years? So it's possible that you could already be dead when he comes back?' Amanda said.

'More than possible,' I said. 'But he's promised.'

'What if you're very old?' Amanda said. 'What if it takes a very long time?'

I just shrugged.

My mother went to John and embraced him. He seemed surprised for a moment, then put his arms around her and held her.

'Look after her,' my mother said into his chest.

He pulled away to smile down at her. 'You know I will. I love her more than anything in the world. She and Simone — the two most precious things in the world to me.'

'He's given up everything for us,' I whispered.

'This is all very delightful and pleasant,' the Dragon said loudly, 'but I have places I need to be.'

John didn't look at the Dragon; he remained holding my mother. 'Wait.'

The Dragon shifted his feet and sighed loudly.

'If you need anything at the palace, tell the staff,' John said. 'You will be allocated servants. If they are insufficient, then just tell the Tiger.'

'Don't worry, Ah Wu, you know I'll look after them,' the Tiger said gruffly. 'I'll bring Michael back with me when I return.'

John dropped his head and released my mother. 'Goodbye.'

'I wish circumstances could have been different,' Alan said.

'So do I,' John said. 'Now, each of you has been assigned a carrier. Go to them. Goodbye.'

'Bye, all,' I said.

Simone ran to my parents. 'Bye, Mr Donahoe, Mrs Donahoe,' she said, reaching up to hug both of them. 'I love you.'

My mother crouched to hold her close. 'Bye, darling Simone. I didn't have a granddaughter until now, and I always hoped Emma would give me one. And she already did.'

'When Daddy's killed One Two Two you can come and stay for a long time,' Simone said. 'Promise you'll come back.'

'I promise,' my mother said. 'And you must come to Australia.'

'Okay,' Simone said, pulling away. 'I think you should go now, otherwise Emma's going to cry.'

My family moved to the Shen and Immortals. The carriers lowered their heads and everybody disappeared.

None of us said a word. I turned and went down the hallway to the student room to collect my stuff and return it to my bedroom. John went to his office. Simone went into her room. We were all very quiet for a long time.

CHAPTER SEVEN

I didn't need to see John's face to know that he wore an expression of amused satisfaction as we entered his office on the top floor of the Hennessy Road Academy building. Chinese New Year had come and gone; there had been no more attacks; and it was time for me to take up my duties as Regent-to-be. But mostly I had to do it because by February I had run out of excuses.

The Generals were already sitting around a conjured conference table, waiting for us. They all rose and saluted formally and carefully. John nodded back and gestured for them to sit.

They turned and saluted me. I hesitated. Then I decided: what the hell.

'Hi, guys,' I said with a small wave.

'Lady Emma,' they all said, not completely in unison, and waited for John and me to sit before they sat themselves.

Damn. I *hated* that. It took most Chinese a very long time to loosen up. Australians were usually cheerful and relaxed right from the start; Chinese stayed stiff and formal for ages.

'Lady Emma's time is limited, she has a class to teach

in an hour, so we will dispense with the formalities,' John said. 'Let me introduce everybody —'

'Don't bother,' I said. 'I'm hopeless with names; I'll just forget them straightaway. Let me ask you your names when I need them, and I'll try to remember them. But I'll probably have to ask you all more than once. If anybody's offended by that, let me know now.'

Nobody said anything. The Generals all watched me, emotionless.

Great.

I looked around the table. Eight of them, standard-looking Chinese men, all very stern, all middle-aged. A variety of shapes and sizes, all wearing old-fashioned Chinese lacquer armour, some with short hair, some with the more traditional long hair. A couple of them looked really severe and scary, but three had definite twinkles in their eyes.

I stole a glance at John. He was already taking notes. I took a deep breath. Okay.

John slid an agenda across the table to me. I didn't look at it immediately; I watched the Generals.

'First item,' John said. 'Demons.'

One of the severe-looking Generals leaned forward and put his hand on the table. 'The Fifth Battalion has had one hundred and fifty demons attain perfection in the last year; the Fourth has had only five or six. The Fifth has no new recruits; the Fourth has had seventy-five. We need to transfer the new recruits to the Fifth.'

'They will stay where they are,' John said.

'The Fifth is undermanned.'

John didn't move or speak.

'My Lord,' the General said, obviously impatient, 'you need to set up some sort of administrative procedure for the allocation of the demons. We need to ask you every single time, and every time it's different.

We need something down on paper to define the methods you use for allocation.'

'Lady Emma?' John said.

I glanced down at the agenda and nearly gasped. He'd read my mind. At the bottom of the first page was a diagram of the table with names where everyone was sitting. He'd even used phonetic spellings, not *pinyin*, so that I could pronounce the names easily. I shot him a quick, grateful glance. His face didn't change but his eyes sparkled.

'General Song,' I said. The General didn't move. 'I thought that all of you had been Raised and were Immortal.'

All of them straightened slightly at that.

'That is true,' General Song said.

'Then why do you want the Dark Lord to write down administrative procedures? You want to make a rod for your own back? You start with the paperwork, it never finishes. You make rules, then you have to make exceptions. Endless exceptions. And the rules give you no flexibility. You can't take each situation as it comes. If Lord Xuan wants to allocate the demons differently each time, then it's his prerogative. He knows what he's doing. He probably doesn't even have a set of rules; he just does it how he sees fit at the time.' The General's face didn't move at all while I made my little speech. 'Frankly, I can't see how you've attained Immortality if you want to put everything down on paper.'

All of the Generals heaved a sigh of relief and relaxed. A couple of them even smiled slightly.

John spread his hands over the table. 'See? What did I tell you.' He pushed his agenda away. 'Right. Now let's have this meeting.'

'You mean that was a *test*?' I said.

'They didn't believe me,' John said.

I glanced around at the Generals. Now *all* their eyes sparkled at me, even though their faces were still grim.

'Will all of you stay in the same seats at the table until I have you worked out?' I said.

All of them nodded without saying a word.

'There are thirty-six of them altogether, Emma,' John said without turning to me. 'Hopefully we'll be able to rotate everybody through so that you can meet all of them. I'll give you a diagram each time.'

'Okay.' I shrugged. 'Meeting. Let's get this over with.'

One of the Generals raised his index finger slightly. 'One Two Two. Tell us.'

'It's easier to tell everybody like this rather than directly one at a time,' John said, explaining. 'Questions can be asked, information can flow, ideas can bounce. One Two Two. Gold has been cultivating a police officer in the investigative squad ...'

I glanced down at the agenda. A short message was written underneath the diagram in John's English scrawl. *I tried to tell them but they wouldn't believe me. Can't wait to see the looks on their faces. Oh, and by the way, give them hell.*

I tapped on the door of John's office. 'Come in, Emma,' he said.

I entered and sat across the desk from him with the school calendar in my hand.

'You know you don't need to knock. I can feel you coming. When's spring break?' he said.

'April,' I said. 'Same time as Easter. About eight weeks from now.'

He didn't say anything, he just watched me expressionlessly.

'If you won't make it that far, then we'll take Simone out of school for a week and leave Michael here,' I said. 'Try not to push yourself too hard, love.'

He glanced down at his hands. His face was still expressionless.

'Simone's not ready. She can't defend herself. If something really big comes after us, there's nothing we can do. You *have* to stay longer,' I said.

He looked directly at me. His eyes blazed.

'Can you sense it?'

He shook his head.

'We *need* you. I knew we should have done it at Chinese New Year.'

'If I go into a coma before April, call the Lady,' he said.

'A *coma*?'

He shrugged and smiled slightly.

'If you go into a coma, how long will we have to get her here?'

'Hours.'

'What if she's in retreat, John?' I said desperately.

He shrugged again, but the smile had disappeared.

'We should do it before April then,' I said.

'I want to leave it as long as I can. I only have two more.' His face was rigid with control. 'I will need at least ten days.'

I glanced at the calendar. 'You'll get it. The break is two weeks altogether. We'll have fourteen days, so we can go to London as well. You want me to organise the trip to Europe?'

'No. I won't make it to Paris. It's too far from my Centre now. I'll arrange something else.'

'How long will you last afterwards?' I said, studying the calendar.

He leaned back, grimaced, and retied his hair. 'December if we're lucky. Earlier if we're not. Probably earlier.'

'December.' I counted the months. 'And then August next year ... the end.'

'Probably before then, love, if we're attacked again,' he said.

'We'll be attacked again, I know we will,' I said grimly. 'That little bastard won't sleep until he has your head.'

'If it comes to a choice between you using that phone and him having my head, give him my head,' John said. 'Do it.'

'His word's not good, you know that,' I said. 'He'll come straight after Simone if he has your head. And me. And Leo, and Michael, and anybody else he can get his hands on. I won't have a choice, love.'

John studied his hands.

'Just make sure you stay with us,' I said. 'As long as you're with us, we'll be okay. *Look after yourself*. For Simone.'

'If I run into the Serpent alone, that will be the end of it,' he said.

I didn't say anything.

He looked me straight in the eye. 'There is a way to hold the Serpent off. We can be imprisoned.'

'What?'

'You can bind us. With the right sort of enclosure, it's possible to bind the Serpent. Stop it from joining.'

'Could the Turtle be bound as well? With the right sort of enclosure?'

'Yes.'

'Even at full strength?'

'Yes.'

'Even the combined creature?'

'Yes.'

'Oh my God. How many people know of this, John?'

'Myself. The Lady. The other three Winds — a similar thing may be inflicted upon them. The Celestial. Others, I don't know.'

'Does the Demon King know?'

89

'I don't know. He's never tried me.'

I put my head in my hands. 'Oh *God*.'

'We should try to enclose the Serpent. That way there is no risk of me running into it alone and rejoining.'

'I couldn't do that to you,' I whispered. 'I love you too much to do that to you. Either of you.'

'Get out! Quickly!'

I shot out of my seat and ran to the door. I fumbled with the handle, eventually managed to open the door and threw myself out. I leaned against the wall of the hallway and breathed. I had to stop doing this to us. Every time we mentioned our feelings for each other, I had to leave the room before he drained me completely.

We won't be going to Paris, I will arrange another place. I am calling the Lady now.

After school the next day Simone and I were spread out in the living room doing her homework. She didn't really need my help, she was exceptionally bright, but we enjoyed the time spent together.

The doorbell rang. 'It's Aunty Kwan,' Simone said, 'and Qing Long. With Jade.'

'Wonderful! Jade's back!' I cried, shooting to my feet.

I rushed to answer the door, but Leo was ahead of me. He opened the door. 'My Lord. My Lady.' He nodded to Jade and she nodded back without smiling.

Qing Long didn't say anything as he stepped through the door. He was in his normal human form, taller than Leo, slim and elegant as a dancer, with turquoise hair and matching eyes, and wearing a grey silk embossed robe.

Kwan Yin stopped and took Leo's hands. 'Hello, Leo. Let me look at you. You look well.'

'Thank you, my Lady,' Leo said.

I took Jade's hands and studied her. 'Are you okay?' I said.

Jade nodded without looking up. 'Just fine, my Lady. Lord Qing cared for me exceptionally well.'

Leo stopped and listened. 'Lord Xuan says Ms Kwan and Lord Qing are to go to the dining room.'

'What's happening?' I said.

Come in too, Emma, John said into my ear.

'I have to go too,' I said to Jade.

'I have work to do,' Jade said. 'The accounts will be backed up for weeks. By your leave, I'll return to the Academy.'

I nodded to Jade and she disappeared.

'Leo, I've been called in as well,' I said. 'Mind Simone for me? Help her with her maths?'

Simone giggled. 'More like I help him with his maths.'

Leo grinned. 'That's right.'

I followed Ms Kwan and the Dragon into the dining room. Qing Long stopped and saluted John before sitting.

John nodded. 'Qing Long.'

I remained silent, wondering.

'For your benefit, Emma, I'll tell you what I'd like to do. Paris is too far; I won't make it such a distance from my Centre, now. But I do want to be as far from the demons' Centre as I can manage.'

'The resort is on the Eastern Rim. It should suffice,' Qing Long said. 'I will provide you with suitable accommodation. Do it there.'

'Where?' I said.

'Kota Kinabalu,' John said. 'Sabah. Borneo.'

'I've heard about KK,' I said.

'It is as far away from the Centre as the Dark Lord can manage in his current state,' Ms Kwan said. 'Far enough away from the demons' Centre, yet still close enough to our own.'

'Is the water there clean enough for you to swim?' I said.

'Dragon?' John said.

'Yes,' the Dragon said. 'The shoreline is slightly polluted, but if you go through quickly it shouldn't be a problem. Out on the islands, in the marine park, absolutely. Should be clean enough.'

'Excellent!' I said. 'You can do both!' I grinned at the Dragon. 'Lord Qing Long, thank you so very much. You have no idea how much we appreciate this.'

'Good,' the Dragon said with a small smile. 'I'm losing a lot of income giving you the Presidential Suite and providing you with demon staff.'

'I'll give you a pile of gold to sit on,' John said.

'Ah Wu! That was uncalled for,' Ms Kwan said.

John and the Dragon flashed each other a quick smile.

'Will we take everybody?' I said.

'Michael is to go to the Western Palace and spend time with his family,' John said. 'So are you.'

I shot to my feet, ready to shout. Then I changed my mind and sat down again. 'I should spend this holiday time with my family,' I said softly.

'Exactly,' John said.

'So I will spend it with you. And Simone, and Leo. And Ms Kwan. My family.'

He opened his mouth to protest.

'I don't have much longer with you. Every second counts.'

He closed his mouth with a snap.

'Good,' I said. 'Can we take the jet to the airport there?'

'Yes,' Qing Long said. 'I will arrange it. Leave it to me. Enjoy. The resort is quite new and very elegant. I think you will like it.'

'What are the chances of us being attacked while we're there?' I said.

'Minute,' the Dragon said. 'I have placed extensive seals on the resort. I will be there. You will be undisturbed.'

'Dragon, thank you so much,' I said.

'You are most welcome, my Lady,' he said with a small blue smile.

CHAPTER EIGHT

It was coming to the end of term in late March. Michael, Simone and I went up to Simone's classroom together, Simone prattling about her schoolwork and Michael silent. I dropped Simone at her classroom and gave her a hug and a kiss. She waved cheerfully to us as we left.

Michael and I threaded our way through the parents and children on the first floor to get to the uniform shop. I was rostered to help out that day, and he needed some new trousers. I kept threatening that if he didn't stop growing I'd chop his legs off. He didn't think it was funny at all.

Michael would be as tall as his father when he was fully grown. He already towered over me. The Tiger was delighted.

Despite the fact that he looked ridiculous in his too-small uniform, Michael still didn't want to go into the shop and buy new pants. He had given me an extremely hard time about me doing it myself, but I wanted to be sure that the pants would fit.

We entered the uniform shop together and he immediately slouched into Sullen Teenager mode. I glared at him. He glared back.

I greeted the two women behind the counter, and they both smiled and waved back. Jessie was a tall, slim Chinese lady who'd been born and raised in the UK, then married an Australian engineer and moved around the world with him, latest stop Hong Kong. Short, blonde Bridget was the wife of an Australian airline pilot and had been in the Territory for many years.

'Michael's getting some new trousers,' I said.

'Sure, Emma,' Bridget said. 'Looks like he needs them. Need to put a brick on his head.'

Michael scowled but didn't say anything.

'Turn around,' I said, and he obliged. 'What size are these ones?'

I lifted his shirt to check the size and laughed. Like most of the boys in his year, he had the trousers pulled down over his hips with a pair of silk boxers from Temple Street showing above them.

'You look ridiculous like that,' I said, and pulled at the waistband of the trousers to check the size.

'Cut it out, Emma!' Michael dragged my hand off and jumped away. 'Let me check the size myself!' He dropped his voice. 'You're as embarrassing as my *mother* sometimes.'

'That's a compliment, Emma,' Bridget called from the other side of the shop, where she was watching us with amusement.

'Go and check the size then,' I said, gesturing towards the changing booths. 'I'll find you some to try that are two or three sizes bigger.'

Michael slunk into the changing room.

Bridget and I shared a smile. Jessie looked confused; she didn't know about the Chen family.

There were some rustles and grunts in the changing room, then Michael called, 'Twenty-nine.'

'Way too small,' Bridget said. 'Thirty-three or thirty-five at least.'

I pulled some larger sizes off the sample rack and handed them through the curtain to him. He grabbed the curtain and wrenched it closed.

'How about his PE uniform?' Bridget said. 'Are his shorts too small too?'

'No!' Michael said.

'Yeah,' I said. 'But if we get uniform pants that fit, the PE shorts just need to be the same size.'

'Thirty-three is okay,' Michael said. 'Can I go now?'

'Come out and let me see,' I said.

Michael sidled out of the changing room scowling. The pants did appear to be long enough, but I wanted to check.

'Lift the shirt, let me see,' I said patiently.

He almost didn't do it, then caved in and raised his shirt. These pants were also pulled way down over his hips, and obviously too small around the middle.

'Go and try on the next size up,' I said.

He scowled, turned and went back into the changing room, jamming the curtain closed.

'What size jeans does he wear?' Bridget said.

'Forty-four,' I said, and she snorted with laughter.

I had no problem with Michael wearing jeans that were ten sizes too big for him. It meant he could carry a small weapon and it was unnoticeable. That was where the fashion for pants that were much too large had originated, and it suited us just fine. He couldn't carry his white katana, that was too big. But he could slip the matching *wakizashi*, a long dagger, easily into one pocket and it was entirely invisible. He'd never been caught with it in a shopping mall or on the street, and he'd already had to use it three or four times, but not on humans. Guys still came after him, but he was a match for any human bare-handed. The weapon was for demons.

John had suggested that Michael be armed at school and we'd had a huge argument about it, me and

Michael both firmly against it. If he was caught with it in the changing room or at the lockers he'd be in serious trouble.

The bell on the shop door rang and Kitty Kwok wandered in, as casual as anything, and strolled up to the counter.

'Michael, have a careful look around right now,' I said loudly.

There was silence from the changing room. Then: 'Nothing,' Michael said. 'Any problem, Emma?'

I went to the curtain and spoke quietly. 'Mrs Simon Wong just walked in.'

'Holy shit,' he whispered over the frantic sounds of him dressing. 'You want me to call someone?'

'Check Simone,' I said softly as he threw the curtain back and peered around.

His eyes unfocused, then snapped back. 'She says she's okay.'

'Are you absolutely sure there are no demons anywhere near here?' I said.

His eyes unfocused again. 'None. Simone says no as well.'

Kitty chatted with Bridget.

'She may have brought humans, Emma,' Michael said. 'Neither of us can sense them.'

'Let's go up to Simone's classroom,' I said. 'Leave the pants. Let's go.'

Kitty ignored us completely as we went out.

'What the hell is going on?' I said as we headed to the stairs.

She's following us, he said silently.

'Can we take her? The two of us?' I whispered as we went up to the second floor where Simone's class was. Kitty wandered casually behind us.

'Easily,' Michael said. 'She's a perfectly normal human being with no training whatsoever.'

'What the hell is she doing then?' I hissed. 'She's on the run from the police right now!'

'You want me to call for help?' Michael said.

At the top of the stairs I hesitated. 'Let's check Simone first.'

Michael nodded and we both went to Simone's classroom. I didn't open the door; I used my Inner Eye to check inside. No demons. Michael's eyes snapped back to focus on me; he had been doing the same thing.

Everything's fine, Emma, Simone said silently.

Kitty came up the stairs behind us. Michael and I readied ourselves.

Kitty walked right past us and tapped on the classroom door, then opened it. She ignored us completely. Michael and I shared a look. When she went in, we followed her.

Kitty went up to the teacher and smiled. 'I'm here to take Helen to the dentist.'

Michael and I posted ourselves either side of the door and waited.

'Sure, Mrs Ho,' the teacher said.

One of the little girls rose from her desk and went straight to Kitty and took her hand. Kitty turned and walked right past us out the door, the little girl holding her hand and smiling.

Michael and I spun and followed her. Both of us ignored the look the teacher gave us.

This is extremely weird, Michael said.

Kitty stopped and waited for us outside the classroom. 'This is my niece, Helen. Say hello to Miss Donahoe, Helen.'

'Hello,' the little girl said, obviously shy.

'What are you going to do to her?' I said.

'I'm taking her to the dentist,' Kitty said.

'You're not taking her anywhere.'

'Go in and ask the teacher. I'll wait for you,' Kitty

said. 'She's my niece. I collect her from school all the time.'

'What are you up to?'

'You have a problem with me taking her?' Kitty said.

I suddenly understood. I went to the little girl. 'Can you give me your hand, please, sweetheart?' I said. 'Double-check for me, Michael.'

Michael came up behind me as I took the little girl's hand. As far as I could see, she was a perfectly ordinary human.

The little girl stiffened and squeaked, her eyes wide. Then she relaxed. Michael had turned his Inner Eye on her.

Perfectly ordinary human, Michael said.

'Is this your aunty, Helen?' I said.

The little girl nodded without saying anything.

'Oh, I'm sick of this. I'll take her to the dentist another day,' Kitty said. 'Come on, sweetheart, I'll take you back to class.' She spun on her heel and went back to the classroom, holding the little girl's hand. The girl glanced back at me, eyes wide, as Kitty pulled her through the door.

We followed them. Kitty came out of the classroom and walked briskly away, passing us as if we weren't there.

What the hell is she up to? Michael said.

I peeked through the classroom door. The little girl had returned to her desk as if nothing was amiss.

I hesitated. Then I went in. 'Can I talk to you privately for a moment?' I said quietly to the teacher, a sweet blonde Australian woman by the name of Jo.

Jo glanced at the class, then shrugged. I led her out of the classroom, where Michael was waiting.

'Is there a problem, Emma?' Jo said.

'That woman's on the run from the police,' I said. 'Underworld connections.'

Jo inhaled sharply. 'I didn't know. You sure?'

'Damn right I am. I know her well. Her boyfriend keeps trying to kidnap Simone.'

'Is that why you're here?' she said, eyes wide. 'You thought she was about to try something?'

'Why'd she take Helen?' I said.

Jo paused, her eyes still wide. 'That's strange. She's in and out all the time. She's always taking Helen for doctor's appointments, bringing her back, all the time. Sometimes she collects her from school. Never had a problem with her. She always treats Helen really well.'

'This is extremely weird,' Michael said behind me.

Jo glanced up at Michael. He was slightly taller than her as well. 'Why aren't you in class?'

Both of us shrugged the question off. 'Do you have the number for Helen's parents? Or her home address? I want to check this out.'

Jo hesitated. She was obviously reluctant about giving out this sort of information.

Michael went rigid behind me. I felt what he did, even though I didn't know what it was.

Jo's face went slack. Her eyes unfocused. 'I'll get it for you,' she said absently. She turned and went back into the classroom, her eyes unseeing.

'That's a neat trick,' I said. 'When did you learn that?'

'Na Zha taught me,' Michael said. 'Please don't tell my dad or Lord Xuan, Emma. I don't think they wanted me to learn how to do it.'

'Why not?'

Michael laughed softly. 'Think about it.'

I understood. 'I don't think you would use it irresponsibly. I think we can trust you. You're a very honourable young man. I know I trust you.'

'Thanks, Emma.'

The teacher came out and handed me a piece of paper.

'Thanks, Jo,' I said.

Jo immediately snapped out of it.

Michael spoke before she could say anything.

'We'd better go and finish in the uniform shop, Emma. My teacher'll be waiting.'

'You're right,' I said. 'And I'm supposed to be working there. Thanks a lot, Jo. I'll leave you to it.'

Jo smiled, turned, and went back into the classroom.

'Have you done anything with metal?' I said. 'That would be very useful.'

'Nothing,' Michael said.

'I'll call Helen's mother,' I said. 'You'd better head back to class. I'll pick up the uniform for you at the same time.'

'Very good, my Lady,' Michael said with a smile.

'You are very cheeky,' I said as we went our opposite ways.

I felt bad about making the call, but it was the only way I could be sure.

'*Wei?*'

'Is Mrs Leung there, please?'

'*Wei?*'

'Can I speak to Mrs Leung, please?'

'Who asking?'

'I'm calling from the Australian School. I want to check about Helen Leung.'

'Wait.' There were rustles, some shouting, then footsteps.

'*Wei?*'

'Hello, is that Mrs Leung?'

'Who is asking?'

'I'm from the Australian School, Mrs Leung. I just wanted to double-check the pick-up arrangements for Helen.'

'Okay. Is there a problem?'

'No problem. I just want to confirm. The people who can collect Helen are you, Helen's father, her *poh poh*,' I used the Cantonese term for 'grandmother', 'and Mrs Kitty Ho.'

'Is correct.'

I was completely floored. I hesitated. I wanted to ask more, but anything I said would probably blow my story. I decided to tackle it head-on and see what reaction I could produce.

'One of the other mothers has claimed that Mrs Kitty Ho is wanted by the police, Mrs Leung. I just wanted to hear your side of the story before we did anything.'

She hung up.

CHAPTER NINE

I held a brainstorming session with John, Michael and Leo. But not a lot of storming happened. We sat silently for a long time.

'Come on, Emma, help us out here,' John said. 'Think.'

'My brain's already worn out from turning this over,' I said. 'I have no idea what's going on.'

'She must be taking the little girl for experiments or something,' Leo said.

'That's obvious,' I said. 'The question is: why? Why do the parents let her? And why did she do it right in front of us? And make such a performance out of it? She came to the uniform shop first, to make sure that we'd follow her.'

'Call the police,' Michael said. 'Let them know. They'll pick her up — end of problem.'

'We have had quite enough contact with the police as it is,' John said. 'Remember, Michael, both Leo and I will die soon. I will die very soon. We want it to be clean and above board, no legal complications whatsoever. I want as little to do with the police as possible right now, so that when I go there are no questions.'

'How soon, my Lord?' Michael said softly.

I dropped my head into my hands.

'I doubt that I'll make it past the middle of next year,' John said. 'In fact, I doubt I'll make it past the end of this year. I have two more sessions with Kwan Yin, including this one coming up. After that, probably less than a year.'

Leo inhaled sharply. He leaned forward over the table and his voice became fierce. 'Simone's not ready yet! She won't be ready! You must stay, my Lord. Once you're gone I won't last long.' He looked down and his voice softened. 'I have a mouth ulcer already.'

'Oh my God, no!' I said wretchedly. 'No.'

John glanced at Leo. 'After Kota Kinabalu I'll be able to clear it again, Leo. It's only two more weeks. Just be careful.'

'What?' Michael said. 'My Lord. Leo, sir. Please. Explain.' He spoke with a very slight desperate edge to his voice. 'Please don't keep me in the dark.'

'I told you I'm HIV positive, and that's why we brought you in,' Leo said. Michael nodded. 'Well, it's more than that. It's already full-on AIDS. I was in second stage. But Lord Xuan can keep me clear of the virus as long as I'm in his service. I've been tested, and given the all clear, since I joined the household.'

'But you said you have a mouth ulcer,' Michael said. 'Does that mean . . .?'

'I'm very drained, Michael,' John said, his eyes burning. Michael was silent.

'I've already taken myself off bladed weapons until after the trip,' Leo said. 'My Lord, please inform all the staff. Infection control, if I'm wounded. It may be best just to leave me if I'm severely wounded; tell one of the Celestial Masters to send me away. I don't want to infect anybody. I should stop teaching anyway. I don't want to put any of the students at risk.'

'You will continue to teach at the Academy. You will continue your duties as if nothing was different. You will not handle bladed weapons in class, but you will still teach them. That is the only difference that I will permit. And that is an order, Leo,' John said.

'My Lord,' Leo said, full of anguish.

'Helen Leung,' John said briskly, returning to the matter at hand. 'What can we do?'

'Has Simone had her over to play?' Michael said.

All of us straightened.

'Very good, Michael,' John said. 'We can have her here and check up on her. We can talk to her.'

'What if that's the intention?' I said. 'What if Kitty lined her up to be brought over here to try something?'

'She's a normal human, yes?' John said.

I nodded a reply.

'Then she can't do anything. Let's ask Simone to invite her here, and see what happens.'

I showed Helen to the door where her Indonesian domestic helper waited for her. 'Bye, sweetheart,' I said. 'I hope you had fun.'

'Bye, Emma,' Helen said. 'Bye, Simone. See you at school.'

'Only one week left!' Simone said with a jiggle of excitement. 'I'm going to Kota Kinabalu for the holidays!'

'I'm going to Phuket,' Helen said. 'Bye.'

The domestic helper took her out. I dropped Simone with Leo, then went into John's office. I sat across the desk from him and we studied each other. I shrugged.

'Why then?' John said.

There was a tap on the office door.

'Enter, Michael,' John said.

Michael came in, his face rigid with restraint, holding something in a towel. He put it on the desk, on top of the pile of papers. 'I suggest you don't touch it, my Lord.'

Both John and I leaned forward and studied it carefully. It was a little stone turtle, a very common household decoration in Hong Kong. It appeared to be made of rose quartz.

John put his hand over the turtle without touching it, then closed his eyes and concentrated.

'The little girl left it here,' Michael said. 'I could sense it from my room.'

'It's not a bug, is it?' I said. 'We don't have to be careful talking near it?'

'Nope,' Michael said. 'No idea what it is. Not a bug, though.'

John pulled his hand away and opened his eyes, then concentrated again.

Gold appeared between Michael and myself. He leaned forward and studied the turtle carefully. He picked it up. 'What do you say, Dad?'

The stone was silent.

'Give it a tap, my Lady,' Gold said.

I tapped the stone.

'Yes, my ...' Its voice trailed off, then went fierce. 'What the hell is that?'

Gold turned it over in his hands. 'No idea.'

'Let me have a look,' the stone said.

'Take the ring off first, my Lady,' Gold said. 'I don't think you should touch it either.'

I removed the ring and handed it to Gold. He touched the ring to the turtle.

'Get it off!' the stone squawked.

Gold jerked the ring away. 'Sorry, Dad.'

'Give me back to the Lady,' the stone said.

Gold returned the ring to me and I put it back on my finger.

'I've opened it. You can see what it is now,' the stone said.

'I see,' John said. 'Have either of you encountered anything like this before?'

Gold shook his head. The stone was silent.

'Would it be safe for me to look inside it?' I said. 'What's so different about it anyway?'

'Look inside,' John said. 'But slowly, carefully.'

I opened my Inner Eye and studied the little pink turtle. Gold placed it on the pile of papers so that I could have a better look. It was like a miniature black hole. It was sucking reality into it. I suddenly knew that if I were to touch it, I would be pulled straight into it.

'So that was the point of the exercise,' I said softly. 'To get one of us to touch that.'

'That bitch is using *human children* to do her dirty work,' John said.

'Would it just kill me, or would it transport me somewhere?' I said.

'Probably a transport device,' Gold said. 'Shades of *Star Trek*.'

'Never seen anything like it before,' the stone said. 'Ingenious. Wait until the Grandmother hears about this. She'll be after this demon *personally*.'

I nodded to Michael. 'Thanks.'

'Sometimes I am extremely glad we have you around, Michael,' John said. 'You are the only one in the household who sensed this thing. Try to keep your abilities to yourself. As long as they aren't aware of them, we're at an advantage.'

'My Lord,' Michael said, then flashed me a quick smile.

'I saw that,' John said quickly. 'Tell me now. That's an order.'

'Damn,' Michael said softly. He sighed, then shrugged. 'Okay, coercion. And PK.'

'You have PK too?' I said.

'What's PK?' John said. 'You've mentioned that before, Emma.'

'Psychokinesis,' I said. 'The ability to move things with the mind.'

'Oh, carrying,' John said, understanding. 'You have ordering *and* carrying, Michael? When did you learn this?'

'A couple of weeks ago,' Michael said.

'Your father taught you?'

Michael dropped his head and didn't reply.

'Na Zha, I think,' I said.

'Damn, I'm impressed,' John said. 'Well done, Michael.'

Michael's head shot up, his blond hair flopping with the movement. 'You're not upset?'

'Every skill you gain is a skill that will give Emma and Simone an edge,' John said. 'We will start you on advanced work immediately. If you do not eventually find the Tao I will be extremely surprised.' He leaned back, his voice full of satisfaction. 'The Tiger is most definitely not having you back.'

Michael grinned broadly. 'Thanks, Lord Xuan.'

I rose. 'I'll get Simone, see if she could sense it.'

I didn't need to. Simone came bursting through the door, with Leo close behind her. She skidded to a halt, cast around, saw the turtle, shouted 'Nobody touch it!', put her hands out towards it, palms facing away from her, and somehow made it explode into a million tiny pieces.

Everybody disappeared in a cloud of dust. I coughed; my eyes were full of turtle fragments.

'Gold!' John said over the sound of everybody coughing.

It was like an exhaust fan was suddenly switched on: Gold somehow vacuumed the fragments into himself. The dust cleared quickly.

'Whoops, sorry,' Simone said, her voice very small.

'No, Simone, you did well,' John said. 'When did you know it was there?'

'I thought something was strange,' she said. 'I could feel it. I was going to ask you to look for me. It was in

my room, then it came in here, then it kind of went ...'
She tilted her head. '*Kablooie*. What was it?'

'If you had touched it, it would have taken you to the bad demon,' I said. 'But it needed to be turned on. The stone in my ring turned it on.'

Simone nodded.

'But you sensed it before it was turned on?' I said.

'Yep. I knew she'd left it there. I knew there was something strange going on.' Her little shoulders sagged. 'I thought Helen was my *friend*.'

'I'm taking her out of school,' John said. 'Until we have dealt with this, it is no longer safe for her.'

'NO!' Everybody shouted it in unison, even Leo.

'I want to go to school!' Simone wailed.

'We can handle it!' I shouted.

'She'll be miserable at home!' Leo said loudly.

I looked at Leo. He shrugged and smiled slightly.

I turned back to John. Everybody was glaring at him. I leaned over the desk and glared at him too.

'You have been outvoted, Xuan Wu,' I said firmly. 'Give it up. She could sense the device. And she is staying in school.'

'She won't be safe,' John growled.

'Time for us to disappear,' Leo said. 'Come on, Simone, Michael.'

'Don't you want to stay and see the fireworks?' I said, still glaring at John.

'I'm staying,' Simone said. 'I'm staying in school.' She ran around the desk and threw herself at her father. He pulled her into his lap. She turned to face him, her hands on his shoulders, and smiled into his eyes. 'Please let me stay in school, Daddy.' She smiled sweetly, wheedling. 'Please?'

John's face was grim but his eyes sparkled with amusement.

'You know you can't say no to her,' I said softly.

Simone put her chin on his chest and smiled up into his eyes. 'Please?'

'Women!' Leo growled. 'Come on, Michael, let's get out of here. You'd better take off too, Gold. When the Dark Lord surrenders to his women it's not a pretty sight.'

I didn't look away but I heard the door close.

'I'll let you kiss Emma,' Simone said slyly. 'For as long as you like.'

John glanced up at me and couldn't hold his face any more. He chuckled.

I dropped my head and shook it. 'I didn't teach her this, John, don't blame me.'

'Come and give Daddy a kiss, Emma, and then you and me are going to check through my room and see if Helen dropped anything else,' Simone said. 'And on Monday you have to tell Miss Atkinson to give me a different desk in the classroom, so I'm not so close to Helen.'

I went around the desk. Simone pulled herself out of John's lap and stood next to him, still holding his hand.

John rose, grabbed me around the waist with his free hand, pulled me in and kissed me hard. I threw my arms around his neck and pressed myself into him.

'Tell me when you're finished 'cause I'm *not looking*,' Simone said loudly.

We smiled into each other's mouth, but we didn't stop. For a long time.

Leo, Michael and I went to Sha Tin, where Helen's family lived, on Monday. Leo parked in the car park of City One, a large estate of high-rise residential blocks, about fifty of them, all white-tiled and around twenty storeys. They were spread around a central market and shopping centre, but still very close together. Some of them had a view over the Shing Mun River. Each floor of the apartment blocks held about eight units.

'Block thirty-three,' I said as we walked out of the car park.

The three of us attracted some attention as we made our way through the estate. A small Caucasian woman, an enormous black man and a blond half-Chinese were hardly the usual sort of people seen in an estate like this.

The entrance to block thirty-three was standard: a large metal gate with a keypad beside it. I pressed the floor and flat numbers for the Leungs' unit and moved back.

'*Wei?*'

Michael moved his head next to the intercom microphone. '*Mgoi, Pak Gai. Hui mun.*'

The door buzzed.

'She *does* order things from the supermarket,' I said as Leo opened the gate and gestured for us to go in. 'Well done, Michael.'

'Gold helped me,' Michael said.

The security guard wasn't asleep. He watched us curiously as we waited for the lift but didn't challenge us. Understandable: Leo was huge. I smiled and waved to the guard and he smiled slightly in return, but still watched Leo.

'I still think we should have brought weapons,' Leo said as we stepped out of the lift into the lobby of the nineteenth floor.

'The guard would be on the phone to the police right away.' I gestured towards the apartment door. 'Michael.'

I opened the door for the stairwell and Leo and I stood inside, out of the line of sight of the apartment. Michael pressed the button for the bell.

The door was opened by a young, innocent-looking Indonesian domestic helper. She studied Michael through the bars of the metal gate.

Michael grinned broadly. '*Pak Gai!*'

'Did we order?' she said with a thick provincial accent.

Michael's grin didn't shift. '*Pak Gai! Mgoi, hui mun!*'

The domestic helper unlocked the gate.

Michael grabbed the gate and threw it open, and Leo and I moved quickly. The three of us stormed into the apartment, pushing past the domestic helper, who shrieked and ducked.

Mrs Leung sat in the dining room, reading the newspaper. She saw the three of us and shot to her feet.

'We won't hurt you,' I said. 'Come with us, we want to talk to you.'

Her English was perfect. 'Who are you?' she said, obviously trying to control her terror. 'It's not a good idea to mess with me. I have friends.'

'We want to talk to you about a little pink stone turtle,' Leo said.

'I have no idea what you are talking about,' she said, but her face was ashen.

'We won't hurt you,' I said. 'We just want to ask you some questions.'

She cast around, looking for a way to escape. Then she gave up. 'Please don't hurt me,' she whispered.

An elderly Chinese lady came in from the hallway. She stopped when she saw us.

'Go inside, Mummy,' Mrs Leung said in Cantonese. 'I can handle this.'

The old lady squeaked and scurried back down the hallway.

I turned and gestured. 'Please, come with us.'

'Who are you?' she said once we were in the car and Leo was driving us back to the Peak. 'What are you?'

'Wait until we get there and then we can talk,' I said.

'Will Helen be okay if this takes a while? If you need us to, we can collect her from school as well.'

'Don't you go near her!' Mrs Leung snapped. 'I have enough trouble with that Kwok woman as it is! You stay away from her!'

'Thought so,' Leo said.

When we reached the front door to our apartment I stopped and studied Mrs Leung carefully. 'There are seals on this apartment,' I said. 'Big ones. If you're a demon, then tell me now. I don't want you destroyed by trying to walk in the door.'

'I am not a demon,' she said stiffly.

'Michael?' I said.

'She's not,' Michael said.

Leo opened the door and we guided her in. We all kicked off our shoes, even Mrs Leung.

John charged out of his office, slamming the door loudly behind him. He stormed up the hallway towards us, his face a grim mask of fury. He raised his hand and Dark Heavens sprang from its clips and flew into it. He quickly drew the sword, throwing the scabbard aside, and charged towards us.

Mrs Leung changed into a fox, ran into the living room and hid behind one of the sofas.

John walked into the centre of the living room, still holding the sword.

Leo softly closed the door behind us and we all moved to stand behind John.

'What is your name?' John demanded loudly.

'Leung Hong Wai Lam,' Mrs Leung said. 'Please don't hurt me. I had nothing to do with it, it was way before my time. My Lord, Celestial Highness, please. Mercy.'

'How old are you?'

'Fifty-seven.'

John lowered his sword. 'You are only a child.'

'Your Celestial Highness,' Mrs Leung said softly, 'I didn't know you were Simone's father. Please don't kill me. I am with child.'

'This is why you have been allowing the demon to control you?'

'I am not working with any demons,' she said, indignant. 'Kitty Kwok is human. She occasionally takes Helen. I don't know why, but she never hurts her, so I let her. The alternative is too horrible to contemplate.'

'Kitty Kwok is in league with a Demon Prince who wants to take my head,' John said.

Mrs Leung was silent.

'Come out, I won't hurt you,' John said with resignation. 'Leo.' He held Dark Heavens out to Leo, and Leo took the blade, collected the scabbard, and returned the sword to the wall.

Mrs Leung came out from behind the couch. She was a small red fox with a white tip on her tail. She cowered as she walked.

'Take human form,' John said. 'I want to ask you some questions.'

She changed back to a normal-looking Chinese woman in her mid-thirties wearing a smart pair of slacks and a designer polo shirt.

'Sit,' John said, gesturing towards the couch. 'I give you my word, I won't harm you.'

Mrs Leung gingerly turned and sat.

'Leo, take Simone to school,' John said. 'Make an excuse for her. Michael, go too. I will talk to this ...' His voice went cold. 'Child of Daji.'

Mrs Leung stiffened. 'I had nothing to do with that. I am not related in any way to that vixen.' Her voice softened and she looked down. 'My husband is human. I am attempting perfection. I live as a human. I have children.' She looked back up at John, desperate. 'You

114

know what my husband would say if he were to discover my true nature.'

'Very well,' John said, sitting on the other couch across from her. 'Tell us the whole story.'

I moved to stand behind John, leaning on the back of the couch.

'Not much to tell,' she said with a shrug. 'Kitty takes Helen and returns her unharmed.'

'Completely unharmed?' I interrupted. 'She doesn't have any minor injuries or small wounds when she's returned?'

Mrs Leung's eyes went wide. 'Helen has no memory of how these wounds occur. What is Kitty doing?'

John and I shared a look.

'Biotech,' I said. 'Demon hybrids for the one hundred and twenty-second son of the King of the Demons.'

'Holy shit,' Mrs Leung said softly. She glanced at John. 'He wants your head?'

'The King of the Demons will promote anyone who brings him my head,' John said. 'To Number One.'

Mrs Leung smiled slightly. 'A grand prize.' The smile disappeared. 'I am sorry, my Lord, you can see I had no choice. She knew I was a fox. She threatened to tell my husband and his family if I did not let her pretend to be my friend, and let her take Helen occasionally. She vowed that she would not harm Helen, and until now she has kept her word.'

'That particular demon is not a creature of its word, and I doubt if Kitty is either,' I said. 'I think it would be a good idea if your family were to go into hiding.'

Mrs Leung lowered her head. 'I don't want my husband to know,' she whispered.

'Bring him here after work this evening,' John said. 'With your child. I will talk to him, then I will arrange a safe place for you. Don't tell anyone you have come here. Try to make the rest of the day as normal as possible so that they don't know you've been here. I will provide a guard for you. Come directly here after your husband returns from work and we'll arrange safety for your family.'

Mrs Leung glanced up, her face full of hope. 'You would do such a thing? After what Daji did to all of you?'

'You are not Daji,' John said. 'All creatures deserve a chance at perfection. All of creation is one with the Tao. To search for the Tao is a noble pursuit. Why would I stand in your way?'

Mrs Leung lowered her head. 'The stories are true, my Lord,' she whispered, her voice thick. 'I could not believe the tales of your merciful ways, knowing your true nature.'

'The Tao is our true nature,' he said. 'Go home. Return this evening. I will arrange a safe place for you.'

'Come on, Mrs Leung,' I said. 'I'll take you home.'

'Thank you, madam,' she said. 'What is your honoured name?'

'Just call me Emma, not madam,' I said. 'I'm nothing special.'

She gasped and fell to her knees, quickly saluting. 'Forgive me, my Lady, I did not know. I am doubly honoured — the Dark Lord and the Dark Lady in one room.'

'You don't need to kneel to me,' I said, exasperated, 'I'm just a human. Come on, I'll take you home.'

I checked my watch. 'Seven thirty. She's half an hour late.'

'Something happened to her,' Michael said.

'Go,' John said. 'I'll stay here with Simone.' He glanced at me. 'Take your weapons with you. I think you may need them.'

* * *

There was no answer from the Leungs' flat when we buzzed the intercom. We shared a look. Michael concentrated and the front door clicked open. There was no security guard this time.

'I have a bad feeling about this,' Leo said as we went up in the lift.

It was completely silent on the nineteenth floor. We came to the Leungs' apartment and stopped dead. Mrs Leung's door had been splashed with red paint: a Triad warning sign. The metal gate hung open, but the wooden door inside it was closed.

Michael concentrated again. The latch sprang open. He carefully pushed the door open with PK; the paint was still wet.

They'd killed Mrs Leung in her fox form and then skinned her. Her husband lay dead beside her in a pool of blood.

The old woman was dead in the kitchen doorway. The Indonesian domestic helper was in the kitchen, decapitated.

We checked the apartment thoroughly, carefully not touching anything. Helen was gone.

Michael locked the door behind us as we went out and we returned to the Peak without saying a word to each other.

Back home, I sat down in the chair on the other side of John's desk. 'We keep making major mistakes,' I whispered. 'We should have brought her family in right away. We shouldn't have waited.'

'Making mistakes is what makes us human,' John said. 'You can only do what you feel is the right thing at the right time. Sometimes it is the wrong thing.'

I glanced up at him.

'This is just one of many, many mistakes I have made in my life that have caused untold suffering to countless people,' he said, his voice mild. 'I could sense the death on her, but I hoped that we could protect the husband and child if we kept the situation normal so that the demons would not notice. I was wrong.'

'You can sense death on a person? You *knew* she was going to die? Why didn't you say something?'

'What would I say? "Hello, Mrs Leung, you are going to die today"?'

I stopped dead. 'Can you sense death on any of us?'

He gazed silently at me.

'Answer me!'

'Yes.' He tied his hair back. 'We are all surrounded by death. There is so much death in this household that it is difficult to say where and when and who. I will die. Leo will die. You and Simone ...' He took a deep breath and exhaled. He shook his head and the anguish showed, just for an instant. 'I hope not. I cannot tell. There is too much death. Everywhere. And I am not perfect.'

'But you've attained perfection,' I said, bewildered. 'You've attained the Tao.'

'And I am not perfect,' he said. 'Nothing on the Earthly is.' He leaned back and sighed again. 'Fate has a hand, even for things as powerful as me. All we can do is try to make the best decisions we can with the information we receive.'

'And people die,' I whispered.

'Yes,' he said. 'And death is part of life.'

'Yang and yin,' I said.

'Exactly. Yang and yin.'

CHAPTER TEN

Simone and Michael finally fell out of bed at eleven o'clock on Saturday morning. School had worn them out, and they'd both stayed up late the night before. Thank God the term was finished. They really needed the break.

I found them in the kitchen, bickering over their cereal.

'Don't call me squirt!' Simone snapped.

'What do you want me to call you? *Princess*?' Michael said, glowering.

Simone straightened. 'Well, I *am*.'

'Simone! Cut it out, both of you.' I sighed. Michael particularly wasn't a morning person. 'Michael's a prince anyway. You're both very special.'

They glared at each other. Simone poked her tongue out at Michael, who turned back to his cereal and pointedly ignored her.

'Ah Yat,' I said, 'where's Lord Xuan? I just had a call from the Academy; he was supposed to be there and never turned up.'

'The Lord is still sleeping, ma'am,' Ah Yat said with a smile.

I glanced at the clock over the kitchen door. Eleven o'clock and he was still sleeping? Simone looked worried. I tried to control my face.

'What?' Michael said.

'That's very late,' I said. 'He wasn't up late last night either. Where's Leo, Ah Yat?'

'In the training room, ma'am,' Ah Yat said, the smile gone. 'Is the Dark Lord all right?'

'I hope so,' I said softly. 'He *is* just sleeping?'

Ah Yat's eyes unfocused, and she nodded.

'We should go and have a look, Emma,' Simone said.

I hesitated.

Simone rose and took my hand. 'Come on, Emma, you're nearly married anyway. It's okay. He won't mind.' She sounded much more mature than her six years. Her eyes unfocused, then she snapped back. 'I told Leo.'

We went down the hall together, leaving Michael in the kitchen, his expression grim. Leo met us outside the training room.

'He has been sleeping much more lately,' Leo said. 'Most days last week he wasn't out of bed before we took them to school.'

I nodded. He was right.

'He said to call the Lady if he went into a coma,' I whispered.

Leo's face went rigid. 'Oh my God.'

'Let's go and see if he's okay,' Simone said, pulling my hand. 'Come on, Leo.'

My heart was in my throat as we approached his door. Simone tapped on it. Not a sound. My stomach fell out.

Simone opened the door for us and led us in. The room was dark and he was asleep, as Ah Yat had said.

Simone dragged me to him. He was on his back, his

noble face peaceful, his dark hair spread in a wild tangle around his head.

'Daddy,' Simone whispered. 'Daddy, wake up.'

He didn't move.

'Oh, dear Lord,' I said softly.

Simone reached under the covers and found his hand. She pulled it out and held it. 'Daddy.' She brushed her hand over his face. 'Look inside, Emma.'

I put my hand on his forehead and concentrated. I sagged with relief. His eyes opened. He smiled slightly at us.

'What are all of you doing in here?' he said, his voice low. He turned to Simone. 'Don't let go of my hand while Emma's touching me.'

I removed my hand from his forehead but Simone didn't let go. I crouched to look at him directly. 'It's after eleven o'clock, John.'

He shot upright. 'I have a class to teach!' He grabbed his forehead and fell back on the pillow.

Simone and I both held him; she by the hand and I by the arm.

'Are you okay?' I said.

He nodded, his eyes closed. He opened them and smiled at us again.

'Are you ill, my Lord?' Leo said from behind us.

John shook his head. 'No. Just . . .' He didn't finish.

'We should get the Lady,' I whispered.

'How long until we go?' he said, his eyes searching my face. 'What day is it today? How long?'

'It's Saturday today. We go Monday,' I said.

'I'll make it.' He smiled. 'Leave me. I just need to sleep.'

I dropped my head into my hands, then brushed my hands through my hair, desperate. 'Leo, please take Simone out.'

Simone didn't protest and I didn't look as they left.

'Can I feed you myself?' I said.

'No, of course not,' he said. 'You are the last person in the world who should try that.'

'You won't make it, John!' I whispered fiercely.

He didn't say anything.

'Can Meredith feed you?'

'I don't want to risk it,' he said. 'I could easily destroy her.' He turned his head to me. 'More than death, Emma. If I were to drain her, it would be *destruction*.'

'Call the Lady,' I said. 'She keeps saying she'll come and do it here.'

'I'll make it,' he said. 'If I call her and she feeds me here, we'll have demons down our throats straightaway. They'll know how weak I am and come after all of us. Every single place will be under attack. Here, the Folly, the Academy, everywhere. Best to wait until we are far from their Centre. She is an incurable optimist offering to come here herself. But the consequences would be disastrous.'

'You were okay to be fed by her here after the Attack,' I said.

'There weren't any demons to come and get us then,' he said matter-of-factly. 'Most of them were destroyed on the Mountain, and the remaining ones were regrouping. But they are stronger now, and they would be here immediately.'

'Oh *God*.'

He turned his head away and closed his eyes. 'Leave me,' he whispered. 'I'll make it.'

I threw myself up and stormed out. It was too late to rearrange the flight plan. I *knew* I should have arranged the flight for Saturday, but we had a lot of loose ends to tie up at the Academy before we left and the three of us had planned to do it together over the weekend with the kids home from school.

I should have arranged it for *Saturday*!

John slept the rest of Saturday and most of Sunday, only coming out occasionally to find something to drink; even so he became very dehydrated. The apartment was like a funeral home the whole weekend. Everybody tiptoed around, talking in whispers. Simone watched him. Wherever she was, whatever she was doing, she would unfocus to check him, and then snap back, her little face grim.

We were due to fly out Monday afternoon. I packed for Simone; Leo packed for John. John wasn't even aware of Leo's presence in his room until we woke him to clean him up. He hadn't shaved in three days; his beard was almost completely white and his greying hair was a mess.

I hovered until Leo carried him into the bathroom and closed the door in my face.

John slept on the boat. When we arrived at Macau, Leo had difficulty waking him. He leaned on Leo as we went through customs and immigration. After he had coerced the staff into not seeing our bag of weapons, his hair was almost completely grey. Simone held his hand, stricken.

'I'll make it,' he said softly. 'A few more hours. We'll get there.'

After we boarded the plane, John passed out. Leo caught him, scooped him up like a child and carried him to the back of the plane, Simone and I following. The airport ground staff closed the door of the plane and rapped the side: we were okay to go.

Leo gently placed John on the bunk bed. He was limp and his face was ashen. He looked very old. I didn't waste any time. I dropped the carry bag on the floor next to the bunk and went forward to the main cabin to tell the pilot over the intercom that we were ready. I threw myself onto one of the chairs, dropped my handbag, and picked up the phone.

We were lucky: it was Brian, a cheerful Australian who did a lot of private contract work and had absolutely no idea of the true nature of his employer for this trip.

'We can go, Brian,' I said.

'Okay, Emma,' he said. 'My co-pilot's arranging clearance for us. We should be given the go-ahead in the next five minutes — the airport isn't too busy right now.'

'Brian,' I said softly, 'Mr Chen is terminally ill. We're going for treatment in Borneo.' Brian began to speak, but I cut him off. 'Don't ask. Just be aware that Mr Chen has already collapsed and we need to get him there *as quickly as possible*.' I tried to control my voice. 'We only have hours. For God's sake, get us there. If there's a delay, we could lose him. We have to make it. Please.'

'I'll do my best,' Brian said. 'Weather is good.'

'Thanks.'

'We have clearance,' said a male voice with a Cantonese accent over the intercom; the other pilot.

'Tell everybody to strap in,' Brian said. 'We're up to go.'

I went through the galley to the little room at the back of the plane. Leo sat cross-legged on the floor next to the bunk, Simone in his lap, both of them watching John.

John was unconscious.

I went to him and took his hand. Leo moved to grab me, but I waved him back. 'It's okay, Leo, he can't hurt me while he's asleep.'

Leo nodded.

I looked inside him and my stomach fell out.

'What, Emma?' Simone said softly.

'Look inside,' I whispered.

Simone concentrated then made a sound of misery. 'No.'

'What is it?' Leo said.

'There's nothing there,' I whispered.

'He's gone?'

'He's still there,' Simone said. 'But there's hardly anything.'

I dropped my head, still holding his hand. 'He won't make it.'

'Call the Lady,' Leo said.

'We'll be taking off in a minute,' Brian's voice said over the intercom. 'Buckle up, everybody.'

'I'll call her when we're airborne,' I said. 'Bring him into the main cabin. He'll need a seatbelt.'

'He's better where he is,' Leo said.

'You know what take-off from this part of China is like,' I said. 'We could hit turbulence. He needs to be strapped in.'

Leo didn't say anything. He gently lifted John and carried him into the main cabin. I took Simone's hand and led her in as well. Leo strapped John in. I took care of Simone. Then we sat ourselves.

The plane taxied onto the runway. The engines roared. We were airborne.

Simone moved to undo her seatbelt but I stopped her. 'Wait until Brian says it's okay, sweetheart.' She nodded and sat back, watching her father with an expression that belonged on a much older face.

I reached for the intercom, then decided against it. The pilots were busy flying the plane. They would tell us when we could move around.

It seemed like an eternity. We hit turbulence twice. Finally we emerged above the clouds and the late afternoon sunshine lit the interior of the plane with an orange glow. The seatbelt light blinked off with a musical chime.

We all hurried to undo the belts and crouched around John. He was limp.

'Take him back into the bunk,' I said. 'Where's the pearl?'

Leo had lifted John halfway. He froze. 'Oh my God.'

'Oh, dear Lord,' I said. 'It's in the hold, isn't it.'

Leo silently carried John to the back of the plane. I sat down and put my head in my hands, then remembered and looked up, full of relief.

'Simone, pet,' I said. 'Call Aunty Kwan now.'

'I am,' Simone said. 'But it's really strange. She's not answering.'

I grabbed her hand. 'Simone, have you checked for demons?'

Simone's eyes went wide. 'The pilot's dead. A demon's flying the plane!'

I shot to my feet, grabbed Simone and ran to the back of the plane. Leo hunched over John, his face full of misery.

'Leo,' I said, gasping, 'the co-pilot was a demon. The pilot's dead.'

Leo spun to the bag on the floor and ripped it open. He scrabbled through and pulled out my sword, then Dark Heavens. He tossed my sword to me. 'Get back, Simone.'

'Get behind us, sweetheart,' I said, turning to face the main cabin. I pulled my sword out of its scabbard and waited.

There wasn't a sound.

Then I felt the plane turning. Turning right. I leaned to keep my balance.

'Towards their Centre,' Leo said softly.

'Damn,' I said. 'If we take the demon out, there's nobody to fly the plane.'

'Before you ask, Emma, no,' Leo said.

'Well, well,' I said. 'There's a first time for everything.'

'I did basic on choppers. Not fixed wing,' Leo said. 'I'm not capable of flying anything solo anyway.'

'What about John?'

'I have no idea,' Leo said. 'But probably not, unless he learned for recreational flying. Never needed to.' He glanced at me. 'He can't fly anything anyway, Emma, he's unconscious.' He went rigid as he understood. 'Don't you dare feed him energy, you'll kill yourself. He wouldn't be able to fly the plane anyway. You stay alive. We need to protect Simone.'

'Simone,' I said, 'keep calling. Kwan Yin, Bai Hu, Qing Long, Zhu Que, Na Zha, Jade, Gold, Michael, everybody. Don't stop, no matter what happens. Okay? Stone, you too.'

'Okay,' Simone said, her voice very small.

'I'm silenced as well,' the stone said. 'Here they come. This demon is stronger every time we encounter it. What is it doing to itself? This is more than just training.'

There was a sound in the main cabin. Leo and I readied ourselves. I suddenly realised: the Demon King's phone was in the main cabin, in my handbag. I'd left it there. I cursed myself for an idiot. I should never have let it out of my reach.

Wong appeared in the door from the galley.

Leo let his breath out in a quiet hiss.

'Hello, everybody,' Wong said. He leaned on the doorway with one shoulder and crossed his arms over his chest.

Leo attacked him, sword raised. Wong didn't seem concerned at all, he smiled slightly. As Leo brought the sword down, he grabbed Leo's arm and held it. With his other hand he hit Leo across the face with a sickening wet crunch.

He grabbed both of Leo's arms and held him. Leo panted and hung limply from Wong's hands.

Wong smiled and looked right into my eyes, then leaned over and bit Leo on the side of the neck. Leo screwed up his face as Wong bit down hard. Simone squeaked behind me.

Wong raised his face, blood smeared over his mouth, and grinned at me. He threw Leo to the floor and kicked him in the head. Leo grunted and lay still.

Simone screamed.

'Stay still, Simone,' I said, moving back to guard her.

'He hurt my Leo!' Simone shrieked. She generated a huge ball of chi and hurled it at Wong.

The demon raised his hand and absorbed the energy.

'I don't want to hurt you, ladies,' Wong said. 'I want you both intact. Are you okay, Simone?'

Simone's face was ashen. I looked inside her. She had very nearly drained herself.

I grabbed her hand and fed her some of my chi. She absorbed it. I felt her terror.

'We'll get out of this, one way or another, sweetheart,' I whispered.

'Oh, well done, Emma,' Wong said. 'I didn't know you could do that.'

'Wake up, Daddy,' Simone said loudly.

John didn't move.

'I don't think he has much longer, dear one,' Wong said. 'I do hope he remembers to leave the human form behind. I need the head. The rest of it isn't too bad, either.'

'You'll have to go through me to get to him,' I said. 'Try me.'

'Oh, with a great deal of pleasure,' Wong said. 'Try you? Something I've wanted to do for a very long time. Kitty?'

Kitty Kwok appeared behind him, moving cautiously.

'What the hell are you doing here?' I said.

'Emma,' Kitty said loudly.

I remained still and silent, waiting, wondering.

'*Emma*!' Kitty ordered sharply. 'Obey me!'

I lowered my sword.

'Well, what do you know,' Wong said. 'It worked.'

'Drop the weapon,' Kitty said.

I dropped the sword and it hit the carpet with a thump.

'What are you doing, Emma?' Simone said. 'Why are you doing what she says?'

'Tell her to come and give me a big wet kiss,' Wong said with delight. 'No, wait.' He pulled Leo up, buried his face into the side of his neck, then dropped him again. 'Now,' he said with a mouth full of blood.

'God, Simon, you are so disgusting sometimes,' Kitty said.

'If she can do this without hesitation then we have her,' Wong said. 'Whoops. Lost it.' He swallowed. 'Wait.' He bent over Leo and sucked some more blood out of his neck. 'He tastes funny. Different. Wonder if it's because he's black, or because he's a girl?' He looked up at Kitty and grinned. 'You should try it.'

'Come here and kiss Prince One Two Two,' Kitty said wearily. 'I don't know why I put up with you, sometimes, Simon.'

Wong pulled himself to his feet and waved me closer.

I didn't hesitate. I went to him, put my arms over his shoulders and raised my face.

'No, Emma,' Simone whispered. 'Daddy, Daddy.'

Wong grinned down at me, his mouth covered in blood. He put his hand behind my neck and held me as he lowered his face to mine.

I kissed him with everything I had. I pressed myself into him and felt his body respond. I put my hands behind his head and pulled him hard into me. He squirted the blood into my mouth and I swallowed it, trying to control the gag reflex. But then I realised: there wasn't one.

The blood tasted *good*.

I pulled away and smiled into his eyes. 'More.'

'Well done, Kitty,' Wong said. 'Lots of new toys. Now let's take the Dark Lord's head.'

'I want more blood,' I said huskily. 'I want you.' I rubbed myself against him. 'You. Now. Blood.'

Wong grinned down at me. 'What a good job, Kitty. You want to share?'

'That bitch?' Kitty said with disdain. 'Kill her.'

'Blood,' I whispered. I reached down, pushed my hand into him and felt him respond. He arched his body into my hand. 'You. Now.' I gestured with my head towards the main cabin. I put my other hand behind his neck and pulled him down and spoke into the side of his throat. 'Blood. You.' I nipped at the flesh of his throat just enough to make him moan without breaking the skin. I shoved my body into him. 'Now.'

'No, Emma,' Simone whispered. 'What's wrong with you?' Her feet thumped on the carpet. 'Wake *up*, Daddy!'

Wong covered my mouth with his again. He tried to swallow me whole. I tasted the blood. It tasted good. He pulled away slightly to speak. He dug his fingernails into the back of my neck, into the pressure points, making me gasp with pain and arch my back.

'Plenty of blood, plenty of pain, plenty of *me* for you, my sweet. Just let me take the Dark Lord's head and then we'll have some *real* fun. You want to feed? You can feed off him, and Leo. Lots of fun. Lots of *sweet* blood.'

'No. You. Now,' I whispered.

'We have to take care of your boyfriend first, honey,'

he said with a malicious grin. 'Then we'll have some fun with *both* the little girls. Simone *and* Leo.'

Okay, this wasn't going to work. I released him and stepped back. I gathered myself, then made a huge leaping attempt to pass him so that I could reach the phone in the main cabin.

He grabbed me in mid-air with one hand and threw me to the floor of the plane onto my back, knocking the wind out of me.

'What an actress,' he said with amusement. 'Had me fooled for a moment.' He dropped to straddle me, sitting on my stomach. 'Well, well. Look what we have here.'

'Please don't hurt my Emma,' Simone whispered. 'Please, Daddy, Daddy, wake up, wake *up*.'

'Oh, don't worry, sweetheart,' Wong said loudly without looking away from me. 'She's much more valuable in one piece.' He lowered his face to mine and dropped his voice, speaking right into my face. 'And much tastier too.' He slowly licked my cheek, taking his time about it. I tried not to let my expression betray my disgust.

He pulled back and put his hands on either side of my throat, with the thumbs on my windpipe. He squeezed. I couldn't breathe. He was strangling me. I struggled but he had me down tight. I grabbed his arms but his grip was like steel. I faded; then he released me and I gasped for breath.

'You didn't go blue,' he said with disappointment. 'Let's try again.'

He wrapped his hands around my throat again and squeezed. I tried to relax into a trance so that I wouldn't need to breathe as much. He saw me do it. He released me to slap me across the face but I ignored it.

He put his hands on my arms and shifted so that he was stretched out on top of me. 'You really don't give a damn about yourself, do you,' he growled into my ear. 'All you care about is the little girl.' He shoved himself into me. 'She has to be intact, you know. But I can still have some fun with her, and I'd love to watch your face while I make her play. Right now is as good a time as any — it'll be a long flight before we get there. I can have some fun with her before I give her to my dad. But I'm keeping you. He won't even know I have you.'

I looked him in the eyes and felt nothing but hate. He had nearly killed Leo. He wanted to hurt my little Simone.

I tasted the blood.

I tasted the rage.

I tasted the pain.

Ice.

Cold.

Fury.

Something between my eyes went *snap*. And suddenly I was huge, and dark, and powerful, and mad as hell.

Wong's face changed from menace to fear.

Both Kitty and Simone screamed.

I easily threw him off, raised myself on my black coils and opened my mouth to strike. My fangs flew out, spraying venom.

Wong and Kitty disappeared. Gone. I tried to follow their movement but they had taken off and gone fast and far.

I looked around. Simone had collapsed into the corner, sobbing. I glanced down at Leo. His neck was broken and he was bleeding profusely from the wound on the side of his throat, but he was alive.

I closed my mouth, refolding my fangs. What was happening?

They'd hurt Leo. They'd frightened Simone. Not good enough. There was a demon nearby. I stalked it.

I slithered silently through the galley into the main cabin. Demon. Kill.

The other side of the door. Demon. Kill it.

I went through the door without stopping. The demon wasn't paying attention. I reared up and bit its head off. It exploded into a cloud of the black stuff. I vacuumed it all into me. Not as good as blood, but it would do.

There was a corpse in the other seat. I nudged it with my nose. Dead. Too bad. I couldn't heal him. Oh, well.

I turned. The door was still closed, but again it didn't stop me. I just went straight through it, as if it wasn't there. I returned to Simone and Leo. I hesitated.

Simone: drained, but okay. Leo: near death. John: also near death.

I touched my nose to Leo and healed him. He didn't wake.

'Call the Dragon. Call the Lady,' I said.

Simone remained frozen, sobbing.

'Call them, child,' I said. 'I won't hurt you.'

I felt them coming. I changed. I fell.

CHAPTER ELEVEN

I gasped and shot upright. '*Who's flying the plane?*'

'The Dragon is,' Leo said.

'John!' I said, casting around.

'I'm fine,' John said from my left. He was sitting on the bunk and smiling. Simone was sitting on his lap, also smiling.

I sagged back and ran my hand over my forehead. 'Whoa. That feels weird.' I tasted my mouth and gagged.

Leo handed me a cup of something strong, sweet and fizzy, and I downed it.

'Thanks, but I need to brush my teeth,' I said. 'My mouth tastes of blood.' I looked around. 'What happened?'

'How much do you remember?' Leo said softly. He crouched next to me, studying me intensely.

I hunted through my memories. 'Oh my God.'

He dropped to sit next to me on the grey carpet. 'Yep.'

'Emma,' John said sharply from the bunk, 'did they have control of you?'

'No, of course not,' I said. 'I was just playing for time. I was hoping he'd try to ...' I stopped. I didn't want to say it in front of Simone. 'I was hoping he'd take me into the main cabin first. The phone's there.'

John and Leo both sighed. Simone didn't seem concerned.

'It was the taste,' I said.

'That was what was different,' the stone said. 'In Central, she injured you.'

'I was bleeding in Central,' I whispered.

'Thought so,' John said.

'What, Daddy?' Simone said.

Nobody said anything.

'You healed me,' Leo said.

'He broke your neck,' I said. 'If he had ripped your carotid you'd be dead. I don't know whether he missed it on purpose or not.'

Leo put his arm around my shoulders and kissed me on the cheek. 'Thanks, Emma.'

I wrapped my arms around him and gave him a squeeze. 'I am so glad I could do that. What happened after I changed back?'

'The Lady and the Dragon came,' John said. 'The Lady gave me enough energy to make it to the resort. She didn't want to feed me too much on the plane, it's not sealed. We'd attract flyers. I'll make it.'

'And the Dragon's flying the plane?' I said.

'No, actually he's on the outside carrying it,' John said with amusement. 'He hasn't stopped complaining about the damage to his claws.'

'Oh, poor baby,' I said. 'Broke a fingernail.'

Leo chuckled and his arm shook around me.

'You were a big black snake again, Emma,' Simone said.

'Yes, I know, sweetheart,' I said. 'Don't be afraid of it, it won't hurt you.'

Simone levered herself over the edge of the bunk and dropped to the floor. She came to me and fell into my lap. I released Leo, wrapped my arms around her middle and kissed the top of her head. Leo's arm didn't shift from around my shoulders.

'It's awfully big and scary, Emma. Was it really you?' Simone said.

'It's really me,' I said.

Leo let go of me and pulled himself to his feet. 'Coffee,' he said, and went into the galley. He poked his head back out. 'My Lord?'

'Tea, *tikuanyin*,' John said. *And a big glass of blood for the Serpent Lady.*

'You are really revolting sometimes,' I said.

'What did he say?' Simone said.

'Don't you like it?' John said. *My Serpent does.*

'No!' I said fiercely. I hesitated. 'Strange. I liked it when I was really mad. Now I can taste it and it's nauseating. I need to wash it out.'

Your Serpent likes it.

'Yeah. I know. But I don't.' I sagged. 'I have a split personality. I need to see a shrink.'

'Perfectly normal insanity,' John said.

'Yeah. I cannot believe I just tried to ...' I didn't say the word, '... Simon Wong. I must be insane.'

'I think the insanity is the most attractive thing about you,' John said. 'That and the black scales.'

'You two are *stupid*,' Simone said.

'Oh, I don't know, Simone,' John said. 'Those who are simple-minded or insane have the easiest path to the Tao.'

'Then I'm already there,' I said. 'Doubly so.'

'You want something, Emma?' Leo said from the galley, ignoring us.

'Yeah,' I said, gently moving Simone off my lap and pulling myself unsteadily to my feet, leaning on the wall. 'I want to brush my teeth. Then coffee sounds really good. Strong. With lots of sugar.'

Simone ran to her father and threw herself onto her stomach on the bunk next to him. She turned onto her back and smiled up at him. 'Are we there yet?'

He didn't say anything, just tickled her until she fell off the bunk onto the floor with a thump.

We sat together in the main cabin. John was drowsy but awake. Simone sat in his lap, her head on his chest. It had caught up with all of us.

'What will we do about Brian?' I said.

'The Dragon will fix it for us,' John said. 'We'll make it look like Brian had a heart attack on the way here, and the co-pilot flew the plane. The Dragon will provide a tame demon to take the place of the co-pilot.'

I tried to remember if Brian had been physically injured. I couldn't.

'Did he have family?' I said softly.

'Yes,' John said.

We were all silent for a while.

'They thought they had control of me,' I said eventually.

'The important thing is that they didn't,' John said. 'Is that the first time they've tried?'

'Yes,' I said. 'As far as I can remember anyway.'

'Then they probably weren't expecting it to work,' John said. 'But they made an attempt anyway.'

'What did they do to me?' I whispered fiercely. 'Did *they* turn me into a snake?'

'If they did, then they made a huge mistake, didn't they,' John said placidly.

'They sure did,' Leo said with satisfaction. 'You *healed* me. The Snake healed me. The ulcers are gone.'

'Uh, Leo . . .' I began.

He understood. 'You couldn't heal all of it, could you?'

'I'm so sorry,' I said, my voice thick. 'More than anything else in the world, I wanted to do that for you. But your neck was broken and you had lost a lot of blood. I did what I could.'

'You couldn't make him better from the bad disease?' Simone said, her voice small. 'He's still going to die?'

I couldn't face them. I got up and went into the galley. Leo followed me. I stood facing away from him.

'Next time, don't bother,' he said softly.

I nodded without looking at him.

He turned and went out.

Two hours later we approached the coast of Borneo.

'Look out the window,' John said.

'I can't see anything. His front foot is in the way.' The window was blocked by the Dragon's huge claws.

'Wait,' John said. The claws disappeared. 'He needs to be invisible to bring the plane in anyway.'

Simone and I rushed to the window to see out. A few tiny islands were dotted through the brilliant aquamarine sea. We approached the land; the shore and the city of Kota Kinabalu came into view. The city wasn't too impressive: there were only a couple of buildings more than ten storeys high; most of the structures were low-rise and shop houses. But the water was a stunning sparkling aqua and the sky was brilliantly clear.

'The resort is below us,' John said. 'On the waterfront.'

Simone saw it. 'There it is, Emma. It's huge!'

She was right. The complex was enormous and embraced the edge of the water. It had bright green grass and a marina with white mooring posts. Two swimming pools glittered below us. A golf course flanked the resort on the landward side.

'The golf course is really big too,' I said. John chuckled. 'You play?'

He shook his head, still smiling. 'Tried for a while, but I gave up. Can't see the point.'

'What, you're no good at it? I find that hard to believe.'

He grinned. 'Apparently my style or technique or whatever is hopeless, but that's beside the point, because I just hit the ball into the hole.'

'You're joking,' I said. 'A hole in one? Every time?'

He shrugged.

'You could make a fortune on the pro golf circuit,' I said, turning back to the window.

'They'd pay me to stay away, I think,' he said.

The bottom fell out of my stomach and I grabbed the arm of the chair. Simone squeaked. We plummeted towards the ground; I could feel it.

Leo jerked awake from where he'd been sleeping in his chair. 'What the hell?'

John went rigid and his eyes unfocused.

The plane stopped falling.

Sorry, the Dragon said into my ear. *That's the way I usually land. I'll take it slowly for you.*

'Is he okay with air traffic control?' I said.

'Yes,' John said. 'They think he's the pilot.'

'Well then, he'd better land like one,' I said.

All taken care of, my Lady, the Dragon said. *No need to put your seatbelts on, you are perfectly safe with me. We will be on the ground in about ten minutes.*

'Thank the Heavens,' John said softly.

So sorry about the damage to the outside of the plane, my Lord, the Dragon said. *My claws are awfully sharp.*

'I don't think he is,' I said.

John just shrugged.

* * *

139

The airport wasn't a big cosmopolitan complex, it was just a large two-storey square block. We went down the stairs out of the plane and towards the terminal.

The Dragon met us and we proceeded together into the terminal building. He had taken the appearance of a good-looking Chinese of about thirty. He was still very slim and graceful, and more than two metres tall, but his long turquoise hair was now standard short and black. He wore a pair of elegant grey slacks and a matching silky shirt.

The customs and immigration counters were deserted.

'Too late,' the Dragon said. 'It's already past six. And we were the only plane coming in.'

'What will we do?' I said.

'Just go through. I'll have my staff take your bags. Don't worry about the paperwork, I'll arrange for it to be fixed up for you.'

'We could get into trouble for this,' I said.

'Wait,' the Dragon said.

A bubbly tingling sensation moved through me.

'Go straight through. Hurry,' the Dragon said. 'I can't make the Dark Lord invisible for very long, he is extremely large. Quickly.'

I took Simone's hand and we rushed past the customs and immigration counters together.

Stay quiet, the Dragon said. *They can still hear you, even though they can't see you.*

A few drowsy security guards didn't notice us, even though our feet probably made some noise.

'This is *so cool*,' Simone whispered.

I hushed her until we were on the other side. The bubbly sensation stopped.

'Can I learn to do that too, Daddy?' Simone said as we went out the terminal to the car waiting area.

'Invisibility? Probably,' John said. 'We'll have a

session together when the Lady is finished with me. We may try a few things.'

'Cool,' Simone said.

A large van with tinted windows waited for us.

'This is it,' the Dragon said. 'The driver is one of mine. He will take you directly to the resort. I will follow when the luggage is secured. I'll meet you there.'

'Thanks, Dragon,' I said.

He smiled slightly. 'You are most welcome. Let's get you sealed and safe.'

I stopped before I entered the van and looked inside. The driver smiled at me. I held Simone back. 'Dragon, please double-check for us.'

The Dragon opened the front passenger door and poked his head in. There was a blinding white flash and the driver disappeared.

'They are certainly on to you, my Lord,' the Dragon said. 'Please wait, I will get another driver for you.'

'Damn,' John said under his breath.

'On second thoughts, I will come with you,' the Dragon said as another grinning driver materialised in the van. 'They're probably planning to ambush us on the way to the resort.'

'How did you know?' John said.

'I have no idea,' I said. 'But I think it's just application of Murphy's Law.'

'What's Murphy's Law?' Simone said as I strapped her into her seat.

'If something can go wrong, it will go wrong,' I said.

'Once you are at the resort you will be safe,' the Dragon said, pulling himself into the front passenger seat. 'The seals there are the most powerful in existence. I had them set when the building was erected. They are part of the structure. Nothing will get in.'

'The seals on my house in Guangdong were breached,' John said grimly.

'These are *blood* seals, my Lord,' the Dragon said.

John stiffened. 'You will tell me more about this later,' he said, his voice a low rumble.

'Let's go,' the Dragon said.

No one tried to ambush us with the Dragon in the car.

The lobby of the hotel was at least five storeys high with a soaring pitched roof. Splashing fountains decorated the centre, and the walls were rich with Malaysian designs and local Borneo handicrafts. The check-in counters were to one side.

'I suggest you go to the end of the lobby and take a look at the resort while I arrange keys for you,' the Dragon said. 'I will need to have the keys put through the computer. How many do you need?'

'How many rooms are you giving us?' I said.

'The Presidential Suite,' the Dragon said. 'Four-bedroom apartment.'

'One for me, one for John, one for Leo should be enough, I think.'

'If they are blood seals then the Lady will not be able to materialise in there,' John said. 'One for her too.'

'Very good,' the Dragon said. He hesitated and his face went blank. 'Good. Your bags are here. I will arrange the keys. Go,' he said and gestured towards the end of the lobby. 'Have a look.'

I took Simone's hand and we walked across the lobby, John and Leo following us.

Simone looked around, goggle-eyed. 'This place is *huge.*'

When we reached the end, we could see over the edge of the lobby to the swimming pool and the ocean beyond. We were about two storeys up; the back of the lobby was higher than the front.

'*Wah!*' Simone said.

Leo chuckled.

The vast pool below us was a deep shade of blue, surrounded by lush tropical plants and vibrantly green lawn. A barbecue had been set out on the lawn, and guests sat at tables spread on the grass enjoying a barbecue buffet. Beyond the lawn was the stone-edged shore of the ocean, which was a deep shade of indigo, rippling with small waves. Across the water, right on the horizon, were four tiny islands.

Above the islands, the sun was setting in a spectacular display of vivid tropical colours. A fresh breeze, full of the smell of the ocean and flowers and tinged with smoke from the barbecue, brushed our hair.

'And I'll be locked up for ten days,' John said ruefully, leaning on the railing.

'Can we go out to the islands?' Simone said, excited.

'Yes, of course. There isn't much beach here on the mainland, the best beaches are out there,' the Dragon said, appearing behind us. 'After you have settled in, we will go out. I have a boat, I will take you, Princess.'

'Thanks, Dragon,' Simone said.

Qing Long bowed and smiled slightly. 'My pleasure, my Lady.' He gestured. 'Your rooms are prepared. Please come this way.' He handed John a small folder. 'Keys.'

John nodded, and immediately passed the folder to me. His hand brushed mine and I knew.

'Leo, for God's sake, quickly,' I said, breathless. 'Catch him!'

Leo moved like lightning to grab John before he hit the floor. He wrapped his arm around John's shoulders and supported him.

'Why didn't you *say*, Daddy?' Simone scolded.

'Let's just get him into the room,' I said. 'When will the Lady be here?'

'She is here already,' the Dragon said. 'She is outside your room, waiting.' He smiled at John. 'Let's get you up there.'

'I'll make it,' John said.

'It is most disconcerting to see you so weakened, my Lord,' the Dragon said as he guided us along the hotel corridor. It was an outdoor breezeway, meandering through the vibrant gardens. 'I have never seen you like this in all the time I have known you.'

John didn't say anything.

A lift lobby was at the end of the breezeway. The Dragon made the lift doors open before we reached them.

'Third floor,' the Dragon said. 'Room 301, of course. Right at the end of the top floor, overlooking the marina and the ocean. Quite a good view. Best room in the house. It's costing me a fortune to put you up here. Usually I have a Celestial in, and they pay for it in fine Celestial jade or equivalent.'

John didn't say anything. His face was rigid as he clutched Leo.

'Are you okay?' I said softly. 'Hold on.'

The lift doors flew open. 'This way,' the Dragon said. He led us along the third-floor corridor, which was flanked on both sides by the dark wooden doors to the rooms. We went all the way to the end, John struggling to walk, Leo almost carrying him.

Ms Kwan waited for us outside our suite. The Dragon pushed the door open.

'Bring him in here with me,' Ms Kwan said to Leo. 'Hurry.' She rushed straight into the suite, through the large living room, and pushed open a door to the right of the enormous balcony.

Leo hoisted John and carried him in his arms like a child. Simone and I followed. Ms Kwan had gone into the master bedroom. It had an enormous king-sized bed and a couple of comfortable wicker chairs next to the window.

'Drop him into a chair,' Ms Kwan said, quickly moving to close the blinds. 'Leo, put a chair across from him for me.'

Leo obliged. John was unconscious.

'Daddy,' Simone said, taking John's hand. She gently touched his face. 'Daddy.'

'Move away, Simone,' Ms Kwan said, throwing herself into the empty chair and grabbing John's hands. I pulled Simone away. Ms Kwan lowered her head, raised their joined hands palm to palm, and the silvery light of shen energy surrounded them.

'Out,' Ms Kwan said without moving. 'You were just in time. Leave us.'

I took Simone's hand and went out of the room. Leo followed us and gently closed the door.

'He nearly didn't make it,' Simone said.

The Dragon waited for us in the living room of the suite. 'Your bags are here,' he said, gesturing towards a smiling porter. 'Tell the demon where to put them. In about half an hour dinner will be delivered. There is a dining room next to the front door, or you may wish to eat on the balcony.' He gestured towards a side table. 'There is an extensive list of hotel activities on the table. We have a small cinema and bowling alley in the country club at the centre of the resort. Of course you have full use of it. The Princess,' he said with a bow to Simone, 'can call me if you require anything. I have informed the concierge and housekeeping that you are to be exceptionally well cared for. If you need anything, do not hesitate to call them. You have an open account at the resort shop.' He spread his arms and his blue eyes flashed. 'My resort is yours. Enjoy.'

I went to him and took his hands. 'Thank you so much, Qing Long.'

The Dragon smiled and nodded. He shook my hands away gently. 'Rest. Look around tomorrow. If you wish to go to the islands, my little boat is yours.'

He saluted Simone, then me, then swiftly turned and went out.

Simone jiggled. 'I want to pick a room!'

'Well then, let's have a look,' I said. 'Ms Kwan will need a room, your dad already has a room, so that leaves two rooms. Looks like you and me are sharing, Simone.'

'I'll sleep on the sofa,' Leo said. 'You take a room of your own, my Lady.'

Both Simone and I laughed at that. I gave Leo a push, ribbing him. 'Those are two-seaters, Leo — you folding yourself up to sleep? I don't think so.'

The suite was enormous. It had a luxurious living room in the centre, with a dining room behind it, and a huge balcony with a spectacular view over the water to the islands. The room was expensively decorated in shades of maroon and cream, with generous use of exotic Borneo timber.

We looked at the remaining two bedrooms. One had two single beds, the other a queen-sized bed. Not really much choosing necessary.

'This isn't right, my Lady,' Leo said as I directed the demon to put his bags in the room with the large bed. 'You should have this room. It's not fitting for you two to share.'

'Simone and I are having a girls' sleepover party,' I said. 'There's a television with a video in here, and we'll be staying up late and watching *Sailor Moon* and *Cardcaptors*. I saw videos for rent at the concierge desk.'

Simone jumped up and down and clapped her hands.

I dug Leo in the ribs with my elbow. 'You can do it instead, if you like. I'm sure you're a big fan of *Sailor Moon*.'

Simone's little face was serious. 'Do you like *Sailor Moon*, Leo? You can come and watch too, if you like. Sailor Mars is my favourite.'

'Not Sailor Jupiter?' I said. 'She does martial arts.'

'Nope,' Simone said, her eyes sparkling. 'Sailor Mars lives in a temple and does magic stuff. That is *so cool*. I wish I could do magic stuff like that.'

I glanced at her. She was serious.

'I think I'll skip it for just one night, ladies,' Leo said, also perfectly serious. 'Maybe another time.'

'Okay, Leo, if we find a really good video I'll lend it to you,' Simone said.

Leo bowed. 'My Lady. Now will you two go out and let me unpack? I *do not* want Lady Emma anywhere near my clothes.'

Simone dragged me out and we showed the demon where to put our bags.

CHAPTER TWELVE

We had breakfast on the balcony the following morning. The Dragon provided us with a vast range of tropical fruit, Western-style eggs, vegetarian congee for John, and four different types of tea. One of the demons hovered to serve until I sent it out.

John and Ms Kwan were both subdued.

'Is ten days enough?' I said.

They nodded silently.

'How long will you hold the charge?'

Neither of them looked at me or said anything.

'Okay, whatever,' I said. 'We'll talk about it later.'

Ms Kwan sipped her tea. John didn't move.

'Emma, take Simone into the pool and around the resort today,' John finally said, his face grim. 'Leo, stay here with us. Stay nearby. Just for today.'

'My Lord,' Leo said. 'I was about to request the day anyway.'

I glanced at Leo. He wasn't eating. He held a cup of water.

'Is it that bad?' I said softly.

'The ulcer's come back and spread to my throat,' he said, just as quietly. 'It's very painful to eat. Anything except warm water is very painful.'

John sat straighter, suddenly brisk. 'Emma, sit next to Leo and take his hands. Let's get the Lion eating.'

Simone moved away so that I could sit next to Leo and hold both his hands. Leo smiled slightly at me.

'Look inside,' John said. 'Leo, warn her if she hurts you.'

I opened my Inner Eye onto Leo. I could see the pain and winced. It was torture for him.

'Whoa,' Leo said softly. 'That feels weird.'

'You know where the meridians are?' John said. 'Meredith's taught you?'

I nodded, concentrating.

'Find the meridian that relates to the pain he's suffering.'

I concentrated and traced the meridians through Leo. He gasped and held my hands tighter.

'Is she hurting you?' John said quickly.

'No,' Leo said. 'It just feels really strange.'

'Found it,' I said.

'Good,' John said. 'Now, start this very slowly, a tiny amount at first. I will supervise.' He came around the table, leaned on it and put his hand on Leo's bare arm, gold on black. 'Good. Use a very small amount of chi and block the related meridian. Use the chi like a needle, stick it into the points.'

I found the points along the meridian. I moved a tiny amount of chi into one of the points, and the point lit up.

'Good,' John said. 'Move up and fill them all, with a similar amount.'

Leo appeared to me like an acupuncturist's dummy, the meridians and points clearly highlighted through him. I moved up the meridian, gently pushing chi into the points.

'How does that feel, Leo?' John said.

'Absolutely fantastic.'

John took his hand away. 'Put a similar amount of chi in again. Double it.'

I did it again. Leo sighed with bliss. 'Damn.'

I saw the ulcers in his mouth and throat. I moved without thinking and covered one of the ulcers with chi, just to blanket it.

'Stop, Emma,' Ms Kwan said from the other side of the table, her gentle voice urgent.

I halted, still with the chi over the ulcer.

'Don't touch her,' Ms Kwan said before John even moved. 'Leo, stay very still.'

We all remained absolutely motionless.

'Move the chi into the centre, then radiate it out,' Ms Kwan said.

'That's what I was about to do.' I moved the chi into the centre of the ulcer, then made it flow outwards until it covered the ulcer. The ulcer disappeared.

'Holy . . .' Leo said, then swallowed the rest.

'How much energy did you just use, Emma?' Ms Kwan said.

'Hardly any,' I said.

'Continue, if you wish,' Ms Kwan said. 'Ah Wu, move away. Let me supervise this.'

I heard them moving but didn't turn. I concentrated on the next ulcer, moved the chi, and healed it.

'Well done,' Ms Kwan said next to me. 'You may continue.'

I healed the ulcers one by one.

'Cool,' Simone said softly. 'That must really have hurt, Leo.'

'Not any more,' Leo whispered. 'Hurry up and finish, Emma, I'm starving.'

I laughed softly, and healed the remaining ulcer.

'Stop,' Ms Kwan said.

I hesitated.

'You must be very, very careful removing your consciousness,' Ms Kwan said. 'Remove your awareness from the Lion very slowly and gently, otherwise you could render him unconscious.'

I carefully removed the tendrils of my awareness from Leo. I felt his gratitude and smiled. I pulled the remaining essence out and snapped open my eyes. 'Done.' I focused on Leo. 'Have something to eat.'

Leo didn't need to be told twice. But he poured himself a huge mug of coffee first.

'Well done, Emma,' John said from the other side of the table. 'That was remarkable.'

'Can I do that to myself if I'm injured?' I asked Ms Kwan.

'Yes,' she said, smiling. 'You can do it for just about anybody, except for Ah Wu.'

'This is the part where you tell me that only Immortals can do that,' I said.

Neither John nor Ms Kwan said anything.

'Can I learn that?' Simone said.

'When you're bigger,' John said. 'You need to have very good energy control to do it. Maybe when you're about twelve.'

'Okay,' Simone said, and returned to her cereal. 'Emma can teach me.'

'I'm sure she will,' John said, his eyes sparkling.

'Hurry up and finish your toast, Emma,' Simone said. 'I want to go down to the pool, and see the bowling place. Can we go to the islands tomorrow?'

'Sure,' I said. 'Leo can stay here and rest today, and go with us to the islands tomorrow.'

'I'm fine now,' Leo said.

'You still need to spend the day here near me,' John said. 'Go out with the ladies tomorrow.'

'My Lord,' Leo said, sitting down to a plate piled high with food.

'Can I talk to you privately for a moment, Ms Kwan?' I said.

Ms Kwan rose. 'Come into my room.'

I followed her. They watched me go, silent.

'Is there a problem, Emma?' Ms Kwan said, sitting on the end of her bed.

I sat in one of the wicker chairs. 'They don't know about this, and Simone didn't really understand. Simon Wong tried to control me on the plane when they attacked us.'

'Ah Wu told me that he had no control over you,' Ms Kwan said. 'Trust yourself, Emma. You will never hurt them, you know that.'

'That's not what I'm concerned about,' I said. 'It's something else.'

'What?' Ms Kwan said gently.

'Wong wanted to test me. To see if he had full control. He took a mouthful of blood and commanded me to kiss him. I did. I swallowed the blood.'

'And that was what brought out the Serpent,' Ms Kwan said, understanding.

'Ms Kwan,' I said, bending forward to speak fiercely to her, 'it was *Leo's* blood. A big mouthful of it.'

'I fail to see ...' Ms Kwan began, then her face went rigid. 'I understand.'

'Can you check me?' I said.

'No,' she said. 'I cannot do it. It is not in my nature.'

'Do you think having the Serpent come out would somehow have cleared it?'

'Emma.' She sighed. 'Emma, I have no idea. You should not have done that.'

'Tell me about it.' I ran my hands through my hair. 'I didn't even think at the time.'

'You were probably more concerned with survival,' she said wryly. 'Quite understandable.'

'You don't know?' I said.

She silently shook her head.

'Okay.' I straightened and pulled myself together. 'Whatever. I'll have myself tested, and won't worry about it until then. The important thing is Simone.'

'Either way, when Ah Wu returns, rejoined, he can heal you,' Ms Kwan said. 'Remember. He has promised. It will be.'

I grinned. She was right. 'Thanks, Ms Kwan.'

She smiled and rose. 'Go and finish your breakfast. Simone is becoming impatient. If she does not have a chance to see the whole resort very soon I think she will explode.'

The Dragon met us at the door of the suite the next morning. He looked similar to the way he had appeared when we had arrived: an ordinary, good-looking Chinese man of about thirty, wearing a pair of smart grey slacks and a silky shirt. His eyes were a milky greenish-brown under his expensive sunglasses.

'You can't change your eyes all the way?' I said as we waited for Leo and Simone.

'Too difficult to bother about,' he said. 'Nobody looks anyway. As long as my eyes aren't bright blue, nobody notices.'

Simone wore her Australian solar swimmers, which were already too small for her. We would have to make a trip down to the resort shop later to buy her some new ones. Leo wore a fluorescent floral Hawaiian print, both shorts and shirt.

'I am not taking you out looking like that,' the Dragon said.

'Looking like what?' Leo lisped.

'Flaming.' I turned and took Simone's hand. 'Come on, sweetheart, let's go and see the islands.'

Leo made a strangling noise as he followed us down the hallway.

The Dragon sighed loudly and brought up the rear.

The marina was right in front of the hotel. It was shiny new and there weren't many boats moored there.

'It will fill up as more people come in,' the Dragon said. 'The condominiums aren't finished yet. I'm expecting wealthy Malaysians to set up holiday villas here. I have a ship's chandlery licence but it's not worth starting business until I have some buyers.' He turned to me as we walked. 'You might consider purchasing a condominium after the Dark Lord has gone. Come here for your holidays. School holidays.'

'Yeah!' Simone said.

'I'll probably be on the Mountain during the holidays,' I said. 'I'll need to find someone to take me.'

'Won't be me,' the Dragon said. 'Won't have the time.'

'I don't expect you to,' I said.

'Here it is,' the Dragon said.

It was a fourteen metre fly bridge cruiser, the *Crystal Dragon*.

'Is this it?' I said. 'It's awfully small.'

The Dragon stared at me, astonished. He pointed to a massive fifty metre yacht moored on the other side of the marina. 'You want to take the big one?'

'That one won't manoeuvre around the islands, will it?' I said.

'Nope. This one is better for viewing the reef.'

'Oh well, then I suppose this'll have to do,' I said wearily. 'We're not going very far anyway.'

The Dragon turned stiffly and boarded the boat.

'Good one, Emma,' Leo whispered.

'Oh, the fun is just beginning,' I whispered back.

The sky was a brilliant crystal blue and the sea was a matching deep blue, almost purple. The breeze was fresh and clean and a welcome relief from the pollution of Hong Kong. It was a brilliantly mild warm day.

The islands were tiny and picture perfect, each with a little head of bristling jungle hair. The Dragon pointed them out in turn as his staff drove us towards them.

'On the right, the large one, is Palau Gaya, Gaya Island. It's inhabited. Not much in the way of reef there. Police Beach around the other side is good, but there are better beaches on the other islands. Next to that, the small one there,' he pointed to the island next to Gaya, 'is Sapi. Very pretty. Some reef off the eastern end. Small but good beach. Probably too many tourists there right now, we'll stop and see how we go.' He turned to Simone. 'Take care, dear, there are monkeys on that island, and the tourists have been feeding them. They can be aggressive.'

'Cool,' Simone said.

The Dragon pointed further to the left. 'That's Manukan. Bigger than Sapi. The sand isn't as soft, but there is some rather good reef off the northern end. We'll stop there after Sapi and you can jump off the boat and snorkel on the reef.'

'Got enough gear for us?' I said.

'I'm not going in,' Leo said.

'Plenty,' the Dragon said. 'Further to the left, Mamutik, very small; and Sulug, only good for scuba. Anybody have a licence?'

Nobody replied.

'Oh well, the Princess is too small for scuba anyway.'

'You didn't learn to dive, Leo?' I said.

Leo didn't say anything. I decided to leave it.

'Okay then,' the Dragon said. 'Easy. Sapi first, then Manukan, off the reef. Then we'll land on Manukan and have a barbecue under the trees, where we won't be accosted by monkeys. Hold; I will inform my staff.' He stopped and concentrated.

Simone jiggled with excitement and leaned over the edge of the boat. I grabbed her around the waist and held her.

'I won't fall in, don't be silly, Emma,' she said, impatient.

'Just being extra careful, pet,' I said. 'Your dad's not here to rescue you.'

'Qing Long can breathe underwater too,' Simone said. 'He's a dragon. Some of them have big palaces at the bottom of the sea.'

'Does he?'

'I don't know,' she said. 'We should ask him.'

The Dragon snapped back and moved next to us. 'All organised.'

'I'm vegetarian,' I said.

'Of course you are,' the Dragon said. 'You are well on the way to attaining the Tao. What does the Serpent eat? I would love to see it. Can you summon it at will?'

'Damn,' I said softly. 'No,' I said loudly. 'And as far as I know, I've never eaten in Serpent form.'

'You never dream about eating babies?' he said softly into my ear.

I went stiff and ignored him.

'Here we are,' he said as we approached the jetty on Sapi. He concentrated, and the boat slowed as we neared the pier.

'Look down,' he said.

Simone leaned over the edge of the boat and squealed. I leaned over as well and nearly squealed too.

There were thousands of brightly coloured fish in the shallow water. The water was only about three metres deep and absolutely clear, as if it wasn't there. The fish glittered as they swam beneath the boat, all changing direction together with brilliant blue and yellow flashes.

'You can swim with them,' the Dragon said. 'You can hand-feed them. They are very tame.' He glanced up at the island. 'This is a marine park. Fishing is prohibited. There is a large amount of exceptional sea life here. The local people are very protective of it. Please take care you do not damage the habitat; we would be in serious trouble.'

'Don't worry,' I said. 'We'll treat it with respect. Look whose family we are.'

The Dragon chuckled. He concentrated again, and his smiling staff brought out bags of snorkelling gear, bamboo mats, an enormous cooler and mountains of fluffy beach towels from the front of the boat.

'Are they all demons?' I said.

'Of course,' he said. 'Human staff are much too expensive for such menial tasks. Most of them are local demons, tamed here myself.' He gestured towards the jetty. 'After you.'

A number of grinning locals stopped to watch us as we disembarked. The Dragon greeted them casually and they waved and smiled.

'What are they all smoking?' Leo growled.

'Leo!' I said. I dropped my voice. 'Please. Not in front of Simone.'

'They are smoking fresh air, a relaxed lifestyle and a friendly culture,' the Dragon said. 'But be careful not to tread on any toes.'

'None of them are smoking, silly Leo,' Simone said impatiently. 'Hardly anybody here smokes, not like China. It's really good.'

'You are quite correct, Princess,' the Dragon said.

I held Simone's hand and helped her off the boat, and the Dragon caught her from the jetty. 'Let's go onto the beach.'

We had a choice. To the right was a narrow sandy beach facing Gaya Island, shaded by huge trees. To the left was a wide beach without shade, ending in a tiny promontory covered in jungle and petering out into rocks that jutted into the water. The beach on the right was packed with screaming Hong Kong tourists. The beach on the left was nearly deserted.

As a group, and without saying anything, we all turned left.

There was a single shady spot under a huge tree. Some American tourists had set up there and were munching on snacks, their snorkelling gear strewn around them.

'Watch this,' the Dragon said, and concentrated.

'Don't you dare!' I cried, but it was too late.

A troupe of small brown macaque monkeys descended on the tourists. They pulled at the snorkelling gear, approaching quickly and then darting away as the tourists gathered the gear closer. A larger male, about the size of a corgi, came down from the trees and sauntered over to the tourists. He opened his mouth wide, revealing long gleaming fangs, and approached them menacingly.

As one the Americans grabbed all their stuff and fled.

'What a rotten thing to do,' I said. 'Please don't do that again.'

'They were only Americans,' the Dragon said, and Leo stiffened. 'Come.'

The monkeys disappeared into the trees and the Dragon's staff laid the mats out for us in the shade.

The Dragon didn't sit. 'I'll stay on the boat, it's more comfortable. I have some calls to make,' he said. 'If you need anything, tell the demons. I'll leave one here for you.' He gestured. 'Nelson here.'

The demon appeared as a youthful Malay who grinned and bobbed his head.

The Dragon turned towards the water. Kota Kinabalu was clearly visible across the ocean, with Mount Kinabalu jutting out behind it. 'These rocks on the right,' the Dragon said, pointing, 'lead to a rather nice small reef. Follow the rocks out to the end, go about three, four more metres. You are on the reef.'

'Thanks, Dragon,' I said. 'But please don't do that to the other tourists again.'

'They were only Americans,' the Dragon said mildly.

'The Black Lion is American,' I said.

'Oh, is he?' the Dragon said, amused. 'Then I shall make him an honorary Japanese, as I am.' He bowed mockingly to Leo. 'You are now a real person.'

Simone got to her feet. 'You are being mean to my guardian, Qing Long, and I don't like that. If you don't stop tormenting Leo, I will have a serious talk to my father about you.'

Qing Long stiffened, his expression rigid. Then he grinned and chuckled. He bowed to Simone, then saluted her. 'As you wish, my Lady. I will in future treat the Lion with the utmost respect.' He turned to Leo and saluted him. 'Lion. My apologies.' He saluted Simone again. 'My Lady. By your leave.'

Simone turned away and sat, ignoring him.

The Dragon chuckled again, saluted me, and turned to walk back to the boat.

What a creep, I signed.

With you there, Leo signed back.

'Is that sign language?' Simone said.

'Yes,' I said.

'What did you say to each other?'

'Grown-up stuff,' I said.

'Bad words about the Dragon,' Simone said with confidence.

'Exactly,' Leo said.

'I want to learn too,' Simone said.

'You don't need to, pet,' I said. 'You can talk right into our ears anyway.'

Oh yeah. Simone switched back to out loud. 'Who'll go out to the reef with me?'

'Have you ever used a snorkel before?' I said.

'No, is it hard?'

'It takes some getting used to. We'll practise here in the shallow water, then see how we go.'

'Okay.'

I fitted Simone carefully with the goggles and flippers. She said something into the snorkel, then laughed into it.

'Pop your head under the water, and breathe through it,' I said.

She nodded and put her face into the water. She squeaked through the snorkel, threw her head back up and said something unintelligible through the tube. She switched to silent speech. *I can see really clearly! There are little fish right near my feet!*

'Don't worry, they won't hurt you,' I said, and she nodded, eyes wide inside the goggles. 'What we'll do now is swim around in the shallow water to practise. Then you and me are going to the reef.'

Simone squeaked into the snorkel, her eyes wide, then thrashed out until the water was waist-deep and launched forward to swim. She swam around in the shallow water perfectly, breathing through the snorkel like a pro, occasionally making muffled comments to herself through the tube.

I glanced at Leo. He watched us from one of the beach mats with a huge grin on his face. I gestured with my head for him to join us and he shook his head, still smiling. I decided to leave it.

I pulled on my own goggles and fins, waded to Simone and grabbed her hand. She squealed and said something unintelligible through the tube. I didn't bother answering; I floated horizontally, put my own face in the water and joined her.

There's an awful lot of fish, she said.

She was right. The water was full of tiny fish only three or four centimetres long. Some larger fish, up to thirty centimetres long, slid casually past, eyeing us warily.

This is so cool, Simone said. *I wish you could talk back. Do you know the names of any of the fish?*

I squeezed her hand.

Okay. Can we go to the reef now?

I had an inspiration. I tapped the stone.

Yes, Emma?

I asked if it could talk to Simone.

Sorry, Emma, not underwater like this. And Gold is too far away to relay for me. Looks like you'll have to be a normal human for a change.

That was unusual. Stone was destroyed by Wood, not Water. Stone was strong against Water.

Ah, you have been learning. Frankly, it's basic physics. I can't be understood! I sound garbled, much as a human would.

I tried not to laugh through the snorkel and inhale water.

Simone chatted inside my head, pointing out the fish, as we swam to the reef. She was concerned about the sea cucumbers; she thought they were the droppings left by a giant sea creature.

When we reached the end of the rocks I shook her hand and we stopped. We put our heads above the water and took out the snorkels.

'Don't worry about those black things,' I said, 'they're just sea cucumbers. You see them dried in the market. They have them in hot pots, remember?'

'Oh, okay,' Simone said. 'Are we at the reef?'

'Should be close by,' I said. 'Don't touch the coral, it will be sharp. Let's have a look.'

I put my snorkel back in and we turned and swam further, Simone merrily chatting inside my head.

The reef wasn't large, but the colours were delightful. There was a splendid variety of coral, and we saw plenty of glittering fish. We floated over the reef, Simone giddy with excitement.

Look at the sea urchins, she said. *They have bright blue eyes. You can see them.*

I nodded and squeezed her hand.

Her voice changed slightly inside my head. *Emma, I forgot to put my snorkel back in.*

I quickly checked her, still holding her hand. She smiled at me. She still had her goggles on, but her snorkel hung loose beside her face. I pulled her above the water and we trod water together. I spat my snorkel out.

'Simone, are you *breathing the water*?'

She didn't bother talking out loud. *Yep.* She grinned broadly. *Let go. I want to go down.*

'Don't go too far,' I said, but she pulled her hand away and dived.

I watched her from the surface. She swam carefully, not approaching the coral too closely. She occasionally turned and waved to me.

It's hard, she said. *I have to keep swimming down, I keep floating to the top.*

Something huge and blue and silver materialised next to me and I went rigid with shock.

It's okay, it's Qing Long, Simone said.

The Dragon's enormous blue and silver head was right next to me. He was in True Form; his head was as big as a small car. His turquoise eyes were clearly visible through the crystal clear water.

The Dark Lord has requested that I test this skill, my Lady, the Dragon said. *With your permission, I will take the Princess on a field trip and we shall see exactly how far she can take this interesting ability.*

I had a million questions, so I pushed my head above the water and dropped the snorkel. 'Can you hear me?' I said above the waves.

Nothing.

I dipped my head under the water. They were gone.

CHAPTER THIRTEEN

Leo stood at the shoreline, watching me with concern. I put the ring above the water and asked it to tell him what had happened.

Too far, the ring said.

'Damn,' I said. Leo would be panicking. I put my snorkel back in and headed towards the shore.

Leo swam out and met me halfway. I stopped and took the snorkel out again. We floated in the water together.

'She's okay, don't worry,' I said. 'She can breathe the water. The Dragon's taken her to try out some stuff. I've had enough. I'm going back.'

Leo swam beside me back to the beach.

When I pulled myself out of the water, I threw off the goggles and fins and collapsed onto the mat, panting.

'You need to do more physical stuff,' Leo said. 'You've been doing far too much energy work lately.'

I gave him a push. 'Thank you *very much*.' I turned onto my back. 'She forgot to put her snorkel back in and was breathing the water. She dived down to look at the reef. The Dragon came and took her out for,' I laughed, 'a *field trip*.'

'Damn, Emma, that's amazing,' Leo said, looking out over the water.

'Not surprising, though. Her father can do it too. If you're with him, holding his hand, you can breathe the water as well.'

Leo glanced at me, then obviously decided against asking. He grinned. 'Want a coconut?' He gestured next to him on the mat. Three young coconuts sat there with their tops chopped off and straws stuck into them.

'Thanks,' I said, and took one. The milk inside was clear and sweet, the flesh like jelly. It was ice-cold and refreshing. 'Nice young one. Where'd you get them?'

'There's a kiosk at the end of the beach,' Leo said.

I faced the water next to Leo. 'You ever seen the Dragon in True Form?'

'Nope.'

'He's at least twenty metres long. Huge.'

'Whoa.'

'Gave me the shock of my life when I turned around under the water. His head was right next to me.'

Leo laughed softly.

We sat silently together on the beach and waited for them to return.

Simone and the Dragon reappeared about an hour later. They climbed out of the water together. The Dragon wore a pair of plain grey swim shorts and had made his hair short and black. He was elegant, slim and muscular.

Simone had lost the goggles somewhere along the way, but she still had the fins. She stopped to pull them off, and fell over in the water. She lay in the water and removed them as the Dragon stood and watched her with amusement.

Simone came up the beach and fell into Leo's lap. She smiled up at him. 'We're going to the other island now. There's better reef there and I'm going to jump off the boat.'

'Lady, Lion,' the Dragon said, still smiling, 'if you will come with me, we will return to the boat and moor for a while off Manukan.'

Leo grabbed Simone and threw her over his shoulder, then hoisted himself up quickly, making her shriek with delight. He carried her towards the jetty, her arms slapping loosely on his back as he walked.

'Faster, Leo!' Simone squealed, and he ran, making her bounce on his shoulder.

The Dragon sighed, shook his head, and gestured for me to follow. A couple of smiling demon staff, in the form of young Malays, walked from the jetty to pack up for us.

'Is she very unusual, being able to breathe the water like that?' I said as we headed back to the boat.

'Not even young half human dragons can do it,' the Dragon said. 'She really is exceptional. Very talented.'

'She needs to be able to defend herself against big demons when her father goes,' I said.

'Yes,' the Dragon said reluctantly. 'That, I'm afraid, will be the most important skill of all.'

'What if she can't handle anything bigger than about level sixty when he goes?' I said. 'What do we do then?'

'She will still be too small to travel to the Plane,' the Dragon said. 'You should just hope that he doesn't go before she can handle just about anything. What about yourself?'

My shoulders sagged. 'Not higher than about level forty bare-handed,' I said.

The Dragon stopped. 'You can handle up to level forty without a weapon?'

I turned to him. 'I know. Similar with energy. With a weapon, nothing bigger than about level fifty.'

'What about the Serpent?' the Dragon said.

I started walking again, the Dragon at my side. 'It's a lot better. Apparently it's taken out a whole heap of level sixty-fives with energy.'

'Apparently?'

'I don't remember any of it,' I said.

'What are you, Lady Emma?' the Dragon said softly.

'I wish the hell I knew,' I said. 'Want to have a look inside? Xuan Wu's looked. Bai Hu's looked. Neither of them found anything except for this enormous damn snake thing, which isn't there most of the time. My guess is that I'm an engineered demon, 'cause I spent a lot of time with the brains behind One Two Two's operation before I went to work for Xuan Wu. She took samples off me and a lot of blood. She thought she could control me. They probably did something to me, and that's why I am what I am.'

'You don't look like a demon,' the Dragon said.

'Have a look inside,' I said. 'If you can tell me what I am, I'd be absolutely goddamn thrilled.'

'You are sure, my Lady?' the Dragon said. 'I would see everything, you know.'

'Everybody else has,' I said miserably. 'One more can't hurt.'

We were at the boat. Simone was sitting on Leo's lap and talking excitedly into his face about what she'd done with the Dragon.

'I think I would prefer to have the Dark Lord's permission first,' the Dragon said after contemplating for a while. He boarded the boat and took my hand to help me on. 'After he has finished with Kwan Yin, he can supervise.' He released my hand. 'I would love to see inside, I must admit. You are rather like an iceberg, Emma. Nothing much on the outside, but a great deal of hidden depth.'

'Can we have lunch before we jump off the boat, Uncle Qing?' Simone said loudly. 'I'm *hungry*.'

'If that is your wish, my Lady, then it is my command,' the Dragon said. He gestured and we pulled away from the dock, the demon staff busy with the ropes. The engines roared and the fresh breeze ruffled my hair. I took a deep breath and decided to live for the now.

The sky was a brilliant crystalline blue, but paler than I was accustomed to. The hill before me rose smoothly, covered in short green grass that almost appeared to be a tailored lawn.

I felt a jolt of joy. Home! Green and crystal and beautiful. If I could have sighed with bliss I would have.

I slithered up the hill, enjoying the feeling of the scratchy grass beneath my belly.

Hundreds of other snakes headed up the hill around me. All about the same size as me, and all as black as I was. We glittered.

Another snake was close enough to talk to, and I spoke to it without stopping. 'What's at the top of the hill?'

'Blood,' the other serpent said without looking towards me. 'Blood and power.'

Suddenly the need for blood, the hunger, was so intense it was almost painful. I slithered faster.

But I woke before I reached the top of the hill.

By the fifth day John was a different person. He was lively and happy and sparkled with energy.

Leo had relaxed as well. He hadn't mentioned it, but he had been feeling unwell; I could see it. The ulcers had stopped recurring by the third day, and I couldn't practise my healing skills on him any more.

On the sixth day John decided over lunch to take a half day to spend with us. Simone was delighted. We went back to Sapi, and John and Simone spent more than an hour together on the reef. After they had emerged, John and I sat at the edge of the water watching Simone as she played. She had a little net and caught the small fish in the shallows, talking to herself as she did it.

'You eat fish?' I said.

'Which form?'

'Either.'

'Human, no. Turtle,' he said as he shifted slightly, 'sometimes.' He smiled gently, still watching Simone. 'I'm not sure you want to know too much about my dietary habits in True Form, Emma.'

'Turtles are cute.'

'Turtles are generally carrion eaters when they crave flesh,' John said. 'Cat food is second best.'

'Yuck.'

'You had to know.' He grinned at me, then his face softened, pensive. 'Nothing quite like a well-ripened whale carcass that's been floating in the sun and the salt for a few days. You humans have robbed us of one of our greatest pleasures.' He laughed, his shoulders moving. 'It revolted Michelle; she didn't want to see me eat at all. Good thing I didn't have both.'

'The Turtle and the Serpent?'

He nodded. 'Hn. Just Turtle.'

As if in answer to his saying the word, a large sea turtle swam right up to the beach and rested its head on the sand between us. Simone dropped her net and raced to stand behind it, her eyes wide with wonder.

'Move away from it, Simone,' John said quietly. 'Come behind me.' His face was expressionless. 'I told you I did not want to see you.'

The green turtle watched him, its eyes sad.

'Go,' he said, glancing sharply away from it.

It transformed and I gasped. Simone squeaked behind John.

For a moment I thought there were two Dark Lords on the beach. In human form, the turtle was a young Chinese man appearing to be in his mid-twenties. He was golden and muscular and had long black hair hanging loose over his shoulders. His face had some softer angles than John's, but there was a remarkable resemblance. He lay on his belly as the turtle had done, half in and half out of the water. He rose to his knees. He wore a simple pair of plain dark green long pants.

'I wish to offer my services,' he said, 'my Lord.'

John didn't look at him. He didn't say a word. His face was an expressionless mask.

'You need me,' the young man said quietly. 'You don't have much more time.'

John shot to his feet, strode into the water and disappeared below the surface.

The young man turned and sat next to me. 'Good day, my Lady,' he said without looking away from the water. 'My name is Ming Gui, but you can call me Martin, if you like.' He smiled at Simone. 'Hello.'

'Hello.' Simone studied him curiously, then came around him to sit in my lap. 'Who are you?'

'I'm your big brother. But our dad is mad at me and hasn't spoken to me for centuries. That's the first word he's said to me in over two hundred years.'

Simone's eyes went very wide. 'You're my brother?'

He nodded quietly. 'Hn.' Something inside me squeezed tight. He was definitely John's son. The resemblance was devastating.

'What are you, Martin?' I said.

'I'm just a little turtle Shen,' he said, turning back to the water. 'If you want me to go, just say so.'

'He's mad at you?'

He nodded again. 'I did something very wrong. He lost a great deal of face. Both of us did. The entire

House of the North was shamed. He still hasn't forgiven me.' He sighed. 'I wonder if he ever will.'

'What did you do?'

'Not in front of my sister.'

He stiffened and froze. His face went blank. Simone's face went blank as well. Then he and Simone turned to each other and smiled.

Simone approached and studied him closely. 'You look a lot like Daddy.'

He nodded, his eyes sparkling. 'Thank you.'

'Can you do the Arts?' she said.

'That's why I'm here,' he said. 'I think you may need me very soon.'

'When Daddy goes,' she said.

He nodded.

'Did somebody just talk to you?' I said.

'Daddy introduced us to each other,' Simone said.

'He doesn't want to be on the same beach as me,' Martin said. He sighed with feeling. 'Still hasn't forgiven me.'

'I'd really like to know what you did,' I said.

'I'll drop by and tell you about it later, if you like,' he said. 'We can talk about the future as well. Whether you are willing to take me up on my offer, after he's out of the picture.'

'I'm asking Xuan Wu if I can trust you first,' I said.

He turned back to the water. 'Go right ahead.'

Leo came up and sat down next to Martin. He reached across Martin and offered me a young coconut with a straw sticking out. 'Thanks,' I said, and waited for it.

Leo offered one to Martin, saw Martin's face and stopped dead. He stared, speechless.

Martin smiled gently at Leo. 'Hello, Lion. My name is Ming Gui and I'm the son of the Dark Lord.'

'You're Martin?' Leo finally said.

Martin's smile didn't shift as he nodded.

'Michelle told me about you.' Leo put the coconuts carefully onto the mat. He brushed his hands on his shorts, then held out his huge hand. 'Pleased to meet you.'

Martin shook his hand and his grin broadened. 'I'm delighted to finally meet you.' He stiffened. His face froze.

'Bye, Martin,' Simone said, her voice full of disappointment. 'Sorry.'

'Bye, Simone,' Martin said kindly. 'I hope I'll see you again soon.'

Simone hesitated, then walked up to him, threw her little arms around his neck and kissed him on the cheek. He smiled with genuine delight and gave her a hug.

'I'm glad I've got a brother,' she whispered.

'I'm glad I have a sister,' Martin whispered back. He pulled away to smile at her. 'He's on his way, I'd better move. If he sees me here he'll have my shell for breakfast.'

He saluted me quickly, shaking his hands in front of his face. 'Lady Emma. I may come and see you later, if you are not with my father.' He touched Leo's hand. 'You're everything I've heard.' Leo's face was a mask of restraint.

Martin transformed into a turtle, pulled himself clumsily into the water, and then disappeared swiftly underneath.

'He was nice,' Simone said. 'I'd like to see him again.'

'So would I,' Leo said softly.

John appeared out of the water and flopped onto his stomach on the beach.

I didn't know what to say. Martin was obviously a problem for him. Eventually I decided to tackle it head-on.

'Can I trust him?'

'Yes,' John grunted, then lay dark, silent and unmoving on the beach. Conversation closed.

CHAPTER FOURTEEN

John knew what Leo and I were doing when we went for a walk along the edge of the water after dinner. He scowled, and took Simone to the play centre. The computers in the business centre next to the playroom had broadband, so he could check his email while Simone was playing.

We headed down the stairs to the edge of the water. The shoreline was mostly rocks, but there was a small strip of sand. There was a park bench on the grass facing the water. Leo and I sat companionably together and waited. The sun was setting over the water, with a spectacular tropical flame of colours. It was still very warm, but the breeze had cooled slightly.

Martin appeared in human form and waded out of the water towards us, his long hair hanging loose over his shoulders. He stopped and concentrated, dried himself, and added a green cotton jacket to the green pants. Leo made room and he sat between us.

All three of us quietly watched the sea.

'Are you as good as your dad, Martin?' I said, coming straight to the point.

'Nobody's as good as the Dark Lord,' Martin said. 'I can take up to level fifty with my bare hands, though.

Weapons, I can take nearly anything. Energy, the same. I think I'll be useful to you once he's gone.'

Leo shifted slightly. 'Good.'

Martin smiled at Leo.

'What did you do?' I said.

Martin turned back to the sea and sighed. 'I did a really stupid thing.' He didn't elaborate.

'Seems to run in the family,' Leo said, his voice a low rumble.

Martin leaned back and threw his arm over the back of the bench. 'Really stupid.' He shook his head. 'I didn't tell my father all there was to know about myself, even though I was living in his house. He arranged a marriage for me.' He smiled sadly. 'I went along. I pretended to be happy about it. She was a lovely girl,' he added, full of remorse. 'Half dragon. It was an excellent match. I was genuinely fond of her. But,' his voice went very soft, 'my partner at the time drank too much the night of the wedding. He'd agreed to the marriage; it was a good thing all round. But he lost control and it all came out. He railed against the situation loudly to everyone present.'

'Oh my God,' I said. 'That's awful.'

'My father was furious,' Martin said. 'He hadn't known about me, about my partner, about anything. He didn't care about that, but he was absolutely devastated that I hadn't told him, and had gone along with a sham marriage purely to please him. I was shamed, he was shamed, she was shamed, both houses were shamed. None of us could hold up our heads in public. We were all a laughing stock.'

'I think you misjudged him, Martin,' Leo lisped. 'If you had told him in the first place, none of that would have happened.'

Martin laughed quietly. 'That's what he said. That I didn't trust him enough to tell him. I suppose ...' He leaned forward and put his elbows on his knees as he looked out at the sea. 'I suppose he was right.'

'How long ago was this?' I said.

'About six hundred years,' he said.

'And he has hardly spoken a word to you since?'

Martin shook his head, looking down at his hands. 'Nope.'

'Well then,' I said crisply, 'I think it's about time you two made up.'

Both Leo and Martin stared at me.

'How many people remember what happened after such a long time?' I said.

'Three.' Martin smiled gently. 'Me, my father and the girl.'

'What about your partner?'

'Moved on a long time ago.'

'You have nobody?'

Martin shook his head. He glanced up at me. 'It would be good to be able to talk to my father again.' He sighed and turned back to the sea. 'I miss him. And very soon, he will be gone.'

'You're a turtle, you'll be able to see him once he's gone,' I said.

'No, I won't.' He didn't look away from the sea. 'It won't work like that. When he's gone, he won't be talking to anybody for a long time.'

I rose. 'Let's go and see him.'

Martin didn't move. 'I don't think that's a good idea.'

'Do I have precedence as his chosen?'

Martin eyed me expressionlessly for a moment, then nodded once sharply.

'Good. Come on then.' I held out my hand. 'Let's go and fix this up.' I smiled wryly. 'That's an order.'

'Damn.' Martin pushed from his knees and threw himself upright. 'I don't think even you can sort this one out, my Lady.'

'That was exactly the wrong thing to say,' Leo said as he rose to join us.

I grinned. 'A challenge.'

'She can't resist a challenge.'

'Let's get these two turtles together,' I said cheerfully, linking my arm in Martin's. 'And then Leo and I can go and work out which one of you is stupider.'

'That will take some working out, my Lady,' Leo said.

The three of us went into the business centre. John and Simone sat together in front of a computer playing a children's game. When Simone saw Martin she raced to him with her arms out. He lifted her to give her a hug, and she kissed him on the cheek again. The look of delight on his face was heartrending. Martin faced John, still holding Simone, who smiled happily with her arm thrown over his shoulder.

John stood and glowered. He didn't say a word. He scowled at me.

'You are coming for a walk with us right now,' I said.

John stood unmoving, stubborn and dismal.

'Don't make me grab you and bring you along,' I said.

His face became expressionless. 'You wouldn't,' he said.

'I would,' I said, moving closer to him.

He moved away. He raised his hands in defeat. 'All right, I'm coming.'

Martin carried Simone and the five of us went out to walk along the edge of the water. The sky had turned a paler shade of lilac and the breeze had freshened, but it was still warm enough for us to be comfortable. The islands off the coast were dark shadows against the purple sky.

'You will forgive your son right now and let him spend time with his sister,' I ordered John brusquely. 'You will apologise to your father sincerely,' I said to Martin, 'and then the pair of you are going swimming together *right now*.'

Martin stopped and his face went rigid with horror.

John's face just went rigid.

'*Now*.' I gestured. 'John, you first.'

Martin didn't let him do it first. He gently lowered Simone, then fell to his knees in front of his father. He touched his forehead to the grass. 'I most sincerely apologise for my mistaken behaviour, my Lord. Please forgive me.'

I sighed with relief. Martin raised his head to look at his father, waiting with quiet hope.

John stood with his face rigid for a long time. He glared sternly at Martin. He didn't move.

'I like him, Daddy,' Simone said. 'Please forgive him.'

Father and son watched each other without moving.

'You are forgiven,' John growled. 'Rise.'

'Neither of you will ever mention this again, okay?' I said. 'Now go and swim together, get to know each other again, and I'll see *both* of you at breakfast tomorrow. Understood?'

Martin rose with a small smile. John still glowered at him. John was about five centimetres taller than Martin and had the edge on him in size; he was quite a lot bigger.

Martin turned towards the water and gestured to his father.

John glowered at me, then a small, fleeting smile lit up his face. He pulled off his black T-shirt and handed it to me. He turned to the water and they walked down to the shore together.

'Make sure he stays in human form,' I called to

Martin as they walked away, and he gestured to reassure me without turning.

'How many gold coins do you have now, Emma?' Leo said.

'Before or after the ones I get from this?' I said.

'Thank you, Emma.' Simone's voice was very small. 'I like him a lot. Nearly as much as I like Leo.'

'I'm glad,' Leo said softly to the ocean.

'They're back,' Simone said as we sat on the balcony eating breakfast. It was another splendid day; the balcony was damp from the overnight rain, but the sun had already become hot.

The door opened and they entered. John went straight into his room; Martin came onto the balcony to sit with us.

'Tea?' I said.

'Western, please.'

I poured him some Ceylon tea and he nodded his thanks. He eyed the food spread out in front of us and selected a quarter of papaya. He picked up his spoon and attacked it with gusto.

'There's congee over on the side,' I said.

He nodded his thanks and returned to the papaya.

'Are you starving?' I said.

He glanced up at me, his eyes sparkling. 'Suddenly I am.'

John had taken a shower and changed his clothes. He came out onto the balcony towelling his long hair. He threw the towel over the back of one of the chairs, quickly tied his hair back, then went to the congee. He studied it suspiciously. 'Does this have meat in it?'

'No, that's mushrooms,' I said.

He ladled some into his bowl, grabbed a spoon, and plonked down at the table next to Martin. They didn't look at each other.

'All fixed?' I said. They both nodded, still without looking at each other. I leaned over the table. 'Tell me about your mother, Martin.'

Leo made a quiet sound next to me, but didn't say anything.

John and Martin glanced at each other. John dropped his spoon and leaned back, expressionless.

'Don't be ridiculous,' I said impatiently. 'I'm not jealous. This was a long time ago. I'd just like to know.'

They looked at each other again and this time they went still.

'Oh no, you don't,' I said loudly, hoping to block them from hearing each other. 'No secrets.'

Both of them looked down at their hands.

'God, you two are alike,' I said.

Leo chuckled.

Both of them glanced up at me. John gestured towards Martin.

'My mother is a turtle Shen,' Martin said.

'Where is she now?'

They glanced at each other again, both of them expressionless.

'Is she dead? Can you kill a Shen?'

Martin sighed. 'She has changed.'

John shifted slightly, but didn't speak.

'Tell me,' I said.

Martin leaned back and studied me. 'I think it would be best if I didn't go into too much detail about this,' he said, looking me straight in the eye.

John visibly relaxed.

Martin gestured towards John. 'One of my parents is him, the Xuan Wu Turtle Shen. I have had very little recent contact with ...' He hesitated. 'With the other.'

'*The* Xuan Wu?' I said.

'Like the Bai Hu, the Qing Long. The Xuan Wu,' John said, 'it is the correct name for it.'

'It is a very strange creature,' Martin said softly.

'They're always saying that,' I said, looking at John, 'but I think that at its core it is just the same as everybody else.'

John looked down, then up into my eyes and smiled affectionately.

I raised my hands in defeat. 'All right, all right, whatever. I'll find out all about it eventually anyway.'

Martin smiled, his eyes sparkling.

'Will you come and help me after the Dark Lord is gone?'

'I would be delighted.'

'Is this okay with you?' I asked John.

John picked up his spoon and attacked the congee. 'Yes.'

'What about in the meantime?' I asked Martin. 'Do you want to stay with us? We could use your help right now.'

John glanced up from his congee. 'I've asked Martin to travel to the Celestial and help with things at that end. Since he has no trouble travelling backwards and forwards, he has agreed to help with the rebuilding of the Mountain and the administration of the Northern Heavens.'

Martin lit up with a huge, delighted grin. 'I am most honoured.'

'Can you carry me to the Mountain, Martin?' I said quickly. 'I haven't seen it yet. It's too far for our household Shen to take me.'

Martin's smile disappeared. 'I'm sorry, my Lady,' he said. 'I am also a very small Shen. Too far for me too. It's a very long way.'

'You will get there,' John said.

'Yes, you will,' Leo lisped.

We were all silent for a while. Martin finished his papaya and went to the side table for some congee. He came back with a bowl, nodded to his father and me, sat down and attacked it with similar gusto. Both of them appeared to be starving. It was a good sign; if Martin was similar to John in this way it meant that both of them were in a good mood.

'Are you finished talking about the boring stuff?' Simone demanded over her cereal.

'Yes we are, sweetheart,' John said.

'Good. I want to go out to the islands with you today, Ming Gui.' She turned to John. 'Can we go?'

John's eyes sparkled at her. 'Of course you can. I think that's a very good idea.'

Martin smiled at Leo. I turned and saw Leo's face. John saw it too.

'You all go,' John said. 'I'll stay here with Mercy.'

Leo and I sat on the beach waiting for them. The two of them had been under the water together for more than an hour.

'I wonder if he can do the same thing for you,' I said.

Leo stretched his dark legs out in front of him. 'He can't. He's too small.' He watched the water. 'Apparently only the most powerful ones can do it.'

I slapped the sand with my palm. 'Damn!'

Leo smiled. 'You just like having me around so that you can take out all your frustrations on me.'

'God, you are such a *bastard*!' I shouted, and pushed him over.

He shot to his feet, scooped me up, ran into the water and dropped me in. I was laughing so much that I choked on the water and he had to thump me on the back when I reappeared.

CHAPTER FIFTEEN

The next day we spent the morning beside the pool, and the afternoon in the suite, resting. I wrote some emails to my family using the dial-up on my laptop. Gold had set up a network in the Western Palace as well and linked my family to the internet. My family weren't finding the palace boring; in fact, the Tiger had arranged some trips down to the Earthly Plane for them. They'd stayed in his posh hotel in Paris for a week, being escorted by a group of his burly sons through all the best tourist spots and dining in the finest restaurants — until they'd complained that they didn't like the food. Much too fancy for everybody except Jennifer and Leonard, who were having a ball. They were giving me a hard time about visiting them, as well. They wanted to show me what they were doing in the palace.

At about three o'clock Simone had a nap and I pulled out a paperback and made myself comfortable on the balcony. There was a knock on the door and Leo shot out of his room. He hesitated at the door, then nodded: John had told him to answer it.

It was the Tiger, Rhonda and Michael. Together.

'Hi!' I said, delighted to see them. 'Come on in. What are you doing here?'

'Holiday,' the Tiger said. 'Family time. And Ah Wu has asked to see Michael.'

'What for?' I said, glancing at Michael.

'No idea,' the Tiger said with a shrug.

'Hi, Rhonda,' I said.

Rhonda was obviously embarrassed. She was blushing. 'Hi,' she said.

'Sit,' I said, gesturing towards the couches in the living room. Leo nodded and returned to his room without a word.

'What's up with him?' the Tiger said.

'Just tired,' I said, and didn't elaborate.

John and Ms Kwan appeared from the master bedroom. The Tiger and Michael both saluted them, falling to one knee for good measure. I watched them, bemused, wondering what was up.

John and Ms Kwan sat on one of the couches. Both the Tiger and Michael gestured for me to sit on the other one, next to Rhonda. It was a competition. And both of them were fully aware of it and playing the game anyway.

The Tiger gestured and a cane chair materialised behind him. He seated himself. 'Xuan Tian.' He saluted Ms Kwan. 'My Lady.' He nodded to me. 'Lady Emma.'

'Ah Bai,' John said. 'Just Michael would have been sufficient.'

Michael didn't have anywhere to sit, so he fell to the floor next to his father and sat cross-legged, completely unfazed. He shook his hands in front of his face. 'Lord Xuan. Lady Kwan Yin. Lady Emma.'

All three of us nodded back. Everybody could see it now.

'The Dragon has been bullshitting about this place for a long time now, and I wanted to see if it's just hot air,' the Tiger said. 'I regret coming though; the blue bastard keeps trying to sell me a condo.'

'You are enjoying every minute of it and you know it,' Rhonda said, glaring at him. 'And the only reason you won't buy property here is because it's in the East and you wouldn't be caught dead owning anything this far east of Centre.'

John and I shared a look. The Tiger was silenced.

'Why'd you want Michael, Ah Wu?' the Tiger said.

'I have a few more days here and I want to do some training,' John said. 'Put Emma and Simone through their paces. Carrying, ordering, flying, things like that. Michael can do it too.'

Michael glanced at John sharply. John ignored him.

'Don't know how much the boy is capable of, Ah Wu,' the Tiger said. 'He has some talent, but I've yet to see him do anything very interesting.'

John still didn't look at Michael. Michael was hard pressed to control his face. Rhonda didn't miss it, but her own expression didn't shift.

'Are you staying here?' I said.

The Tiger and Rhonda both nodded. 'Got a two-bedroom suite on the other end of the resort,' the Tiger said. He leaned forward over his knees to speak intensely to John. 'The Dragon claims to have put in blood seals, Ah Wu.'

'Michael, leave us,' John said. 'I wish to speak to your father privately about this.'

'I will retire,' Ms Kwan said, and returned to her room without another word.

Michael rose as well. 'You want me to go back to our room? Mom? Dad?'

'Anywhere in the resort is okay, except the bar,' the Tiger said without turning away from John.

'There's a games room and business centre downstairs with broadband,' I said. 'The pool is very good as well.'

Michael shook his hands in front of his face. 'By your leave.'

I had a sudden inspiration. 'Leo!' I yelled.

Leo's door opened. 'My Lady?'

'Show Michael around? Maybe take him downstairs and do some hand-to-hand? He could probably use the practice. You up to it?'

'Just wait, I'll put a shirt on,' Leo said.

'Good idea, Emma,' John said.

After Leo and Michael had gone out, John and the Tiger went grim. 'Emma and Rhonda, could you leave us?' John said.

Neither Rhonda nor I moved.

'Waste of time, Ah Wu,' the Tiger said.

'I want to know,' I said.

'Me too,' Rhonda said.

'I always knew he was a complete bastard, but this is way past the boundary of acceptable,' the Tiger said. 'It's one thing to encourage Celestials to stay here, but *blood seals ...*'

'Have you asked him about the source of the blood?' I said.

'He claims he bought it,' John said. 'He claims not to have harmed a single human.'

'Oh, and sticking big needles in them isn't harming them?' the Tiger growled. 'He's taking advantage of you, Ah Wu. Don't let him get away with it.'

'He will keep,' John said.

'But he's given us an awful lot of help this trip, John, you have to admit,' I said.

'Is there some rule about harming humans?' Rhonda said.

'More a matter of honour than a rule,' John said. 'Humans are weak. It is simply not honourable to harm them, particularly when they are defenceless. And besides, the Earthly is their plane. We are Celestials. This is their world, not ours.'

'You talk as if neither of us is human,' I said softly. 'I'm not sure how I feel about that.'

'Both of you are already more than human,' the Tiger said. 'Both of you are much, much more. I know for sure that Rhonda is well and truly Worthy.'

Rhonda blushed furiously.

'How's Louise?' I said, and instantly regretted it.

The Tiger and Rhonda both stiffened. The Tiger scowled. 'She had a girl, number two hundred and forty. Both mother and child are doing well. She says to say hello, and to come and see her soon.'

'Maybe when my life has returned to something slightly less interesting,' I said, and smiled at Rhonda.

She smiled back. 'Never going to happen,' she said. 'You will be cursed with an interesting life, I think.'

'So what will you do, Ah Wu?' the Tiger said, changing the subject.

'Take this under advisement,' John said. 'In the past it was unthinkable; blood seals were only achievable through injury. Now, with modern technology, it is possible to harvest blood without harming the donors.'

'You're not actually saying this is *okay*?' I said.

'Blood seals are impregnable,' John said matter-of-factly. 'Not even the Lady can pass through them unassisted. Not a single demon can enter this complex without a suitable escort. The Dragon does have a point.'

'Trust a yin creature to say something like that,' the Tiger said. 'The use of blood is unthinkable. Not even that red-headed bastard would do something like this.'

Rhonda stared at John, wide-eyed.

'I don't believe him myself sometimes,' I said.

'You are altogether too damn yin right now,' the Tiger said. 'Hurry up and get that goddamn Serpent back.'

I put my head in my hands.

'Sorry,' the Tiger said softly.

'If you have nothing else you wish to discuss,' John said, rising, 'I have things I need to do. You are dismissed.' He bowed to Rhonda. 'Lady. Please join us for dinner this evening.'

He went into his room without saying another word. Ms Kwan emerged from her own room, nodded to us, and followed him, closing the door behind her.

'How long are you staying?' I said.

'Just a couple of days,' the Tiger said, then smiled affectionately at Rhonda.

'Go out to the islands, they're fabulous,' I said. 'Oh, Simone's started to breathe water.'

'She is more impressive all the time,' the Tiger said. 'Where is she?'

'Asleep,' I said with amusement. 'Worn out. You'll see her at dinner. You'll come?'

'Sure,' the Tiger said, and rose. 'Let's go and have a look around and see if we can find that son of ours. I'd like to see him sparring with the Lion, that should be good.'

'You're not having him back, you know,' I said as I saw them to the door.

The Tiger grinned. 'Not even if I promoted him?'

I stopped dead. 'How ... Promoted? You wouldn't.'

'What if he were my Number One?' the Tiger said. 'Would you still hold on to him?'

'You can't promote him to Number One, he's not Immortal,' I said as I opened the door for them. 'So don't try that stuff with me.'

The Tiger shook his hands in front of his face. 'My Lady.'

Rhonda took my hand and kissed me on the cheek. 'Look after yourself, Emma.'

I kissed her back. 'You too, Rhonda.' I squeezed her hand, then released it. 'See you at dinner.'

* * *

At the end of the eleventh day, John and I sat on the balcony overlooking the water and shared a pot of tea. Simone was asleep, exhausted as usual. Michael was busy in the business centre, chatting with his friends over the net. Leo had disappeared, probably taking a solitary stroll along the waterfront.

Frogs sounded in the garden pond below us, and crickets chirped all around. The night was a blaze of stars; the clear air seeming to magnify their brilliance. We couldn't see the ocean or the islands, but the small waves hissed as they washed against the beach below us. Smoke rose lazily from the mosquito coil inside the decorative ceramic frog next to the balcony rail.

'You still have two more days,' I said. 'Relax. Enjoy the time.'

'I intend to,' John said, pouring more tea. 'But there is something else I want to do as well.'

'No work,' I said.

'Work for you. The Dragon has an executive development centre here. Team building, focus groups, things like that.'

'I don't think our team needs much building,' I said wryly.

'No, you are quite correct. But the facilities can be used to teach some advanced techniques. As I said, I never did get you flying.'

The door to the suite opened and I stiffened.

'Leo,' John said softly, and I relaxed.

'Alone?'

John hesitated, concentrating. 'No.'

'Martin?'

John's voice was very soft. 'Yes.'

'Good.' The door to Leo's room opened and closed. 'I'm pleased for him. Can you get Jade in to catch?'

John laughed quietly.

I realised, and joined him. 'That was unintentional.'

'I'm sure it was. Jade's busy doing the taxes. I'll get the Dragon to catch.'

Both of us laughed quietly together. John poured more tea.

Lightning flashed across the ocean on the horizon. The sound of the thunder echoed deeply across the water.

'There is an enormous storm out there,' John said. 'It will hit us in about half an hour. The rain will be torrential.'

'Let's just stay here and enjoy the remaining time we have then.'

He didn't reply.

The executive development centre was mostly outdoors. There was a military-type obstacle course, artificial rock walls for climbing and abseiling, and a large open area used for corporate paintball tournaments. It was perfect.

'Revise the wall-running first,' John said, gesturing towards the rock walls. 'Show Michael. He could probably learn the skill as well.' He turned to Qing Long. 'Could you take True Form about four, five metres long?'

Qing Long eyed John with disdain. 'The smallest I can manage is about ten metres. I am an extremely large Shen, you know that. Take it or leave it.'

John's face went rigid and he looked the Dragon right in the eye. The Dragon went completely still. Then he smiled, bowed slightly, and changed into True Form of about five metres long. His Dragon form was glittering turquoise and silver with scales that rattled with a metallic sound as he moved. He thrashed his tail with its enormous silver fin and wiggled his head from side to side.

'Close enough,' John said.

'Come and watch, Michael,' I said. 'This requires a lot of concentration.'

'You know what you have to do?' John said.

'Yeah,' Michael said. 'It sounds hard.'

'If the energy gets away from you, be sure to drop it,' John said. He gestured for the Dragon to position himself underneath me.

I readied myself and studied the wall appraisingly. 'Ready, Dragon?'

'My Lady,' the Dragon said.

I ran to the wall, took three strides up it, and lifted myself from the inside using the energy centres. I had it. I ran all the way to the top of the wall, about ten metres. I grabbed the top and jumped to stand on it. It was difficult to balance; the wall was a thin layer of what appeared to be fibreglass over a metal frame, only about a centimetre thick. I turned and looked down.

Try something, John said into my ear. *Jump off. Use the centres again, this time in the opposite direction, to slow your fall.*

'What if I lose it?' I shouted down.

Call, John said. *The Dragon will catch you.*

'If I come down too fast, catch me,' I called to the Dragon.

My Lady, the Dragon said, his voice hissing in my ear.

I hesitated. This would be even more difficult; I would have to be very careful. It was much easier to move the centres when I was already going in the same direction.

I concentrated. I wanted to let myself simply fall off the wall, but it was at a slight angle and I might hit it on the way down. I had to leap clear of it.

I jumped. I tried to ignore the sensation of falling, and instead concentrated on the energy centres. All three, moving in the opposite direction, smoothly. Smoothly, upwards.

I slowed my descent, but not enough to avoid injury when I hit. The ground came rushing up to meet me.

'Catch me!' I yelled into the air and spun onto my back. I dropped the energy and sped up. I hit the Dragon's forearms with a jerk that jarred through my body.

'Thank you,' I said.

'You are most welcome,' the Dragon said. 'Was that really the first time you have attempted that?'

'Yes,' I said. He tipped me out of his arms onto the ground and I turned to study the wall again. 'Slowing my descent is much harder.'

'Have another try,' John said, 'and then we'll let Michael attempt it. Don't tire yourself too much; you need to try horizontal holding as well.'

'How long have you been training this one, Ah Wu?' the Dragon said.

'I think about a year and a half,' John said. 'Emma?'

'That's about right.'

'Let me know if you tire of her, Ah Wu,' the Dragon said. 'Despite her plain appearance, she would make a worthy addition to any household, untouched or not.'

I faced the Dragon. John did the same thing.

'You will need to line up,' I said softly. 'The White Tiger and the King of the Demons have both attempted to win me away from Xuan Wu already. But you are all completely wasting your time. I'm a lot like him, and his number is one. For me, there will never be any other.'

The Dragon's expression was unreadable. He gazed at me with his enormous shining turquoise eyes. Then he spoke. 'You are quite correct, my Lady, and I most sincerely apologise.' He lowered his massive silver-fanged head over his front legs. 'Please believe me, I meant no offence. Permit me to present you with a gold coin later.'

I turned back to the wall. 'Let me have another try.'

You'll have two coins when you get back, John said into my ear.

I didn't reply. I ran to the wall, hurled myself up it, and made it to the top without difficulty. The skill was easier each time I did it.

I turned at the top and concentrated. I gathered my energy and jumped away. I ignored the fact that I was falling and concentrated on moving the energy. I gently moved the centres upwards, then with more force. I slowed myself; I had it. I floated down. At about five metres up I put my arms out and rotated so that I was feet first, balancing for a soft landing. I studied the ground, readying for the impact.

I completely lost it. I fell straight into the ground and hit it hard, left side first, winding myself.

John raced up, crouched next to me and put his hand behind my head, lifting it. 'Are you all right?' he said. 'Are you hurt?'

'I'm fine, I'm fine,' I said, trying to suck in enough air. 'Nothing's broken. Just had the wind knocked out of me.'

'Thank the Heavens,' he said, and took my hand in his. He smiled into my eyes and I realised. Too late. I opened my mouth and inhaled deeply, trying to get enough air in to shout at him. Too late.

The great gaping dark vortex opened in front of me and I was sucked in. My ears were full of rushing wind and my eyes full of raging darkness.

Something brilliantly blue and silver flashed and then everything went black.

'This time she really will tear strips off you,' Leo said, his voice full of amusement.

'I know,' John said.

Damn. I couldn't move.

'She moved,' Simone said.

'Squeeze my hand if you can hear me,' John said.

I tried. I didn't know if I did it.

'She squeezed *my* hand, Daddy,' Simone said.

Okay. I tried the other one.

'That's me,' John said.

'Hold,' the Dragon said. 'Ah Wu, Simone, let go.'

My hands were released and a warm breeze washed over me, making my hair flutter. I inhaled deeply, breathing in the sweet air. It filled me; my blood flowed back.

'Whoa,' Michael said softly.

'She is extremely large, my Lord, are you sure she's human?' the Dragon said as the warm air flowed over me.

'Fat chick,' Leo said.

Simone giggled.

'You will keep,' I croaked.

'Michael, get her a drink of water,' John said.

'That's the best I can do,' the Dragon said, and the warm air stopped. 'She will be weakened, but still able to complete the training, I think.'

'You can open your eyes now,' John said.

I did. I was still on the training course, on the ground. All of them crouched next to me, concerned, except for Michael, who quickly appeared holding a water bottle.

'Help me up,' I said. Leo took my hand and gently raised me so that I was sitting. Michael handed me the bottle and I took a huge drink, then gasped a breath. 'Thanks, Qing Long.'

'You are welcome,' the Dragon said, his turquoise eyes glowing.

'You really are a stupid damn Turtle,' I said. 'You

haven't been able to touch me for more than a year now, and you completely forgot.'

John didn't say anything but his eyes were full of amusement. Simone giggled again.

'Has Michael tried it yet?' I said.

'No,' John said.

'How long have I been out for?'

'Only a few minutes.'

'Good,' I said. 'Give me a couple of minutes while Michael tries. Then I want to have another go.'

'You sure you're up to it?' John said.

'What do you say, Qing Long?' I said.

'Let me look at you. Yes. Not a problem,' the Dragon said. 'Sit, drink some water, rest for a few minutes, watch Michael. Even better, I will get you an energy drink. If you get some carbohydrates into yourself you will be fine.'

He nodded his huge blue and silver head and a bottle of sports drink appeared on the ground next to me.

'Thanks,' I said, grabbed the drink, twisted the lid off and took a swig.

Michael, John and the Dragon went to the climbing walls together. Simone and Leo stayed with me.

'What are you guys doing here?' I said. 'I thought you were having a swim, Simone.'

'Leo won't go in with me. It's *boring*,' Simone said. 'The pool's too small. I want to go back out to the islands and feed the fish. And Leo won't let me go to the kids centre and play there.'

'They won't let him stay and guard you,' I said. 'It's not safe.'

Simone crossed her little arms in front of her chest. 'Humph.'

'Don't you want to stay and watch me and Michael learn to fly?'

'No,' she said, irritated. 'I want to learn to fly too.'

She concentrated on her father, arms still crossed over her chest. He turned to her, then a big grin spread across his face and he gestured with his head.

Simone threw her arms up, whooped with delight, and charged over to him. *He's going to teach me to fly too! He says it won't hurt my bones at all!*

'Great,' I said. 'Another thing she'll be better at than me.'

'One day she'll probably be protecting you,' Leo said.

'Help me up,' I said, putting my hand out. 'I think one day she'll probably be protecting both of us.'

CHAPTER SIXTEEN

It took Michael five tries before he could do the wall-running, but once he had the skill he could float off the wall easily.

'My turn,' I said, moving forward. 'I want to have this right.'

Everybody moved back and I ran to the top of the wall. 'What do you think is the highest I could go?' I called down to them. 'Could I make it to the top of a skyscraper?'

No, John said into my ear. *You could probably manage about five, six, storeys and then run out of energy and fall off. Don't try it; you wouldn't have any energy left to slow your fall! Be very careful with this.*

I didn't reply, I just hurled myself from the top of the wall. I concentrated on moving the energy centres upwards to slow my fall. I had it. I held out my arms, rotated, and floated gently down to land on my feet.

'Oh my God, that feels so good,' I said softly. I glanced up at John. 'How about if I jumped off a building? How high could I do that safely from?'

'Once you have the skill, there is no limit,' John said, amused. 'Slowing your fall requires much less energy, just more control. The Tiger and I have taken energy students skydiving without parachutes more than once — it's great fun.' He smiled. 'When I return, I'll take you up and we'll try.'

'Where will you find a skydiving plane in Hong Kong?' I said. 'There isn't space for small aircraft.'

His smile didn't shift. 'It won't be Hong Kong, unless that is your wish. And I won't need a plane.'

'Me too,' Simone said softly.

John grinned. 'Okay, sweetheart. Now, who wants to learn to fly?'

'*Me first! Me first!*' Simone squealed, jumping up and down. She ran and tackled her father hard, nearly knocking him over. 'I want to do some too!'

John hoisted her high and she squealed again. He lowered her gently. 'Let Emma try first, you watch. Then you can try.'

'Okay.' Simone gestured to me. 'Come on, Emma.'

I went forward. John led me to the obstacle course. 'This will do.'

It was a military-style obstacle course, with walls, ropes and nets. 'Ignore the obstacles, we just need the space,' John said. 'Run alongside.'

He stepped back to stand next to me, still facing the obstacle course. 'Run. Run fast. At the same time, lift the centres. This should be easier than slowing your fall; the centres are moving in the same direction as you.' He grinned. 'Lift yourself. Not too high — you'll probably manage some good momentum, if you fall you'll hit the ground hard.' He gestured. 'Try it. Watch carefully, Michael, Simone. Emma will probably have it correct first time.'

I ignored him. I readied myself, concentrating, then threw myself forward and ran as fast as I could. I felt a thrill of shock. I hadn't run like this ever before — there wasn't space and privacy to do it in Hong Kong — and I was moving extremely fast.

I used the centres to lift myself. My feet cleared the ground. I had it. I flew about five metres, then landed. It was like a huge running stride, but as light as being in water. It was incredibly exhilarating. I kept the motion for a few more metres, then carefully slowed, stopped and turned.

I was a good three hundred metres away from them and I'd only run for about five seconds.

If you're wondering, John said into my ear, *you did the first hundred metres in about three seconds. World record?*

I shook my head. I felt ridiculous.

You look like a cartoon, Simone said. *You fly, but your legs are still moving like you're running. You look really stupid.*

'No more *Sailor Moon* for you,' I said softly.

I heard that.

I ran back to them. I managed about two hundred metres of it in the air, and carefully didn't run while I was flying. I just let myself hang off the energy centres, revelling in the sensation. I landed, ran, slowed and stopped.

'That is one of the most fun things I have ever done in my entire life,' I said, gasping through the huge grin. 'What a shame there's nowhere to do it back home.'

'You are incredibly fast,' John said, glancing at his watch. 'You did the last fifty metres in two point five seconds.'

'Why don't any of the students ever compete in the Olympics?' I said. 'If the training can make you that fast?'

John smiled indulgently at me. I turned away. 'Damn.' I turned back to him. 'What's the fastest any of them has done?'

'A very good student can be close on the time of a world-class athlete,' John said. 'Some of them have

crossed over into the professional field. Not many —
maybe two or three at the most; they're more interested
in the Arts, that's why they're good enough for the
Mountain in the first place. I will only take the most
dedicated young people who love their Arts more than
anything else.' His smile became more gentle. 'You
knew you were fast, Emma.'

'Michael's turn,' I said, gesturing. 'I'll bet he's faster
than me.'

'No *way*!' Simone shouted. 'Me next!'

'Emma, take Simone, hold her hand,' John said.
'Help her with the centres, make sure she does it right.'
He moved closer to me and spoke softly. 'I'm counting
on you. Keep her safe. You know this can be
dangerous.'

'You know what to do, Simone?' I said, taking her
hand.

'Lift the energy centres, the dan tian,' she said. 'I saw
what you did.' She hesitated. 'Watch me carefully; let
me know if I do it wrong, Emma.'

'Okay, sweetheart. Ready?'

'Ready,' Simone said, and gathered herself.

We ran together, holding hands. She wasn't as fast as
I was, but she was still very fast.

She grabbed the centres and lifted them, and I lifted
myself as well. We hung on the air together, then both
dropped and hit the ground running. Simone stumbled
and I held her up. We skidded to a halt together and
turned. I felt her excitement through her hand.

'Again!' she squealed, and jerked my hand.

'One, two, *three*!' I shouted and we ran together
again. She lifted herself, I lifted myself, and we flew
together.

When we touched down again, Simone continued to
run and this time didn't stumble. She didn't stop; she let
go of me, ran straight into John and tackled him, nearly

knocking him over again. She grinned up at him with her eyes sparkling. 'Can I go again?'

He grinned. 'Go.'

She laughed, turned and ran again, lifting herself on the centres. She had it.

I moved closer to John. 'I wish we had the space to do this at home.'

'So do I,' he said. He gestured and Michael approached us.

'You want me to go with you?' I said.

'Can I try by myself?'

'Go. Try,' John said. 'Take care, but I think you can do it.'

Simone returned, her face flushed and her eyes sparkling. 'That's more fun than swimming. Can I try jumping down?'

'Jump down off the obstacle course,' John said, and she ran to climb the ladder. The Dragon moved to catch her.

'She won't need him. She'll get it right first time, same as Michael,' John said, motioning towards Michael who was flying along the side of the obstacle course.

He was right. Both Simone and Michael were like children in a playground. They couldn't get enough of the flying and falling. John and I watched them with amusement.

After five minutes I moved to sit under a tree, leaving John to supervise. I faced the water and enjoyed the view, relaxing.

I caught a movement out of the corner of my eye and leaned forward to see.

Leo and Martin stood at the end of the beach, watching the water together and talking. Leo had his arms crossed; Martin had his hands folded behind his back.

They faced each other. Leo reached up and stroked Martin's cheek and lowered his face to Martin's. Martin put his hand around Leo's neck and pulled himself closer.

I faced the other way.

A couple of minutes later they strolled past me along the beach, hand in hand, talking softly. They didn't notice me. But they dropped their hands when they were within view of Michael and Simone.

I sighed.

'Don't wear yourselves out,' John called after about half an hour of Michael and Simone flying and leaping from the obstacle course. 'There's one more thing we need to do.'

He gestured for us to approach and we gathered around him.

'Simone should do this first, she has good control of her shen,' John said. 'Projecting your consciousness into your chi. Generate chi, and move a very small part of your shen into it.'

'But that's shen work,' I said, protesting. 'I can't do that on the Earthly Plane, only on the Celestial Plane.'

'Not quite shen work,' John said. 'Joining the energy together, working with them together. Just more advanced chi work. You should be able to do it.'

He gestured for Simone to approach. 'Generate about this much.' He indicated about a tennis ball's worth.

Simone nodded, concentrating, held out her hands and generated the energy.

'Try something for me, Simone,' John said gently. 'Try turning the chi white. Don't turn it into shen; you know what the difference is. Try to make it white.'

Simone concentrated on the chi, her little face rigid. The chi turned silvery-white, almost identical to shen energy except that it had golden bands through it.

'Very good,' John said softly. 'Change it back to yellow.'

Simone inhaled slowly and deeply and the chi changed back again.

'If you tire too much tell me,' John said. 'Now, leave the chi there, concentrate, and move a very tiny part of your shen into it.'

Simone's face was stiff but her eyes were very wide.

'Can you move a little more in?' John said.

Simone didn't move.

'Good,' John said, his voice so soft it was almost a whisper. 'Now. Turn and float the chi gently away from yourself.'

Simone did as he said, and the chi floated off her hands and moved about two metres away from her. Her face changed from concentration to rapt awe.

'That's really amazing, Daddy,' she whispered.

'Slowly call it back,' he said.

The chi gently returned to her. As soon as it was absorbed into her hands she flopped down to sit on the sandy ground.

He crouched next to her and took her hands, studying her face. 'Are you okay?'

'I'm okay,' she whispered. 'Just let me sit, Daddy.'

He held her hands and concentrated, then gently pulled her to her feet. He led her to one side and sat her under a tree. 'Ah Qing, could you get her a drink?'

The Dragon nodded his huge blue and silver head and a sports drink appeared on the ground next to Simone. John opened it and passed it to her.

She took a sip and made a face. 'That tastes yucky.'

'Apple juice?' the Dragon said, nodding again.

Simone took another sip, then a large swig from the bottle, her throat moving as she drank. She finished, gasped, and smiled up at her father. 'I'm okay.'

He took her hand again and smiled. 'Yes, you are. Emma. Your turn.'

'Is she really okay?' I said as I approached him.

'She'll sleep very well tonight,' he said with amusement, then shared a quick glance with the Dragon. 'Try.'

'Is standing or sitting better?' I said.

'Standing,' John said. 'The chi starts higher.'

I nodded, put out my hands and concentrated. I generated a similar-sized ball of chi to Simone's.

'Can I try to turn it white?' I said. 'Is white chi somehow better?'

'Try,' he said. 'White chi is much more destructive to demons. In all other respects, the colour of the chi makes no difference.'

I nodded again, concentrated and turned the chi white. It was much harder than making it blue; it took a great deal of concentration.

'This is like starting all over again,' I said as I felt the chi trying to move back into my hands.

'Precisely,' John said. 'But it's a useful type of energy to master. Change it back before you drain yourself too much.'

I released the whiteness of the chi. It went black. I held a ball of roiling black energy in my hands.

'I didn't know you could do that,' I said. 'What is black chi good for?'

John was silent. I glanced up and saw his face. It was rigid with restraint.

'Stone, are you awake?' he said.

The stone didn't reply.

'Do not move, Emma,' John said very softly. He gingerly reached out to tap the stone on my finger, carefully not touching the black chi. 'Stone,' he said, his voice quiet and fierce.

'I am looking,' the stone said. 'Hold.'

'Hold very still, Emma,' John said. 'Don't move, physically or mentally.'

'Is this the first time you've seen anything like this?' I said.

John was silent but his face said it all.

'Not yin,' the stone said. 'Hold.'

John raised his hand to the chi and the stone yelped. 'Don't approach it, Turtle! It will harm you!'

'Oh shit,' I said softly, trying to retain my concentration.

'Emma,' the stone said, its voice soft and insistent, 'turn and see if you can move this chi off your hands.'

I did as the stone instructed, turning away from John and moving the chi off my hands. 'It feels like normal chi,' I said. 'I can't feel the unusual colour at all.'

'I wonder what it would do to a demon,' John said.

'Move it back,' the stone said.

I nodded and returned the chi to my hands.

'Do you have a demon jar here, Ah Qing?' John said.

'Of course not,' the Dragon said. 'This resort is thoroughly sealed; no untamed demons in or out.'

'It will have to wait until we're home then,' John said. 'Fascinating. You never cease to amaze me, Emma. The Celestial Masters will all want to see this.'

'Is it demon essence, stone?' I said, trying to control my voice.

'Nope,' the stone said. 'It's definitely black chi. Never heard of it before. Must contact the Hall of Records, Turtle, there may have been other instances.'

'Good idea,' John said.

'Change it back to gold,' the stone said.

I concentrated, and the chi returned to its usual golden colour. I didn't feel the colour change.

'Why could I do that?' I whispered.

'Because you are what you are,' John said.

'And what am I?'

'You are my Lady. Now,' John said, more briskly, 'try moving shen into the chi. Try.'

I concentrated. I left the chi on my hands, moved my awareness to my upper dan tian, found my shen and carefully moved a tiny amount into the chi. The feeling hit me. Part of my awareness was inside the chi; it was as if my Inner Eye had moved into it. I saw my surroundings from two distinctly separate angles.

'Now try moving the chi off your hands, only a short distance,' John said.

I moved the chi off my hands, as he said, and floated it closer to Simone. I saw two images of her: one through my physical eyes and another through my chi.

'Oh my God, this feels so good,' I whispered. I tried something; I moved the chi higher. Nothing happened, so I carefully moved it level with the treetops. I could see the horizon through my chi. A huge thunderstorm had gathered out to sea; the lightning flashed inside it.

I pulled the chi back down to me and absorbed it. 'Michael should quickly try, and then we should all hurry back to the resort,' I said. 'It'll rain cats and dogs in about twenty minutes.'

'Sooner than that,' John said. 'Try, Michael, but don't hurry; you have all the time in the world. You should be able to master the skill easily. If you're not too drained, Emma, go to one side and practise generating that black chi. I'd like to experiment with it when we return home.'

'Permission to take a look at the black chi,' the Dragon said. He was still in True Form. 'It is fascinating.'

'Good idea,' John said. 'Emma, go to the side, make some and let the Dragon see.'

'He can have a look inside me at the same time,' I said.

'That is not necessary; we have seen all we need to,' John said.

'I want him to,' I said.

'No need, Emma,' John said gently.

'If the Dark Lord objects then I have no option,' the Dragon said. 'I won't go against his wishes.'

'I'm doing it anyway,' I said. 'Come on, Dragon, let's have a look inside this unusually snaky female who can generate black chi.'

The Dragon didn't move.

'Come on,' I said, waving him forward. 'Tell him.'

'Let her,' John said with resignation. 'If that is what she wishes, then I really have no choice.'

The Dragon shook his enormous turquoise head and followed me.

'Look at the black chi now,' John called to us. 'Look inside Emma later, back at the resort. That storm will be here soon and you don't have time.'

'The Dragon can move it away for us,' I said.

'I will keep you dry if we are caught in the storm, but I will not tamper with the forces of nature unless it is absolutely necessary,' the Dragon said.

'Okay,' I said. 'I understand.'

The Dragon returned to his preferred human form: turquoise hair, silken grey robe, serene long face. 'Generate the black chi.'

I held my hands out and put some chi into them, then turned it black. It was easy.

'Not difficult?' the Dragon said, his bright blue eyes focusing on the chi.

'Can he touch it?' I said.

'Yes,' the stone said. 'Such a small amount should be all right for a powerful Shen such as he, at full strength.'

'That stone is quite useful,' the Dragon said, raising his hand to the energy. 'Let me see.' He held his hand above the energy and concentrated. His long turquoise hair floated around his head. He very slowly lowered his hand until it was just above the chi. 'Fascinating.' He quickly dipped his hand in and out of the chi. 'Remarkable.'

'Well?' I said.

'You can release it now. Michael has finished. We should return,' the Dragon said.

'And?'

'To inspection, to touch, to feel, it is perfectly ordinary chi, nothing special about it at all,' the Dragon said, bemused. 'Please invite me along when you throw it at a demon. I would be interested to see what it does.'

I released the chi back into my hands and gasped with shock. I hadn't changed it back to gold and the skin of my hands flashed black for a split second as it went in.

'Oh my, that was good,' the Dragon said, taking my hands and studying them. 'Please do that again.' He glanced up at my face. 'That didn't hurt you in any way, did it?'

'No,' I said. 'It just felt perfectly normal. Are you okay, stone?'

'It felt normal,' the stone said. 'It just looked black. As you say, Lord Qing, most fascinating.'

'Do it again,' the Dragon said, releasing my hands.

I generated chi, turned it black and dropped it into my hands. They flashed black again.

'Try generating black chi right from the start,' John said. He had approached us without me noticing and stood beside the Dragon.

I concentrated, held out my hands and generated a ball of black chi.

'Try moving your shen into it,' John said. 'Just a very small amount. See if you can move your consciousness into it.'

I came around on my bed back in the hotel room with John and Simone holding my hands.

I closed my eyes. 'I really must stop doing this to myself.'

CHAPTER SEVENTEEN

We waited until the next day for the Dragon to look inside me. John had some indoor things to teach us as well. These required privacy and quiet, so the Dragon chased all the staff out of one of the large function rooms and gave it to us.

The function room was like a ballroom, with a huge chandelier and elegant wallpaper and carpet. We took a corner, and had an area of about five by five metres partitioned off. Chairs had been stacked against one of the walls and John pulled a few down for us to sit in the centre of the room.

John sent Leo, Simone and Michael off to the country club while the Dragon looked inside me. The Dragon sat me in a chair and sat behind me, placing his hands on my shoulders. I relaxed and let him in.

'I am honoured that you permit me to do this when you dislike me so much,' the Dragon said.

'I don't dislike you that much,' I said.

The Dragon didn't reply.

He hunted around inside me, same as John and the Tiger had. I was accustomed to the feeling and stood back to watch as he rummaged around.

'And the Tiger could bring the Serpent out?' the Dragon said.

'Yes,' John said from his chair in front of me. 'He dug his claws into her and dug deep. It came out.'

'Depth. Depth,' the Dragon said softly. 'Depth.'

'Interesting,' John said. 'You seem to become deeper every time one of us looks inside you. The stone was correct.'

'Of course I was,' the stone snapped.

'And I will be astonished,' John said. 'I think I am astonished already, stone.'

'Why will he be astonished?' I said.

'Please remain silent, my Lady,' the Dragon said. 'Stay still so I can look at you.'

I subsided and let the Dragon see me.

'And the taste of blood brings it out as well,' the Dragon said. 'I have some here. Just hold on, I'll get someone to bring it.'

'No,' John said. 'I forbid it. That is wrong.'

'Very well,' the Dragon said, shrugging inside my head. 'Would have been an interesting experiment, though.' He continued to shuffle through my thoughts and feelings. 'Worthy.'

'Of course,' John said. 'Anything?'

'No ... no.' The Dragon stopped and pondered inside my head. 'Hold out your hands and generate some black chi. Let's see what happens from the inside.'

'Are you sure that's a good idea?' I said.

'Don't move shen into it, just make the chi,' John said. 'Shouldn't hurt you. Ordinary chi can be generated in these circumstances without any risk, and watching the process from the inside can be very informative.'

I held my hands out and generated a small ball of black chi. I could tell that it was black without even looking at it.

The Dragon ripped himself out of my head, tearing the inside of my brain and making my entire head explode with agony. He moved swiftly behind me and his chair fell over. He held me bound, with my hands out holding the black chi.

'Destroy it,' the Dragon hissed fiercely. 'Do it now!'

'Don't be ridiculous,' John said calmly.

I snapped open my eyes. John still sat in front of me. He had turned the chair sideways and was leaning one arm over the back. He appeared perfectly calm and relaxed. He smiled at me. 'Don't worry, and don't move.'

'Destroy that thing *now*!' the Dragon said more loudly. 'It will be the end of you all!'

'You don't even know what she is,' John said. 'You're just panicking.'

Oh my God, he was talking about *me*. I tried to remain still but my throat was thick and I found it difficult to breathe.

'I saw *that*,' the Dragon said, somehow indicating something. 'I don't know what it is, but I really don't like the look of it.'

'Am I a demon?' I whispered. 'If I'm a demon, please, John, destroy me now.'

'No demon can come into the resort, Emma,' John said. 'The Dragon is just being an old woman about this. You are not a demon.'

'No. She isn't a demon. If she were a demon I wouldn't be reacting like this.' The Dragon's scales rattled behind me. He'd transformed. 'You should destroy that thing *now*.'

'You are a Serpent yourself,' John said mildly, not shifting from his relaxed posture.

I reabsorbed the chi, but couldn't turn to speak to the Dragon. He still had me bound. 'What did you see?' I said.

'It cannot be put into words,' the Dragon said.

'Well then, show us,' John said.

He did. Right in my centre, at my very core, was a heart of deepest darkness that seemed to absorb everything around it. It was a roiling ball of such merciless destructive power that it terrified me. It thirsted for blood and slaughter and would stop at nothing to get it. It was huge and dark and monstrous and scared the living daylights out of me — and it *was* me.

I inhaled sharply. The Dragon was right. I knew what I had to do. I desperately struggled to move, but the Dragon had me bound tight. I had a quick inspiration. I generated an enormous ball of chi and threw it straight at John. He'd absorb it, drain me, kill me: easy.

I closed my eyes. I *knew* it.

I saw a blinding flash of white light through my eyelids and then everything faded. I heard sounds, but they disappeared. No vacuum vortex this time, just a gentle fade. Goodbye.

Ms Kwan spoke, full of her sad smile. 'Emma.'

'Wake up, Emma!' Simone's little insistent voice.

'And if you do that again, I will be extremely cross with you,' John said.

I opened my eyes. I was still in the chair. All of them were there: John, Simone, Michael, Leo, Ms Kwan. Even the Dragon was behind them, in human form, watching.

'What happened?' I said.

'Daddy says you did something really silly and nearly died,' Simone said, her voice miserable. She climbed into my lap, threw her arms around my neck and put her head on my chest, burying her face into my shirt. 'Please be careful, Emma. Daddy and Leo will leave me

210

and you'll be all I have left.' She shook soundlessly, and I wrapped my arms around her and kissed the top of her little tawny head.

'Promise me you won't do anything silly like that again,' Simone said, gasping through the sobs.

I was silent.

'Promise me!' Simone said, jamming her head into my chest. 'Promise!'

I pulled her tighter into me. 'I promise,' I whispered into her hair.

''Cause you're all I'll have left,' she whispered. 'And I don't want you to leave me.'

'I won't leave you,' I said.

'You are a complete fool,' the Dragon said, and disappeared.

'Who was he talking to?' I said.

'I think, all of us,' Ms Kwan said.

'Now that Emma's finished being extremely silly,' John said with an amused edge, 'it's time to learn our last few lessons. Emma and I can talk in private about her extremely advanced silliness later.'

Simone squeezed me but her head didn't move from my chest.

'I promise, Simone,' I whispered. 'I won't do it again.'

'Good,' Simone said, a huge gasp. She climbed down off my lap, took Ms Kwan's hand and led her out.

'I have something I want to teach you, Simone,' John called after her.

'I'm going to the bathroom to wash my face and blow my nose,' Simone shouted back, irritated. 'Don't do anything without me. Ms Kwan's looking after me. You stay there and tell Emma that she's very silly.'

I couldn't help myself. I laughed softly.

You will never harm them, Emma, Ms Kwan said into my ear.

I sighed. She was right.

'When I am back at full strength I will make that Dragon suffer most dearly,' John said with amusement.

'But what was that inside me?' I said. 'It was horrible.'

'It wasn't horrible,' John said, the small smile still there. 'It was just you, Dark Lady.'

'But it was dark and heartless ...' I stopped, speechless.

'Precisely,' John said.

'See?' the stone said.

'Did she freak the Dragon out?' Leo said, pulling one of the chairs over and sitting with us. Michael grabbed a chair as well, spun it around and sat backwards on it.

'Yes,' John said. 'He was ready to kill her. He was terrified of her.'

'Whoa. Excellent,' Leo said with a huge grin. 'I wish I'd seen that.'

'And then the stupid human tried to kill herself by forcing me to drain her,' John said softly. The amusement was gone.

'Stupid's the word, my Lord,' Leo said.

'Was it really that bad, Emma?' Michael said.

'Yes,' I whispered. I dropped my head and ran my hands through my hair.

'One: you will never hurt any of us. Two: Simone needs you. Three: let's see if the dark and heartless monster can turn itself invisible,' John said.

'Invisibility? Sweet,' Michael said.

'You can try first, if you like,' John said, turning to Michael without rising from the chair. 'Nothing to do with energy, but I can't do it right now. Just concentrate and think yourself transparent.'

'Is this how the dragons fly around without being seen?' I said, curious despite myself.

'Sometimes, yes,' John said. 'Most of the time, though, they don't hide themselves at all, because frankly most humans don't look up much; they're usually looking at the ground or straight ahead. If the dragons are seen, they take the form of a bird, or a plane, and then they're simply not interesting.'

Michael had his head down, concentrating. He was already getting there; he rippled like thick glass bricks.

'Excellent,' John said. 'You are very talented, Michael.'

I lowered my head, centred my chi and concentrated on being transparent.

Simone came in, still holding Ms Kwan's hand. She stopped close to us.

'*Boo!*' Michael shouted behind her and grabbed her around the waist. She squealed and jumped, and turned to shout at him, but he was invisible.

'Don't you dare do that again, Michael,' Simone huffed, 'or I'll tell my Daddy. You could have *hurt* me. I'm only little, you know.'

I had to laugh. She could take him down with one hand tied behind her back using either physical or energy skills.

'Come and learn to be invisible too,' John said. 'That way you can sneak into his room and steal all his games CDs.'

'She keeps stealing my copy of MOHAA, logging onto my server and playing as me anyway,' Michael said from somewhere in the air above me. 'The guys in my clan are always emailing me asking what happened, my average went through the floor.'

'You shouldn't be playing so much during term time anyway,' I said. 'Now. Simone and me. Whoever is first to be invisible wins an ice-cream beside the pool.'

Simone dropped her head and concentrated. I did too. She was invisible within five minutes. I never got there.

'Give up, Emma, let's try ordering,' John said. 'We need an ordinary human to practise on and unfortunately we only have one.'

'You're not practising coercion on Leo; that is simply not fitting and I won't let you,' I said. 'Do it to me, or find somebody else.'

'That's why I'm here, Emma,' Leo said softly. 'So that you guys can try this skill on me.'

'But you don't know what this involves, Leo,' I said with desperation. 'This is thoroughly inappropriate.'

'I volunteer to be a subject in coercion training, my Lord,' Leo said loudly.

'Accepted,' John said, and rose. 'Get up, everybody, let's see what we can do. Look inside Leo, find out where his "engine" is — the part that makes things happen. Then you can try steering him the way you want him to go. Michael, demonstrate for Simone.'

Michael reappeared and hesitated. He didn't move to take Simone's hand.

'It's okay, Michael, she has to learn this,' Leo said gently. 'Do it.'

Michael shook his head slightly and took Simone's hand. 'We'll learn this and then we won't do it any more,' he said. 'Emma's right.'

'It's a useful skill,' Leo said. 'Try making me walk.'

Michael's expression went even darker. He frowned and held Simone's hand tight.

Leo's face went blank. He turned, walked towards the door, then turned and came back to us.

He snapped out of it and shook his head.

'Let me try,' Simone said.

Leo went rigid again. He turned, walked and returned.

'See if you can make him sit on the floor,' John said softly.

Leo snapped out of it.

'No, Daddy, that's enough,' Simone said. 'I can do it, and I won't do it any more.' She turned back to Leo. 'Are you okay?'

214

'I'm fine, sweetheart,' Leo said. 'I don't even know what you made me do.'

Simone shook Michael's hand free. 'I don't like that skill. Are we finished yet? I'm *hungry*.'

'Emma should try it,' John said, gesturing. 'Michael, show her.'

Michael took my hand. I felt him reach inside Leo and pull the strings. Leo walked away and back again. My throat thickened; Leo didn't care at all. He trusted us completely.

When Michael had finished I attempted to reach inside Leo and pull the strings as well, but I simply didn't have the strength to make them move. I struggled, trying to gather enough power to control him.

'You can't do it, Emma,' John said. 'Maybe after a year or so more of training you may be able to. Right now, I don't think so.'

'Good,' I said, and I meant it.

'One more,' John said. 'The most fun one of all. Carrying. Michael can already do it, he'll show you.' He looked around. 'Anybody have a pen?'

Nobody replied; nope.

'How about we have some lunch beside the pool and do it there?' I said. 'Simone's starving.'

'Yeah!' Simone said.

'You'll have to be careful that nobody sees you,' Leo said.

'Not a problem,' John said. 'We'll do it at the end of the pool nearest the lobby, to one side, and if anybody sees us Michael can just blank out their memory.'

'I really don't like messing with people's heads, my Lord,' Michael said as we rose to go out to the pool. 'I thought it was cool when Na Zha showed it to me, but every time I do it I feel lousy afterwards.'

'What, it makes you feel ill?' I said. 'Drained?'

'No,' Michael said. 'It makes me feel bad. It's wrong.'

John moved to walk beside me as we went through the lobby to the stairs that would take us down to the pool. 'It's a shame Leo won't be around to help you, Emma,' he said softly. 'He is the finest judge of character I have ever seen.'

'I know. And I think he and Martin are developing something very special.'

John sighed. 'I know.'

Michael and Simone could do PK. I couldn't. John said I was the weirdest mix of talents he'd ever seen. Great. Even the Xuan Wu thought I was weird.

After lunch we returned to the suite. I sat on the balcony enjoying the scenery and putting photos together for the Tiger to take to my family. John was with Kwan Yin having a quick top-up. Michael had gone with his parents to the islands. Leo and Simone were playing Go Fish in the living room.

A commotion erupted inside. '*Leo*!' John shouted. 'Guard!'

I heard thumping and doors banging, and rushed into the living room.

John and Ms Kwan raced in too and stared at the front door. Leo had pushed Simone behind him. John and Ms Kwan went forward to stand in front of them.

'Emma,' John said. 'Stay back.'

'What's going on?' I said.

'He would not do this. I cannot believe this,' Ms Kwan said. 'Why?'

The Dragon appeared next to John and Kwan Yin. 'You are entirely much more trouble than you are worth, my Lord,' he said evenly. 'The seals are blown. I will never have them back to what they were. No

Celestial will be able to stay here unmolested for a very long time. I will lose a great deal of money on this.'

Nobody said anything.

The doorbell rang.

'Leo, weapons, quickly,' John said.

Leo raced to the hall cupboard, scrabbled through the bag and pulled out swords for each of us. He threw Dark Heavens to John, my Serpent sword to me, and hefted Michael's white blade in his own hand.

'Back, Leo,' John said. 'Guard.'

Leo moved to stand in front of Simone and me.

'What's going on?' I whispered.

Ms Kwan answered the door. Martin stood there, smiling slightly. Next to him was an enormous demon. It had taken the shape of an ordinary-looking Chinese man in his mid-fifties wearing a plain shirt and pants. It was the biggest demon I had ever seen short of the Demon King himself. Way into the nineties in level. Absolutely enormous. None of us had a chance against it.

'What have you done, Martin?' I whispered.

'Hold,' Martin said loudly. 'Number One will not harm you, he is here to talk terms. Remember, he has a similar goal to us. He has given his word that during this visit he will harm no one.'

John lowered his sword. 'Go,' he said. 'Leave us.'

Ms Kwan disappeared. The Dragon also vanished.

'Is his word good?' I said.

'Yes,' John said. 'He is renowned for it. Leo.' John held Dark Heavens out, hilt first.

Leo collected the blades and stood holding them, guarding.

'Enter,' John said. 'Leo, take Simone into her room. Emma, please go with them.'

Leo took Simone gently by the hand and led her, wide-eyed and unprotesting, into her bedroom. I didn't move.

Martin and the demon carefully entered and approached John.

'Emma, please,' John said without turning around.

'I am staying here and hearing what he has to say,' I said.

'Come. Sit,' John said, gesturing towards the couch.

Martin smiled at me but I scowled at him.

Martin and the demon sat together on one of the couches. John sat on the other couch. I pulled the chair away from the desk and sat behind John. I folded one of my feet underneath me and leaned on the back of John's sofa.

'My Lady,' the demon said, giving me a small smile.

I ignored him.

The demon gestured and a cup of black coffee appeared in front of him. 'Tea, my Lady?' I shook my head. He nodded to John. 'Xuan Tian?'

John didn't move. 'Ming Gui,' he said, 'after this is completed, you will remain. I wish to speak to you.'

'My Lord,' Martin said with a wry smile.

'Well?' John said.

'Anyone who presents your head to the King will be promoted to Number One,' the demon said. 'I will be out.'

'I am well aware of that,' John said.

'If One Two Two gets your head, it will be only the beginning. He will be promoted. I hate to think of the consequences.'

'The most immediate ones are for you,' John said.

The demon smiled slightly but didn't say anything.

'What is your offer?' John said softly.

'Give me your head —'

'*No!*' I hissed.

'Give me your head,' the demon continued, 'and I will remain as Number One. One Two Two will remain as he is. I will do my best to ensure that your family remain unharmed.'

'Can you guarantee our safety?' I said. 'Simone's safety?'

'You will be safer than you are now,' he said.

'If I go to the King, he guarantees her safety,' I said.

'If you go to the King it will mean that One Two Two has taken the Dark Lord's head and has been promoted,' the demon said. 'You certainly do not want that, my Lady.'

'Can you take out One Two Two?' John said.

The demon leaned forward, picked up his coffee and took a sip. He put the coffee back down and put his elbows on his knees. 'No.'

'Why not?' John said.

'He has done some things to himself and to his closest allies. He has made himself immensely powerful. I can't take him.'

'He's more powerful than you?' I said.

Number One nodded, his face grim.

'What about the King?' John said. 'Why hasn't he destroyed this one? It's obvious where this is headed. He should have destroyed it a long time ago.'

'That's what I think,' Number One said. 'The King is overconfident. They get that way after a few centuries of being able to handle anything thrown at them.'

'Am I correct in understanding that a lower-level demon can destroy the King and take over?' I said.

'Exactly,' John said. 'This particular King was Number One himself for about five hundred years before sneaking up and stabbing his father in the back.'

'I have vowed not to try against my father, and I am renowned as a creature of my word,' Number One said. 'That is the only reason I am still here today.'

'I really can't see the advantage in giving you the Dark Lord's head,' I said. 'The only real benefit seems to be to you.'

'Please consider my offer, Turtle,' the demon said. 'You do not want to see One Two Two promoted, believe me. He has no hesitation in using modern technology.' The demon leaned back and its voice remained mild. 'He has contacted the other Centres. He is attempting to make pacts with the other Kings.'

John inhaled sharply. 'No.'

'Oh, dear Lord,' I said softly.

'The Celestial must be informed immediately,' John said. 'Martin.'

'My Lord,' Martin said.

'I will consider your offer, One. Go. I will contact you if I decide to give you my head. If I do not contact you, do not approach, because I may take *your* head instead. Martin, remain.'

'Okay, whatever you say,' the demon said, and disappeared.

Martin remained on the couch. He smiled wryly again.

'I should give you to the Dragon,' John said mildly.

'Please, go right ahead,' Martin said, the wry smile not shifting. 'I know it'll take me a long time to work this one off.'

'Did he tell you the deal before you brought him?' I said.

'Yep.'

'Then why did you bother to bring him? That deal wasn't anything we'd take him up on, unless we were desperate,' I said.

'You really are extremely stupid sometimes, Martin,' John said. 'It's almost as if you *want* to stay out of my good favours.'

'I did what I had to do,' Martin said, still smiling.

'Oh geez, you haven't fallen for that bastard, have

you?' I said. 'I can't believe a Celestial like yourself would have anything to do with a high-ranking demon.'

'It's happened before, Emma,' John said. 'But I also find it difficult to believe, considering who Martin is, and whose son he is.'

Martin didn't say anything.

'Does he return it?' I said.

Martin's face didn't shift.

'Holy shit, but you are an extremely stupid little turtle,' I said. 'It's hard to believe that you're his son.'

'I should disown you completely and send you to Hell for eternity,' John said, his voice a low rumble.

'There is a place for me there,' Martin said, so softly I could hardly hear him. He straightened and spoke more loudly. 'I'll go. It'll take me at least two years to return. You'll be gone before I come back. You won't see me again for a long time. Satisfactory?'

I couldn't believe this. 'Geez.'

'Report to the Jade Emperor first,' John said without emotion. 'Tell him what Number One just told us. Wait to see if he wants to talk to me about this. If he doesn't, then go. I look forward to not seeing your face for quite some time.'

Martin rose and smiled at each of us. He moved forward and knelt on the plush rug next to the coffee table. 'My Lord,' he said, saluting John carefully. 'My Lady,' saluting me. He rose and disappeared.

John bowed his head and sat silently. I didn't move either. Neither of us spoke.

'I cannot believe he did that,' Leo said as we sat beside the pool watching Simone. 'He used me, he used Simone, he used all of us. He brought that waste-of-time huge demon straight through our front door to make an offer he knew we wouldn't take. He broke every single seal on our apartment.' His voice became more vehement. 'He *used* me!' He dropped his head. 'I thought he was different. I thought he was ...' He didn't finish.

'Well, he's in Hell now,' I said. 'He said it'll take him a couple of years to come back out.'

'Lucky for him,' Leo said, raising his head so that he could watch Simone again. ''Cause if he comes out when I'm around, I'll damn well send him straight back down there.'

'I hope you get your chance,' I said softly.

'Not going to happen, Emma.'

'I'll send him back down there for you then.'

'My Lady.'

'God, the lifeguards here are useless,' I said. 'Simone's been swimming around under the water for more than five minutes without coming up for air and none of them have noticed.'

'They probably see that she's still moving and don't try to rescue her,' Leo said.

'Oh yeah. God, Martin was amazingly stupid.'

'You got some useful information out of that demon anyway,' Leo said. 'It's all happening at once, isn't it. Xuan Wu out of action. This little demon bastard using all the new technology stuff. New hybrids. Contacting the different regions. Shooting for Number One.'

'Shooting higher than that,' I said, and he stiffened. 'Interesting times. You know that isn't a Chinese curse at all?'

'What?'

'You know, the curse: "May you live in interesting times." I've asked people. Nobody's ever heard of it.'

'Neither have I,' Leo said.

'Ah,' I said. 'So you haven't read *all* my books yet.'

'No idea what you're talking about.'

Bastard, I signed.

I saw that, he signed back.

222

CHAPTER EIGHTEEN

I woke with a start. John stood next to my bed, leaning over me.

'Quietly,' he said. 'Come with me.'

I didn't ask any questions; I just levered myself out of bed and followed him.

'I'm not properly dressed,' I whispered as I followed him through the living room. I wore a pair of old shorts and a tank top to sleep. 'Where are we going? Is everybody okay?'

'Everyone is fine,' he said. 'Just come with me. I want you to see something.'

He led me down the stairs, both of us barefoot. He wore his usual plain black pyjama pants without a shirt, his long hair braided down his back. I retied my untidy hair as we walked.

'This had better be good, John,' I said as he led me across the damp, cool grass towards the water. 'I have to get up early tomorrow and pack. We're supposed to be out of here by eleven to go home.'

'I think you'll like it,' he said. He stopped. 'It's a beautiful night, isn't it.'

I stopped next to him and looked up. The sky was completely clear and the stars blazed. There was no moon. A fresh breeze, full of the smell of the sea, made the dark water before us ripple. 'What time is it?'

'About midnight.' He smiled, his dark eyes shining in the starlight. 'Come.'

I followed him to the edge of the water. We stood and waited on the small beach.

'The Dragon is coming in True Form,' John said softly, his voice carrying over the gentle sound of the small waves. 'Don't be concerned, he's coming out of the water ... now.'

The Dragon emerged in full majestic True Form, nearly twenty metres long. His turquoise eyes glowed. He lowered his massive silver-fanged head over his front legs. 'My Lord. My Lady.' He turned so that his back was towards me. 'Climb on, Emma. Right behind my head. Don't worry, my scales won't hurt you. Hold on to my frill.'

I stopped dead. 'You want me to *ride* you?'

'Hop on. We don't have much time,' John said. 'Let's go.'

I moved next to the Dragon's head and he lowered his shoulders so that I could climb on. John didn't move. 'What about you?'

'We are going under the water,' John said. 'Don't worry, you'll be able to breathe. Just hold on to the Dragon, he'll take you. Let's go.'

'You're not coming?'

He gestured impatiently. 'Of course I am. I don't need a ride. Now *hurry up*!'

I pulled myself onto the Dragon's neck and held on to the massive silver and turquoise frill that surrounded his head. I couldn't ride him astride; he was too big. I had to sit side-saddle. He wasn't cold and sharp; he was warm and the edges of his scales were smooth and fine. He had horns, like a deer, with two prongs; I hadn't noticed that before. The horns towered over me.

'Ready?' the Dragon said.

'Yes,' I said.

'Hold on tight,' John said. 'Here we go. No! Wait!'

The Dragon hesitated.

'Emma, while we are under the water, the Dragon and I will be able to speak to you, but you won't be able to talk to us.'

'That will kill her,' the Dragon said wryly.

'I'll survive,' I said, nudging his frill. 'Let's go. This had better be good, I'm missing my beauty sleep.'

I think it will be worth it, John said. *Let's go.*

The Dragon launched himself into the water but I didn't feel the movement. The water pounded past us but there was no pressure.

Don't hold your breath, the Dragon said. *You can breathe.*

I nudged his frill to show that I understood. I looked right. John swam next to us, matching the Dragon's velocity without moving a muscle. He was stretched out as if he was flying. He noticed my gaze and smiled.

Not many humans have seen me swim like this, he said. *I feel self-conscious swimming in human form, I know it looks strange. I hope you'll see me swim in True Form one day.*

I nodded. I hoped so too.

The Dragon's body whipped beneath me but there was still no other sensation of movement.

The water became very dark as we plunged deeper. I gripped the Dragon's frill tighter.

If the darkness bothers you, close your eyes, the Dragon said. *I will let you know when there is something to see. Some of my human wives have found this part of the journey quite claustrophobic.*

The wives were right. The water was dark and pressed in all around me. I couldn't see a thing. I wasn't sure whether the flashes of illumination that sped past us were real or just my eyes playing tricks. I closed my eyes and lowered my head. I wondered how deep we were.

About a hundred metres, the stone in my ring said. *But we are a good twenty kilometres from shore. We are travelling very fast. We will drop off the continental shelf any second ... There.*

There was a definite change in the movement; the Dragon seemed to be using more effort to travel.

Not more effort, the stone said. *He just sped up. Before, he was going about three hundred kilometres an hour. He has just doubled his speed. I must say, Emma, this is quite exhilarating.*

That was pretty damn fast. I hoped that John could keep up.

The Dark Lord has absolutely no problem at all. I suspect he may be able to travel faster than the Dragon.

It is about a twenty minute trip, my Lady, the Dragon said.

If you are feeling unwell, give the Dragon a kick, John said. *I know it's quite a trek.*

I opened my eyes. Nothing but darkness around me. I relaxed and closed them again, enjoying the sensation of travelling without motion through the warm darkness. The Dragon's scales were smooth and silky, and his frill felt like a velvety chamois.

Don't go to sleep, John said, jarring me out of my slumber. *You need to hold on. Here we are.*

I opened my eyes and nearly fell off.

'Here' was a fairytale castle, glittering with multicoloured lights. It seemed to stretch forever, with curved towers and arched walkways. The walls were transparent around the edges, milky white in the centre. It had a traditional tiled Chinese roof, with upwardly curving edges and sweeping corners, covered with glistening white tiles and edged with coloured lights. It was enormous.

I opened my mouth to exclaim my astonishment and nothing came out. John chuckled into my ear.

I nudged the Dragon's frill.

Thank you, the Dragon said. *They all say that.*

A pair of small gold dragons emerged from the arched entranceway that glittered with coloured fairy lights. They bowed to us. I nodded back as we passed.

Number One and Number Two, John said into my ear. *He honours us.*

We swept through the archway and a pair of enormous pearly doors opened before us.

I asked the stone if it had ever been to a place like this before. It was silent. Eventually it spoke.

No. I am speechless.

I laughed quietly to myself.

Yes, you are quite right. I also think it is the first time.

We travelled through a corridor that was at least twenty metres high, with towering walls of what looked like ice, but appeared to be glass or crystal. Flowing crystalline chandeliers provided sparkling light above us. The white floor was polished to a high reflective sheen.

There was another set of huge doors at the end of the corridor. They opened by themselves and we went through.

On the other side was an elegant formal garden, glowing with colour. But the garden wasn't flowers; it was coral, and sparkling reef fish flitted between the tiny spires and archways.

I'm rather proud of this, the Dragon said. *Huge amount of upkeep, but the wives like it.*

I nudged his frill and he slowed as we passed through the garden. It was in a courtyard with towering walls on all sides made from a glistening semi-transparent material. They were at least five storeys high, and people and dragons watched us from the arched walkways on higher floors.

They're not here to see the North Wind or the East Wind, Emma, John said into my ear. *They're hoping to catch a glimpse of you.*

I dropped my head and tried to hide behind the Dragon's enormous frill.

Won't work, my Lady, the Dragon said, and abruptly changed direction, heading straight up. At the top floor he changed direction again and flew onto one of the walkways.

And here we are, John said. He landed lightly next to us and stood on the balcony. His long hair had come completely out and floated around his head, but he had no trouble standing. He smiled, his eyes sparkling, and gestured. *Follow me.*

I slid off the Dragon and gave him a friendly pat to thank him.

You are most welcome, the Dragon said. His voice gained an amused edge. *Enjoy.*

I turned and looked around. Above was the dark ocean. Below was the bright, glittering multicoloured reef garden. I leaned over the balcony, and John waited patiently for me. The balcony rail was transparent at the edges and milky in the centre; it was made of crystal. I looked out and saw a vibrantly pink, lilac and gold dragon on a balcony directly across from me on the other side of the courtyard. It raised one gold-taloned claw in greeting and I waved back.

Come on, Emma, John said, and I turned to him, wondering why he was so impatient. He led me off the balcony into a room and closed the pearly doors behind us.

There was a shining mirror in front of us, swirling like quicksilver.

Go through, John said. *You will be perfectly safe.*

I walked through without hesitation, trusting him completely.

I stopped dead. I was in air, not water, inside a large, white-walled bedchamber with an enormously high ceiling. The four-poster bed had white gauzy linen and appeared to be made of huge staghorn corals that had grown into the frame's shape.

I looked down: I was dry. John stopped and dried himself completely as well.

'What do you think?' he said.

'This place is truly marvellous,' I said. 'I'm so glad I was able to see it. Where are we going next? I want to see everything!'

'Are you sure?' John said. 'Because that's not the reason I brought you here.'

He moved closer to me and his smile broadened. Before I knew what was happening he swept me into his arms and I buried my face in his bare chest. He kissed the top of my head. I threw my arms around him and tried to squeeze the life from him.

'Hey,' he said softly, and I looked up. He smiled down at me. He held the back of my neck, lowered his face and kissed me. We were lost in each other for a very long time.

His hands moved to my waist and worked at the hem of my top, eventually pulling it free so that he could draw it over my head. He threw it to one side and buried his face in my throat. He bent, scooped me up and carried me, dropping me onto something soft and silken.

He leaned over me. 'We don't have much time,' he whispered. 'It's already two. It will take us an hour or so to return against the tide. We have to make the most of the short time we have.'

I gazed into his wonderful brown eyes without saying a word. I loaded my hands with chi and brushed them over his back. He dropped his head and grimaced.

I moved my hands over his back and down, running them just beneath the top of his pants, over the indentations at either side of the base of his spine.

'I love you,' I whispered, and his whole body went rigid.

The skin of his back was smooth and fine. I moved my loaded hands further up his back and brushed them over his shoulders, feeling the outline of the muscles beneath. He breathed heavily and his face jerked up so that he could look at me. Then he buried his face in my throat, running his lips along my neck and down to my collarbone, sending shivers of response through me.

'You are the only one I will ever love,' I whispered into his ear.

He pulled back to gaze into my eyes. He couldn't speak, his face was rigid with the effort of maintaining control. He kissed the edge of my chin and along the line of my throat.

I pulled him down next to me, added more chi to my hands and lightly floated them over his shoulders, feeling him flex his muscles in response. I held my hands on his shoulders and ran my mouth down the silken side of his throat. He tasted salty, like the sea. He quivered under my lips but still didn't lose it.

'I will wait for you forever.'

I worked my mouth over him until he arched his back and a deep, vibrating sound of pleasure escaped from somewhere inside him. He pulled me up so that my face was level with his, planted his mouth on mine, and pushed into me as I ran my hands along the chiselled muscles of his back.

He pulled away and studied me. He ran his hand

through my hair and down the side of my face, tracing my features.

I ran my fingertips over his cheek, feeling the gritty stubble over the silken skin. 'Let go. Let go for me.'

I slid my hand down his throat, lightly running my fingers over his shoulder and down the muscles of his chest. He inhaled sharply and his eyes went very dark, but he still had control.

Not for long.

I smiled gently at him, moved my hand lower, loaded it with even more chi and pushed it right into him.

He exhaled in a huge gasping breath and completely lost it. The dark shutters rolled up over his eyes and his face went rigid. He grabbed my shoulders, rolled me onto my belly and shoved me into the silky white sheets. One of his hands held my shoulder down while the other ripped my shorts away, pulling impatiently as the fabric shredded. He crushed me into the sheets so hard I had to turn my head to one side so that I could breathe.

Then he threw himself on top of me, grabbed me around the middle and tugged me into him. He pulled at his pants, then his arms went around me like a vice. His face was a fierce grimace next to mine, his breath rough in my ear.

'Yes!'

He flopped onto his back next to me.

'You bastard. You tried to hold it back,' I said.

'What did you just call me?' he said, rolling over to face me.

I moved my face right into his. 'A turtle egg.'

He rolled onto his back again and shook with silent laughter. I pulled myself on top and straddled him. He brushed his hands over my back and drifted them over my shoulders.

'I wanted to see how long I could hold out,' he said. 'I think I lasted about twice as long that time. But you were no help at all. You like pushing me over the edge, despite my best efforts to retain control.'

I leaned my arms on his chest and put my nose right next to his. 'Don't bother.'

He kissed me. I closed my eyes and drifted into him, and then suddenly I knew. I snapped open my eyes and jerked back. He didn't move; he watched me silently, his face expressionless.

Neither of us said anything.

I threw myself on top of him and held him tight. I kissed him frantically, and he returned it just as frantically, because we knew. We both knew. It was perfectly clear. The truth was obvious.

This was our last chance.

I jerked awake. I'd been half asleep in his strong arms, my own wrapped around him, our bare skin touching wherever it could. I had a sudden inspiration. I carefully looked up at him: he was dozing, his noble face serene. I gave him a tremendous push and completely launched him out of the bed, his long hair flying. He woke before he hit the floor, landed on one hand, somersaulted, and touched down lightly on his feet into a long defensive position.

I didn't give him a chance to do anything. I threw myself at him, both feet aimed straight at his chest.

His face didn't move. He caught my feet and turned me over. I somersaulted with the movement, landed back on the bed, and jumped right over the top of his head. He spun to face me.

I went for him with a series of roundhouse kicks, one after the other, as fast as I could. He easily blocked them all. On about the fifth one he was close to the wall, so he grabbed my foot again and attempted to flip me over.

I wrapped my other foot around his hand and used the energy centres to twist him, trying to take him off his feet. It didn't work; he moved with the force, rolled, flew back upright, and threw my foot away.

I used the energy centres again and this time, instead of moving away, I moved closer to him. I landed in front of him, spun, grabbed his arm, pushed, twisted and threw him onto his back.

'That,' he said, holding out one hand for me to help him up, 'was absolutely pathetic. I've seen first years do better.'

I reached down, took his hand and jerked him right into me.

He wrapped his arms around me and pulled me close. I put my hands on his back and pulled myself into him. He smiled down at me. 'I made you a promise a long time ago. Want to try?'

'No, of course not,' I said. 'Don't waste your energy. We should take the chance to do some hand-to-hand instead.'

He shrugged. 'Not a problem. Won't take too much energy down here.'

'You sure?' I said, eyeing him suspiciously.

He squeezed me briefly. 'Of course. Move back, give me room.'

I released him and moved away. He lowered his head, concentrated and took Celestial Form.

He was nearly four metres tall, his hair a wild tangle around his head. His face was square and dark and ugly, with a long thin black beard. He wasn't wearing armour; his traditional black robes flowed around him, held at the waist by a wide black belt.

He held his arms out. 'Try.' His voice sounded exactly as it always did.

'This is weird,' I said. 'I've never touched the Celestial Form.' I hesitated. 'It doesn't feel like you.'

He bent so that his face was level with mine. He looked me in the eye and his eyes crinkled up.

'Okay, it's you,' I said. I spun, grabbed his arm and threw him onto his back, the robes flying everywhere as he hit. I didn't give him time to rise; I quickly moved to sit on his chest. It was like sitting on a horse, he was so big.

'Freud would have a field day,' I said, then moved my face into his and kissed him. It wasn't as good with something so huge; he was far too big and the beard felt strange.

He put his enormous hands onto my back and then circled my waist. He gently pushed me so that I slid down his body, moving easily on the silk robes. He raised himself on his elbows to see my reaction, his expression full of amusement.

I'd wondered about that, and now I knew. The Celestial Form was complete and he was huge *everywhere*.

I grinned wickedly and climbed back up to his face. This was interesting.

'Can you shrink down to about three metres tall?' I whispered.

He became smaller beneath me. Now it was *very* interesting.

'Tell me if it's too much,' he whispered. 'I can change my size.'

'I wonder if Louise knows about the Tiger's Celestial Form,' I wondered out loud.

'They all do,' he said. 'But his Celestial Form requires more than one.'

'One what?'

He smiled gently. 'Wife.'

'What about you?' I said, running my hand through the wild tangle of silken hair around his head.

'I'm sure one of you is more than sufficient,' he said, brushing his hands up and down my back.

I leaned closer. 'How do I get you out of these robes?' I said, fingering the black silk at his neck.

'You don't,' he said, and the robes were gone. The skin of his Celestial Form was dark all over. Not completely black, like Leo; more a dark silken mahogany colour. It still felt smooth and fine, stretched over the toned muscles, same as his human form. The Celestial Form was as magnificent as the human form, but on a grander scale. *Everything* was on a grander scale.

I traced my finger over the muscles of his chest, enjoying the silken feeling, then sat back and admired him. He watched me with amusement.

'John Chen Wu,' I said, throwing my arms around his neck, 'you never cease to amaze me.'

He sat up and towered over me, then bent so that his mouth was next to my ear, his beard tickling my throat. His voice was very soft as he put his hands under my thighs and lifted me. 'Good.'

I cuddled into him and he pulled his arm tighter around my shoulder. I brushed my hand over his chest. He was easier to hold in human form.

'Promise me you'll come back for me,' I said.

'I promise.'

'I wish I knew how long it will take.'

'So do I.' His voice was a low rumble through his chest, and I could feel his heart beating, strong and slow. 'I will return for you.'

'I have a feeling,' I said.

'So do I.'

'What's the line? "I have a very bad feeling about this."'

He laughed softly, his chest moving beneath my head. 'It never ceases to astonish me how perfectly innocent expressions quickly become clichéd. With modern media the way it is, very soon all of language will become one huge cliché.'

'There's a lot of stuff waiting for us just around the corner.'

He shifted slightly to look down at me. I twisted my head to see his face. I could tell from his expression that I was right.

He squeezed my shoulders. 'We will make it through this. The greatest prizes require the greatest effort. And I will find you, and Raise you, and marry you, and take you to live on my Mountain. I promise.'

I lowered my head into the side of his chest. 'I want to see the Mountain.'

'I know,' he said with a sigh. 'It is very hard not being able to take you there, not being able to see it myself. The photographs that Gold brings do not capture the true essence of the Celestial Mountain.' He wriggled down to make himself more comfortable and pulled me tighter. 'It drains the household Shen far too much to take humans backwards and forwards. Jade nearly killed herself when the Celestials moved the students to the Western Palace; and, of course, being a dragon all she did was take herself away and hide without telling anybody.'

'Is that what happened to her,' I said. 'I wondered where she'd gone; she was away for a couple of weeks. It must be a very long way.'

'It is about as far as anywhere,' John said. 'It is further than any part of the Celestial. It is a very, very long way so that it is difficult for demons to get there.' He squeezed me. 'You are already too big inside for any but the largest Shen to take you. I doubt if even the Tiger or the Dragon could take you now.'

'You're joking,' I whispered.

'You are the finest human student it has ever been my privilege to teach.'

'You're just saying that because you want to get into my pants,' I said, twisting my fingers in his hair where it fell in a wild tangle over both of us. 'Unethical, you know, student–teacher relationships.'

'Happens all the time on the Mountain,' he said, amused. 'Both the students and the Masters have the wisdom and discipline to keep professional and personal completely separate, otherwise they would not be on the Mountain in the first place.'

'I noticed,' I said. 'But Leo would never touch any student.'

'Leo is the wisest of us all.' He pulled me in again and sighed. 'We have to go soon.'

'I'd like to return here some day.'

He rolled over to face me and ran his hand along my arm. 'You will. I promise you. And you will one day be presented to the King of the Dragons as my Empress, and you will see the finest undersea palace in existence.'

'Do you have one?' I said. 'You're Water.'

'I have a small holiday place under the North Pole, only about ten rooms,' he said. 'Cold and dark, the way I like it. I use it to get away sometimes, to have time alone. I don't need anything bigger. I spend most of my time on my Mountain and in the Northern Heavens. When I have a choice, that is.'

'Holy shit, you have a *Fortress of Solitude* at the North Pole,' I said, barely controlling the giggles.

'I don't understand,' he said, bemused.

I pulled myself into him. He put his arms around me and buried his face in my hair.

'You have one last chance if you wish,' he said into my hair. 'We have time, and you know that I have the ability.'

I didn't look up at him. I left my cheek against his chest. 'Can we just stay here like this?'

'It is what I would prefer as well.'

We held each other close.

He sat upright and levered his long legs over the edge of the bed. He tapped me on the shoulder. 'The Dragon's here to take us back.' He rose and pulled on his pyjama pants. I giggled. 'What?' he said.

'I don't have any pants,' I said, sitting cross-legged on the bed and lifting the remains of my shorts. 'After we're married I'll have my entire wardrobe made with Velcro fastenings, otherwise I'll spend my whole time buying new clothes.'

'Good idea,' he said, turning away and concentrating. 'Michelle . . .' He stopped.

'Michelle what?' I said gently.

He hesitated and looked down.

'It's okay, tell me.'

He looked back up at me and smiled. 'Michelle enjoyed having new clothes made. But she'd shoot me anyway.'

'I wish I could have met her.'

A light cotton robe appeared on the bed next to me. 'Wear that,' he said.

'No way am I riding the Dragon wearing that,' I said fiercely.

'Put it on anyway,' he said. 'They'll have something else for us.'

I rose and slipped on the robe. He approached to help me, pressing himself into me from behind while he wrapped the belt around my waist. He pushed his face into my neck, then shoved his hand inside the front of the robe and ran it over me, making me gasp. My skin burned in trails where his fingers touched me. He gently drew the top of the robe down over my shoulders and ran kisses over my skin, making me writhe with need.

Both of us breathed heavily as he pushed into me from behind. I felt him hard against my back. He ran his hands under the hem of the robe and drifted his fingertips up my thighs and further. My knees went weak and I sagged as he held me.

'To hell with it,' he said, yanking the robe up and pushing me forward to bend me over the bed. 'They can wait.'

I didn't have the breath to say anything. But I still hoped they didn't hear me.

CHAPTER NINETEEN

Once again Leo couldn't meditate on the boat back to Hong Kong from Macau. I sat next to him on the couch in the lounge and moved to take his hand, but he pulled it away.

'Tell me what happened,' I said.

He closed his eyes and pretended to meditate, his dark face rigid with concentration.

'They found out, didn't they.'

He didn't move.

'What did they do to you?'

He remained completely still.

'One of the Celestials could help you, you know. Meredith could clear it all up for you.'

'Not an issue,' he said, then threw himself up and stalked down the stairs into the cabin at the front of the boat.

I moved to sit near John, and he looked at me over the top of his book. 'Do you know what happened?' I said.

'No. He's never told anybody. Most of them think that somebody sabotaged the seatbelt in the helicopter rescue simulation.'

That was too horrible to be true. 'I know about that,' I said. 'They put you in a mock helicopter, strapped in, high above a big pool. Then they tip it upside down and drop it into the water. You have to release your own seatbelt and swim out after you're submerged, still unsure about which way is up. Sounds terrifying.'

'Imagine what it would be like if the seatbelt wouldn't unfasten,' John said, turning back to his book. 'And the safety crew were hanging back, enjoying the sight of watching you drown, only rescuing you when it was obvious you were in serious trouble.'

'No. They're much too professional to do something like that.'

'That's where the money is. Some of the Celestials agree with you, that the crews are more professional than that. There's also money on a Nitrox accident at very extreme depth.'

'They have a book running on it?'

'Since Leo arrived and it became obvious.'

'That is so wrong.'

He shrugged almost imperceptibly. 'Most of my staff are Chinese, Emma.'

'You don't have money on it, do you?'

'I'm running the book.'

'Oh my God, you *bastard*!' I hissed. 'Does Leo know?'

'Yep. He finds it highly amusing. I think he asked Gold to wipe the records in the States so that nobody will ever know.'

'Good.' I jumped up and went to talk to Simone and Michael at the back of the boat.

I stood against the long wall of the training room back at the Peak, unsure. We hadn't invited the Dragon along; we wanted to see what would happen first, just the two of us.

'Let's try it on a little one,' John said. He reached into the jar. 'Level five.' He glanced up at me, eyes

241

sparkling. 'It was a level three that nearly broke your nose that first time. Now you can handle a whole battalion of these with one hand.'

He threw the demon under the mirrors, and it formed: a normal-looking Chinese female. He released it and it went for me.

I generated black chi and threw it at the demon. The demon imploded completely, taking my chi with it — a visible suction into a shrinking black hole that quickly disappeared. The chi was gone.

John didn't move at all. Then he pulled another demon out of the jar. 'Do that again.'

He threw the demon onto the floor. It was a level ten, a small humanoid in True Form.

'Can you lose that much chi without draining yourself?' he said.

'Yep,' I said. 'Not a problem at all. Let it go.'

He released the demon, it went for me, and I threw black chi at it.

It melted like a wax sculpture, losing its form slowly, the black stuff oozing into a puddle on the ground. The puddle moved towards me and I realised with a jolt of horror that the demon was still alive.

'Black again,' John said.

I threw another bolt of black chi at it and it reformed and shook its head.

'Again,' John said. 'Stop if you become too drained.'

I threw black chi at the demon and it imploded, disappearing completely. But this time the chi returned to me.

'This is ridiculous!' I said. 'It's different every time.'

'Fascinating,' John said. 'Want to try something bigger? How's your energy level?'

'Let's try a level twenty,' I said. 'I'll hit it with ordinary chi to top myself up if I'm too drained.' I stopped dead as I understood. 'If I can use both types of chi alternately, I'll never drain myself or explode from absorbing too much. If I balance it out correctly, I'll be able to use energy for as long as I like.'

'Precisely,' John said, and reached into the jar. He pulled out a bead, threw it under the mirrors, and it formed. It was a small cockroach, about a third of a metre long.

'Oh God, you hate me, Xuan Wu,' I said, running my hands through my hair.

'Let's see what the black chi does to one of these,' he said. He released the insect and it waved its feelers at me.

'Don't you dare turn,' I said softly. 'I hate you things.'

It raced towards me and I hit it with a big ball of black chi. Nothing happened. Damn, now I had to take it out hand-to-hand; my weapon was too far away.

'Shit!' I shouted. 'I don't want bug goo all over my hands!' I hit it with a huge ball of gold chi instead and it exploded into feathery streamers of black stuff. Some of it hit my pants, but not enough to worry me.

'You okay?' John said.

'Fine. Let's try that again. Another level twenty.'

'Another bug?'

'Yeah, I think so, then we'll try a humanoid.'

'Okay.' John shuffled around inside the jar. 'Here we are.' He threw the bug demon onto the mat under the mirror and it formed. He released it and it went straight for me.

I hit it with black chi and the bug changed into a miniature Mother, only about a metre tall. It slithered towards me.

'Again,' John said.

I hit it with black chi again, and it exploded exactly as if it had been hit with gold chi, returning the energy to me.

'Different every time,' I said with exasperation. 'This is ridiculous.'

John shuffled in the jar and pulled out a humanoid. He tossed it in front of the mirrors and it formed. He released it and it went for me. I hit it with black chi and it changed into a young human Chinese female of about sixteen years old.

She fell to her knees. 'I plead! I swear allegiance! I am yours!'

'Get up,' John said.

The demon didn't move.

'Rise,' I said, and the demon shot to its feet. 'Go and take the Dark Lord's hand.'

John waited patiently with his hand out. The demon winced. It sidled towards him and took his hand. Nothing happened.

John's eyes widened. 'Emma, what have you done?'

I moved to John and the demon. The demon still held John's hand, its face rigid with awe.

'Has it definitely turned?' I said. 'It didn't change to True Form.'

'This is its True Form,' John said softly. 'Release my hand, dear.'

The demon dropped John's hand, burst into tears and fell to her knees. He stood over the demon, seemingly unable to decide what to do.

'What's the problem?' I said. 'Where will we put her?'

'I don't know,' John said. His face was as full of awe as the demon's was. 'I've never seen anybody do anything like that before.'

I was thoroughly confused. 'Like what? I just tamed her, that's all.'

'Emma, you changed her into a *human*. She's not a demon any more, she's a perfectly normal human female.'

The demon fell over her knees and sobbed more loudly.

'Holy shit,' I said softly, studying her. I was speechless. I dropped to crouch so I could face the demon ... the girl. 'Are you okay?'

She glanced up at me and wiped her eyes, still gasping. Then she threw herself into my arms and held me tight. 'Thank you. Thank you. Thank you so much.' She pulled away and tried to say something more, but the words wouldn't come.

I moved back to sit on the floor and John did too.

'Nobody's ever done that before?' I said.

'Nope,' John said, beginning to smile. He glanced at me, about to say something, then turned back to the girl. 'You have your freedom now, little one. What will you do with it?'

The girl looked helplessly at both of us. 'I don't know.' She shook her head. 'This is all so sudden. I have no idea. It will take me a while to become accustomed to having a mind and a will of my own.'

'You can stay with us until you've worked out what you want to do,' I said, my heart going out to the poor thing. 'We'll look after you.'

She threw herself into my arms again and clutched me. 'I think I would like to serve you, if you will let me.'

'You can't,' I said, holding her. 'You're free. You're not tamed. You're your own woman.'

'Would you like a job with us?' John said.

The girl fell back from me and smiled through the tears. 'A *job*? Earning money, like a human?' The smile broadened. 'It's true. It's all true. You *are* the most generous creature on the Plane.' She shook her head, her face still alight with the beautiful smile. 'Yes, I'd love a job, thank you, Dark Lord.'

John pulled himself to his feet and held his hand out to the girl, who took it, still smiling.

'I can't believe this is happening,' she said softly.

'You'll need to find yourself a name, pet,' I said.

'Set her up in the other student room,' John said. 'Then I think you'd better take her shopping — she was extremely lucky she was able to conjure the clothes the way she did. I'll put the jar away, I've seen enough. If that happens again, I'll have to take back the unit downstairs.'

'Come on, sweetheart,' I said, taking the girl's hand. 'I think you need some very speedy lessons on being human.' I turned back to John without letting go of her. 'Call Ah Yat, tell her to come into the room and help us. I think she'll understand.'

The girl clutched my arm as I took her out, obviously wobbly on her legs. Whether it was from the shock or the change in form it was hard to tell.

I was sitting cross-legged on the couch watching a DVD in my room when there was a tap on the door. 'Ma'am, it's me.'

'Come on in, Ah Yat. What do you want?'

Ah Yat opened the door and smiled at me.

'Is the human girl okay?' I said.

'She is fine, ma'am,' Ah Yat said. 'She's learning quickly. She has chosen the human name of Sonia, but she is trying to work out a family name. I had to explain to her that Donahoe wasn't appropriate.' She hesitated, obviously uncomfortable about whatever was coming next.

'You want me to teach her the facts of life?' I said.

'She knows about that already, ma'am,' Ah Yat said. She looked down, still uncomfortable.

'Okay, ask me, Ah Yat. What do you want to know?'

'She says that you did it to her.'

I sighed. 'Yes, I did.'

Ah Yat fell to her knees in front of me. 'Please do it for me, ma'am. Can you? I will stay with you, I swear,

I will not leave your service. But I would give anything,' she took a huge gasping breath, '*anything* to be human.'

'You're nearly there anyway, Ah Yat, the Dark Lord said so himself.'

'You could do it *now*, my Lady.'

I turned off the television with the remote and turned to face her, leaning over my knees. 'Get up, Ah Yat, I can't talk to you like that.'

She pulled herself up from the floor and stood twisting her hands together.

'She doesn't know the rest of what happened before I changed her,' I said.

Ah Yat was silent.

'We were testing out an unusual type of energy that apparently only I can generate. It destroyed about half the demons I used it on. Others, it changed. It turned a humanoid into black goo, but it was still alive.'

Ah Yat winced.

'It turned a bug into a tiny Mother. And then it changed Sonia into a human. About one in ten, I think.'

'The others were destroyed or changed?' Ah Yat whispered.

'Yes. Except for one, which was undamaged.'

'Can I see the energy?'

'It's black, Ah Yat.'

'Can I see, ma'am?'

I held my hand out and generated a ball of black chi about the size of a tennis ball.

Ah Yat inhaled sharply. 'I have seen that before.'

I reabsorbed the chi and shot to my feet. 'Where? Who?'

'It was during the Trouble Times, ma'am, just over a thousand years ago. The King had been destroyed by his Number One son. The son could produce that.' She pointed at my hands.

247

'But that would be the current King,' I said.

She bowed slightly. 'That is correct, ma'am.'

'Did his black chi produce similar results? Just random effectiveness?'

'No, ma'am, it just destroyed things. It destroyed everything. It was very scary.'

'And you want me to use it on you? I don't think so.'

'I have one chance in ten?'

'I think so. Maybe more, maybe less. I'm not trying it out on anything else, the results are too unpredictable.'

She fell to her knees and touched her head to the floor. 'Please, ma'am. *Ngoh kow nei*. I beg you.'

'If you continue to serve us as you have, how long before you attain perfection?'

'Not more than twenty years, ma'am.'

'You would give that up for a one in ten chance?'

'I could be human *now*, ma'am.'

I went to her and held out my hand. 'Up you get, Ah Yat.'

She took my hand and rose, then bowed slightly.

'Ah Yat,' I said, patting her shoulder, 'as far as all of us are concerned, you're already human. Would you like a salary? We could pay you. You could have a job, exactly like Sonia. The difference at the moment is purely academic. To us, you're human.'

'If you give me an order I am forced to obey, ma'am,' she said softly, head bowed. 'If I were human I would have free will.'

'Ah Yat, I want you to consider something. Say you were human and were still working for us. If the Dark Lord gave you an order, would you obey him?'

'Of course, ma'am,' she replied.

'Well then,' I said, patting her hand, 'there you go. No difference whatsoever. I won't do this to you, Ah Yat, the risks are too high. Stay and attain perfection, and be glad for Sonia. Will it be the same for you when you get there?'

'No, ma'am, it will be completely different for me, but I can't tell you how. It is one of those things that cannot be shared with mortals, even nobility such as yourself.'

I laughed. 'Nobility? I think I'm about the furthest you can get from nobility and still be human.'

'If you say so, ma'am,' Ah Yat said diplomatically.

I laughed again and patted her back. 'If you ever want an evening off to go and do human things, like shopping, let me know. In fact, I just had an idea. You show Sonia — take her shopping, show her how to buy and how to budget, how to dress.'

'Yes, ma'am,' she said, and turned to leave.

'Ah Yat,' I said, and she turned back. 'You don't have to do it if you don't want to. It's your choice. You're free to decide whether or not you want to do this.'

'No, I'm not, ma'am,' Ah Yat said, and went out.

John was in the television room, watching a tape of an appalling Cantonese period drama with martial arts so laboured that you could actually see the actors counting as they performed the moves. *Yat, yee. Yat, yee.*

'I don't know how you can watch that trash,' I said, leaning on the arm of the couch. 'I need to talk to you.'

He switched off the television and paused the video. 'What?' He moved to the end of the couch so that I could sit and turned to face me.

'Ah Yat asked me to change her into a human.'

'I'm not surprised,' he said, pulling his feet up to sit cross-legged.

'She asked to see the black chi, and when I showed it to her, she said she'd seen it before.'

He straightened, suddenly much more interested. 'Who? Where?'

'Apparently when the current King of the Demons took over, he used this black chi.'

He rubbed his hand on his chin and studied me appraisingly. 'I've never seen him use it. Interesting.'

'*Are you sure I'm not a demon?*' I said fiercely. 'Is there any doubt at all in your mind?'

He shifted, making himself more comfortable, flexing his bare feet. 'I am sure. No doubt whatsoever.'

'Then what am I?'

'Stay still,' he said, and leaned to tap the stone.

'Hm? Yes?'

'She's worried she's a demon again. Apparently the King has used black chi similar to what she produced.'

'Really? Interesting,' the stone said. 'Not surprising, though.'

'Why?' I said.

'Because, young Emma, you are becoming more yin all the time. The more time you spend with this yin creature, the more yin you become yourself. When you first arrived in his household, you were extremely yang. Now, his influence is affecting you, in more ways than one.'

'Is it because he is such a powerful creature, even though he's drained?' I said. 'He's inundating me with himself because he's so big and I'm so little?'

'You have it precisely, Emma,' the stone said. 'I think you knew that all along.'

'But he can't generate black chi.'

'Never tried,' John said, bemused. 'But if I wanted to, I probably could. Must try it when I return.'

'I'm losing my personality into yours,' I said.

Both the stone and John snorted with amusement. 'Not very likely,' John said.

'No way,' the stone said. 'You have an extremely powerful personality, and I don't think you're in much danger of "losing" it as you say. In fact, I think you have changed him just as much.'

'You are quite correct,' John said. 'Go back to sleep.'

'I certainly will,' the stone said. 'I was having a lovely dream. I dreamed I was an active volcano and I had erupted, driving hundreds of fleshies from their homes.' It sighed with bliss. 'You interrupted me right in the middle of it.'

'You are a small, square, green creep,' I said.

The stone was silent.

'Still worried?' John said.

'Oh no, nothing to worry about. There aren't any demons after us, you aren't on the edge of losing your life, Leo isn't dying, Simone is quite ready for both of you to go, and I'm absolutely nothing out of the ordinary,' I said. 'Everything is perfectly peachy.'

'Come and do a slow set with me,' he said, pulling himself up from the couch. 'Something nice and yin.'

I ran my hands through my hair. 'God, you hate me, Xuan Wu.'

'You know I don't,' he said softly as he opened the door.

A week later I got a call from our doctor, Regina Chow. 'Come on down to the infirmary, please, Emma. I have the results of your test.'

My stomach fell out.

'Sit, Emma,' Regina said when I arrived at her office. Regina was a delightful Chinese human in her mid-twenties who lived with one of the Mountain dragon staff. She closed the door behind me. 'Before we do anything else, the result was negative. No sign of the virus at all. You're clear.'

I sagged with relief. 'Thanks,' I said, and rose to leave.

'Wait, Emma,' she said gently.

I flopped back into my chair. I knew what she was going to say.

'Sometimes it takes a while for the virus to appear. Up to six months. You will need to come back for another test then.'

'I know,' I said.

She sighed. 'Also ...' She shuffled the papers on her desk. 'I'm sorry, Emma, but the test was really a waste of time. I asked Leo to provide a sample too, and of course he's clear as well.'

'I understand,' I said. 'Waste of time testing me again until Xuan Wu is gone.'

'I'm sorry,' she whispered, not looking up from the papers.

'Why? This isn't your fault.'

She smiled sadly at me. 'You have enough misery in your life without this adding to it.'

'I'm not miserable,' I said. 'Right now, if I had the choice, I would not be anywhere else doing anything else. Here and now, I'm happy. The future can take care of itself.'

'You sound like one of the Immortals,' Regina said.

'Yep, most of them are pretty stupid too.'

I sat in the back of my car with the door open, reading a book. The late May weather wasn't hot but summer was just around the corner and there was a humid edge to the air. I was waiting to pick Simone up from school.

Gold appeared in the front passenger seat.

'Yes?'

Gold's face was rigid as he studied me.

'What's the matter, Gold?'

'Lady Emma, may I hold your hand, please?' he said, his face still rigid.

I shrugged and held my hand out. He examined me carefully, then sighed, dropped my hand, and ran his hands over his face. 'Thank the Heavens.'

'It's me, Gold,' I said.

'When does school finish?' he said, turning to face the front of the car.

'In about twenty minutes.'

He concentrated, then nodded. Obviously he'd just talked to somebody.

'My Lady, I think it's important that we take the Princess and the young guard home immediately. There are ...' He hesitated. 'There are *people* there that wish to see you.'

'What do you mean?' I said, bewildered.

Trust him, Emma. Take them out of class and bring them home now. You are needed here immediately.

I felt a shock of concern. 'What the hell is going on? Is everybody okay?'

Gold smiled slightly. 'Everybody is fine. This is not a Celestial matter.' He shrugged. 'The police are at the Peak and wish to see you.'

'Gold, pass this on to Lord Xuan for me?' Gold nodded and I continued. 'Tell me what the hell is going on *right now* or you are in serious trouble.'

John's voice was amused. *They found you dead in a dumpster in Kowloon City. They want me to identify the body. They also think I killed you and they want to take me in for questioning. Come home, I think.*

I flung down the book, leaped out of the car and bolted up the stairs into the school.

The police were in the living room with John. They all turned to me as we walked in.

'Go into your room and do something, Simone,' I said softly.

'Okay, Emma,' Simone said, just as softly.

Michael followed her down the hallway, his back rigid. He didn't want to attract any police attention; they might have a file on him because of his brief connection with the gangs.

253

The police rose. There were two of them: a European in his mid-fifties, obviously quite senior from the amount of metal on his uniform; and a younger Chinese male with the red shoulder flash indicating that his English was good.

I nodded to both of them and they sat. I shared a glance with John and he shrugged without saying anything. I couldn't sit down next to John — we'd be too close — so I remained standing. This body language wasn't good but I had no choice. John was unaware of the problem; he was probably still getting over the shock of the police arriving at his front door to tell him that I was dead.

'I'm Inspector Parry, Miss Donahoe,' the older police officer said. He gestured to the younger man. 'Sergeant Cheung.'

I nodded to both of them, then had an inspiration. I wandered over to John's couch and leaned casually on the side, folding my arms over my chest. Much more acceptable body language. The stupid damn Turtle still didn't get the message. Obviously shell-shocked. I smiled slightly.

'I got a message to come home,' I said. 'Is there a problem? My visa is fine.'

'Nothing like that,' the inspector said. 'We found the body of a young European woman in a dumpster in Kowloon City. Sorry to be blunt about it, but the corpse was quite badly mutilated, and when we compared the face to the ID card records it seemed to match you.' He turned to John. 'I don't think you'll need to come with us now, sir.'

'You have my details; please feel free to call me any time,' John said, very calm. 'I'd be happy to help you any way I can.'

'Both of you were hospitalised recently,' the Chinese sergeant said. He held a thick manila folder with papers

254

inside. Damn; there was a file on us. The policeman looked at John. 'You were kidnapped January last year.' He flipped through the papers and glanced at me. 'You were attacked last October, and hospitalised with head injuries.'

John and I were both speechless. *Think quickly, Emma.*

'I'm sure the police are doing their best to keep the streets of Hong Kong safe,' I said mildly, turning the problem back to them. 'Fortunately, neither of us was badly injured when we were attacked. John ...' I glanced quickly at him. 'Mr Chen was kidnapped, but we paid the ransom and got him back. And the guy who attacked me last October was after my handbag. When I wouldn't give it to him he laid into me.'

The sergeant flipped through the file. 'At the time you said you couldn't remember anything.'

I tried to stay calm. 'No, that's not correct. I said that I was attacked by a young man, thirty-ish, well-dressed, good-looking. I even sat with the identikit policeman and we did a sketch of the guy.'

And they'd never picked Simon Wong up, even though they had to know he was the head of all the underworld activity in the Territory. I wondered if it was incompetence, or they didn't have enough on him, or it was something more sinister.

'Maybe you should be looking for those who attacked us, instead of interrogating us,' John said, matching my mild tone.

'What happened to the woman in Kowloon City?' I said, deliberately changing the subject.

'There wasn't enough left of her to work out exactly what happened to her,' the inspector said. 'But she appeared to have been poisoned.'

Demon. The essence comes up as poison. Wonder why it didn't disintegrate? May have been a hybrid.

I tried to control my face. 'Anything else?'

The inspector rose. The sergeant hesitated, unhappy, then rose too.

'Nothing else. Sorry to take up your time. But the body in Kowloon City did look a lot like you. You don't have any relatives here, by any chance?' the inspector said.

'No,' I said. 'Must just be a coincidence. That poor woman. I wonder what happened to her.'

The inspector smiled, suddenly paternal. 'Don't worry, we'll track them down.' He sobered. 'Next time somebody tries to grab your handbag, just give it to them, okay?'

I shrugged and rose to show them out. 'Sure. I don't know what I was thinking, refusing to give it to him. Just overconfident, I guess.'

'Some of these young thugs are trained in martial arts,' the inspector said. 'Kung fu, you know? Be careful. Some of them look small and harmless, but can kill you with their bare hands.'

'Really?' I said, feigning astonishment. 'I thought that was all movie stuff.'

The inspector grinned. 'Don't worry, we keep a close eye on their activities. If they're learning martial arts, then we know about it. We know the location of every school in the Territory and watch them closely.'

'That's reassuring,' I said, carefully controlling my expression. 'I'm glad you're on top of it.'

'Sorry to take up your time,' the inspector said to John, who nodded.

I guided them out, closed the door behind them, and sagged.

I was so worried about you, love. I'm too weak to sense anything. I had no idea.

'If Wong had a copy of me then why did he kill it?' I said as I fell onto one of the sofas.

256

'Maybe it died,' John said. 'But I don't like the concept of him copying you at all. I've never seen that done before. Shapeshifters, yes. But not copies.'

'We should get together and work out a set of identifying codewords,' I said. 'We need to do it right away.'

John's eyes unfocused, and then he rose to guide me into the dining room.

'Oh, and next time, try to remember. I can't sit next to you on the couch,' I said wearily, 'it's too close. That looked really bad, me standing over them like that. Next time move so that I can sit.'

'I'll send someone to buy a matching armchair for the living room,' John said. 'You are quite correct, I was totally unaware.'

'Were you that upset?' I said softly as he opened the door to the dining room.

He didn't look at me. 'Yes.'

'You weren't sure everything would be okay? I thought you would know.'

'I don't know everything,' he said, sitting in one of the dining chairs and resting his elbows on the table and his head in his hands. 'Nobody does. The future isn't fixed, it's moving all the time.'

'We'll get there,' I whispered as Simone and Michael entered. The grim expressions on both their faces made them look much older.

John didn't say anything.

Later I had the chilling realisation: it had probably been a *toy*.

CHAPTER TWENTY

On Saturday evening I was in my room when the sound of the television blasted out. It was guitar music, a sweet riff that meandered through the scales, but Simone had it awfully loud. I hesitated before I went in to ask her to turn it down; I was enjoying it, but John would want the volume lowered if he was meditating.

I opened the door to the television room and found Simone directly on the other side, about to emerge.

'You need to turn that down, Simone,' I said. 'If you're going out, don't forget to turn the television off.'

'It's not on,' Simone said. 'That's Daddy.'

I turned and listened. 'That's Daddy?'

She nodded. 'I've never heard him play that before. I didn't know it was his.'

We went to the music room together, and hesitated outside.

'Let's leave him,' I said.

Come on in.

We shrugged and entered. The music stopped.

'Don't stop, Daddy,' Simone said. 'I like it.'

John returned the black electric guitar to its stand, then switched off the amp in the corner. 'You do? I'm awfully rusty.'

'That was rusty?' I said. 'That was wonderful.'

'You both like it?' he said. 'Michelle ...' He stopped.

'Mummy didn't like it?' Simone said.

John didn't say anything, he just shook his head.

'Well,' I said, '*we* like it, so you're going to play it for us *right now*.'

'Yeah,' Simone said, climbing on the piano stool. 'Play for us.'

I leaned against the stand holding the *guzheng*, next to the wall. It was a horizontal stringed instrument, similar to a Western zither. 'Do you play this too?' I said, 'I really like *guzheng*.' I plucked one of the strings absently.

'*No, Emma*!' Simone shouted, but it was too late.

The force of the blast threw me across the room and I slammed side-on into the piano. The keys hit me in the ribs and I fell over.

John and Simone both rushed to me.

'Careful you don't touch her, Daddy,' Simone said as she took my hand. 'Now it's okay.'

'Are you badly injured?' John said with concern, taking my other hand.

I checked myself internally. 'Cracked ribs and a bruised liver. Give me a couple of minutes to heal it and I'll be as good as new.'

Neither of them said anything; they just held my hands and watched me as I started to move the energy.

'What hit me?' I said as I moved the energy through my ribs.

'That is the Celestial *guzheng*,' John said. 'The one that carries the Mark —'

'— of Six Fingers? That's Six Fingers' *guzheng*?' I said, my voice hoarse.

'I thought you knew,' he said.

'That thing's legendary.'

'So am I,' John said with amusement. 'I think you've ruined the piano. The whole front of it is smashed in.'

'Yay! No piano practice!' Simone cried with glee.

'Simone, are you okay?' I said.

'I'm fine,' Simone said. 'Somehow it went right through me and didn't touch me.'

Leo tapped on the door and entered. He stopped when he saw us. 'What the hell happened here?'

Simone giggled. 'Silly Emma touched the *guzheng*.'

'You were supposed to tell me what to avoid,' I said fiercely from the floor. 'When I first came to work here, you showed me around, but you didn't mention that thing at all.'

'Oh, by the way, Miss Donahoe,' Leo said, moving further into the room to tower over me, 'the Chinese musical instrument in the music room used to belong to a demon. It's enchanted, and if you play it, it will destroy just about everything around it, so don't touch it.'

'Oh, so now you tell me.'

'Shut up and heal yourself,' John said. 'It'll take all day if you keep talking like this.'

'Yeah, Emma, you can talk underwater,' Simone said cheekily.

John and I shared a look.

'Leo, take Simone out,' John said, releasing my hand. 'I'll stay here and supervise Emma.'

Neither of them said a word as they left the room.

'Concentrate, Emma, you can do this,' John said. 'Do you want me to put on some music?'

'Some of *your* music?' I said with derision. 'That would make it take ten times longer.'

'Suit yourself.'

'I checked some of that German stuff you play. I found translations to the lyrics. Some of it's really dark, John.'

260

'I only play clean disks,' John said. 'Hard as they are to find. And since those ones are in German it doesn't really matter.'

'Some of the music you like is very dark.'

'Dark is my first name.' He pulled himself up, went out, and quickly returned with a cushion from the couch in the television room. He fell to one knee and passed it to me. 'Put this under your head.'

I pushed the pillow under my head and made myself comfortable on the floor. I moved the energy from my ribs to my liver. A lot of the soft tissue had been crushed and it would take some time to bring it back. I worked carefully; soft tissue was much more fiddly to heal than simple cuts or breaks.

'Good,' John said. 'You're doing very well.'

'Have you ever killed a human, John?'

He looked me in the eyes and didn't say anything.

'How many?'

He remained silent.

'When was the last time?'

He flopped onto the floor to sit cross-legged next to me. 'Nanjing. A long time ago.'

'Tell me,' I said softly as I moved the energy through my liver.

'I'm very old, Emma. I've been around for a long time. I am the Arts of War. I am yin incarnate: cold, darkness, death. And times change.'

'Tell me. Nanjing.'

'They were mad.' He looked away. 'Berserk. Crazed. They killed everything in their path. Some of them did it in cold blood as well.' He turned back to me. 'Humans are astonishing sometimes.'

I didn't say anything.

'They were killing children,' he said softly. 'The children of my people; *my* children.'

'How many?'

'Them or us?'

'Them.'

He dropped his head. 'I have no idea.' He raised his head and gazed at me. 'A lot.'

'You protected your children.'

He dropped his head and was silent again.

I concentrated on the energy in my liver. Some of the damage was very deep. I would be sore for a while.

'They were your children as well,' I said. 'They are all subjects of the Eastern Centre.'

'I know,' he said softly, almost a moan of pain. 'And they are all human, regardless of the Centre. They are the ones who seem to ignore that fact the most.'

'Have you ever killed anyone in cold blood?'

He wiped his hand over his face. 'Everything I kill, I kill in cold blood, Emma. I am cold-blooded.'

'Have you ever killed anyone without honour?'

'Nearly everybody I killed was without honour.'

'No,' I said, 'I meant, have you killed anybody in a dishonourable way? Have you ever stabbed anybody in the back?'

He pulled his knees into his chest with his ankles crossed and wrapped his arms around them. 'Of course not. But I can't really see how that makes a difference. Dead is dead.'

'You know I love you anyway, and I always will,' I said. 'I know you. I know you have only killed when there was no other alternative. And I know that times have changed. What was acceptable even a hundred years ago is completely unthinkable now.'

He dropped his arms from his knees and moved away. 'You are much wiser than your years, little Emma Donahoe.'

I sighed and finished healing my liver. I rounded up the energy and put it back. I sat up and the room spun around me. 'I need to sleep now.'

Leo opened the door and entered. He didn't say anything, he just came to me and put one massive hand under my arm to help me up. He lifted me as if I didn't weigh anything.

I leaned on him as he led me back to my room. He scooped me up and put me on the bed, pulled off my slippers, and tucked me in like a parent. He kissed me on the cheek and brushed his hand over my forehead.

'He hasn't played that guitar since Michelle died. He'd only play it when she wasn't around, before.'

'He's very good,' I said.

'One of the best. You brought it back for him.'

'I don't deserve him,' I said softly.

'I know,' he said, his voice a low rumble. 'You don't deserve any of us.'

'I know,' I whispered as I drifted away.

The next day was Sunday and both John and Leo forced me to rest so I could heal. Simone demanded sushi for lunch, and John and I trailed along. She loved raw fish so much it was like she was a sea creature herself. We could find something vegetarian later.

It was only a half hour wait before we were given three stools at the bar in front of the conveyor belt that held the small plates of covered sushi.

'Can you come to the end of term concert, Daddy?' Simone said as she munched on her third plate of raw tuna.

'When is it, sweetheart?'

Simone quickly swallowed. 'I don't know. Emma knows.'

'I'll talk to your daddy about it,' I said. 'We'll look at his diary.'

'Then you don't need to talk to him,' Simone said cheekily. 'He doesn't do his own diary. You and Two Five One do it.'

'That's right,' John said. 'I can't do anything without my Emma. Are you in the concert?'

Simone nodded, her eyes wide.

'Then I'll come.'

Simone squealed and hugged him, dropping her chopsticks. 'Whoops.'

I gave her a new set of chopsticks from the box on the bench. 'There's hardly any vegetarian sushi going past,' I said, watching the plates meander on the conveyer belt in front of us. 'It's all raw salmon and seaweed, and I've already had seaweed.'

The conveyer belt had a mirror behind it, reflecting the dishes. I saw something in the glass and froze. I spun on my stool to look out through the floor-to-ceiling windows behind us. The busy street was packed with people, but I was right.

'April Ho just went past, John,' I said urgently. 'By herself.'

John concentrated and Gold appeared, crouched under the bench.

'Mind Simone,' John said.

Gold nodded and pulled himself out to sit on a stool. Nobody noticed. John and I hurried out of the sushi bar and followed April along the busy Causeway Bay street.

'April!' I called, and she hesitated, then continued.

'April! April Ho!'

April stopped and turned. She looked around, saw me, but didn't appear to recognise me. She turned to continue walking.

'April Li!' I called again, using her maiden name and running to her. She stopped and turned. I grinned as I approached her. 'It's so good to see you! I was worried about you.'

Her face was stiff. 'Do I know you?'

'It's me, Emma,' I said with a huge grin. 'I haven't changed that much, have I? Look.' I gestured towards

John behind me. 'You can finally meet him. John Chen Wu.'

'Pleased to meet you, April,' John said politely. 'I hear you had a baby not long ago. Congratulations.'

April's face went even more rigid. 'I think you are talking to the wrong person.'

I studied her closely. 'April, it's me, Emma.'

I think she's had her memory wiped.

I inhaled sharply. 'April, you went to China and had your baby.'

'I have no idea what you are talking about.' She spun and walked quickly away.

I raced to follow and walked alongside her. 'April, it's me, Emma. Don't you remember me? We looked at your wedding photos.'

'I am not married,' April said grimly.

'You were *pregnant*, April!' I said desperately. 'You were living in Discovery Bay. You went to China and had the baby, by caesarean. The ultrasound scans showed it was a boy.'

'I do not think this is funny,' April said, walking faster.

'What about Andy?' I said.

April stopped. 'How do you know about Andy?'

'He's your *husband*,' I said.

'Not yet,' April said through the frown. 'I am marrying him in Australia later this year, and then we are going to Australia to live there together.'

Memory's definitely been wiped. You're wasting your time, Emma. She doesn't know you at all. I wonder what happened to the baby. The grandparents had to know about it ...

'Oh, dear God,' I said softly. 'You're getting married? What did your family say?'

April pushed her face right into mine, her features screwed up in a fierce grimace. 'My *family* were killed in a car accident in Australia earlier this year.' She put her hand to her forehead and saddened. 'I don't know why I'm telling you this, I don't even know you.'

'We were friends at the kindergarten.'

'What kindergarten?'

'Kitty Kwok's kindergarten,' I said. 'Saint LaSalle Kindergarten, in Kowloon Tong.'

April's face lit up. 'Aunty Kitty looks after me.' She took my hand and shook it. 'If you know Aunty Kitty then you are a friend. She has been wonderful, caring for me after my family were all killed.' She saddened again. 'I shouldn't be out like this; she says I'm not ready to be shopping by myself. But I wanted to go out for a while. I haven't been out in a long time.'

'Come with me, April. I'll look after you,' I said, squeezing her hand.

April's mobile phone rang and she pulled it out of her bag. It still had the glittering aerial that flashed with coloured lights when it rang, but she had changed the pink furry Hello Kitty case for a blue Doraemon one.

'*Wei?*' she squawked into the phone. She smiled, pulled the phone away from her ear and pointed at it. 'Aunty Kitty,' she whispered. She put the phone back to her ear. 'Yes, Aunty Kitty. I'm on Canal Street in Causeway Bay, I just went for a walk around.' Her shoulders sagged as Kitty's shouts were audible at the other end of the line. 'Sorry,' she mumbled. 'I'll be right back.'

She closed the phone and brightened. 'Do you want to come with me and see Kitty? Our apartment is close by.'

'Where is it?' I said.

'It's ...' April hesitated, then turned, pointing. She stopped and her face went blank. 'I don't remember.'

They're coming to collect her. Very big demons. Let's get out of here.

266

'What's your phone number?' I said.

April's face was completely blank. 'I don't know. What's yours?'

Don't give it to her. They'll know it's you and probably try to use it to get to you. She'll be safer if they aren't aware that you've talked to her. John stiffened. *We have to get out of here right now.*

'Bye, April,' he said, and gestured for me to follow him.

'Bye,' April said, her face still blank.

I glanced back as we raced away. She stood on the pavement with people flowing around her. She seemed completely lost. Some burly men appeared behind her and spoke to her. She turned, one of them took her elbow, and they led her away. She glanced back, looking for me. She didn't see me.

Back at the sushi bar I threw myself onto my stool and put my head in my hands. 'I will get that bitch one day,' I whispered, so softly that Simone couldn't hear me. 'April trusted Kitty. Look where it got her.'

They are taking a huge risk by not killing her immediately, John said. *Why didn't they kill her the minute they had the baby? They had no problem with killing her entire family. Why have they kept her and wiped her memory?*

'Even worse, what have they done with the baby?' I whispered.

'Hurry up and finish your sushi, Simone,' John said. 'We're going home and having another energy session.'

'Oh, come *on*, Daddy,' Simone whined. 'We spent the whole morning on sword. I want to rest.'

John dropped his head. 'Okay, sweetheart. Tell me if I tire you out too much.'

'Lately it seems to be all we do,' Simone grumbled. 'Just wushu. Nothing fun.'

'It's not fun any more, sweetheart?' I said, my heart breaking. 'It's never been not fun before. You've always enjoyed it a lot.'

'Too much,' Simone said, still grumbling. 'I want to spend a whole day having *fun* instead.'

'Right,' John said, putting his hands on either side of the stack of plates in front of him. 'Tomorrow, we will have fun. No wushu at all. What would you like to do?'

'Tomorrow's a school day, John,' I said softly.

'We're skipping school for a day and having some fun, Emma,' John said. 'Simone can go anywhere she likes.'

Simone squeaked with delight. 'Anywhere?'

'Anywhere.'

Simone jiggled. 'I don't know where I want to go. What I want to do. Can I think about it?'

'You sure can,' John said. 'You can tell me later. Okay. Are we finished?'

Simone and I both nodded.

'Both of you ate more than me,' John said, waving his hand at the stacks of plates on the counter in front of us.

'Simone ate the most,' I said. 'So she has to pay.'

John levered himself off the stool and took Simone's hand to help her down. 'That's right. I'm not paying for you to eat all this food when I can't have anything.'

Simone glanced at me, her face cheeky. 'Next time we come without Daddy.'

I was about to open my mouth to say something cheeky back when I saw John's face. It was completely rigid.

Next time we *would* be coming without Daddy, and Daddy knew it.

When we arrived home, Simone went straight into the television room and sat in front of the TV, zoning out. We left her and went into John's office together.

'Andy didn't want to stay married to April. He wanted her to have an abortion,' I said.

'He asked her for a divorce?'

I suddenly remembered. 'No, he didn't. He wanted her to stay married to him, just out of the way. But he did want her to have an abortion.'

'Why wouldn't they want the baby? The baby was probably the whole point of the exercise.'

I ran my hands through my hair. 'It was a *boy*, John. The ultrasounds showed it was a boy. April told me so herself.'

He was obviously confused. 'But if you're traditional, a boy is better. Why would he want her to abort a boy?'

'Because they wanted a girl.'

He suddenly understood. 'Simone.'

'Or me.'

'The copy of you in the dumpster.'

'But I'm thirty years old, John. They couldn't make a baby into a copy of me. It's just not possible.'

'You know that demons are hatched fully grown, Emma.'

'But this one is at least half human! How could it be hatched?'

He rubbed his hands over his face and tied back his hair. 'I don't know. I have never encountered anything like this before. I have no idea how they are making these copies. I suspect that April's baby boy was used in the experimentation and they let her keep the baby when they realised it could be useful. But that is just an educated guess.'

'We have to go in and get her out,' I said fiercely. 'She's my *friend*.'

'We have no idea where she is.'

'She's in Causeway Bay. Somewhere. With a lot of big demons.'

'You will go in and face that many powerful demons?'

'Yes,' I said firmly. 'To help my friend, I will.'

'Simone needs you, Emma,' John said. 'Simone needs both of us. They have not harmed April. She does not appear to be in any danger; in fact, she said that Kitty is caring for her.'

I couldn't believe it. 'You don't think we should go in?'

'I would love to go in and clean out that nest. But right now we are unable. We must protect Simone.' His voice softened. 'We have no choice, Emma. Our first duty is to Simone. She is the one who is in real, immediate danger here.'

'Send in some Disciples.'

'No.'

I glared at him.

'I will not send my Dark Disciples against a powerful demon on its own turf. That would be a useless waste of life.'

'Send in some Celestials.'

'The Celestials are protecting the human Disciples, Emma.' He sighed and leaned his elbows on the table. 'Face it. Right now, there's nothing we can do.'

I crossed my arms on the table and dropped my head onto them. He was right.

CHAPTER TWENTY-ONE

The next day, while John and Simone were at the theme park in China, I saw Louise for lunch. We met at the atrium that connected Sha Tin station with the shopping mall. Having the baby had made her softer and rounder. She held the baby in a sling strapped in front of her, and was accompanied by a demon, who appeared as a middle-aged Filipina domestic helper, carrying an enormous baby accessories bag. A hefty young bodyguard — one of the Tiger's sons — stood behind her watching the crowd carefully.

Louise raced to me and hugged me around the baby, who squirmed at the pressure. Then she stepped back to see me. She studied me carefully, looking me right in the eyes, then smiled broadly.

I cooed at the baby and took her hand. She grasped my finger, her little rosebud mouth nearly forming a sweet smile, and my heart melted.

'What's her name?' I said.

'Four —' Louise said, then stopped. 'Oh, her *name*. Kimberley. Kimmy.'

'She's gorgeous,' I said, brushing my hand over the baby's downy white hair.

Louise grinned with pride, her bright blue eyes sparkling under her spiky blonde hair. 'Come on, let's get some lunch. Let's go to the Japanese place the Tiger owns. We won't have to wait, and we can have a private room.'

She turned and we headed past the fountain, the bodyguard hovering and alert, the demon servant trailing after us lugging the huge bag.

'Lady Emma,' the bodyguard said, nodding.

'Hi,' I said. 'What's your name?'

'Two Eight Five.'

'Matt,' Louise said, and the bodyguard nodded again.

'You haven't changed a bit, Louise,' I said as Matt cleared our way through the Monday lunchtime crowd in the centre of the mall.

'Yeah, right,' Louise said with a grin. 'Put a lot of weight on, but the Tiger's dietician and personal trainer are working with me. I'll be back in shape in no time.' She looked me up and down. 'You need to see them too, Emma.'

I sighed. 'Yeah, I know. Need to do more physical stuff. I do too much energy work.'

Louise laughed softly. 'I heard about that. You have to show me.'

'Not in public, but you can come over to the Academy and see,' I said.

'But you look amazingly healthy,' Louise said, glancing sideways at me. 'You actually look younger than you did last year.'

That completely floored me. 'What?'

'You only look about twenty-five.'

I was bewildered. 'I'll be thirty-one in October, in four months,' I said. 'I can't look that young, don't be ridiculous.'

'You do.'

We arrived at the Japanese restaurant. There were about twenty people waiting outside, and five more at the reception desk collecting numbers to wait. When we reached the desk, the receptionist scowled at the baby. Louise wasn't fazed. She reached around the baby into her shirt, pulled out a platinum tiger that she wore on a chain around her neck, and dangled it in front of the receptionist.

The receptionist's face immediately went blank, then she smiled warmly and gestured for us to follow her, bobbing her head.

'Oh my God; that bastard,' I said softly.

'What?' Louise said as we were led into the private room.

'He tried to trick me into taking one of them.'

'One of what?'

'One of those little platinum tigers,' I said.

Louise grinned, then burst out laughing. She pulled her shoes off and went into the room. The demon servant followed her and sat quietly in the corner on the tatami mats.

'I'll wait outside, ma'am,' the bodyguard said. 'I'll be right outside the door.'

'Okay, Matt,' Louise said. She undid the straps holding the baby and gently lowered her as we sat. 'You want to hold her?'

I nodded and carefully took the baby. She squeaked and waved her little hands. I held her close and tried to control my reaction.

'What?' Louise said. 'What's the matter?'

I couldn't say anything. I just held the baby close and watched her.

'What's the problem, Emma?' Louise said.

'I'll never have one of my own,' I said, my voice thick. 'Never.'

'Why not?' Louise said softly. 'He's promised to come back for you, hasn't he?'

I carefully passed the baby back. 'It will take him years to come back, Louise. I'll probably be too old.'

Louise leaned forward over the table, holding the baby in front of her. 'Human Immortals can have children, Emma. The Jade Emperor has dozens.'

I silently shook my head. Then I snapped myself out of it and grabbed a menu. 'I hope there's something vegetarian for me.'

'See?' Louise said. 'Vegetarian, looks young, not worried by anything. Immortal.'

'Oh, cut it out.'

The baby started to squall and Louise handed her to the maid. 'Beanie, I think she needs changing.'

'Ma'am,' the maid said, and took the baby into the corner of the tatami mats. 'I'll feed her as well, ma'am, I think she's due.'

'*Beanie?*' I said.

'Ma'am?' the maid said, turning back to me.

'Go and change her, Beanie,' Louise said, and the maid turned away again. 'It's great I can put her onto the bottle now — I have a lot more freedom. The Tiger likes all the wives to feed the babies themselves for at least the first four months. That reminds me.' She pulled out a notebook and flipped it open.

'What the hell are you doing?' I said. 'We haven't done that in ages.'

'I have a bet with wife number One One Six and wife number One Two Zero,' Louise said. 'I have some questions for you, and you have to answer them truthfully for me.'

The waitress turned up and Louise dropped the notebook and grabbed the menu. 'But let's eat first, I'm starving.'

'Why is the demon called Beanie?' I said after we'd ordered.

'What demon?' Louise said.

I gestured towards the maid who was busy preparing a bottle. 'Demon.'

Louise glanced sharply at her. 'Are you a demon, Beanie?'

The maid bobbed her head. 'Yes, ma'am, tamed by Lord Bai Hu's Number One son himself.'

Louise turned back to me, grinning. 'I didn't know that; I thought she was a domestic helper. How about that? You could see she's a demon?'

'Of course I could,' I said. 'Why is her name Beanie?'

'No idea,' Louise said. 'Beanie?'

'I don't know, ma'am,' Beanie said. 'When I was tamed, they opened a large book, crossed out a dark word and said that was my name.'

I collapsed forward over my knees laughing.

'What?' Louise said, bewildered.

'Dictionary,' I said. 'They go through the words and use them as demon names.'

Louise's face lit up with delight and she laughed as well.

A waitress passing our room closed the door to keep the noise level down. Matt opened it again slightly so that he could keep an eye on us.

'How old are you, Beanie?' I said.

'About twenty years, ma'am,' the demon said.

'What?' Louise said. 'Only twenty years old? She looks mid-forties.'

'They hatch as adults and don't age,' I said.

'That's incredible.' Louise studied Beanie then turned back to me. 'How come you know all this stuff? No, wait.' She lifted the notebook and raised her hand. 'I need a pen, Beanie.'

'I'm sorry, ma'am, I don't have one,' the maid said.

I scrabbled through the mess in my bag and passed Louise a pen.

'Okay,' Louise said, flipping the notebook open again. 'You have to answer these questions truthfully, okay?'

I shrugged. 'Only if they're not too personal.'

Louise grinned broadly. 'What's he like in bed?'

I reached over the table and pushed her. Her grin didn't shift.

'Okay.' She looked down at the notebook then back at me. 'Can you pick demons from a distance?'

'Yes,' I said.

'How far?'

'About twenty metres.'

She made a tick in the notebook. 'Next. How much chi can you generate?'

'A ball of about two metres across, at the moment, but I'm working on it,' I said.

'Whoa.' She made another tick and glanced up at me. 'Can you take out level forty demons with your bare hands?'

'Yes,' I said, pouring some green tea.

'Wow,' Louise said; another tick. 'Can you take down Leo Alexander hand-to-hand?'

'Yep,' I said, sipping the tea. 'I can take down both Leo and Michael at hand-to-hand.'

'Whoa, *really*?' Her eyes were wide. 'That's Michael, the Tiger's son? The good one? Really? You can take him down as well?'

'The *good* one?' I said, grinning. 'I can take them down *together*.' This was beginning to be fun.

'Crikey, Emma,' Louise said, and I giggled. 'Can you generate black chi?'

'How the hell do you know about that?' I demanded loudly.

'Oh, word gets around,' she said. 'Can I see?'

I held my hand out, generated a small ball of black chi, and reabsorbed it. Louise's eyes were huge.

'Your hand went black. Do that again.'

I did it again for her and she put down her tea and scribbled furiously in the notebook. 'I'm going double or nothing on that one,' she said. 'I should have brought a video camera.' She glanced up at me. 'Can you tame demons?'

'Yep,' I said, and she ticked the book.

'Oh, wait,' I said. 'I can't complete the process; Xuan Wu needs to do it for me.'

'Not important,' she said. 'Can you use your Inner Eye?'

'Yep.'

'What colour bra am I wearing?' she said.

'You're not wearing one,' I shot back, and we both laughed.

'Can you do telepathy?'

'No.'

'Damn,' she said, and made a cross in the notebook. She picked up her teacup and sighed. 'Can you fly, Emma?'

'No.'

'Damn,' she said, shaking her head. 'There was a lot riding on that one too. They said you can run and then lift yourself and float, and I believed them.'

'Oh, I can do *that*,' I said. 'But I can't fly like superman, that's what I meant.'

'*Yes*,' Louise hissed, scribbling in the notebook. 'Excellent.' Her face changed and she looked at me more seriously. 'Do you turn into a snake, Emma?'

I hesitated.

'Tell me,' she said softly.

I ran my hands through my hair and looked down. 'Yes,' I whispered.

'Good,' Louise said loudly, and put another tick in the notebook. 'Really?'

'Really,' I said quietly.

There was a tap on the door and it opened.

'Okay,' she said. She handed the baby sling to the demon. 'Beanie, take the baby out for a walk, please.'

'Oh shit, Louise, don't do this to me, please,' I said. 'I won't hurt your baby, I swear.'

Louise grinned. 'I just want to eat in peace, Emma. The food's here.'

'Really?' I said.

She reached across the table and gave *me* a push. 'Sure. I'm not worried.'

'I am.'

'Don't be, you'll be fine.'

She waited until the plates had been placed on the table and the waitress and Beanie had gone, Beanie carefully closing the door behind her.

'Matt, go with her,' Louise called at the door. 'I'll be safe with the Dark Lady.'

'Ma'am,' Matt said from the other side of the door.

'Does the ring talk?' Louise said.

'Yep.'

'Show me.'

'Oh, no, Louise, it's asleep right now. Don't wake it up, it's a pain in the neck.'

'The stone *sleeps*?'

'It's a Building Block of the World. It's really old. Like an old man, it sleeps a lot.'

'It's a what?'

I sighed. 'You know the story of the Dark Goddess?'

'Nope,' she said, shaking her head over the udon.

'Okay,' I said, and took a deep breath. I tapped the stone.

'Yes, Emma?'

'Say hello to Louise,' I said.

The stone didn't say anything.

'It's really rude sometimes, don't worry about it,' I said. 'Okay. Anyway, a long time ago there was a battle between two elementals, or between a demon and an elemental.'

'Two elementals,' the stone said. 'Thunder and water.'

'Was that it?' Louise said.

'Yep.'

'It sounds English.'

'I know. Anyway, one of them knocked down one of the Four Pillars holding up the Heavens, so the Dark Goddess, Nu Wa, had to build it again. She collected stones, made a new pillar, destroyed all the monsters that had entered the world and were terrorising her children —'

'Her children were humanity. She created humanity,' the stone said. 'She fashioned the human race from clay. But she became tired, and after a while simply dipped a rope in the mud and threw the clay to make people. Noble people are those she created directly. Common people are those from the rope.'

'It's hard to tell what's true and what isn't with this stuff,' I said. 'And there are so many different versions —'

'She also started the Shang-Zhou wars because the Shang King insulted her,' the stone said. 'She was mortally offended by his disgraceful behaviour, and sent a fox spirit to take over the body of his favourite concubine and lead him into performing such atrocities that his own generals rebelled and toppled him. It led to a civil war so vast that the whole country was plunged into anarchy. Many, many people died. At the end of the war, the mightiest and most courageous warriors were all Raised.'

'Xuan Wu was one of them, wasn't he,' I said.

'Yep,' the stone said. 'In human form. The White Tiger too. A lot of them had their human forms Raised because of their noble deeds.'

'Was the fox spirit called Daji?' I said quickly.

'Yes, she was. But back to me, I'm the important one,' the stone said, and Louise snorted.

'Anyway,' I said, 'when the sky fell down, the Dark Goddess built a pillar to hold it up. She had some stones left over from building the pillar, and they are old and powerful and *extremely annoying*.'

'How did you come by this one?' Louise said.

'I think Xuan Wu's had it for a very long time,' I said.

'Yes,' the stone said. 'A very, very long time.'

'Go back to sleep,' I said.

'I certainly will,' the stone said. 'I was in the middle of a lovely dream: I was a mighty snow-capped peak with the frozen corpses of failed mountaineers adorning my slopes.'

'Is it useful for anything?' Louise said. 'Or is it just annoying?'

'It can come in handy, but I really wonder sometimes whether it's worth the suffering.' I shrugged. 'Enough.'

'Yeah, that was the last one,' Louise said. 'I thought you could do all of those things, so I mostly win. But some of the stories they tell about you are obviously ridiculous. Like, they say that you took out a level fifty demon with your bare hands —'

'Yep,' I said through the udon.

'Damn,' she said softly, 'I really should have brought a video camera. They say you told the King of the Demons to his *face* to piss off —'

'Yep,' I said. 'You should have seen the look on John's face.'

'John? You call the Emperor *John*?' she said, incredulous.

'It's his English name. Sounds like Xuan. Xuan Wu.'

'Oh, that makes sense.'

'That's not the only thing I call him,' I said into the udon, and Louise giggled.

'They say that you can jump off high places and float down without getting hurt —'

'Yep,' I said. 'Just learned that one not long ago.'

'Geez, Emma,' Louise said. 'I really should have brought a video camera. If I could get a video of this I'd be in the Tiger's bed every night for six weeks.'

'*What*?'

'You don't think we bet for money, do you?' Louise said with a grin. 'We bet nights with Tigger.'

I couldn't hold back the laughter. '*Tigger*?'

'He's very bouncy,' Louise said, her eyes sparkling. She glanced down at her notebook. 'Damn. I really should have brought a video camera. They won't believe me without proof on those last ones.'

I pulled out my mobile phone and called home.

'*Wei*?'

'Ah Yat,' I said, 'could you grab the video camera and bring it to the Tokyo private room in the Japanese restaurant in the hotel in Sha Tin?'

'Ma'am,' Ah Yat said. 'Give me about five minutes, I need to find it.'

'Okay, no rush,' I said, and hung up.

'Thanks, Emma,' Louise said. 'You're great, you know.'

I shrugged.

'Did you really tame a level seventy demon?' Louise said.

I nodded, sipping some miso soup.

'Tell your helper to hurry with the video camera,' she said.

I studied her. All of my exceptional abilities didn't seem to have fazed her at all.

'Louise,' I said.

'Hm?'

'None of this stuff I can do seems to worry you at all. You don't seem to be jealous, or bothered by it, or anything.'

'Jealous?' she said with a grin. 'I'm *privileged*. Do you have any idea how impressed people are when I say that you're my friend, and that we shared a flat for a couple of years? You're a legend in your own lifetime.'

'Oh, great,' I said, lifting the last piece of yam tempura with my chopsticks. 'That's all I need.'

'Can I come to the wedding?'

'Do Chinese weddings have matrons of honour? 'Cause that's what I want you to be.'

'Who cares whether they do or they don't,' Louise said. ''Cause I'm coming, and I'm wearing something frilly and awful in pink with a dreadful cocktail hat.'

'You'd better be careful what you wish for, mate,' I said. ''Cause it could very well come true.'

'Coronation too,' she said. 'My roommate, Empress of the North. Do you get a crown?'

I thumped my chopsticks on the table with mock fury.

She grinned and her eyes sparkled. 'Have you heard from April?' She saw my face and the grin disappeared. 'Is she okay?'

I sighed and dropped my head. Then I pulled myself together. April was Louise's friend too. She had a right to know.

'Okay,' I said. 'You know this demon bastard who's after us? After my family?'

'Yeah,' Louise said softly. 'It once broke into the stables in Ireland and did some really bad stuff to the wives who were managing there. One of them'll never walk again, and the other was horribly disfigured.' She bent over the table to confide in me. 'And the Tiger still sees them both, you know. He loves us all.'

'Okay,' I said. 'Well, that particular demon is the head of all the underworld activity in Hong Kong ...'

Louise inhaled sharply, eyes wide.

'... and Kitty Kwok was helping the demon to launder its dirty money through the kindergartens —'

'Holy *shit*, Emma. Kitty Kwok? The woman you worked for?'

I continued. 'And Kitty Kwok's been building demon hybrids for him, and taking samples from the children in the kindergartens — blood and tissue samples —'

'No,' Louise said. 'No.'

'Kitty Kwok has labs in Dongguan where they're building the demon hybrids —'

'Hybrids?'

'And Andy, April's husband, was involved in triad activity —'

'I knew there was something wrong with that guy,' Louise interrupted again. 'He was a total creep to her. He was in league with the demons?'

'I think he is a demon. He just married April to get her pregnant. So that they could ...' I stopped.

'What, Emma?' Louise whispered.

I dropped my head. 'Kitty sent April to Dongguan to have a caesarean delivery,' I whispered.

'She got the baby!' Louise shouted, furious. 'She killed April! No!'

'I saw April last week,' I said, and Louise relaxed. 'She doesn't remember anything — her marriage or her pregnancy. She told me her family were all killed in a car accident in Australia, and Kitty is looking after her.'

Louise straightened. 'Okay, Superwoman, go in and get her and her baby out.'

'I wish I could,' I moaned. 'But I have no idea where she is, and nobody else does either. All we know is that she's in Causeway Bay somewhere.'

'What about Xuan Wu?'

'He won't leave Simone,' I said. 'And neither will I.'

'That makes sense.' Louise smiled. 'I'll talk to Tigger about it. See if we can't send some Horsemen in and get April out.'

'I doubt very much that the Tiger will send his sons to certain death,' I said. 'That demon is incredibly powerful, and it would be on his own turf.'

Ah Yat appeared in the corner with the video camera and Louise jumped. 'I still have to get used to that,' she said.

Ah Yat handed me the video camera, and I set it up to record, then passed it to Louise. 'What were those questions you wanted to ask me?'

'We will get April out, Emma,' Louise said as she pressed the button. 'Now, generate some black chi first — that was great.'

I sighed and put my hands out.

CHAPTER TWENTY-TWO

I taught a first-year energy-work class straight after lunch. Everybody froze when Monique managed to generate chi.

'Hold it carefully, Monique,' I said softly, moving the other students away so that I could sit in front of her. 'Concentrate. Everybody else, to one side, silence. Don't move.'

Monique's face was a mask of concentration. She hadn't generated much chi, only about a golf ball's worth, but it was an achievement for someone from a Western background to be able to do it at all. Her mother had studied in China and learned Tai Chi and had taught Monique from an early age.

'Do you have it?' I said.

She didn't say anything. Her face was rigid, her green eyes very dark from her dilated pupils. Her brown hair drifted slightly with the static from the energy.

I put my hand on her arm to supervise: she had it.

'Very well done,' I said softly. 'Now, you know what to do. Slowly and carefully, let it drop.'

Her face stiffened as she prepared to let go of the energy.

My mobile phone rang.

The chi rocketed back into her hands, her eyes rolled up and she collapsed.

'Damn!' I said, catching her. 'Anybody here her roommate?'

A black girl stepped forward: Sofie, from Ghana. 'Me, ma'am.'

My phone was still ringing but I ignored it.

'Okay, Sofie. Take Monique down to the infirmary, lie her down and let her rest. She'll be fine.'

I pulled my phone out clumsily, still holding Monique, and checked the screen. Leo. I pressed the 'reject' button.

'Brad, Joe, help Sofie to carry Monique. I'll be down shortly.'

'Ma'am,' the three of them said. Brad was a huge black kid and he gently lifted Monique, the young Cambodian, Joe, helping him. Sofie hovered, concerned.

I pulled myself to my feet. 'She'll be fine, guys. I'll come down to the infirmary and apologise personally, *on behalf of Leo*, later.'

They all grinned and nodded, and Brad carried the unconscious Monique out. The other students stood frozen with wonder.

'Well, she did it. When will you guys manage it?' I said cheerfully. 'Go and take a break. I'll see what Leo wants.'

The students filed out, chatting.

I pulled the phone out and called Leo back.

'One of my energy students had just generated her first chi when the phone rang,' I said.

'Why didn't you switch it off then?' Leo shot back.

I hesitated. 'You know why.'

He was silent as he understood. Then his voice returned, more brisk. 'I need your help down in my office. You're really gonna love this. One of the new students has a major problem with his roommate at the New Folly.'

'On my way,' I said and snapped the phone shut.

286

I passed the tea urn on the way to the lift. 'Be right back, guys,' I called to the students clustered around the tea table. 'I expect all of you to be able to generate chi the size of a basketball when I come back.'

'Yes, ma'am,' the students said in unison, grinning.

Leo's office door was shut. I tapped on it and went in.

Leo's desk was free of paperwork; he didn't have much to do with the administration side of things. The room was more of a bolt hole for him. The bookshelf held an extensive library of martial arts books and videos, though, and he had been trusted with many of John's older and more valuable scrolls on the Arts. A signed poster of an American college football team was the only decoration on the wall.

Leo saluted me without rising, but the kid just sat and scowled. I didn't recognise him; he must have been very new.

'This is Scott,' Leo said. 'He's just been recruited from Gold's latest run through the US and Canada. Canadian. Arrived last week.'

'Hi, Scott,' I said, and took the chair next to him. 'What seems to be the problem?'

The kid was silent, still scowling, and it dawned on me: he didn't know who I was.

'He's been told everything, Leo?' I said without looking away from Scott.

'I don't think he completely believes it yet, my Lady,' Leo said.

Scott's face went slack as he realised and he quickly rose and saluted me, falling to one knee. 'Apologies, my Lady.'

'Maybe I won't throw you out, after all,' I said, amused. 'If I did, I think you would be the quickest ejection in the history of the Hong Kong-based Mountain. Do you believe it yet? Tell me the truth.'

Scott glanced down and didn't say anything.

'Sit,' I said, and he sat in the other chair. 'Are you willing to go along with us crazy people to learn the Arts?'

Scott nodded, his face serious. 'Anything. I want ...' He paused. 'I want it to be true, you know? I've seen chi. I've seen some of the stuff you guys can do. But it's hard.'

'Have you met the Dark Lord?' I said.

Scott nodded. 'But,' he said with a small smile, 'he's not really that impressive. He just looks like an ordinary guy.'

'You'll get there,' I said, rising. 'Can't see a problem here, Leo. He'll get there.'

'Sit, Emma, that's not the problem,' Leo said. His expression became wry. 'He has a major problem with his roommate at the New Folly.'

'The guy's a freaking *faggot*,' Scott said viciously. 'You put me in with one of *them*. I want out right now.'

I fell back into my chair, speechless. Leo's face remained wry.

'I don't know what he'll do to me in the middle of the night. You know they're all ...' He paused, and pulled himself together. 'You can't trust them. And he could be diseased, or anything. We'll be sharing the same goddamn *bathroom*. You've gotta move me out *now*.'

I struggled to find words. Leo began to look amused at my reaction.

'I cannot believe you let one of *them* learn here,' Scott said fiercely. 'Don't you know about him? He told me like it was the most natural thing in the world, you know: "I'm from Holland, here's a photo of my family, by the way I'm gay." I could not believe it.' He dropped his head. 'I've heard they're more relaxed about that stuff in Europe, but geez, he just came out with it like it was completely normal. And he didn't even *look* like one of them. Usually you can spot them a mile off — they're totally gross.'

Leo leaned back and waited.

'Hold out your hand,' I said.

Scott seemed surprised at the strange request, then shrugged and held his hand out. I took it and examined him.

'Definite energy potential, Mr Alexander,' I said, releasing his hand. 'But I think we should throw him out anyway. How good is he in hand-to-hand?'

'Brilliant,' Leo said. 'Feel free to have some fun with him if you like, my Lady, this is the first one I've had in a while.'

'You're going to throw me out? Don't throw me out!' Scott looked from me to Leo. 'I didn't do anything! What — you think this is *okay*?'

'How many staff of the Mountain have you encountered so far, Scott?' I said kindly.

'Of course, Gold,' Scott said. 'He recruited me, showed me the quarters in Happy Valley, set me up, that sort of thing.'

'Do you like Gold?' I said. 'You know he's really a stone, not a human being at all.'

'Yeah, somebody said that, but I can't really see how the guy can be a rock,' Scott said. 'But he looked after me, he's an okay guy.'

'After Gold had you settled in, what happened next?'

'I had the orientation with Master Leo. I've spent the last week being issued gear, being shown around, things like that. Everything was explained. I was presented to the Dark Lord and had to swear allegiance.'

'It's been a busy week,' Leo said.

'They haven't sworn allegiance to me yet,' I said.

'We'll get there,' Leo said. 'Sometimes it's better if they don't know who you are for the first few weeks.

I mean, they know you're there, they see you wandering around, but they don't connect the stories with *you*.'

'My plain appearance,' I said, understanding. 'They've heard stories of the Dark Lady, and they expect me to be about two metres tall, raven-haired and spitting fire, not short, plain and scruffy.'

'Exactly,' Leo said. Scott appeared astonished.

'You're really clever sometimes, Leo,' I said. 'Good lesson for them: nothing on the Mountain is ever as it seems.'

Leo made a soft sound of amusement.

'I want to meet his roommate,' I said. 'Can you get him?'

'Tymen!' Leo yelled without moving. 'Come on in.'

Tymen tapped on the door and came in, carefully closing the door behind him. He was similar in appearance to Scott; they could almost be brothers. Both were tall, angular, and bony, with the gangly limbs that signalled some growing still to do. Both were fair with sandy blond hair. Scott was younger, probably only seventeen, while Tymen could have been nineteen or twenty.

I rose. 'Sit, Tymen.'

Tymen sat in my chair. Scott went rigid and Tymen sagged.

'Do you know who I am?' I said kindly.

Tymen shook his head, his blue eyes wide.

'This is the Dark Lady herself, Tymen,' Leo said in a low growl. 'Watch yourself.'

Tymen shot to his feet and fell to one knee, saluting. 'My Lady.' He rose and studied me closely, then offered me his seat.

'Sit,' I said. 'I'll stand.'

'Do as she says,' Leo said when he saw Tymen hesitate.

I leaned against the wall. 'Young Scott here has a

problem with you, Tymen. He thinks you're going to rape him in the middle of the night.'

Leo made another soft sound of amusement. Scott's scowl became defiant. But Tymen sagged again. He was obviously accustomed to it.

'Please find me alternative quarters, ma'am, sir,' Tymen said softly. 'I have no wish to offend anyone with my presence. I know some people have issues with people like me. I thought ...' His voice trailed off and then he pulled himself together. 'I thought the environment would be more accepting here, after talking to both Gold and Master Leo. I spoke too soon.' He glanced desperately up at me. 'Please don't throw me out, ma'am, I want this more than anything. I'll keep my head down and my mouth shut, I promise.'

Scott glared at Tymen with contempt.

'Did you have a boyfriend back home?' I said kindly.

Scott looked horrified.

Tymen sighed. 'I had a lot of friends. Nobody special; I think I'm too young. But I gave up a lot to come. Please don't throw me out.'

'Hold out your hand.'

Tymen didn't hesitate, and I took his hand and examined him carefully. 'Hand-to-hand?'

'Just as brilliant,' Leo said. 'These two could be brothers.'

I suddenly knew with a certainty that left me breathless that one day they *would* be like brothers. The shock of the feeling nearly knocked me off my feet.

'Are you okay, Emma?' Leo said softly, seeing my reaction.

I dropped Tymen's hand and pulled myself together. 'Two of the Masters you have already met and spent time with are gay, Scott. I won't tell you which two, because you said you can pick them.'

Scott's mouth dropped open.

'You haven't had much contact with many of the staff of the Mountain, so it shouldn't be too difficult to work it out. One of them can't really be said to be gay because he's not human, despite the fact that right now he's dating another guy. But the other one,' I said, carefully not looking at Leo, 'is one hundred per cent pure flaming fairy queen, right the way through.'

Scott's eyes were very wide, but he still hadn't put it together and didn't look at Leo. I saw Leo's reaction out of the corner of my eye and nearly lost it. Tymen made a small choking sound but I couldn't see his face.

'If you have a problem with learning from a Master whose private life is absolutely none of your goddamn business anyway, say so now,' I said. 'If you have a problem sharing with Tymen, tell me right now and I'll throw you out.' I leaned forward to speak intensely to him. 'We will not have discrimination on our Mountain. We take the best; it doesn't matter where they come from or what they are. Some of the students are perfected demons. Many of them aren't even *human*. The Dark Lord himself is a reptile, Scott. You will encounter a great deal of very strange stuff in the near future. Compared to that, a gay roommate will be a refreshing dash of normality.' I straightened and folded my arms. 'So say the word. If you aren't prepared to learn to be more accepting of those around you, I will quite happily throw you out right now.'

Scott's eyes were still very wide. 'Who?' He turned to Leo. 'Who?'

Leo made another amused sound but didn't say anything.

'Scott,' I said, and he turned back to me. 'Are you scared of snakes?'

Scott's face went blank. 'I don't like them, but I wouldn't say I'm *scared* of them ...'

'I change into a snake when my family are threatened,' I said, very calmly. 'How big is it, Leo?'

'Oh, it's a good ten metres long, Emma,' Leo said, still amused. 'Big, black, ugly thing too.'

'Big, black and ugly, just like you, Leo,' I said.

'Yep,' Leo said with a grin.

Both Scott and Tymen stiffened.

'Weirdness is the order of the day at Wudangshan,' I said. 'About the only thing that's not weird around here is the fact that some of the staff and students are gay.'

Scott didn't say a word.

'I'm leaving you with Tymen, Scott, and I know for a fact that you two will be good friends one day,' I said. 'Tymen, don't hide yourself. There's absolutely no need. Scott, try to learn, open your mind. 'Cause if you don't do it yourself, the first time you see a Snake Mother it'll get opened so wide and so fast the damage will be permanent. Enough, Leo?'

'I can handle the rest, my Lady,' Leo said. 'Gold can help me.'

'Don't tell him who they are,' I said as I turned to open the door. 'Let him try to work it out himself.'

I winked at Tymen. 'Don't you tell him either; it's obvious you know.'

'You read my mind, Emma,' Leo said softly as I went out to find Monique and see how she was doing in the infirmary.

Tymen's grin completely made my day.

On my way to the infirmary to check on Monique, I passed Sonia in the lift lobby. She was pushing the mail trolley. When she saw me she stopped and fell to her knees.

'Up you get, Sonia,' I said kindly. When she was back on her feet I moved forward and gave her a little hug, just enough to make her feel wanted without embarrassing her too much. 'Is everybody looking after you?'

Her face lit up. 'I cannot believe the kindness I have been experiencing. And some of the other staff here are demons as well.'

I let the fact that she wasn't a demon slide. 'Are you coping okay with the work? It's not too hard for you?'

Sonia glanced down at the contents of the trolley. 'At first I was frightened — I didn't know where anything was supposed to go. But,' she smiled up at me, 'I can ask anyone. Nobody will harm me.' She hesitated, her eyes wide. 'It's a strange feeling to know that I have nothing to fear from anyone here.'

'When are you moving over to the Folly?'

'I can't believe that happened. The students who asked me to share with them are so kind. They *want* to teach me to live as a human. They say they enjoy my company and like having me around.'

'Good.' I smiled down at her. She was much shorter than me, slight and slim. Her tiny blue jeans were too big on her, and she wore a typical Hong Kong T-shirt with a random English phrase that made absolutely no sense: 'High Fashion Ice-cream'. 'I'd better go. One of my students drained herself and she's in the infirmary.'

'My Lady.' Sonia dropped to one knee and saluted me.

I sighed. 'You really don't need to do that, you know, Sonia.'

She smiled up at me. 'I know, ma'am, but I want to.'

I pressed the button for the lift. Sonia rose but didn't move.

I turned back to her. 'What?'

'Uh ...'

'Ask me, Sonia,' I said. 'You can ask me anything.'

She glanced up at me, her face full of hope. 'I would

294

like to attend evening classes, after work. I would like to study.'

'What do you want to study?'

She dropped her head, unsure.

'I'm thoroughly impressed, Sonia,' I said, reaching out and squeezing her hand. 'If you want to study, I'll support you any way I can.'

Her face lit up again. 'I want to study bookkeeping and typing. I want to help more in the office.'

'Good,' I said. 'If you need time off from work for the study, then just tell me. If you want help getting into a course, or a reference, ask me. Did Gold handle your identity papers yet?'

She nodded. 'Yes, ma'am.'

'Good.' I turned back to the lift. 'You'd better get on, Sonia, we can't stay here chatting all day, we both have work to do.' I grinned at her. 'Let me know when you want to take your stuff over to the Folly and I'll drive you.'

'Thank you, ma'am,' she choked, and hurried away.

I bent over Monique in the infirmary. She was unconscious.

'Will she be okay?' Sofie said.

I sat next to Monique and took her hand, examining her. A first-year student like this had very little chi to start off with; and Monique was tiny.

'Everybody stay very still and don't touch either of us,' I said.

I took a deep breath, concentrated, and fed her enough chi to bring her back. The chi moved through her like a golden flowing wave, the energy meridians lighting up.

Monique gasped and her eyes snapped open.

'Don't move, Monique,' I said urgently. 'Stay very still. Relax.'

Monique heard me. She had the concentration of a true energy worker, and controlled her reaction to the feeding of the energy.

I saw what happened when the energy hit her lower abdomen; her face screwed up. This sometimes happened the first time a student was fed with energy and could be tremendously embarrassing for them, particularly the male ones.

'Everybody out,' I said. 'She's fine.'

Monique was gasping. All the other students quickly went out. I stopped the feed, rotated her energy through her, gathered it and put it back into her dan tian. I gave her a small mental pat on the head and smiled. I carefully withdrew my consciousness, but retained my hold on her hand.

'I'm so sorry,' she said, breathless. She blushed furiously. 'I don't know why that happened . . .'

'It's quite normal the first time,' I said. 'I don't normally talk about it, because if it happens, it happens, and it's not that big a deal.' I leaned forward and whispered. 'It's ten times worse for the guys.'

Monique laughed quietly and struggled to sit. I helped her up.

'How do you feel?' I said, still holding her hand. Internally she looked fine, but emotional damage was possible; she could have been concerned about the helplessness she had felt.

'Warm and tingly,' she said with a cheeky grin. She laughed softly. 'But I did it.' She jiggled with delight. 'I *did* it!'

John's voice spoke in my head. *Emma, it's happened again. Top floor, please.*

'Oh my God, *damn*!' I said loudly. 'Not again!'

Monique blanched. 'What happened?'

'Nothing to do with you, Monique,' I said. 'Go to the rest of the class, tell them they're dismissed, but they're not to return to the New Folly, they have to remain here. A demon's found its way into the Folly again. Happens every time we get a new batch of students.' I dropped her hand and rose. 'I'd better go.'

I called John on his mobile phone as I stormed out to the lifts.

'*Wei?*'

'John, it's me. Are you coming back? Where are you?'

'I'm still in Splendid China, Emma, but I'm coming back.'

'*John Chen Wu, don't you dare!*' I yelled. Some students in the lift with me turned away and smiled. 'You stay right there and spend the day with Simone! Is that understood?'

One of the senior students in the lift behind me tittered.

'You will keep,' I growled. I raised my voice to speak to John again. 'You stay there. You enjoy yourselves. We'll handle it. How big is it? Where is it?'

'Level seventy,' he said, and I inhaled sharply. 'In the New Folly, cornered on the fourteenth floor.'

'I'll get some Celestial Masters. We can handle it. You stay there and have fun. We'll be fine.'

He was silent for a while and I could easily visualise the expression on his face.

'We'll be fine,' I said again, and exited the lift on the top floor.

CHAPTER TWENTY-THREE

When I arrived at the lobby of the Folly there was a crowd of students outside and the fire alarm was ringing. One of the seniors raced forward when he saw me.

'It's on the fourteenth floor,' he said, breathless. It was LK Pak, one of the best seniors we had, in his mid-thirties and Chinese. He continued to keep me informed as we charged to the lift. 'It's holding the student who brought it in and won't let anybody near. It says it wants to talk to the Dark Lord, it won't take anybody else. It's threatening to kill the student if we don't bring it the Dark Lord. Where is he? We need him!'

'He's over the border in Shenzhen,' I said, trying to stay calm. 'Maybe I'll do. How many Celestials do we have up there?'

'Three,' LK said. 'Tae Kwon Do, and two *Wudang* Weapons Masters.'

The lift doors flew open and we stepped out together. The corridor was deserted. LK led me to the apartment. The door hung open.

The demon was in the living room, standing in front of the television in True Form, holding the student by the scruff of the neck. The student was very new, I didn't even know his name. He was unconscious and there was blood on him.

The demon was a huge red humanoid with three eyes, nearly three metres tall. The three Masters faced it, ready.

'Out, LK,' I said. 'This is too big for anybody but Celestials.'

LK nodded and went out to call the lift.

I carefully entered the apartment and the Masters made room for me.

'Park,' I said softly to the Tae Kwon Do Master, 'pass on everything that happens to the Dark Lord, okay?'

My Lady, Park said.

I studied the demon carefully. No wonder everybody was hanging back — this one was huge. At least level seventy; absolutely enormous. Had to be minor nobility.

'What do you want?' I said.

'Who are you? *What* are you?' the demon said.

'Emma Donahoe. Heard of me?'

The demon stiffened. 'You'll do.'

I didn't move. 'What do you want?'

The demon dropped the student, who crumpled. It fell to its knees and took human form: a Chinese girl in her mid-teens, small and slim, with long hair. 'I swear allegiance. Please protect me. I am yours.'

'Shit,' I said softly. John wasn't there to confirm that the demon had turned.

Park moved to help the student but I raised my arm to stop him. 'Why did you hurt the student?'

'Self-defence,' the demon said. 'He went for me. He's not badly injured; it looks much worse than it is, I assure you. Come and get him, I won't hurt you.'

I lowered my arm and nodded. Park inched carefully forward, grabbed the student and pulled him to one side.

The demon is correct, Park said. He and the student disappeared.

'Master Sit,' I said, nodding to one of the *Wudang* masters, 'find somebody who can tame demons for me right now, would you?'

'JC is on his way,' Sit said.

I nodded. JC Poon was the Demon Master.

The demon pulled itself to its feet and we all readied ourselves.

'I'll sit on the couch and wait,' the demon said without moving. 'Is that okay?'

I nodded, and the demon moved to sit on the couch.

'Sit with me, Lady,' it said, gesturing. 'I won't harm you. I'd like to tell you what I know now, so that it can be quicker when it comes.'

The living room was too small to have more than one couch. I hesitated.

The demon saluted. 'I give my word. I will not harm you.'

'Get Meredith,' I said. She was about the only Master powerful enough to take out something this big if it wasn't tamed. The other Master, Liu, was held up on the Celestial Plane, doing some job in the Northern Heavens that everybody refused to talk about.

'My Lady,' one of the Masters said behind me.

I carefully moved to sit next to the demon on the couch. It smiled slightly, its fresh young face innocent.

'I have offended One Two Two,' the demon said. 'It was planning to use me as a toy.'

One of the Masters inhaled sharply.

'What are his plans?' I said.

'If I may, my Lady,' the demon said, 'I think it would be a very good idea if you were to take this.' She reached into the back pocket of her jeans and I leapt to my feet. 'It's okay, it's just a card.' She raised one hand while she pulled the card out with the other. She held it out and I took it, sitting to look at it.

The name on the card was 'Cynthia Chow'. It was the card for a law firm: Wong and Associates. I felt a jolt of excitement. One Two Two's law firm. Offices in Central, Tsim Sha Tsui, Sham Shui Po and Kowloon City. Got him.

'Now you know where he is,' the demon said.

'Thanks,' I said. 'I think in the very near future, a Turtle, a Tiger, a Lion and me are paying him a visit.'

'I wish I could be around to see it,' the demon said, smiling slightly. It took a deep breath and dropped its head into its hands. 'Please make them come quickly, I want this over with.'

'What's he going to do?' I said.

'I honestly don't know,' the demon said, looking back up. 'He's been making really incredible hybrids — you should see some of the things he's produced. Some of them are pretty scary.'

I tried to control my face.

'Look,' the demon said with a shrug. 'I just want it to be over. Can you do it for me now? It won't make a mess, and I just want to be gone. Please.' Its voice became anguished. 'Help me!'

'Any weapons around here?' I said.

'I can call my sword, my Lady,' said Lionel Chan, the other *Wudang* Weapons Master. 'I can do it now if it is your wish.'

'No!' the demon said. 'Only the Lady. None other.'

It fell to its knees in front of the couch and touched its head to the parquet flooring. 'My Lady, I beg you. Only you. You are the only one I trust. No other.'

'Okay.' I pulled myself to my feet in front of the demon. 'Call your weapon, Lionel.' I glanced down at the demon. 'Anything else you want to tell me?'

301

The demon carefully pulled itself to its feet. 'Yes. One other thing.' It lowered its voice. I strained to hear. 'This,' it whispered, and leaped.

It felt like someone had stabbed me in the neck. The pain was excruciating. I grabbed its head where it had buried itself into my neck and ripped it away. It grinned at me, still in human form, its long black pointed tongue clearly visible.

'You little *bitch*!' I shouted, and backhanded it across the room. It crashed into the window, but didn't break it. It pulled itself to its feet and came for me again.

Lionel jumped in front of me, sword raised, and the demon smiled. It moved so fast it was a blur. It leaped and buried its head into his throat, holding his arms. Lionel struggled but the demon had him.

I raced forward and punched the demon on the head where it was biting Lionel. It held him, then let go and moved back. Lionel sagged to his knees, then fell over like a dead tree and disappeared. Master Sit moved forward to block the demon, and it hit him right in the middle of the chest with a blast of something black and horrible. He disappeared.

The demon straightened and grinned. 'You and me.'

I straightened as well. 'Try me.'

'The toxin is already moving through your bloodstream,' the demon said. 'You don't have much longer anyway. As soon as you're out, we'll visit my Master.'

I put my hand to my neck and pulled it away covered in blood and clear sweet-smelling venom. She was right. I readied myself. 'I won't let you take me, sweetheart.'

The demon rushed me. I dodged under its attack and hit it with my feet as it went through. I knocked it down but it rolled, turned and was back on its feet facing me.

The toxin was in my neck. It *was* moving through my bloodstream; I could feel it. But it didn't feel too bad at all. I could deal with it.

'Does it burn?' the demon said with a grin.

'Nope,' I said. 'Doesn't worry me at all.'

If I hit the demon with chi I would blow myself up; it was too big. I had to do this one with physical.

The demon came at me again, so fast it was a blur, but I was way ahead of it. I hit it across the neck with the blade of my hand, then used the momentum to swing my foot into its abdomen. But its human shell was thick and I didn't get through.

The demon latched onto my neck again. I hit it across the windpipe, but it had injected more venom into me before I freed myself. The little bitch was like a dog humping my leg; she just wouldn't let go.

The venom was really starting to move through me now. I could feel it, but it felt *good*. It seemed to be making me stronger, not weaker.

I didn't have time to wonder about it. The demon was at me again, but this time she seemed to be slower. I clasped my hands and used them together in a crushing hammer blow right at her temple. I was through her.

She disappeared.

The venom burned through me and everything looked really weird: the colours were all wrong and all the furniture seemed to be a strange shape. A strong smell of acetone filled the room. The television was on its side, and I could see the threads of the rug, sideways, right in front of my eyes. No, that wasn't right . . .

It was hard to hear the voice talking to me through the roaring in my ears. I couldn't see anything.

'Emma, concentrate. You have to clear this out of your system.'

'Meredith?'

'Emma, thank the Heavens. Concentrate. Help me.'

I shook my head but still couldn't see. 'What happened?'

'Demon poisoning, dear.' Meredith's voice was crisp. 'We need to clear this out of you. Now. Concentrate on the sound of my voice. This will hurt.'

Her cool hands were on my forehead. Before I could do anything my veins filled with needle-sharp, ice-cold fire. The pain was unbelievable. I screamed and thrashed.

Emma, keep still, John said into my head and I subsided. *Concentrate. Let Meredith help you. Try to control your reaction to the pain.* He hesitated. *I know it hurts, love, but this must be done.*

'John?'

'I'm here, love.'

I exhaled a huge sigh of relief and let Meredith hurt me for a million years.

'We came so close to losing her,' Meredith said softly.

'I must stay nearby,' John said. 'If I had been nearby this would not have happened. This demon waited until I was out of range and then came.'

'Was the student poisoned too?' I said without opening my eyes.

'No,' John said, his voice soft and warm. 'All he had was a bloody nose, and he fainted at the sight of the blood. He's fine, his nose isn't even broken.'

'God, what a wimp,' I whispered, my voice hoarse.

'He brought the demon in,' Meredith said. 'It took the form of a pretty girl and he led it right in the front door. There's some disagreement as to whether we should let the stupid little bastard stay.'

'He's very talented; he just needs to mature,' John said.

'He's probably only been here a week. Let him stay,' I said.

'Yes, ma'am,' John said, and I tried to raise my hand to thump him but I was too weak. I struggled to open my eyes and saw the ceiling of the Folly apartment. I was lying on the living room couch. I wanted to pull myself upright but I couldn't.

Meredith pushed me back. 'Rest some more, then we'll take you home.'

'Holy shit, not directly,' I said. 'That'd kill me.'

'You are quite correct,' John said. 'So Meredith will carry you down to the car and I will drive you home. But we want to make sure that you'll survive the trip first.'

'I'm fine.' I wanted to pull myself to sit but I couldn't even raise my arms. 'Whoa. I'm so weak.'

'Look at your chi level,' Meredith said with amusement.

I felt a shock as I checked my central dan tian. I was running on empty. 'So that's what it feels like.' I closed my eyes. 'Can you top me up, Meredith, to get me strong enough to go home?'

'Sorry, dear, you were too badly poisoned,' Meredith said. 'If I were to fill you with chi now, the energy would kill you in your current weakened state. You will need to go home and rest for quite some time, building the chi slowly yourself.'

That made sense. I heaved a huge sigh.

'Do you realise what you just did?' John said quietly.

'Yep,' I said. 'I fell for the oldest trick in the book and nearly got myself killed.'

'You took down a level seventy, Emma.'

'With your bare hands, no less,' Meredith said.

I was silent.

'You took down a demon that was more than a match for two Celestial Masters,' John said. 'And you

305

did it full of demon venom. You just get better all the time.'

'Astounding,' Meredith said. 'Wish I could have seen that.'

I wanted to run my hands through my hair but I was too weak.

'Rest,' Meredith said. 'Then we'll take you home.'

The next day I was up and tottering around the house like an invalid. I could barely lift my cup of tea in the morning, but after a good sleep I could actually eat something at lunchtime. John and I shared a huge pot of vegetarian *ho fan* in the dining room.

'How long before I'm back to normal?' I said.

'About five days, give or take,' John said. 'You will be too weak to practise anything for a while. Your already injured liver is slowing the healing process; there is still poison in your system that needs to be filtered out.'

'Damn,' I said into my noodles. 'Monique just generated her first chi and now I can't help her.'

'Meredith will take over,' John said with amusement.

We shared the noodles in silence for a while.

'The Tiger has a suggestion,' John said. 'Simone is at school for another two weeks until the end of term. She is cared for by Leo and Michael. I am here. You are too weak to do anything except rest. Why don't you go to the Western Palace and see your family? Recuperate there? You'll recover much faster on the Celestial.'

I glanced at him. 'Will I really?'

He nodded through the noodles.

I shrugged. 'Okay.'

His eyes filled with amusement and I glared at him. 'What?'

'I was expecting more resistance from you,' he said.

'If I'm back to normal faster then it can only be good,' I said.

'I can't go, Emma, if that's what you're thinking,' he said softly. 'We need the Tiger strong.'

'I know you can't go, John,' I said, just as softly. 'I know.'

I knew. We both knew. There would be no more opportunities for us to be together.

I came around on a couch with my parents' concerned faces hovering above me. I pulled myself upright and ran my hands over my face. I looked around. I appeared to be in a comfortably furnished living room with modern tan-coloured leather furniture and cream carpet.

'Oh, come on, Emma, say the line,' the stone said.

'No,' I said. 'Go to sleep.'

'If you don't mind, my Lady,' the stone said, more seriously, 'it's been a long time since I was on the Celestial. I was wondering if I could ...' Its voice drifted off.

'Do you want to leave the ring and wander around?' I said.

'How did you know I can do that?' the stone said.

My parents watched the exchange with amusement.

'Go,' I said. 'Have some fun. Enjoy. I'm perfectly safe here. I don't need you.'

'Humph,' the stone said. 'Lovely to be wanted.'

'Just go,' I said.

'If you want me back, say "Jade Building Block",' the stone said. 'I'll be right back, I promise.'

'Will you just go!' I said, and the stone disappeared, leaving the empty ring on my hand.

'Bet it's gone to find Amanda's opal,' my father said. 'There's some serious history there.'

'Wouldn't be surprised.' I pulled myself to my feet, holding the back of the couch for support. 'Damn. I'm still weak.'

My father rushed forward to help me, and guided me into the kitchen and sat me at the table. A smiling young demon servant, appearing as a Mongolian girl in her mid-twenties, was packing the dishwasher.

'Would you like a drink?' my father said.

'Tea, *sow mei*,' I said, and the demon filled the kettle and flicked it on.

'The Tiger says you were poisoned,' my mother said. 'Are you okay?'

I showed them the bandage over the wound in my neck. 'Apparently it was pretty bad, but with a few days' rest I'll be fine.'

My father opened his mouth to say something then closed it, smiled and shrugged.

'What?'

'I was about to ask you if he's really worth it,' he said. 'But I already know the answer to that question.'

CHAPTER TWENTY-FOUR

After I'd finished the tea my parents gave me the grand tour of their apartment. It was a luxurious two-bedroom suite with all mod cons, even air conditioning. Amanda and Alan had a four-bedroom apartment next door, and Jennifer and Leonard had something similar across the outdoor breezeway.

The Tiger had placed my family in a guesthouse complex slightly away from the main palace, joined by a covered walkway that meandered through the desert gardens with their many fountains. They had their own grassy lawn, a leafy glade of shady trees, a small swimming pool, and a playground for the boys, all surrounded by a large red stone wall. On the other side of the guest complex was the large school and crèche buildings for the Tiger's many children.

'These weren't here last time I was here,' I said, studying the new electrical appliances in my parents' apartment. 'I don't even think the room I had was wired for electricity.' I glanced at my father. 'You did this, didn't you? You haven't been able to stop working.'

My father smiled and shrugged. 'Have to keep busy. You should see what I did in the women's quarters. Those poor girls were suffering horribly in the summer, so I put a reverse-cycle ducted air-con system in for them. They all love me.'

'The Tiger lets you in with the *women*?' I said with disbelief.

'Sure,' my father said, confused. 'Why?'

'I wonder how he generates the power,' I said, almost to myself. 'We're on the Celestial Plane.'

'This place is really incredible, Emma,' my father said. 'There *is* no generator. I just wire up the appliances and they work. It's like there's electricity in the air.' He rose and went into the living room, returning with a light bulb and a length of copper wire. 'Watch this.'

The wire was about forty centimetres long. He touched an end of the wire to each contact on the bulb and it lit up. He removed the wire and the bulb went out.

'As long as the wire is long enough, I can get anything working,' my father said with pride. 'And I can't be electrocuted, it's like the voltage can't hurt me. But sometimes when the Tiger's in the room, everything goes haywire. I've had to put in overload circuits, because just his presence blows things up.'

'Do you think it's him generating the power?' I said. 'He's Metal, you know.'

'I'm damn sure it's him,' my father said. 'When he's away for more than a couple of weeks we have a definite brownout in the supply. But there seems to be enough lingering electricity to keep everything working for a while.'

'Dad's keeping himself busy. Are you okay?' I asked my mother.

'We're all fine,' she said with a smile. 'I made friends with some of the wives, the ones who are slightly closer to my age. I joined a few of the clubs — mah jong, the book club, and the needlework club. I've made some really good friends; some of the wives are delightful.' Her eyes sparkled at me. 'I'm having a great time actually. Amanda's helping in the crèche, and Alan's negotiating some travel insurance policies for the travelling wives.'

'What about Jennifer and Leonard?' I said, more softly.

My parents both laughed. 'Jennifer's having a ball,' my mother said. 'She's acting as liaison between the Tiger's clothing stores here in the palace and the fashion houses on the Earthly Plane, flitting backwards and forwards between here and Paris and Rome and New York, having the time of her life. Leonard's doing some legal work for the Tiger that he said should have been sorted out over five hundred years ago.' She shrugged. 'Everybody's happy and busy.'

Her face went strange and she glanced at my father. My father's face went rigid as well and I looked from one of them to the other. 'What?'

They didn't say anything.

'What?'

My father looked down at his hands on the table. 'We were making plans to retire anyway, Emma. We're thinking about staying here.' He glanced up at me. 'There's precedent, you know: there are a few human families here, helping the wives run the palace. It's a big job. We love it here. There are some ...' He hesitated, and took a deep breath. 'Some *advantages* to staying here, as well.'

My mother looked down too. 'We never get ill. We'll live about twice as long as ordinary people —'

'You'll live longer on the Celestial Plane?' I said sharply, interrupting. 'I didn't know that.'

Both of them nodded. My mother looked up at me. 'Of course, that means that once we reach a certain age, if we return to the Earthly Plane it will kill us.' She smiled and shrugged. 'Shangri-La. "Lost Horizon".'

'I am going to *kill* him,' I said. 'He never told me that, and if I can live longer then there's more of a chance for us.'

My parents were obviously amused at my reaction.

'We'd like to stay here,' my mother said. 'What do you think?'

I stopped to consider what this would mean for us. I'd still be able to visit them; they seemed truly happy; and I was planning to move to the Mountain on the Celestial Plane myself, eventually, anyway.

I shrugged. 'If that's what you want, I'm happy for you. You can go home any time you like if you change your minds. We will look after you. What about Amanda and Jennifer and their families?'

'Amanda and Alan want to go home,' my father said. 'Jennifer and Leonard want to stay here, but Leonard says it's up to John, because he's John's Retainer.'

My mother became very serious. 'We didn't realise when we met John. He's so ...' She searched for the word. 'He's so *powerful*. Everybody speaks his name, "Xuan Wu, the Emperor Zhen Wu, the Dark Lord", with awe. I mean, the Tiger's a god, but Xuan Wu's ...' Her voice drifted off.

'John's like more than a god,' my father finished for her. 'Some of the things he's supposed to have done over the centuries defy belief. He's supposed to have defeated an entire demon army single-handed. He's the Tiger's boss, and the Tiger himself is incredibly powerful. The Tiger says he would be deeply honoured to have us stay here, as your parents.'

'John's a force of nature,' I said. 'And a normal sweet guy.'

'They say things about you too, Emma,' my mother said, studying me.

'Yeah,' I said. 'I know there are stories about me.' I smiled. 'I had lunch with Louise a couple of days ago.

312

She had a bet running with the other wives that the stuff I've done is true. The other wives didn't believe it.'

'That's part of the reason we want to stay here, Emma,' my mother said, and she shared a look with my father. 'Being your mother makes me royalty. Everybody treats us like we're something very special.'

'They couldn't believe I was just an ordinary Australian electrician,' my father said with amusement. 'They thought I had to be a demi-god or something, to have a daughter like you.'

'You are,' I whispered.

'Do you think you could manage a walk through the gardens?' my mother said. 'You could come and visit Amanda in the crèche, see Jen in the shops. The Tiger has a complete shopping mall attached to the palace —'

'Full of *women's* shops,' my father said grimly. 'Not a single hardware store there. Going to fix that as soon as I've finished the air con in the women's quarters, and then I'm wiring up that mall so you can actually *see* when you're in there. A couple of sons have asked to come along and learn from me. I have apprentices.'

'I thought you were planning retirement,' I said with amusement as I rose, leaning on the back of the chair. My mother moved to help me and I waved her away. 'I should be fine to walk around. If I'm too weak I'll let you know.'

'For your father,' my mother said, linking her arm in mine to help me anyway, 'this *is* retirement.'

I didn't hear the Tiger appear as I sat on the viewing podium watching the show-jumping competition. Michael was competing and they'd put me in the VIP box, right in front of the arena. A smiling demon waiter made sure that I was well cared for with cool drinks and vegetarian snacks. I hated receiving special treatment, but at least the competition was good.

313

'Lady Emma Donahoe, chosen of the Dark Lord,' the Tiger said, lounging next to me as if he'd always been there.

'Lord Bai Hu, Emperor of the Western Heavens,' I replied, watching the riders.

'You'll be terrific in Court,' Bai Hu said.

'Oh, thanks a *lot*.'

He turned and grabbed a tall drink of something cold from the demon waiter who had appeared next to him. 'Your family is great. Your dad has already wired up nearly half the women's quarters. Your mother has made friends with just about everybody. Your sister Jennifer can be a bit hard to take sometimes, but the other one — I don't remember her name — she's a cutie. I offered her half a million US dollars for that Southern stone Shen and she wouldn't take it, despite its protests. She said it was worth more than money to her.'

'Amanda,' I said. 'I can believe that she wouldn't take money for it; it's saved her family's lives more than once. But the stone tried to convince her to take the money?'

'I think it was planning to sneak back to her after I'd paid for it,' the Tiger said with amusement.

The loudspeakers crackled to life over the arena. 'Two Nine Seven, riding Sun Bird.'

A young son of the Tiger, slim and well-built with mid-brown hair, rode a large strong chestnut horse into the arena. He came to the front of the box and saluted us with his whip. The Tiger and I nodded back, the Tiger raising his drink. Two Nine Seven then faced the judges and saluted, and the bell rang for him to commence his round.

'And you keep your paws off my sisters, they're married,' I said.

'You're not married,' the Tiger said softly, watching the young man take the horse over the jumps. A rail went down and he winced.

I sighed. 'We've had this discussion before, Bai Hu. And if John knew, he'd pull your whiskers out one by one.'

He shrugged. 'Can't blame a guy for trying.'

We watched the rider in silence for a while. He finished the round with eight faults — two poles knocked down — but he had the fastest time.

'Good horse,' the Tiger said. 'He's done well with it.' He didn't turn away from the arena. 'Is it all right if your family stay? I'd be truly honoured by their presence. I would be able to keep them safe for you.'

'If that's what they want, I have no problem with it.'

A group of gorgeous young wives appeared, escorted by a couple of guards. They sat in the stands and waved cheerfully to the Tiger. He waved back.

'Three One Five on White Flame,' the announcer said. Michael rode out on a small grey horse, only about fifteen and a half hands. He stopped and saluted us in front of the podium. As we nodded back he went rigid, then relaxed.

'Michael MacLaren on White Flame,' the announcer said, sounding unhappy.

The Tiger made a soft sound of amusement as Michael turned away to salute the judges.

'What do you do if one of the sons has a fling with one of the wives?' I said.

'Doesn't happen,' he said firmly.

'Oh, come on,' I said. 'There are supermodels, actresses, the whole works in there. A smorgasbord for any red-blooded guy. You can't tell me it doesn't happen.'

'Doesn't happen,' he repeated. 'Not red-blooded guys.'

I inhaled sharply with horror. 'Oh my God, you *don't*. Not any more. Tell me it doesn't happen any more.'

'Yeah,' he said with a grin. 'Used to happen. I never did it to them, they'd do it to themselves. Stupid bastards. I kept telling them it's a waste of time, you can't kill all the hormones, all you can do is make yourself useless, but they wouldn't listen. Being a member of the Seraglio Elite Guard is one of the greatest honours in the West. So they did it. Cut *everything* off. And so, as much as I hated it, I had to give them a job. It was a vicious cycle. Same as in Beijing.'

'But you *have* stopped it now?'

'Of course.' He shrugged. 'Found a clever way around it. One of the wives thought of it. When they turn twenty, they can apply. A Shen inspects them. If they show no interest at all in chicks, and they have the talent, they're promoted. The numbers are just right: about one in ten. The situation works well.'

I was speechless, a huge grin on my face.

He continued with a perfectly straight face. 'They all go out clubbing together. I think they have more fun in Gay Paree than the wives do.'

I collapsed over the railing laughing. When I'd regained control I wiped my eyes. 'If Leo knew about it he'd be here with Michael every Sunday. Some of those Elite Guards are incredibly cute.'

'Oh, Leo knows,' the Tiger said. 'But he is completely devoted to his Lord, his Lady and their child. He never wants to be too far from you. He told me that himself.'

'She's not our child,' I said softly. 'She's his child.'

'Yes, she is, Emma,' the Tiger said. 'She's yours just as much as she's his. One day you guys must make it formal. You could make a declaration at Court after you're married. Permit me to arrange it for you when the time comes. I'd love to see it.'

I hesitated. It was disrespectful to Michelle's memory for me even to consider this.

'Michelle would have wanted it, Emma,' the Tiger said.

'You knew her?'

'Clear round for Three ...' the announcer said, his voice trailing off as Michael glared at him. 'For Michael MacLaren.'

'That's an exceptionally talented little horse he has there,' the Tiger said. 'Yes, of course I knew her. I was best man at the wedding.'

Everybody applauded and Michael gave me a cheery wave. I waved back.

'If you guys have a Western wedding, though, I'm not coming,' the Tiger said. 'Western weddings are as boring as hell. Those things take forever, altogether too much ceremonial garbage. The Chinese way's much better. Serve tea to the elders, have a big dinner, lock the bride and groom away to do their thing, and then play mah jong for the rest of the night. And a few days later have a declaration in Court, making Simone your own.'

It made my heart ache to think of it. We'd be a family. John would be my husband. Simone would be my daughter. A family. And then a chill went through me.

'What if I'm the White Snake?' I said.

'You can't be,' he said. 'Ah Wu and I discussed it. The Pagoda has not fallen. The Red Snake has not appeared. You are not the White Snake.'

'What would happen to his vow to marry me if I was the White Snake? If I was his daughter?'

'How do you know she was his daughter?'

I smiled grimly. 'I saw the look on his face.'

'He vowed to marry you. It would happen. If you are the White Snake, you would not discover it until after you are wed. That is the nature of a vow such as this. I felt it when he made his oath to you, all the way from here. Such a vow from one such as he is a thing of incredible power.'

'What would be our punishment for marrying in a situation like that?'

'I don't know,' he said. 'Something like that has never occurred among us. And it's already too late, you know that.' He suddenly appeared wistful. 'The White Snake was a delightful girl. A loving wife, faithful, everything a man could want. Her human husband was very lucky. What they had together was a rare and precious thing. Even after he discovered her Serpent nature, he still loved and trusted her.'

I tried to control the bitterness in my voice. 'And a Taoist priest convinced her husband she was evil. Just because she was a snake.'

He smiled gently. 'There is nothing evil about snakes. They are just cold-blooded.'

'And eat babies. Alive.'

He shrugged. 'Young antelope are the best. Sweetest.'

'But serpent Shen in human form can't do the things that I can do,' I said. 'I checked.'

'Is it true that you lifted Leo one-handed?' he said softly.

I didn't reply.

'Ah Wu is not concerned, but I have to admit that I am. That is more than Serpent nature, Emma. Do you thirst for blood? Do you have dreams?'

I dropped my head. 'Yes.'

'Clear round for Two Eight Seven,' the announcer said. 'With the fastest time, Two Eight Seven is now in the lead.'

Everybody applauded.

'Do you harm any of them in your dreams?' the Tiger said.

'No.' I glanced at him, trying to hold my emotions in. His golden face was full of sympathy. 'One Two Two and Kitty Kwok had me for a year. They experimented on me, I know they did. The Serpent is probably a result of that. If it is, then it's demon, it's inside me, and they may be able to bring it out.'

'Shit.' He looked away. 'Shit.'

'I dream I'm a Mother.'

'Having children is life's greatest gift.'

'I dream I'm a *Snake Mother*, Bai Hu.'

His voice was almost a whisper. 'Shit.'

I ran my hands through my hair. 'I vowed to Simone that I would never take my own life. I promised her.'

He looked into my eyes. 'You have wanted to?'

'When I see what's inside me, sometimes, yes.'

He turned away. 'I wouldn't blame you.' He sighed, his shoulders moving. Then he held his hand out. A bright glow appeared in his hand, and coalesced into a large silvery claw, gleaming on his palm. He held it towards me. 'Take this.'

I lifted the claw out of his hand. It was about ten centimetres long and the point was sharp. It appeared to be made of platinum.

'It's one of mine,' he said. 'If you feel that the dark urge is too strong, hold it in your hand and concentrate on me. I will come.'

'Thank you.'

He turned back to the arena. 'Time to present the trophies. Will you do them the honour?'

I checked the board. 'Michael came second. I'd love to give him the trophy. But we'll need to find a place to put them soon; his room is full of them.' I glanced at the Tiger. 'What would Xuan Wu do if you had to kill me to protect Simone?'

'He is not vengeful by nature, Emma. But his grief would be punishment enough.'

Both of us rose, smiling, to present the riders with their prizes.

CHAPTER TWENTY-FIVE

Louise's face changed and she looked up at me, more serious now. Her voice softened. 'Do you turn into a snake, Emma?'

I hesitated.

'Tell me,' she said softly.

I changed, and grabbed her. I quickly wrapped my coils around her. Squeeze this one. No venom; I wanted to feel her struggle. The demon in the corner and the delicious child would be next.

'Emma, what are you doing? Stop it!' Louise yelled, struggling frantically. Her arms pushed against my coils, only encouraging me to pull tighter. The feeling was fabulous.

'Emma, you're killing me, let go. *Let go*!' Louise shrieked.

If I could have grinned I would have. I checked the baby in the corner; yep, still there. If they tried to make a run for it I wasn't worried; I'd be faster than them.

Louise's voice became strangely deeper, sounding more masculine. 'Emma, you're hurting me, ease up!'

Something clicked inside my head. What?

'Emma, let go! You're hurting! Let *go*!' Louise's voice

was even deeper now, and her face was darker, and it wasn't the beautiful black of asphyxiation.

'Emma, you're *killing* me!'

Leo?

Something crashed and I was struggling with Leo; I had my arms around him and held him tight. I released him and cast around: I was in my bed back home at the Peak and Leo was sitting on the edge of the bed facing me. John stood just inside the door where he'd come racing in.

Leo's face was blank with horror. I threw myself into his arms. He hesitated for a moment, then held me and buried his face in my hair, stroking the back of my head.

'Leo, I'm sorry, I'm so sorry,' I said, gasping. 'I was dreaming. I didn't mean to hurt you.' I pulled back, hands on his arms, so that I could see his face. 'Are you okay?'

Leo smiled slightly. 'That's a hell of a grip you've got there, sweetheart.'

'Any cracked ribs?' John said softly without moving from the doorway.

I quickly checked Leo for injuries, and shook my head through the tears. 'No.'

'I think you'd better talk to Mr Chen,' Leo said, releasing me and rising. 'That was a hell of a dream.'

I wiped my eyes. Leo turned to go out. As he passed John, John put his hand on his shoulder and they shared a look that spoke volumes. Then John released Leo's shoulder and Leo went out.

John came and sat on the bed, far enough away not to hurt me. 'You dreamed you were the Serpent,' he said, and it wasn't a question.

I just nodded. Then I glanced at him. 'How did you know?'

'Emma can't do telepathy, but the Serpent obviously can,' John said. 'We all saw it. Simone's in with Ah Yat, too terrified to come near you.' He glanced down. 'Leo came in first, and saw the snake. He went to you anyway. Then you changed and grabbed him.'

'Oh my God,' I said softly. 'He came to me anyway, even though I was a snake?' I shook my head with disbelief.

John concentrated, and I heard a soft sound in the hallway outside the door. 'Emma?'

'Come in, Simone, I won't hurt you,' I said, full of misery.

Simone crept in, and then her little face filled with relief when she saw it was me. She threw herself into my arms. 'You dreamed you were a snake, Emma. You were killing your friend. It was horrible.'

'I know, pet,' I said, burying my face in her hair. 'It was horrible for me too.'

'It was just a dream,' John said. 'In dreams, we have no control. Emma would never hurt her friend or the baby in reality. Do you understand?'

I clutched Simone and both of us nodded.

Simone pulled away to smile at me. She put her little cool hand on my cheek. 'Daddy's right, Emma, don't be afraid. Your snake won't hurt anybody you love. It was just a dream.'

John moved closer and put his arm around my shoulders and the three of us held each other.

'Daddy, can I sleep in your bed tonight?' Simone said, her voice muffled.

'No,' John said. 'I need to sleep well and rebuild my energy. I'm sorry, sweetheart.'

'I understand,' Simone said. She glanced up at me. 'Emma?'

I hesitated, then decided. 'I nearly hurt Leo while I was dreaming, sweetheart. I don't think it would be a good idea.'

Simone dropped her head and nodded into my chest.

'Go and ask Leo,' I whispered.

'Leo says I kick too much.'

'I think, tonight, he won't care,' John said. 'I think he'll be glad to have you safe there with him.'

The Saturday after I returned from the Tiger's palace, I sat with Leo in his office during the morning break between classes and we had a coffee. It was one of the first times since my return that we could talk in peace and privacy. School was nearly finished for the year and we were making arrangements for the holidays.

'So we'll continue the roster,' Leo said. 'Just not staking out the school any more, minding her at home instead.'

'Works for me. She can come down to the Academy sometimes too.'

'Mr Chen said that's okay?'

'He said he'd prefer her here actually. With the Masters around her, on call.'

'What about Michael?'

'He can go to the Western Palace for a while,' I said. 'I've made arrangements: some time with his father, some with his mother. He'll be helping out in her shop, in between classes here at the Academy. He's asked to do some intensive energy work and advanced Weapons during the holidays. But the first three weeks he'll be in the West.'

'I'll miss him,' Leo said. 'He's good company.'

I nodded. I understood. I'd miss Michael as well.

Leo's face grew serious and he leaned over the desk to speak intensely to me. 'Any more dreams?'

I ran my hands through my hair. 'No.'

He leaned back. 'Probably caused by the shift in location, and the stress that you've been through — when that demon poisoned you. You'll be fine.'

I sighed. He was right. 'I don't know what I'd do without you sometimes, Leo.'

Leo smiled slightly, his small brown eyes sparkling.

Gold interrupted us. *Lady Emma, are you free to talk? I have something I would like to ask you.*

I tapped the stone to wake it. 'Can you talk to Gold, or should I call him?'

The stone paused, checking. 'No, I can talk to him.'

'What, Emma?' Leo said.

'Gold,' I said. 'Wants to ask me something. I'll get him to conference call. Tell him to talk to Leo too, stone.'

Okay.

'This would be easier using the phone,' Leo growled.

I have seen an extremely talented practitioner, Gold said, ignoring him. *Only been learning a year, but appears to be close to generating energy already. Very talented at hand-to-hand. I'd like to bring her in.*

'Where are you?' I said.

Christchurch.

'Where the hell is that?' Leo said, still growling.

'You *American*!' I said with scorn. 'It's in New Zealand. I can't see the problem, Gold. Does the family object? And if they do, why are you asking us? You know that if the family objects that's the end of it.'

She is twenty-eight years old. Married. Separated. Divorce will be final very soon.

'Children?' I said.

Of course not.

'Too old,' Leo said. 'Waste of time.'

'Talented at hand-to-hand?' I said.

Exceptionally talented.

'Bring her in,' I said. 'Not a problem at all.'

'She's too damn old, Emma,' Leo said. 'She'll be a total waste of both our time. Don't worry about it, Gold.'

'You think if somebody's twenty-eight they can't learn to generate energy?' I said.

'Nobody who started above the age of about twenty-two has ever made it,' Leo said with conviction. 'Ever.'

'Don't be ridiculous,' I said. 'You can start it older than that, it's just harder. We should give her a chance. Gold.'

My Lady.

'Ask her if she wants to come. She may need some convincing —'

They always do, ma'am.

'But get her to come. I want to teach her.'

'You are totally wasting your time, Emma,' Leo said. 'It's just not possible. Absolute maximum is twenty-five.'

'Absolute maximum?' I said.

'Absolute.'

'I bet you a beer that there's been a student who did it older.'

He walked right into it. 'No way. You're mixed up. We sometimes take older people for hand-to-hand, but nobody for energy that's older than twenty-two.'

'I bet you a beer. Older than twenty-five. Generated energy for the first time.'

He eyed me sceptically. 'Human?'

I nodded. 'Human.'

He pushed his huge dark hand over the desk and I shook it firmly.

'Okay then, smarty chick, who?' Leo said.

I crossed my arms over my chest. 'Me. I was twenty-nine when I generated my first chi.'

He looked at me blankly. Then he grinned. 'But you're not human.'

'Damn straight I am.'

'You're a goddamn *snake*, Emma. You're not human, and that's why you could do it.' He waved his hand over the desk at me. 'Look at you. Completely cold-blooded. One minute freaking out about your weird

325

dreams, the next minute making stupid damn bets that you've obviously lost, because you're *not human*.'

'I. Am. Human. And you owe me a beer.'

'I want a second opinion as to your humanity,' Leo said sternly. 'Lord Xuan.'

'Whoa,' I said. 'High stakes. Okay, a beer and dinner as well. If he says I'm not human, I'll buy.'

Leo pushed his chair away from the desk and rose. 'And if he says you are human, I'll buy. Let's go.'

John was sparring with the Weapons Master, Miss Chen. She swung a vicious metal spiked chain whip with three hooks on the end. He was bare-handed.

I winced. If she hit him with it, anywhere along its length, it would shred him. The spikes were on every link of the chain, razor-sharp and more than two centimetres long.

'He is completely crazy,' Leo said softly beside me, crossing his arms and leaning on the doorframe. 'Overconfident.'

Miss Chen was a tiny Chinese woman, around one and a half metres tall, who appeared to be in her early sixties with a round, grandmotherly face and a plump, matronly figure. Her hair was braided into a long queue that was almost completely white. Like most things on the Mountain, though, she was much more than she appeared. As Master of Weapons she was matched in skill only by John himself. The chain whip was one of the most difficult weapons of all to master.

Chen swung the whip at head height and John ducked easily underneath it. She snapped it back immediately, again at head height, and he backflipped. The chain spun between his head and his feet, missing both completely. He landed on his feet facing her, spread into a standard defensive position.

She snapped the whip back and paused.

Neither of them moved.

She performed a magnificent handless cartwheel and snapped out the whip just as her head brushed the floor. The whip snaked across the floor and wrapped around John's ankle. As soon as her feet hit the floor she snapped the whip back, but it was too late. He back-flipped again, using his bound ankle to jerk her off her feet. She fell onto her belly and slid across the floor, eventually conceding and releasing the whip.

The whip spun in the air as John flipped, and he somehow snapped his ankle so that the whip was released and coiled into his hand. He landed on his feet, once again in a defensive position, holding the coiled whip in his left hand.

'Damn,' she said loudly. 'You do that every single time.'

'What, win?' he said, relaxing out of the stance.

'Yeah,' she said, pulling herself to her feet and accepting the whip from him.

'Overconfident?' John said.

'Are you injured?' I said.

'It's nothing.'

'*What*?' Miss Chen said fiercely. 'What do you mean, *nothing*?'

'I knew it!' I shouted, racing as close as I could to John. I pointed at the ankle that had taken the whip. His black pants were shredded and dark with blood. 'Look. Bleeding. You stupid goddamn Turtle, I will *kill* you! Quick, look at it, Leo.'

Leo knelt and John tried to pull away. Miss Chen grabbed him and held his wrist. 'You stand right there, Dark Lord,' she said grimly. 'Don't you dare move.'

Leo pulled the bottom of John's track pants up and hissed. I knelt beside him and watched. 'Some of these are nearly two centimetres deep. He'll need stitches,' Leo said.

'Get Meredith,' I said.

'You can't, my Lady,' Miss Chen said. 'Nobody can heal him with energy — it would destroy anybody who tried it. And he can't heal this himself, he's too drained. This will have to heal normally, and it will take a long time in his current state.' She glared at John. 'You said it would be *okay*.'

'It is,' John said.

We took him down to the infirmary where the Academy doctor saw to him. She used local anaesthetic to numb the wounds before she would stitch them, despite John's protests. Normally an energy worker would numb any injury sites using the meridians, but nobody could do it for John without putting themselves in major peril. And we couldn't find a set of acupuncture needles; we never needed them.

'You should never have done that!' I said.

'You cannot stop me from being what I am,' John said calmly as Regina worked with the needle on his lacerated ankle.

'The pain will wear you out and use your energy,' I said fiercely. 'We'll all suffer for this. Being in constant pain is exhausting.'

'Is it?' John said, sitting straighter. 'I didn't know that.'

'We have a choice,' Leo said. 'Either feed you pain-relieving drugs or let you suffer. Either way, you will burn energy. This is a no-win situation.'

John was silent, his face rigid.

'You didn't know, did you?' I said softly. 'You've never been in real pain for any length of time before. You've always been able to heal yourself.'

'He was in pain after the Mountain,' Leo said. 'In the hospital.'

'They fed him some heavyweight stuff there,' I said.

'Nearly pushed him over the edge, I think. And then Ms Kwan fixed him up.'

'I'm right here,' John said.

'We are well aware of that,' I said. 'Decision time. Drugs, or leave it?'

'Leave it,' John said.

'Try the drugs first,' Regina said. 'Watch his energy. When the medication wears off, check again. Compare. I think you will find that the drugs make it easier for him.'

'No Western pills,' John said. 'Only herbs.'

'Whatever,' I said.

'The herbs and the Western medicine have the same effect, but the herbs must be boiled for at least an hour and a half and taste foul,' Regina said. 'I'll give him some analgesics and anti-inflammatories.' She paused, musing. 'I wonder if it will become infected, considering his current weakened state.'

'I'm still right here,' John growled.

'Leo?' I said.

Leo paused, then understood the question. 'I'm okay.'

'Don't worry about antibiotics. I don't think he'll need them if Leo's okay,' I said.

Regina studied Leo. 'What?'

Leo didn't say anything and I slapped my forehead with my palm. '*Men!*'

'Oh, dear Lord,' Regina said softly. 'Why didn't anybody tell me?' She raced to her desk and scrabbled through the drawers. 'I'll need prescriptions right away. It will take *weeks* for me to get the right cocktail of drugs from the States or Australia, and acquiring them without giving anything away about our operation will be incredibly difficult. *Damn!*' She rounded on Leo. 'How bad was it? It was before you went to Malaysia, wasn't it? Tell me *now*.'

Leo slowly and gracefully rose to his feet, towering over all of us. His face was rigid.

He fell to one knee before me and saluted, head bowed. 'My Lady,' he said, his voice hoarse. 'I wish to make a request.'

I didn't move, watching him. 'Regina,' I said softly without turning to her, 'don't worry about the AIDS drugs. DNR. I'll manage the pain for him as much as I can.' I heaved a deep sigh. 'Leave it.'

Leo rose with a great deal of dignity and bowed from the waist to me. 'I thank you, my Lady,' he said softly. He bowed to John. 'My Lord.'

John didn't say anything but his face was tight.

Regina turned away and thumped the desk.

'Let's take him home,' I said with resignation.

'I don't need to be taken home,' John said.

'No, what you need is to be left in the middle of the street across the tram tracks,' Leo said with feeling. 'Let's get Simone and go.'

We put him in the front of the car. As Leo guided him in, he hissed with pain. 'I took the drugs,' he said. 'They didn't work.'

'I think they did, but not completely,' I said, buckling Simone into the seat in the back. 'You'll still be in quite a lot of pain anyway.'

'I don't know how you humans live with it,' he said.

'Is Emma human?' Leo said quickly as he pulled himself into the driver's seat.

John paused, the seatbelt buckle halfway into its slot. He pushed the buckle all the way in and faced the front. 'Interesting question. Hard to say.'

'We need an answer. There's dinner riding on it,' I said.

John didn't turn. 'Let me think about it.'

'If you need to think about it then she's not human,'

330

Leo said. 'If she's human, you'd be able to say so right away. If you have to think about it then she's not.'

'I think he's right,' John said.

'Emma is human,' Simone said with conviction. 'But the snake isn't human.'

'Does that mean that I'm not the snake?' I said.

'That's right,' Simone said, facing the front of the car. 'Emma's human, but the snake isn't.'

'I think she's right,' John said.

'We can't both be right,' Leo said.

'I am human,' I said. 'I can't do anything that a very talented human can't do.'

'Yes, you can,' John said. 'Humans cannot work with shen. Humans cannot heal with energy. Humans cannot run one hundred metres in three seconds.' He gestured at Leo next to him in the front. 'Absolutely no human could lift him with one arm.'

'I win, Emma,' Leo said. 'Face it. You're not human.'

'What am I then?'

Nobody said anything.

We went to the American restaurant in the Peak Tower and Leo ordered the most massive steak that I had ever seen, so rare it was still mooing. I ordered vegetarian pasta.

I took a sip of the beer and winced.

'What?' Leo said.

I studied the bottle. 'Ever since I started working with energy, alcohol tastes strange. Wrong. I don't like it any more.' I put the bottle down and glanced around for a waiter. 'Mineral water.'

After the waiter had brought the mineral water I poked my fork into my pasta with amusement. 'I might as well shave my head and start wearing brown Taoist nun's robes,' I said. 'No meat, no alcohol, no sex. I'm a freaking nun.'

'At least if you dressed like that you'd be tidy,' Leo said. 'You wouldn't always look like you fell out of bed in the clothes you wore the night before.'

I reached across the table and gave him a push. 'Oh, thank you *very much*.'

'Not no sex,' he said, grinning.

I stiffened. 'How the hell do you know about that?'

The grin didn't shift. 'Obvious. I heard you two sneak out. Gone all night.'

I dropped my head. 'That was the last time, Leo.'

He leaned across the table and took my hand. 'You can't be sure of that, sweetheart. You two might have another chance. Remember what the Tiger said.'

'No,' I said, looking up into his eyes. 'That was the last time. I know. You know those kids — Scott and Tymen? They'll be like brothers one day. I *know*.'

'How do you know?' Leo said, his face becoming sterner. 'What do you mean, you *know*?'

'I just know,' I moaned, leaning my chin on my hand. 'I know absolutely for a fact. Scott and Tymen will be like brothers, and John and I will not have another chance before he goes.' Suddenly I knew something else, and I was so sure of the feeling it took my breath away. 'And we will accept the girl from New Zealand and she will do remarkable things.'

'You had that look on your face again,' Leo said, studying me.

'I had that feeling again,' I said. 'I *know*.'

Leo dropped my hand and pulled his own away. 'You really *are* becoming an Immortal.'

I ran my hands through my hair. 'I hope so, Leo, and I hope you do too.'

'Eat your dinner,' he said, picking up his steak knife and slicing into the enormous slab of bleeding meat. 'I can't become an Immortal. If I had to go vegetarian it would kill me.'

CHAPTER TWENTY-SIX

M y parents insisted on coming down from the palace to attend Simone's end-of-school concert. Simone was delighted, and my parents were too. She really was becoming like a granddaughter to them.

I drove my parents and Michael in my car, and Leo drove John and Simone. Before we left, Leo jokingly told me that we needed to buy a van to carry our growing family. I glared at him.

We parked at a nearby shopping centre; our special parking treatment wasn't valid on a night where everybody would be attending. A couple of the Tiger's Horsemen met us at the car park — my parents' guards.

We were all alert as we walked over to the school, even my parents. They'd been attacked by demons before while out with us. John was doing his best not to limp, but it was obvious that the ankle was still giving him trouble, even after a week. Regina had taken the stitches out that morning.

Simone was entirely unaffected by the danger. She held my hand and skipped beside me, prattling excitedly about her part in the performance. Her class was reciting a poem in Putonghua about tigers, complete with tiger masks and costumes.

When we reached the school, the White Tiger was waiting for us at the door with a satisfied grin. He wanted to see Simone's class recitation too. Simone was thrilled and ran to him. He hoisted and spun her, making her squeal.

We went inside and sat without incident. The Tiger made himself invisible and stood near the stage, guarding. The Horsemen guarded the doors, and Leo leaned against the wall at one side of the auditorium, dark and unmoving.

Michael was doing something behind the scenes with the lighting for the production so we didn't see him, but Simone's little class doing their tiger poem were delightful. John had a proud smile a mile wide as he watched his daughter perform. I glanced at him questioningly a few times and he silently shook his head. About halfway through I began to relax; obviously they weren't willing to try us with so many people around.

When the show was finished we all met outside the auditorium.

'Do you want to come back to the West now, or go up to the Peak for a while?' the Tiger asked my parents.

'Is it safe for us to stay?' my father said.

'Should be okay if you're with me,' the Tiger said.

'Ah Bai,' John said, 'it would be better if you take Simone directly to the Peak. I will take Emma. Leo and Michael can take Brendan and Barbara. We know who they're after.'

The Tiger gestured and the Horsemen approached from where they'd been guarding the perimeter of our little group. 'One in each car.'

'My Lord,' the Horsemen said.

'I'll see you at the Peak,' the Tiger said. He glanced down at Simone. 'Come on, little tiger. I'll take you home and you can play with the big tiger.'

'She's really getting far too old for this,' I said as they disappeared together, Simone wearing a cheeky grin.

All of us were tense and alert as we walked back to the car park. John concentrated, and Gold appeared in the middle of the group.

'Can you sense anything?' my father said, his voice low.

'No,' John said. He concentrated again and his eyes turned inward as he walked. 'Ah Bai and Simone are back at the Peak, and they are fine.' He shrugged. 'Maybe they won't try for us with so many guards.'

'I hope not,' I said as we paid the parking tickets.

We reached the cars without incident.

'Anything?' I whispered.

John and Gold shook their heads.

'I'll take Emma. Gold, Two Sixty, with us,' John said, gesturing towards the smaller car. 'Leo, Michael, Two Seven Three with Emma's parents in the big car.'

Leo pulled himself into the driver's seat of the big car. The Horseman sat in the middle of the back seat, with one of my parents on either side of him. As my parents entered the car the Horseman pulled a short sword out of a scabbard he'd had hiding on his back under his shirt and rested it across his knees. Michael retrieved his white katana from the trunk of the big car and sat in the front passenger side with it across his knees.

'In, Emma,' John said, having a last look around before he entered the smaller car.

I moved to sit in the front passenger side.

'No, in the back, between Gold and the Horseman.'

I shrugged and sat between them; I knew why.

'What are the chances?' the Horseman said softly.

'No idea,' Gold said. 'Last time they attacked before we made it to the car park.' He hesitated. 'Emma, please wake my parent, it may be useful.'

335

I tapped the stone.

'Hm?' it said.

'We're driving home from the concert, Dad,' Gold said, looking around as John eased the car towards the exit. Leo followed us. 'Help keep a lookout, will you?'

'Not a problem,' the stone said. Its voice became petulant. 'I missed Simone's poem? I was looking forward to seeing that.'

'Gold,' John said, 'pull down Seven Stars. Lay it on the passenger seat.'

Gold lowered his head and concentrated. The sword appeared, leaning on the seat next to John. I peered around to see it; I'd never had a good look at it before.

Gold hadn't worried about the scabbard: the blade was bare. The sword was jet black, with seven large circular indentations running down its length. Each indentation centred on a hole, about two centimetres across, right through the sword. The guard was a traditional Chinese style, silver and elaborately carved, but I couldn't see the details of the carving. The handle appeared to be white stone. The sword must have been nearly two metres long. No wonder he needed to be in Celestial Form to wield it fully.

'Whoa,' the Horseman said. 'Seven Stars. Wish I had a camera.'

'It's exquisite,' I said over the back of the seat.

'One day you'll see it shine,' John said.

'Is it usable even if you can't load it?' I whispered.

'It's a blade. It's big. It's sharp. It will do the job,' he said. 'Lean back between your guards. Provide less of a target. We cannot use firearms against them, but they can certainly use them against us.'

I huddled back between Gold and the Horseman. Gold concentrated and took battle form: his human shape made of quartz with gleaming veins of gold. The suspension of the car shifted underneath his weight.

'You sense something?' I said.

'No,' Gold said, his mouth not moving. 'Just being careful.'

We travelled up Waterloo Road, long and straight with high rises on either side. The ground-floor levels of the apartment blocks weren't gardens, they were paved car parks. We travelled through three or four sets of traffic lights.

'Shit,' John said softly, checking the rear-view mirror. He concentrated, then raised his voice. 'He can't hear me, Gold, and he's getting out of the car. Get back there *now*!'

Gold lowered his head and disappeared.

I didn't say anything. John was concentrating on driving, and besides, I had a good idea what had happened. John couldn't do a U-turn — there was a large concrete divider between the traffic lanes.

'Damn,' John said. His voice became fierce. 'I don't care, stop him!'

He cut through three lanes of traffic from the right lane to the left, causing cars to screech their brakes behind us. He drove like a maniac for three hundred metres, then exited to the left so quickly that the tyres on the Mercedes squealed.

'This is a direct order, Michael, Gold. Kill him now,' John said. 'Take his head immediately. Do it.'

When he was on the exit road he raced at a dangerous speed up the right lane, looking for a place to perform a U-turn, but once again the road was separated by concrete dividers.

'Kill him! I know he's controlled. Kill him anyway!' John shouted.

We came to a place where the dividers were removable metal gates rather than concrete, to allow access by emergency services. John put the hazard lights on, stopped the Mercedes next to the dividers, and concentrated.

The dividers collapsed inward. Every weld on the metal disintegrated, turning the gates into useless pieces of metal pipe. John eased the Mercedes through into the oncoming traffic, ignoring the horns from other drivers. The underside of the car grated painfully on the pipes, then we were clear.

John took off again, going the other way. 'Kill Leo *now!* He's far too dangerous to let live. Just take his head!'

We raced for about five hundred metres, then took an overpass to go back on Waterloo Road, in the opposite direction from before.

John's eyes unfocused and he relaxed. 'Michael stopped him. Your parents are okay, Emma.'

'Michael killed Leo?' I whispered.

John slowed the car as we merged with the Waterloo Road traffic. 'No,' he said. 'Michael and Gold both disobeyed a direct order and are in serious trouble. Leo is still alive.'

'Were they hit from behind?'

'Yes. Somehow the demons in the car that hit them gained control of Leo. Leo killed the Horseman and was about to grab your parents when Gold and Michael subdued him together. They are both in extremely serious trouble. They should have taken his head when they had the chance.'

The Horseman next to me hissed under his breath.

We reached the scene of the accident. John checked them carefully as he drove past the other way, then turned left. We travelled through the quiet backstreets of Kowloon Tong until we found a place where we could turn right to return to Waterloo Road. We passed Kitty Kwok's kindergarten on the way; it was only about five blocks from the school.

'Were Gold or Michael injured?' I said.

'Michael,' John said. 'Your parents are okay. Gold is uninjured. Apparently Leo received the worst of it.

Gold and Michael had to use a great deal of force to subdue him, and the demons tried to kill him after he went down.'

'How did they gain control of him?' I said as John turned on the hazard lights and pulled in behind the ambulance attending the two cars.

'I don't know. And we may never have the chance to find out, love,' John said, gesturing towards the gurney being lifted into the ambulance.

Michael was taken in the ambulance as well, Gold accompanying him. John drove me and my parents directly back to the Peak with the remaining Horseman. The Tiger and Simone waited for us in the living room, quiet and subdued. When we came through the door Simone ran straight to her father. He lifted her and held her close.

'Is Leo okay, Daddy?' she said into his shoulder.

'Michael says they don't know yet,' John said, holding her tight. 'But Meredith is there, looking after him. We'll just have to wait and see.'

She pulled back so that she could see his face. 'I want to go to the hospital and see Leo.'

'If you don't mind, Brendan, Barbara, could you care for Simone for a short time while we discuss this?' John said.

My parents didn't say anything, they just nodded grimly. John lowered Simone, and my mother came forward to take her hand and lead her into her bedroom.

My father turned to speak over his shoulder to me. 'Don't worry, Emma, we're fine. Go and talk to John.'

John, the Tiger and I went into the dining room. Ah Yat brought us a pot of tea without being asked.

'Is Leo still controlled?' I said.

'It's hard to say,' John said. 'He hasn't come around yet. Right now, though, he isn't capable of hurting anything. Gold and Michael did an extremely good job on him. They came very close to following my orders. Then the demons tried to kill him outright.'

Gold appeared beside John, still in his battle form, all of stone. He held his hand out. 'We stones have been arrogant for years about our ability to transcend normal animal energies. We have thought ourselves aloof and superior. And boy, have we been wrong.'

Gold placed a small jet-black pebble, about two centimetres across, onto the table. 'This was in the Lion's pocket,' he said. 'Somebody probably slipped it onto him while we were at the concert.'

We all leaned forward to study the stone.

'Let me see, Emma,' the stone in my ring said. 'Put me on the table next to it.'

I took the ring off my hand and moved it near the black stone. 'Not too close!' it squawked, and I placed it about ten centimetres away.

'Damn,' the stone said. 'I'm speechless. How the hell did he manage to do this?'

Gold changed back to his normal human form, wearing a pair of tan slacks and a tan polo shirt. His face was very grim. 'This was once one of us, my Lord. Now, it is less than nothing.'

I inhaled sharply with shock. 'This was a stone Shen?'

Gold nodded. 'I knew this one too. She was a wonderful person. There is nothing left of her that can be salvaged.' He looked away, his face full of pain.

'My Lord Bai Hu, Exalted Emperor of the Western Heavens,' the stone in my ring said very formally.

'Jade Building Block of the World,' the Tiger said.

'My Lord,' the stone said, not quite as formal, 'I'd like your permission to bring the opal in on this. The opal can take this ...' It hesitated, as if taking a deep breath. 'This *thing* and show it to the Grandmother. It is vitally important that she sees this.'

'The Grandmother speaks to us all,' Gold said, turning back so that he could see the black stone. 'If she is aware of this ... *thing*, then we are all aware. We will have the knowledge to avoid such a thing happening in the future.'

'Granted,' the Tiger said, just as grim. 'Gold can come with me to the palace to talk to Amanda, then the opal can go and report.'

I glanced at Gold. 'Does Leo know that he was controlled and that it wasn't his fault?'

'He hasn't come around yet, but he'll still think it's his fault anyway, ma'am,' Gold said sadly. 'He'll be full of guilt that they managed to place this thing on him in the first place.'

'Come on, Gold, let's go and talk to this opal,' the Tiger said, and both he and Gold disappeared, taking the black stone with them. I put the jade ring back onto my finger.

'What's your name, Two Sixty?' I asked the Horseman.

'Derek,' he said with a sad smile. 'I hope my dad remembers to come back for me. This is the second time this year he's left me stranded on the Earthly.'

John's eyes turned inwards. 'Leo will survive. They moved him into intensive care. Meredith is with him, she appears as his wife.' He smiled slightly. 'Two Sixty, your father left you here deliberately, I think, to take up Leo's duties while he recuperates.'

'No! Really?' The Horseman's eyes unfocused; obviously his father was speaking to him. He grinned broadly. '*Hot damn!*'

'I'd like to go and see Leo,' I said. 'I know Simone would too. How can we do it so we're safe?'

'I will take you,' John said, rising. 'Obviously they are still too cowardly to face me. Leo will be harmless now that the stone has been removed. Two Sixty, stay here and guard the Dark Lady's parents. Ah Yat!'

Ah Yat poked her head through the doorway.

John gestured towards Derek. 'This one is staying in the room next to Michael's. Arrange it while Emma, Simone and I go to the hospital.'

'My Lord,' Ah Yat said, and her head disappeared around the door.

'You know what to do,' John said.

Derek saluted. 'My Lord.' He was hard-pressed to keep the delight from his face. 'I am extremely glad the Lion will be all right. All of us Horsemen have a tremendous amount of respect for him. We'll be gunning for him to recover quickly.' He grinned again. 'And *damn*, this is an honour to be serving you in his place.'

'Come on, Emma,' John said. 'Let's go to the hospital and try to convince Leo that he isn't the worst guard on Earth.'

'Not going to happen, John,' I said softly as I followed him out.

The staff said children weren't allowed in intensive care. Meredith came out in the form of a portly black woman in her mid-thirties and coerced them into letting Simone in. We went into the ward together. Leo was on a number of life-support machines, but they were completely silent; there wasn't the usual heartbeat blip sound that was so popular on television.

My heart twisted when I saw the signs above his bed. A brilliant black-on-yellow 'Biohazard' sign, and next to it a card with 'HIV+' scrawled on it in marker. Meredith had told them.

Meredith sat next to Leo and took his hand. She appeared to be holding his hand like a stricken wife, but she was actively healing him through the contact.

342

Michael leaned against the wall in the far corner of the room, his arms crossed, his school shirt bloodied on one shoulder. He didn't attempt to salute John, he just nodded. 'My Lord.' He winced. 'Leo tried to take my head off, and missed. He hit my shoulder. I healed the wound, but I'm afraid I'll be unable to salute you correctly for a while.'

'Are you sure you're okay?' I said quickly.

'I'm fine,' he said, but he didn't shrug. 'Wait until Katherine sees the scar. You'll have to help me think of a story to tell her.'

'I thought it was Betty,' I said.

'Katherine right now,' Michael said, his eyes sparkling.

'Go outside and wait,' John said. 'Rest the shoulder.'

'My Lord,' Michael said, then hesitated. He dropped his voice. 'My Lord. I know I disobeyed a direct order, but I couldn't kill him. Not Leo. Permission to remain here with him.'

'Granted,' John said, and Michael leaned back against the wall.

John sat down on the other side of Leo from Meredith and Simone wriggled into his lap. Simone's eyes had become very wide when she saw the tubes and machines, but now she seemed only concerned. She reached over and took Leo's hand, holding it tight.

I moved behind Meredith and put my hand on her shoulder, examining Leo through her. I gasped when I saw the extent of the injuries.

'How bad is it?' John said softly.

'It's like someone hit him with a sledgehammer,' I said. 'Everything inside is bruised and bleeding. Most of his ribs are cracked. His breastbone is fractured. Even his heart is damaged.' I glanced over at Michael. 'You did this?'

'I had to hit him hard to stop him, but I didn't do that,' Michael said. 'When he went down, one of the demons hit him with some sort of black energy, right in the middle of his chest. I think if it weren't for Master Liu's healing skills, he'd be dead.'

Meredith nodded without saying anything.

'Was it like black chi?' I said, desperate.

'No,' Michael said. 'Nothing like anything I've ever seen before. It wasn't chi, I'm sure. It was more like ...' He paused and thought. 'It was more like pure demon essence, thrown straight at Leo.'

'Not possible,' John said. 'They can't throw demon essence.'

'And they can't kill stone Shen,' I said.

'A stone Shen was killed? Not *Gold*?' Michael cried, horrified.

'Gold's okay,' I said. 'Somebody slipped a stone into Leo's pocket that put him under their control. It was a stone Shen that had been changed somehow into an object. No longer intelligent or sentient, just a rock. Gold is reporting to the Grandmother.'

'He's coming around,' Meredith said softly. 'Lord Xuan, take his hand.'

John didn't question her, he just took Leo's hand out of Simone's and held it himself. I sat carefully on the bed next to Leo's massive thighs. I checked with Meredith and she nodded: I was okay to sit there.

Leo's dark face screwed into a grimace of pain and then his eyes fluttered open.

Michael quickly moved to stand behind Meredith.

Meredith lowered her head and concentrated. 'I'm just relieving some of the pain that he's feeling when he breathes. You can talk to him for a few minutes, then I'll put him under again. It's hurting him too much to breathe.'

'My Lord,' Leo said, staring at the ceiling. 'Lord Xuan. Simone.' His eyes closed again. 'Emma? Michael?'

'We're all here, Leo,' John said, leaning forward over Simone and holding Leo's hand tightly. 'We're all safe.'

Leo breathed a huge sigh of relief, then coughed, a strangled sound. He gasped with the pain. 'What happened to me?'

'Your mind was controlled by a demon. You probably don't remember anything,' I said. 'Everybody's safe. If it hurts too much, say so, and Meredith will put you under again.'

'Meredith's here?' Leo said. 'Master Liu?'

'I'm here, Leo,' Meredith said. 'We're all here. Michael too.'

'Hey, Leo,' Michael said, his voice full of affection. 'That demon certainly hit you hard.'

'Hey, Michael,' Leo said. He turned his head, not seeing. 'Simone? Simone, sweetheart? Are you okay?'

'I'm fine, Leo,' Simone said, her little voice as stricken as her face. 'Does it hurt?'

Leo coughed again, then moaned. 'It hurts a little bit. But I don't care, sweetheart, 'cause you're okay.'

Simone was silent, her eyes still wide.

'What happened wasn't your fault, Leo,' I said, rubbing the blanket that covered his leg. 'You were controlled by a demon. Rest, get better, and then we'll take you home. I think you should put him back under now, Meredith.'

'Wait,' Leo gasped, a heavy breath.

We all hesitated.

Leo was silent for a while. Then, 'I don't know what to say.'

'You don't need to say anything,' John said, still grasping Leo's hand. 'Concentrate on recovering. That's all you need to do.'

'Somebody needs to guard Simone at school,' Leo said. 'Somebody needs to guard Emma, and Simone.' His strained voice became urgent. 'The family must be guarded. I have to get out of here!'

'Simone's school is finished for the year, Leo,' I said gently. 'She can spend her holidays at the Academy where she'll be safe. I'll be in the Academy too. You don't need to worry about us.' I patted his leg. 'Worry about yourself for a change, and concentrate on getting better.'

'Is that an order?' Leo breathed with some of his old defiance.

'Damn straight it is. Now Meredith's putting you back to sleep, and I'll be here to visit you tomorrow morning, first thing. Okay?'

'Okay,' Leo said, but he was already asleep before he'd finished saying it.

A week later we brought Leo home from the hospital. He was still very weak, even with the additional assistance in healing from Meredith. I held one arm and John held the other as we guided him into his room.

We led him to his bed, turned him around, and gently lowered him to sit. He winced; he was still very sore inside. I bent and pulled his loafers off, and John moved to undo the buttons on his shirt.

'Stop,' Leo said, and we both hesitated. 'Emma, Mr Chen, please don't do this.'

I rose to speak to him at his level. His face was full of misery. 'Who else can do it?' I smiled and shrugged, patting his arm. 'You're like a brother to me, Leo.'

Leo glanced from me to John.

'I'll go out,' John said.

'Wait,' Leo said, and John hesitated. 'My Lord, could you ask Michael if he would be willing?'

John concentrated, his eyes unfocusing. 'Michael is on his way. Are you sure?'

Michael tapped on the door and came in.

'I'm sure,' Leo said. 'Out. Both of you.'

Michael stood to one side and let us leave.

'Leo and Michael?' John whispered as he closed the door.

'Of course not,' I whispered back impatiently. 'Leo's like a father to Michael, that's why he asked for him.' We went back up the hall towards the training room; we'd decided by silent mutual agreement to do some weapons work together. 'You really don't understand people very well sometimes, John.'

'I don't think I ever will,' John said as he held the training room door open for me.

'What about me?' I said as I collected my sword.

'Especially you,' he said as he studied the weapons on the wall, and eventually selected a pair of *sais*. He turned to face me, spinning them appraisingly in his hands.

I pulled out my sword and tossed the scabbard aside. 'Okay, Raphael, do your worst.'

'See?' he said, and attacked.

CHAPTER TWENTY-SEVEN

The New Zealand woman Gold had recruited was called Amy. She was half-Chinese and exceptionally talented. She and I became good friends very quickly; not surprisingly, we had a lot in common. She knew about Chinese culture from her Chinese father, and the Australian and New Zealand cultures were very similar. She was friendly and happy and the difficulties she'd had in her marriage didn't seem to have affected her much at all.

I began to suspect there was something special about her when she generated chi the first time she tried. I sat her in my office to speak to her.

'Amy, you remember you swore allegiance?' I said.

'Yes, ma'am.'

'Okay then, keep that in mind. I want some answers.'

Amy straightened.

'First: have you really been studying the Arts for only a year?'

'Yes. I wanted something to get me out, something different. Something that would make me feel ...' She hesitated, searching for the words. '*Strong* again. I was surprised that I turned out to be so good at it.'

'Okay,' I said. 'Second: are you completely human?'

Her face went strange and I interrupted her before she could say anything. 'Wait.' I tapped the stone.

'I was sleeping, Emma.'

'You will be sleeping in the water if you talk back to me again,' I said. I saw Amy's face. 'The stone in this ring is sentient, abusive, noisy, arrogant and lazy.'

'You forgot bad-tempered,' the stone said.

'Yeah.' I asked it silently to check whether Amy was telling the truth. It agreed just as silently. Both of us turned back to Amy.

'Amy,' I said, 'are you human? Tell me the truth.'

Amy hesitated, then sighed. 'I hope so.'

True.

'Do you suspect you may not be human?' I said.

Amy shrugged. 'I'm really talented. Everybody else reacted so badly when I generated the chi; I didn't even know I wasn't supposed to be able to do it yet.'

I had a sudden feeling of *déjà vu*.

True.

'I would like to look inside you,' I said. 'Do you give your permission?'

Amy's eyes went wide.

'It won't hurt,' I said. 'In fact, I won't do it myself at all; only a Shen can do it. It is a completely painless process, the only discomfort being the fact that the Shen will be able to see everything inside you. Everything. But I would like to confirm that you are completely human.'

'Are you worried about me?' she asked quietly. 'I know *I* am.'

True.

I smiled and patted her hand. 'I'm sure we won't find anything.'

She smiled slightly in response. 'Which Shen?'

'Probably Gold,' I said. 'He's the best one available

349

right now. All the other Academy Shen are flat out with the new recruits, and Jade's off doing some sort of dragon thing. Besides, as a new student, you know Gold already.'

She shrugged, the smile widening a little. 'Okay.' She shook her head. 'Who would believe it? That I'm in a martial arts school run by a turtle, taught by a snake, side by side with a dragon and a stone?'

'Freaked my parents out completely,' I said. 'Don't tell your family.'

'They think I'm a NET teacher, getting away from my husband while the divorce papers go through,' she said. 'Native English-speaker Teaching scheme.'

'Most of our older students' parents think that,' I said. 'If they're underage of course we tell the parents they're coming to learn the Arts, but if the student is an adult, like you, it's up to you to choose what to tell them.' I paused, then decided. I took the ring off my finger and handed it to her. 'Put this on for a moment.'

She studied it, turning it over in her fingers, then slipped it onto the smallest finger of her left hand.

'Okay,' I said. 'Give it back.'

She shrugged and returned it to me.

'Good,' I said. 'I'll arrange a time for you to be examined by Gold. Don't worry, you know him already. He's okay.'

'Is that the ring?' she said.

'Yep. I just had the stone look at you as well.'

'Did it find anything?'

'No,' the stone said. 'Amy, you are a perfectly normal human being. Just extremely talented.'

She sagged with relief.

I didn't tell her it was exactly the same thing the stone had said about me.

She smiled. 'Why does it sound English?'

'To annoy me,' I said. 'Go back to the Folly. I'll contact you later and we'll have you checked out.'

'Why do you call it the Folly?' she said. 'Both the student residences are called the Folly — the Old Folly and the New Folly.'

I laughed. 'Full name is Turtle's Folly. Mr Chen bought the Old Folly at the top of the market, paid double the current market value for it. He lost a serious amount of money on it.'

She smiled wryly. 'I thought gods didn't make mistakes.'

'This one has made some absolutely spectacular ones.' I spread my hands. 'I'm one of the biggest, according to him.'

'Isn't calling someone a "turtle" here in Hong Kong an insult?'

'Damn straight. Don't call it Turtle's Folly when the Chinese kids are around; some of them are sensitive about it.'

'And if someone mentions it in front of the Dark Lord, does he get very mad?'

'No,' I said. 'He's thoroughly delighted with the name. I wish I'd never thought of it, because he had it translated, and has a piece of calligraphy hidden away somewhere that he wants to put in brass above the door.'

Her mouth dropped open.

'Go home, and don't worry. The worst we'll probably find is that you're a lost Shen, or half Shen, or something like that, and you'll have extra talents we can bring on.'

'I just want to be completely human,' Amy said. She saluted me and left, closing the door softly behind her.

'Well?' I said.

'There's something there,' it said, 'but I'm not sure what it is. Wait until Gold has a look at her. We'll both see inside.'

'Is it possible that she's a demon?'

The stone hesitated. I heard it hesitate.

'Well?'

The stone's voice was completely emotionless. 'Yes, Emma, it is quite possible.'

'But she doesn't know if she is?'

'Correct,' the stone said.

'Has this happened before? Somebody was a demon but didn't know about it?'

The stone hesitated, then obviously decided to answer before I could shout at it. 'Yes, of course. It was a favourite trick of the previous King. Create a half demon, half human. Plant a trigger in it, similar to a program. The demon itself is unaware of its true nature. When the time is right, the trigger is activated and the demon usually self-destructs, taking all around with it.'

'Holy shit,' I said softly. 'Why didn't John tell me about this?'

'Two reasons,' the stone said. 'The first is obvious. The second is that the current King is slightly more honourable than its predecessor and does not engage in this sort of underhand activity.'

'He can be pretty underhand when he wants to,' I said grimly.

'He is a Demon King.'

'Will Gold be able to tell if Amy is a demon?' I said.

'Yes.'

'You sure?'

If the stone could sigh it would have. 'Of course. He is my son.'

'You mean *child*.'

The stone didn't speak to me for a long time after that.

I arranged the examination for two days later so that John and Meredith could be present as well as Gold and me: John for his demon-spotting skills, and Meredith as the best demon-binder on the Mountain. JC Poon, the Demon Master, was on call, but didn't need to be present unless Amy was a demon and was either bound or tamed. If she turned and attacked us we would destroy her and he wouldn't be needed at all.

We used a training room on the twenty-second floor by silent mutual agreement. It would be the best place if she turned; the seniors and Celestials would be close by.

Amy walked in and stopped dead when she saw all of us. Her face went ashen, then she remembered and fell to one knee, saluting us all.

'Come in, Amy,' I said, as gently as I could. 'I think you know everybody. Do you know Meredith?'

Amy shook her head, her eyes wide. She was panicking. She knew something was up.

I gestured towards Meredith. 'Master Liu, Energy Master, Tai Chi Master.'

Amy saluted Meredith and Meredith nodded back, her angular, intelligent face serious. She was already examining Amy.

'Okay, Amy,' I said, trying to be brisk and businesslike. She broadcast raw terror. 'Sit cross-legged on the floor in the centre of the room and Gold will have a look inside you.'

She did as she was told.

Gold knelt behind her and put his hands on her shoulders. 'Relax, dear. I won't hurt you. Everything will be just fine.'

Amy was shaking.

Gold didn't move, but I saw him contact Meredith. Meredith silently moved forward and put her hand on top of Amy's head.

Amy went rigid at the touch and then her face went slack. Gold nodded and Meredith moved away.

Human at the top level, Gold said. *My Lady, could you bring my parent here, please? I would like it to provide a second opinion.*

I moved quietly to Gold and put the stone in front of him. I released it, and it hovered in front of Gold's face, between his nose and the back of Amy's head. Gold nodded, his face still full of concentration.

Going deeper. Dad?

Human. No apparent demonic attributes at any of the top levels, the stone said.

Gold stiffened. *What a bastard.*

With you there, the stone said. *No wonder she wanted to learn to defend herself.*

Gold sighed, his shoulders moving. *Going deeper.*

What was that? the stone said.

What? Gold said.

For a moment there ... nothing.

My Lord Xuan, please take a quick look, Gold said. *Through me, so that you cannot harm her.*

John approached them and bent to place his hand on Gold's shoulder. His face went rigid with concentration, then he released Gold and moved back.

Definitely not a demon, John said. *Could be something else there, but it's so well hidden it's hard to say. Probably just exceptional talent. I have seen humans this talented before. If a talented human suffers such as she has, it can also bring forward the energy control.* He smiled. *Suffering brings wisdom and control.*

The ring rose above Gold and returned to me, and I picked it out of the air. Gold took his hands away from Amy's shoulders and rose.

Meredith crouched beside Amy and put her hand on Amy's shoulder. 'We're finished now, dear.'

Amy shook herself out, then heaved a huge sigh and pulled herself to her feet, swaying slightly. Meredith held her elbow to help her.

'That was weird,' Amy said. 'You knocked me out or sedated me or something, didn't you?'

Meredith smiled but didn't say anything.

'I thought I could hear people talking but there wasn't a sound,' Amy said.

'You are quite correct, Amy,' John said.

I went to Amy and took her arm. I looked her right in the eyes. 'You are a completely normal, talented human who has had her talents boosted by a prolonged period of suffering.'

Amy's eyes widened. 'You know about that? You know?'

'Nothing to be ashamed of, Amy,' Gold said. *May I see her back to the Folly?*

'Go,' I said. 'Amy, Gold will escort you back.'

'The long way,' Meredith said. 'Not directly; she wouldn't be able to handle it right now.'

'Oh, I'm taking the long way,' Gold said, smiling into Amy's eyes. He gently took her elbow to lead her out. 'Are you free Friday night? A group of us grown-ups are going to Lan Kwai Fong to try out the new Italian restaurant there. And to get away from the little ones for a while. You're welcome to come; you spend a lot of time with the younger students as well.'

'Little ones?' Amy said. 'You look the same age as most of the students.'

'Appearances can be deceiving. I'm slightly older than I look,' Gold said, amused. 'You are a very interesting person, you know that? A lot of depth to you. I'd love to see more of it.'

'Tell Gold I heard that and he's seeing somebody already,' I said quickly, and the stone relayed the message.

Broke up with him a month ago, Gold said.

'He's to tell her all about himself up front. And if she's too traumatised by what she's been through then it's strictly hands off.'

Of course.

Another bolt hit me. They would be great together. Totally made for each other. And she *was* something special, but it wasn't ready to come out yet.

I shook myself out of it. Meredith and John stared at me. 'What?'

'We saw that,' John said. He pointed at the floor. 'Your turn.'

I hesitated, then moved to sit cross-legged in the middle of the room. Meredith took up position behind me and put her hands on my shoulders.

I relaxed and let her in.

It didn't take long. She flipped through me like a magazine, then put me back and released me.

'Well on the way there,' she said, rising. She reached down and helped me up. 'Impressive.'

'Have you had any flashes about us? You and me?' John said.

'No. Only the students.' I gestured towards the door. 'Amy and Gold are made for each other. They'll be great together.' It hit me again. 'In fifteen or twenty years, their kids will be some of the best students you and I have ever seen, and we'll teach them together.'

I heard what I'd just said and dropped my head as my throat thickened. John looked away, but Meredith grinned broadly.

'See?' she said, and linked her arm in mine. 'It will be. Let's go and buy the young Immortal-to-be some lunch.'

The next afternoon I paired up my energy students and they worked with chi together, one manipulating the energy and the other supervising. It was incredibly satisfying to have half a dozen students all taking their first steps together.

I paired Amy with Brad, a hefty young black man from Argentina. We didn't recruit many young people from South America; there wasn't much interest there in the Asian Arts. But the movie industry was helping us immensely. Young people saw Hollywood wire-fu and wanted to learn some for themselves. Many were disappointed when they realised that the stuff they saw on movies was pure fantasy, but others were intrigued by the real Arts and continued. And some eventually came to the Mountain and discovered that the stuff depicted by wire-fu was the *least* of what they could do.

John said that he had never seen so many talented students in a single year. He pondered out loud that the Mountain didn't just need to be rebuilt, it needed to be extended. And then he grinned at my moans of dismay.

As I passed Amy, I gently placed my hand on top of her head. I felt her working under Brad's supervision and suddenly realisation hit me like a thunderbolt. Amy was a dragon. *And Brad was a demon.* I had to think quickly; now that I knew the truth I didn't have much time.

'Call the energy back, guys,' I said casually. At the same time, I tapped the stone and silently ordered it to get Gold in *right away*.

'Everybody up,' I said, and they all rose. 'Remain in your pairs and move so that you are an equal distance apart in the room. Spread out and make space.'

Gold appeared beside me.

'Brad, grab Amy *right now*!' I shouted fiercely. 'Standard arm lock! Amy, if you can understand me, let him do it.'

Brad jumped to obey me. He held Amy from behind, towering over her. Amy didn't fight him.

'Everybody out!' I ordered loudly.

Amy's face went ashen. Brad's face tightened into a grimace of effort. The other four students went out, closing the door behind them.

'What did I do?' Amy said. She didn't attempt to struggle.

'Gold, get Jade here,' I said. 'I don't care if she's in the middle of laying eggs, I want her here *right now*.'

A long minute of agony passed before Jade appeared. She looked around, then saw Brad holding Amy and stiffened. 'Get the next of kin,' I said. 'Tell them to hurry.'

I told the stone to explain the situation to Gold, who passed it along to Jade, and both of them nodded without saying a word.

Amy's face twisted into anger. 'Don't move, Amy,' I said. 'Brad, hold her.'

'I didn't do anything!' Amy shouted, struggling.

'Hold still, Amy, trust me,' I said. Amy subsided. 'Hold her, Brad, a tight grip.' Brad nodded, his face rigid.

'What did I do, Emma?' Amy said. 'Why are you doing this?' Her face filled with horror. 'Oh my God, am I a demon and I don't know?'

'Just trust me and stay still,' I said. 'If I'm right, we won't hurt you at all. Trust me. How long, Jade?'

'Five minutes,' Jade said. 'It was a long way.'

'Amy,' I said gently, 'give us five minutes, and it will all become clear. I won't let Brad release you, because you may get hurt. Trust me, stay still. Brad, concentrate. Hold her.'

'Ma'am,' Brad said.

Tears ran down Amy's face; she was terrified, but she remained motionless in Brad's grip. Brad didn't move at all.

'Two minutes,' Jade said.

'Jade, Gold, on the count of three: as much chi as you can generate, right at her head,' I said. 'One.'

'*NO!*' Amy shrieked. 'I didn't do anything!'

'Two.'

Jade and Gold moved into position. We generated three balls of chi, each at least a metre across.

Amy struggled harder. Brad held her tight.

'Three!' I shouted, and all three of us let loose with the chi right at Amy's head.

Amy transformed into a small black dragon, about two metres long. The chi missed her completely and hit Brad at neck height. He was completely destroyed and dissipated quickly.

Amy, still in the form of a black dragon, threw her mouth open and roared, then hurled herself at me.

Jade transformed, leapt onto Amy's back and held her down. Amy's black dragon form struggled against Jade, writhing and roaring with fury, but Jade was bigger and held her.

Gold and I waited patiently.

A magnificent dark blue dragon appeared in front of me, facing Jade and Amy. Its scales were so dark they were almost black, and its fins and tail were gold. It was about twice the size of Jade and had to bend its long tail to fit in front of me.

Amy froze completely when she saw the dark blue dragon. The dragon transformed into a short, round Chinese man in his late fifties. He stood still and silent, studying Amy.

Amy's dragon form sagged, then she changed back to her human form. She collapsed onto the floor. Jade also transformed, and put her arms around Amy.

The Chinese man went to Amy and stood silently over her for some time. Eventually, Amy pulled herself to her feet, Jade helping her. Then Amy fell into the man's arms, weeping. 'Why didn't you *tell* me?'

'What would be the point?' he said. 'Either you are one of us or you aren't. If you are, it will happen. If you aren't, it is better that you never know what you could be.' He turned to me with Amy still in his arms. 'Hello.'

'Hi,' I said. 'Have you heard of the Academy?'

'Of course I have,' he said. 'But I didn't connect it with what Amy was doing in Hong Kong.' He pulled away slightly to smile down at her and stroke her hair. 'I should have realised. She isn't here to teach English and avoid her husband at all. Like most dragons, she is unusually talented in the Arts and was recruited by the Dark Lord.'

'You never knew?' I said.

'She never showed any inclination before,' he said. 'Before she started learning kung fu, she never displayed any signs whatsoever.' He pulled her tight. 'I am so *proud*, Amy. My own beloved daughter, a black dragon.'

Amy was gasping. 'A black dragon?'

'Black as night,' I said.

'Is that why you tried to destroy me?' she said. Her face filled with horror. 'Oh my God, Brad! You killed Brad! How could you do that? No ... no. You missed me, and killed him — he was helping you!' She breathed in ragged gasps. 'He died for me!'

'He was a demon, Amy,' I said. 'I was counting on you changing so that I could destroy him without him knowing we were on to him.'

'He was a demon?'

'The stories are true, my Lady,' Amy's father said.

'I'm sorry, sir, I don't know your name,' I said. 'You'll have to forgive me, I don't remember Amy's last name.'

'Amy Wu,' Amy said.

Amy's father released one hand and held it out to me.

I shook it. 'Mr Wu.'

'You can call me Richard, it's easier,' Amy's father said. He turned and smiled at Amy. 'A black dragon. Wonderful.'

'Am I a bad dragon?' Amy whispered. 'If I'm black?'

Both her father and I laughed. 'Colour has nothing to do with it,' I said.

'By your leave, Lady Emma, I would like to take my daughter to try out her new abilities,' Amy's father said. 'And then, of course, I must present her to the King.'

'Of course,' I said. 'Say hello to the Dragon King for me. You *were* something special, Amy, it was just very well hidden. Happens all the time with you dragons. You're the third one this year. I should be getting used to it.'

Amy released her father and embraced me. 'Thank you so much, Emma.' She turned to Gold and saddened. 'Does this mean I won't see you again?'

Gold smiled gently. 'Once you've been presented to the King you'll probably be back here joining the advanced classes with the other dragons. I'm thinking of setting up a special school for you guys, so many of you keep turning up.'

'The world is shrinking and we are finding more mates among the wider human population,' Amy's father said. He turned back to Amy. 'Now, we will transform, and I will show you how to fly and how to swim, and then you will see the most magnificent palace in existence.'

'Bye, Amy,' I whispered as her father took True Form. 'Have fun.'

'How do I change?' Amy said, but before she'd finished she was already in her dragon form. Her frill, fins and tail fin were all gold; the rest of her was shining jet black. She was magnificent. Her golden eyes flashed.

'Whoa,' Gold said softly.

'Bye, Gold,' Amy said.

'Au revoir,' Gold said. 'Come back soon.'

'Thanks, Emma,' Amy said.

I bowed slightly. 'You are most welcome, Dragon Lady.'

'Follow me. Watch closely,' Amy's father said and disappeared.

Amy glanced at me with her golden eyes, then disappeared as well.

Gold sighed with bliss.

'She'll be back soon,' I said softly.

'I know,' Gold said.

'Now we will sort out my students, and then the three of us will have a contingency meeting on how Brad the demon made it halfway through second year without any of us knowing,' I said.

Jade and Gold both looked sheepish.

'Not good enough from any of us, guys,' I said. 'Stone, did you see all of that?'

'Yep,' the stone said.

'Good,' I said. 'I'll want you to replay the part where Brad was destroyed. I want a good look at that demon; obviously he was something very special. We'll do a post-mortem on that thing and find out how we were duped.'

'Good idea,' Gold said.

'I think it would also be a good idea if I kept you busy for the next week or so,' I said to Gold.

'Forgive me, my Lady, but I was sitting on a clutch,' Jade said, miserable.

'Oh, for God's sake, why didn't you *tell* me?' I said. 'Go! Before they get cold. Why don't you dragons ever tell anybody anything?'

Jade disappeared.

'Because they are truly wonderful,' Gold said.

'I wonder who the father is?' I said.

'No idea,' Gold said.

CHAPTER TWENTY-EIGHT

A couple of the Masters wanted to come along later that afternoon when we replayed the Amy/Brad incident. Meredith as Energy Master, the Demon Master JC Poon, and Gold were present. Meredith and JC had passed Brad in the hallway many times without picking him; Meredith herself had examined him as an energy candidate. JC was a charming good-looking Northern Chinese who appeared in his mid-forties. Both he and Meredith wanted to see how Brad had made it past them.

Much as Leo wanted to see it, he and Michael took Simone out. She was sick of spending her summer holidays at the Academy and had demanded a day out with both of them, and Leo was strong enough to take her now.

We watched the replay in John's office, around a conference table that one of the Celestials conjured for us. I put the ring in the centre of the table and everybody leaned forward to study it.

Once I discovered that the stone kept a perfect record of everything it heard, I often used it as a memory aid. It was almost like a personal assistant for me; it even reminded me when I had appointments. I knew it could record images as well, but I hadn't tried it until now, and I was interested to see the results. I was expecting something like *Star Wars*: an image projected above the stone.

'Everybody ready?' the stone said. 'This will feel queer.'

The room expanded, then collapsed, and we were back in the training room. The students were frozen, Brad holding Amy. The figures of Jade, Gold and I stood facing them.

John and I approached Brad and Amy, the other Masters behind us.

'Can you rewind it to where I put my hand on Amy's head?' I said.

The images didn't move backwards; instead, the scene shifted. The image of me stood next to Brad and Amy with its hand on Amy's head.

I studied myself. 'I really need to do more physical stuff.'

'Everybody's been telling you that,' John said. 'It's obvious you don't enjoy it as much when you can't do it with me.'

Meredith couldn't hold her amusement and made some most undignified noises.

'This is where you knew,' John said, crouching to study Amy and Brad. Amy held the energy in her hands, her face a mask of concentration. Brad sat across from her, his hand on her arm, supervising.

'Yes,' I said. 'Amy was distracted, and I saw right through her. I saw through her into Brad, who was also concentrating. It was there for a fleeting second before Brad closed up — I saw what he was. He was busy closing up so he didn't see what Amy was. I had both of them for a split second.'

'I didn't see that,' the stone said behind me.

I turned. It had taken human form to join us. Both Meredith and I collapsed over our knees laughing. It had taken the form of Sean Connery.

364

'What?' the stone said.

'You don't sound like Sean Connery, you sound like John Cleese,' I said, gasping.

'I do not sound like that buffoon,' the stone said stiffly. It changed to a distinguished-looking European man in his mid-sixties wearing a smart dark green suit and tie. He held his arms out. 'How about this?'

'Much more like it,' I said, and turned away. Meredith was still grinning like an idiot. Gold had a similar expression on his face.

'I'll have a lot of trouble working with it now that I know what it looks like,' I said softly as I bent over Brad and Amy.

'You know what it looks like,' John whispered. 'It's small, square and green. Ignore it.'

We both studied Brad. I reached out and touched his image on the head.

'Move slowly forward, second by second,' I said. I felt the movement even though the images themselves were unmoving; at the time we had all been still. 'Stop.' I straightened and gestured. 'Here. I saw what she is, and what he was.'

Meredith, Gold and JC moved closer to study Brad. John touched him on the head, his face a mask of concentration, his noble features glowing in the reflected light of Amy's chi. Meredith and JC put their hands on Brad's head as well.

The stone approached to stand behind John, watching.

All three of the Masters rose together and shared a look.

'Move forward to where the demon was destroyed,' John said without turning.

The scene changed. Amy was a roaring dragon on the floor; Brad was in the process of dissipating.

John moved to stand next to what was left of Brad's exploding form.

I inhaled sharply when I saw it, then had to turn away, my stomach churning. Meredith quickly moved to catch me, and set me gently to sit on the floor. 'Breathe, Emma,' she said urgently. She saw my face and pushed my head down over my knees. 'Don't look.'

'I shouldn't be this squeamish,' I whispered through the gasps. 'I'm a Master of the sword.'

'You've never harmed a human, or seen a human like this,' John whispered next to me. He put his arm around my shoulders and I flinched away, but he held me. 'It's okay, we're not really here.'

I threw myself at him and buried my face into his chest. He held me. 'Of course seeing that has upset you. You have never harmed a human being, and you never will.'

'But I was okay after we saw what happened to Helen's mother,' I said into his chest. 'The domestic helper had her head cut off and that didn't worry me at all.'

He pulled away to smile at me. 'You were ready for battle then. You weren't ready for this. I think the snake part of you is a long way away right now. It's just all *you*.'

'Is she all right?' the stone said with concern from above us. 'Here.' It had produced a mug of Ceylon tea for me.

'Thanks,' I said, and took a sip. It was more than just tea. As the liquid went down my throat I felt calm and strong and in control.

I glanced up at the stone. 'Thanks. I needed that.'

The stone smiled, its pale blue eyes twinkling under its shock of grey hair. 'My pleasure.'

I passed the cup back and pulled myself to my feet, assisted by John. 'Okay. Let's see what we have here.'

'You don't have to look if you don't want to,' John said, still holding me around the shoulders.

'Once you're gone I'll need to be able to handle anything,' I said. 'Better get used to it, I think.'

John held my hand as we went back to the demon.

'Is this one of the half human demons that the stone was talking about?' I said.

'Something similar to that,' the stone said, studying the demon. 'But in many ways, different.'

'Rewind until it is whole again,' John said. 'Try to do it frame by frame, like a movie.'

The appalling mixture of red and black and white pulled itself back together.

'This is like something out of a very poor horror movie,' Meredith said softly.

'I don't like horror movies, I don't watch them,' I said.

'Me either,' John said, watching Brad carefully. 'I do not find the depiction of humans being harmed entertaining. Forward and back slowly, stone, run through it a few times. This is extremely interesting.'

Every time it happened it was newly horrifying.

'Was Brad human?' I said.

'No,' JC said. 'Definitely a demon.' He sighed. 'A human–demon hybrid, but still one hundred per cent demon. Do not be concerned that you may have harmed a human, my Lady. This thing was demon right through.'

'But inside,' I said, gesturing, 'it's physically very human.'

'You okay?' John said softly.

I nodded. 'Thanks, stone,' I said without turning.

'My Lady,' the stone said behind me.

'It has a skeleton and everything,' I said. 'You can see its brain.' I stopped. 'I'll probably have nightmares when the stone's tea wears off.'

'If you do, call me,' Meredith said.

John reached over and squeezed my hand.

'How long did it take to completely dissipate?' John said.

'Less than half a second,' the stone said.

'Run it at full speed,' John said.

The chi hit Brad and he exploded.

All of the Masters shared a look, except for Gold, who was studying Amy's dragon form with longing. The stone watched Gold, its eyes sparkling with amusement.

'Well?' I said.

'Take us out,' John said.

Everybody else except for the stone disappeared. The room was empty except for me, John and the stone. The stone didn't say anything; it gestured and a chair appeared. It turned the chair away from us and sat.

John pulled me in and held me close. I looked up at him and he lowered his face to mine. His arms tightened around me and our lips met.

Nothing around us moved. Time stood still.

Suddenly John went rigid. The stone threw itself up from the chair and we were back in the conference room.

I collected the ring and put it back on, silently thanking the stone.

My pleasure, it said with amusement.

Realisation hit me like a thunderbolt. Oh my God, it *was* a voyeur.

The stone didn't say anything.

I smiled to myself. It wouldn't have anything to watch for a very long time now. And when John did return, it would be left outside the room.

I would like to remind you that I work very hard for you, my Lady. I serve you well.

I didn't know whether to laugh or explode with anger.

'Are you okay, Emma?' John said. He stood on the other side of the table.

'We need to talk privately later,' I said.

John didn't reply. He quickly turned to the other Masters. 'Well?'

Meredith and JC were on their feet as well, their faces grim. 'Both of us can identify them now,'

Meredith said. 'We've already locked down everything, now we'll go through the students and clean up. We have a busy day ahead of us.'

'What, you think there are *more*?' I said, shooting to my feet as well.

'Three of them turned in the past ten minutes, while we were in the stone,' JC said. 'Two students were killed before the demons were contained. They are level forty-five equivalent.'

'But Brad was considerably bigger than that,' Meredith said, still grim. 'He was about level fifty-five.'

JC's voice was fierce. 'We have been infiltrated. We are full of them. And I didn't pick a single one.'

'We do not have time for regrets,' John said. 'We need to move, and move now. Each of us will take one-third of the building and show the other Masters how to identify the demons. Do not attempt to work alone; obviously some of them are very large. We will clean here first, then we should have enough Masters trained in spotting to do both Follies at the same time. Gold.'

'My Lord?'

'Find Simone, Michael and Leo. Escort them home immediately.'

'My Lord,' Gold said, and disappeared.

Master Liu, the Shaolin Master, appeared behind me.

'Take Emma home directly and guard her,' John said.

'No!' I shouted. 'I'm staying here and helping!'

'Not this time,' John said, his eyes blazing.

We materialised in the training room of the Peak apartment. I fell over, but Liu caught me before I hit the mats.

'Take me back!' I shouted.

'At this stage I do not think that would be a very good idea,' Liu said calmly. 'Unless you want to see your students dying.'

I sagged in his arms. 'No.'

'The demons know we are on to them. There is a very large number of them. This is very, very bad.'

'No.' I buried my face into his shoulder and he held me.

'Emma, we may be attacked here. They may take advantage of the fact that the Dark Lord and most of the senior Masters are occupied defending the students.'

'Oh my God, *Simone*! Is she okay?'

He gently pushed me away so that he could study my face. 'Emma, she is fine. She will be home soon. Then we will lock down and prepare to defend ourselves here.'

'Liu,' I said fiercely, 'this apartment is sealed. They can only come in one at a time. Please. Go. Find Simone and defend her; she's out there with only Leo, Michael and Gold, and none of them can handle anything bigger than about level fifty. I can handle higher than that with energy myself. They need you much more than I do. Send Gold back if you like, he can help me. But please, for God's sake, find Simone and defend her.'

Liu hesitated.

'You know I'm right,' I said. 'Go.'

He released me. 'Where is your sword?'

'In my office in Wan Chai,' I said. 'Forget it. Go.'

'Call it. Hold out your hand and call its name. It may come to you.'

I did as he said. I held my hand out, closed my eyes and called the Silver Serpent to come to me.

I opened my eyes. I was holding the sword, but I hadn't felt it appear. It felt like it had been there all the time.

Liu disappeared without saying a word.

I pulled the sword from its scabbard and threw the scabbard aside. If Simon Wong didn't come for me I would be very, very surprised.

I checked the back pocket of my jeans: the phone was there. I didn't take any chances any more: I kept it with me everywhere. Even in the bathroom, next to the basin, when I was taking a shower. But if Simone was okay then I wouldn't need to use it. The worst that could happen would be that I was killed, and that was infinitely better than either Wong or the King getting their hands on Simone.

As I readied myself I wondered if Xuan Wu could find me and Raise me in the next life if I was killed. If there *was* a next life. All the Taoist teachings said there was, but a great deal of the stuff that had come out over the years was wrong in many important details. And none of the Immortals would talk about it; not even Kwan Yin, who was an icon of both Buddhist and Taoist faiths; and Buddhism was firmly based on the concept of reincarnation.

I silently pondered if I would ever meet any of the Bodhisattvas. Once again none of the Immortals would talk about it. But Immortals were pretty much the same thing as Bodhisattvas anyway. One day I would have to make a trip to India and check it out. And visit the Kun Lun mountains in the West.

But first. I hefted my sword. I had to survive this.

I felt them coming.

I silently asked the stone if Simone was okay.

She is fine. They haven't gone after her. They are coming for you. Liu, Leo and Michael are returning as quickly as they can, but they cannot come directly, Simone is too large to carry.

I wondered where Gold was.

Gold is here. He is hiding. He will help you with a surprise attack if necessary. He has taken True Form and is very, very small. You can't see him.

I'm here, Gold said. *Here they come.*

CHAPTER TWENTY-NINE

I felt them on the other side of the door. I saw them with my Internal Eye. Yep. It was Wong. He had a Mother with him. Just the two of them.

They can only come in one at a time, the stone said.

He'd send the Mother first. He was too much of a damn coward to come and face me one on one.

The doorbell rang down the hallway. Oh my God, Ah Yat. She would answer the door and he'd kill her.

Don't worry, she's not here, Gold said.

I sighed with relief and then stiffened as the door was knocked off its hinges. I heard its footsteps coming down the hallway. It appeared in the doorway.

I hesitated in confusion. My Inner Eye saw it as a Mother, but my physical eyes saw April. I panicked: what if it *was* April? I desperately asked the stone, but it had been silenced.

April stood in the doorway, bewilderment all over her soft, round face.

'April?' I said.

Her face was blank.

I stepped forward, holding the sword ready. I studied her. My Inner Eye still saw her as a Mother.

'April?'

'Do I know you?' she said.

'It's me, Emma. Do you remember me?'

Suddenly she smiled with recognition. 'Hi, Emma, long time no see. I had a girl, you know that? A beautiful baby girl. She's at home in Discovery Bay with the *amah*.'

I didn't lower my sword. Something really didn't feel right. It was extremely confusing. Mothers didn't shapeshift. They only had two forms: human female form and True Form. If this was a Mother, then it couldn't take April's form unless ... unless it *was* April.

April continued speaking as if nothing was amiss, not even appearing to notice the sword in my hand. 'I'm going back to work soon, you know? It's funny.' Her smile widened. 'All the scans said it was a boy, but I had a girl. A beautiful fat girl. Andy thinks she's wonderful.' An expression of bewilderment swept swiftly across her face. 'Andy?'

I was stumped. I didn't know what to do. As far as I could see, it was April. But it appeared to be a Mother as well.

There was a sound in the hallway and Simon Wong walked up behind April, grinning.

'Hello, little Emma,' he said. 'It's been a while. According to my research, you only turn into a snake when Simone's threatened. You don't care about yourself at all. I wonder how true that is?' He turned his head to smile down at April, who still grinned with her eyes blank. 'You like what I've done to your friend?'

I didn't move. I waited for him to come to me.

Wong grabbed the side of April's head and wrenched her around. She moved like an automaton. He kissed her, holding the back of her head with one hand. She didn't return it; she was completely still. He moved his mouth over hers and she screamed and struggled. He grabbed her with his other arm and held her, muffling her screams with his mouth.

He released her and turned back to me. His mouth was bloodied. So was hers. He'd bitten her.

I didn't move. I still wasn't sure.

'You wanna kiss?' he said, grinning.

April's face went strange. Her eyes widened and her whole body went rigid. She transformed. She took the True Form I had seen with my Inner Eye: she was a Mother.

'I won't kill my friend,' I said loudly.

'Good,' Wong said. 'That means you'll have to let her kill *you*.'

The Mother slithered forward, its skinless head nearly brushing the ceiling. Its serpent back end didn't leave the usual slimy trail.

I readied myself. I would defend myself if I had to, but I wouldn't kill April. I studied it with my Inner Eye. It appeared to be a Mother right the way through; no trace of April at all. But I wasn't willing to take the chance.

'You can take off now, coward,' I said.

'No, I think I'll stay and watch,' Wong said, crossing his arms over his chest and leaning against the doorframe. He glanced up at it. 'Still got the chip that Leo took out of the frame last time I was here. You should get that fixed.'

I made the sword sing. The Mother still came at me.

I silenced the sword, dropped it, and readied myself for hand-to-hand.

'This would be a good time to come out,' I said loudly.

The Mother lowered its front end so that its eyes were level with mine. Its serpent-like forked tongue flicked out; so long that it brushed the top of its skinless head. It lunged for me on its black coils. I dodged and struck it in the face.

'Very good,' Wong said with amusement.

'Where the hell are you, Gold?' I said as I lunged back out of the way of another swinging strike.

'Oh, *Gold*,' Wong said as I ducked under a vicious swing and struck twice at the Mother with my feet, hitting it in the abdomen and having absolutely no effect whatsoever. 'Gold's gone. Pissed off.'

'No way,' I said. 'Not possible.'

I managed to dodge the punches that the Mother aimed at my head, left and right. It wasn't trained in the Arts, but with its speed and strength it didn't need to be. It just used brute force.

It feinted at my abdomen with its left and I spun around it, but I was too slow. It grabbed me by the throat with its right hand and lifted me.

I rose. It had me by the throat and lifted itself on its coils. We were close to the ceiling. The Mother charged forward and slammed my back into the wall. It held me, ignoring my struggles. I tried to grab its hand where it held me but it was too strong. My efforts to break free were useless.

I concentrated, filled my hands with chi, and slammed them into its shoulders, blasting it with energy from the outside in. Absolutely nothing happened. No damage at all, except that I had wasted nearly half my chi.

It remained unmoving, holding me pinned against the wall. I waited for it to taste me with its tongue but it had learned from the one that Leo had destroyed.

Wong sauntered closer and stopped beside the Mother, his head level with my stomach. He still had his arms crossed over his chest, casual and relaxed.

He raised one arm and punched me viciously in the centre of the abdomen. I wasn't ready for it. The blood gushed internally, and I quickly concentrated to heal myself.

'Let's go,' Wong said softly.

I came around on the floor of Kitty Kwok's office at the kindergarten in Kowloon Tong. I shot to my feet and looked around; the shock of the incongruity of the location nearly knocked me over again. This was the desk where Kitty had sat and asked me to spy on John Chen Wu. I'd promptly resigned and walked out. It seemed like a million years ago.

I raced to the door: solid wood, and locked. I shoulder charged it and tore a tendon in my shoulder. Stupid.

I went to the window as I healed the shoulder. I couldn't afford to do too much more healing; my energy reserves were running low.

The window, like most windows in Hong Kong, was barred. And not just the usual decorative grille; these were half centimetre square steel bars ten centimetres apart. I tried to bend one but I didn't have the strength.

I concentrated, put my hand on the bar and hit it with chi, attempting to melt it. Not possible. The bar was too hot to hold way before it was hot enough to melt. I couldn't throw chi at it; the energy would go right past it. I had to hold the bar to hit it with chi. Waste of time. I gave a few of the bars some optimistic pulls and was unsurprised when they didn't shift.

I tapped the stone as I opened my Inner Eye to look around.

Holy shit. The kindergarten was full of *kids*. *Human* kids. They were right outside the goddamn *door*. The bastard was using them as a shield to ensure that I wouldn't explode myself.

The stone didn't make a sound, but it was probably me that was deafened, not the stone silenced.

'If you're talking to me I can't hear you,' I said. 'But I'm out of ideas.'

I cut off a shriek as my hand was stabbed with pain. The stone had grown some sort of appendage and was cutting into me.

I tried to rip the ring off my finger, but it wouldn't let go. The stone continued to slice into the back of my hand, then moved to the vein on my middle finger and sliced that as well.

The appendage disappeared back into the stone as I watched it with horror. Then, of all things, the stone grew a little smiley face on its surface.

I rushed to the desk and grabbed some tissues to staunch the flow of blood from my lacerated hand, silently cursing the stone. What the hell had gotten into it?

Then I saw them coming with my Internal Eye. Wong, and Kitty Kwok. Both of them.

I went ice-cold with fury as I frantically mopped up the blood. That bastard would not get me; I would blow myself up with chi first. And take him with me if I could.

The stone had done a good job; the finger was dripping; it had definitely hit a vein. The blood was everywhere. I concentrated, ready to heal the wounds, and the goddamn stone stabbed me *again*. I pushed the tissues into the wound, trying to stop the blood.

Blood.

Sweet.

Oh, *yessss*.

The door opened. Wong and Kitty sauntered in. The children sitting on the floor behind them were visible before Kitty closed the door.

'Thanks,' I said, and shoved the back of my hand into my mouth.

Sweet. My own blood wasn't as good as somebody else's, but the bitch in front of me looked extremely tasty, and the Demon Prince was powerful. But not nearly as powerful as me.

I pulled my hand away and grinned.

Kitty shrieked and spun. Wong pushed her aside and ran to open the door. He went through and closed it on her hand, making her shriek again. He opened the door, pushed her hand out of the door, then closed and locked it in her face.

She turned, leaned against the door, and slid down it to sit on the floor.

I went up to her, still grinning. I crouched in front of her. Her terror was delicious.

I picked up her hand and dropped it. She was limp with fear. Her mouth was open in a silent scream.

'*Simone*!' somebody shouted, and I remembered.

I changed and jumped through the open window between the bars. I was three storeys up, and I smiled as I fell.

A while later the sky was becoming dark and I was running out of puff. I was causing panic wherever I went, and I wasn't even very big. I found a perfect place to hide.

'Emma.' Something prickled the back of my head and somebody was whispering my name.

'Emma, wake up.'

There was a stone right in the middle of my back and it *hurt*. I grimaced.

'Emma. Come on, I know you can hear me.'

'Wha'?'

'Simone needs you!'

I shot upright and cast around. I was next to a tall chain-link fence. On the other side were railway tracks. I was sitting in the dirt. It was dark. I was completely naked.

'Where am I?'

'You are in a vacant lot near the Kowloon Tong KCR station. You came here after you escaped from them. You went through the links of the fence and hid at the back here, in the tall grass, where nobody could see you. Then you changed back. I think you were too weak to conjure the clothes.'

'Oh *damn*, not again!'

'It saved your life, I think.'

My left hand hurt like hell and I checked it. It was covered in a network of cuts. I remembered, concentrated, and healed it.

'Thanks for that,' I said. 'I didn't know what you were doing.' I looked around. 'Could you call Gold for me?'

The stone was silent.

'Oh my God, they got him, didn't they?'

'I am afraid he is not answering my calls,' the stone said.

I felt a stab of pain and dropped my head. Gold was gone. Then I pulled myself together. 'Well,' I said, 'I need to contact somebody to come and take me home. I can't go anywhere like this. Any suggestions?'

The block was covered with construction debris, trash and tall grass, and surrounded by a chain-link fence. I'd chosen a good place to hide. The fence was nearly three metres high; it would take a good jump to get out, and I'd have to do it carefully so that nobody saw me.

'I'll see if I can contact any of my other children,' the stone said. 'They may be able to relay a message for you.'

I looked down. A snake's trail wound across the dirt next to me. I was concerned there may be snakes in the long grass of the lot. Then I relaxed: the snake's trail was from *me*. I curled up to sit with my knees in my chest behind the grass. It was high enough to hide me from anybody passing. I'd chosen a good spot.

Mid-July was always blistering hot, day and night, and the evening was very humid. The fact that I didn't have any clothes didn't make me any more comfortable; the dust clung to the sheen of sweat on my skin. I brushed at the dirt on my arm, then stopped to study it. The dust had stuck to my arm in a scale pattern, obviously left over from when I'd changed. I ran my finger over the edge of the scales, not completely sure how I felt about that.

'Agate in Shantou. No,' the stone said. 'Amber, Xian. No. Hold on, Amethyst's answering. Damn, he's under the ice of the South Pole, having a holiday. Can't contact anybody for us.'

'You going through your address book?' I said, amused.

'Bauxite isn't answering, that's strange. He has a human family in Russia, Siberia. Should be there, I wonder what happened to him? Anyway ...' The stone fell silent again.

I waited patiently. I dozed off over my knees; I was exhausted. The lights above the train tracks blinked on. Crickets chirped. I hoped that everybody was okay: the students in the Academy and the Follies. And Simone. I sighed. Simone, more than anything. A train rolled past and I curled up in the grass and sat very still. I felt the vibration through the ground. Nobody in the train noticed me; they were moving too fast.

It occurred to me that John might be gone. I searched for him with my consciousness; I hoped that when he left I would be aware of it. I smiled slightly into my knees. Yeah, right. Not likely.

'Found one,' the stone said. 'This is most unusual, Emma, a great many of my children are not answering my calls. To tell you the truth, I am concerned about them. Anyway, I managed to contact Fred in Lingnan — he's calling the Dark Lord on his mobile. May take a while, the phones there are a bit dodgy.'

'Fred?'

The stone didn't reply.

'Are you Chinese?' I said. 'Most of your children are in China, but you take European human form.'

'Of course I'm Chinese,' the stone said impatiently. 'I took the European form to honour the present company.'

'You were just stirring.'

The stone was silent.

'You really like to watch?' I said softly.

It stayed silent.

'How does that work? You're a *rock*.'

'The Dark Lord made me promise to behave after I woke, and I have been extremely good,' the stone said. 'I meant it when I said that I was asleep, and he does me the honour of taking my word for it.'

'Geez,' I said into my knees. 'I'm going to kill him.'

'I have been extremely useful, you have to admit, Emma.'

'Yeah, you just chopped up my goddamn hand,' I said.

'And it got you out of there.'

I sighed. I wanted to curl up and cry my eyes out. What I really needed was a hug from my man.

'We will have you home soon, and you can have a long hot shower and sleep,' the stone said.

'Holy shit, I wear you in the goddamn *shower*!' I said fiercely, curling up tighter.

'Makes no difference to me whatsoever,' the stone said.

'Yeah. I really believe you.'

'Really. You can ask the Dark Lord for confirmation. In that respect, I truly am a genderless piece of rock.'

'You are extremely weird,' I said.

I could picture the stone's human form shrugging with a wry smile. 'Aren't we all? Leo is the only really *normal* member of the Chen household, Emma.'

I sighed into my knees again.

'He's onto them. They're okay,' the stone said.

'All of them?'

'All of them, Emma. They are all fine.'

I heaved a huge gasping sob of relief into my knees and went still.

'Leo is on his way to collect you. Lord Xuan has remained at the Peak with Simone, because the apartment has no door.'

'How many students did we lose?'

'You will be home soon, Emma.'

I buried my face in my knees and waited.

'That's him, dear,' the stone said, waking me. 'He's looking for you.'

The dark Mercedes rolled slowly past the block, its headlights bright.

'There's nobody around to see you,' the stone said. 'It's okay.'

I rose and staggered towards the fence. The car stopped, then reversed slightly.

I raised my hand. Leo came out of the car and hurried to the fence. 'What happened to you?' He looked at the fence, each side and up. 'How are you going to get out?'

I went closer to him and checked carefully around. 'Move away, I'll just come over.' I decided against jumping; I'd use the energy centres. I took three steps back, then ran to the top of the fence. At the top I carefully placed my feet between the knots in the barbed wire, and floated down the other side. I touched down lightly. My knees buckled; I couldn't hold myself up. I fell to my knees.

Leo pulled off his jacket and quickly wrapped it around me. He scooped me up and laid me on the back seat of the car. His huge dark face was right in mine, his voice gentle. 'Do you need to go to the hospital, Emma? Are you injured? You have blood on you.'

'She's okay,' the stone said. 'Just exhausted. Take her home.'

The door slammed far away. I wasn't aware of Leo climbing into the car, but I did feel it moving.

I didn't know he carried me up to the apartment on the Peak.

I broke through the clouds and hovered about thirty metres above the ground.

The houses were scattered over the top of the mountain, some of them still swathed in the edges of the clouds. The ground was covered in soft, short grass; there were manicured shrubs and hedges, but no trees.

I swooped over the houses and landed on a narrow cobbled road next to a hedge. Nobody was around. I slithered along the road to see, but there wasn't much. I climbed up the hill, towards a beautiful house with a garden surrounded by a low red brick wall. I could smell the flowers in the garden; I could taste them.

Home? No. But something close.

I threw myself up into the air again and flew over the houses. The entire mountain top was deserted. Why? Everything seemed perfectly normal. Something told me that there should have been damage, but I didn't know why. Something also told me that the houses shouldn't have looked like standard Western thatched cottages; they should have been more Chinese. What a strange idea.

I tasted blood and looked around, distracted. A bird flew past.

Dinner.

I raced to follow it. I could smell its blood from thirty metres away, the hunger driving through me.

Both of my hands were held and I jerked them away and threw myself upright with a gasp. I cast around desperately.

I fell back. I was in my room at home, in my own bed, clean and warm and in my pyjamas. John was on one side of me, Simone in his lap. Leo was on the other.

'Simone, are you okay?' I said.

'I'm fine, Emma. The stone told us what happened,' Simone said, taking my hand back and holding it. 'How do you feel? You've been asleep for a long time.'

'I'm okay.' I rubbed my free hand over my face and pulled myself up to sit again. 'Could someone get me a drink of water?'

Leo turned to my bedside, then turned back and handed me a cup. I took a huge drink and gasped, then handed the cup back with a nod of appreciation.

John gently slid Simone off his lap, but she didn't release my hand. He moved to sit next to me on the bed and put his arm around my shoulders, studying my face.

'I'm okay,' I said.

'Leo, take Simone out,' John said gently.

'I want to stay with Emma,' Simone said.

'I need to talk to her,' John said, moving away again. 'You can come back later. Okay?'

Simone hopped off her chair, grumbling about 'bad Daddy'. Leo took her hand and gently led her out.

'I was in the kindergarten in Kowloon Tong,' I said. 'I thought she had to give all that up, that they'd been closed down.'

'She sold them,' he said. 'But to another company that was a subsidiary of Tautech.'

'How many students and Masters did we lose?'

He returned to the chair and leaned his elbows on his knees. He studied his hands. 'Two junior Disciples, and about ten seniors.' He hesitated, still studying his hands. 'And all but three of the Celestial Masters. Three Celestials remain: Liu, Au and Chow. Meredith is gone.'

'Shit. How many demons were there?'

He glanced up at me, his face grim. 'About fifty.'

'Holy shit. How big were they?'

'Between forty and seventy.'

'*Seventy*? Good God.'

'If they had managed a surprise attack, I hate to think what we could have lost. I am very glad you caught that one.'

'Geez. Me too. Was it Wong or the King?'

'Of course One Two Two. They were hybrids.'

'Wong went for me rather than Simone,' I said.

'He probably felt you would be easier to carry. Simone is very large inside, much bigger than you. He is also a shocking coward, and you are the weakest of the three of us. Besides, if he holds you, then of course I must do what he wants.'

'If you let him blackmail you by holding me I will be very, very cross with you.'

'Of course you will.'

I sighed. 'And I'm cross with you anyway. You didn't tell me about the stone.'

'Nothing to tell,' John said mildly. 'It has promised to behave, and it is a Building Block, so it will keep its word.'

'I wear it in the *shower*, John. Doesn't that bother you?'

'Your state of undress means nothing to it; it is a stone.'

'Really?' I said.

'Really.' He sounded amused. 'Absolutely. Its little predilections are in a slightly different direction.'

'You should have *told* me,' I said fiercely.

'Nothing to tell.'

'This doesn't bother you at all, does it,' I said.

He made a soft sound of amusement and moved slightly away. He opened his mouth to say something, then obviously changed his mind and closed it again.

'Tell me,' I said.

'I don't think it would be a good idea. You are very accepting, but I think this would be too much for even you to accept.'

'Try me,' I growled.

'I don't want to lose you, Emma,' he said softly.

'Oh *shit*,' I said with despair. 'Not *you* too? Where did my normal life go?'

'She'll find it amusing, my Lord,' the stone said. 'You'd better tell her; right now she thinks it's much worse than it really is.'

'Okay, I'll take your word for it.' John didn't move but his face changed. 'Spring of 1978,' he said wistfully. 'About three years after I'd lost the Serpent. The water around Hainan Island was unusually warm, and crystal clear. I ran into a stunning female turtle Shen. Pursued her for ages, both of us in True Form. She teased me, and evaded me, for days. Every time I thought I had her, she would take off again. She drove me mad.'

I was silent. I could picture it.

'I finally had her; I had my flippers over her shell.' His eyes were very dark. 'I heard a sound behind me.' His face twisted into a wry grin. 'The *Calypso*. They were *filming* us, very excited. They launched a Zodiac and circled us, filming. I was the largest marine turtle they'd ever seen, and they'd caught us in the act. First time on film, marine turtles mating. They were delighted.'

I collapsed backwards onto my pillow, laughing silently.

'See?' the stone said.

I gasped for breath. I couldn't speak I was laughing so hard. I wheezed with the effort.

'She wants to know if you bothered to stop,' the stone said.

John hesitated, then, 'Nope.'

I rolled onto my side and clutched my stomach. I laughed so hard I felt like I was about to throw up.

'I've ... I've ...' I tried to suck in enough air to speak.

'She thinks she's seen it,' the stone said.

'*Everybody's* seen it,' John said. 'It's a standard piece of footage now. Whenever they bring up the subject of marine turtle reproduction, there we are, large as life.'

I gasped for breath.

'Yes, Emma, we are a matched set,' the stone said. 'He is an exhibitionist, and I am a voyeur.'

'The Tiger is three times the exhibitionist that I am,' John said. 'I don't think I'm an exhibitionist at all. I'm just a Turtle, and when my flippers are over a nice piece of shell everything else falls beside the way.'

I wiped my eyes, my hands shaking.

'And the fact that you don't have one makes absolutely no difference at all to me,' John said softly. 'It is the inside that counts more than anything else. And the inside of you is the most ...' His voice trailed off.

'He can't finish it, Emma,' the stone said.

I wiped my eyes with my palms. I was still shaking.

'Rest,' John said. 'Simone is safe, you are safe, the remaining students are safe. That is all that is important in the world.'

'Thank Leo for me,' I said softly, my voice quivering. 'For cleaning me up.'

'I will,' he said. 'He refused to let Ah Yat do it. You were only semi-conscious and he was concerned she would drop you. He said you would not mind. Rest.'

I reached over to my bedside table, pulled a couple of tissues out of the box, and nodded into them.

John rose to leave.

'Porn star,' I gasped loudly as he went out.

He laughed softly as he closed the door.

CHAPTER THIRTY

I stepped out of my bathroom, clean and feeling much better. I rummaged through the disaster area that was my wardrobe, searching for something comfortable to wear; my back was sore from lying on the rock in the vacant lot.

I stopped dead.

'That was the phone digging into my back, wasn't it?' I said.

'The King's phone?' the stone said. It hesitated, then, 'Oh, yes. You were lying on it, and you didn't take it with you.'

I rummaged through the clothes again. 'I need to go back and get it.'

The stone didn't say anything.

'How come I came around with no clothes, but you and the phone were there?' I said as I finally found a clean pair of jeans.

'The phone follows you, Emma,' the stone said. 'When you returned to human form, it materialised.'

'Oh,' I said. 'What about you? I don't have hands to hold you when I'm a snake. Where did you go?'

'I stayed with you,' the stone said.

'How? On my tail?'

The stone was silent.

'Oh my God, this is something really weird, isn't it?'

'Depends on your definition of "weird". I move inside you,' the stone said.

I sat on the bed. 'No. I don't want you in there.'

'It's not what you think,' the stone said. 'I become lodged in the muscle tissue of your back, about a third of the way along your serpent length.'

I didn't feel very relieved. 'That is extremely weird.'

'It's extremely claustrophobic. I don't like it at all.'

'I'm not sore there,' I said. 'That's strange.' Then I flexed my left shoulder and felt a definite twinge, as if I had torn a muscle and it had nearly healed. 'Whoa.'

'Put your clothes on,' the stone said. 'The Dark Lord is coming; he sensed that you were awake.'

We need to get together and work out what to do, Emma, John said. *We have some major problems and your help would be appreciated, if you are feeling up to it.*

I grabbed an old T-shirt from the wardrobe and tugged it over my head, then went to the door and opened it. John waited on the other side.

'I'm okay. What's the problem?'

'Come into the dining room and we'll talk about it,' he said.

Leo and the Shaolin Master, Liu, waited for us, with the two other remaining Immortal Masters, the junior Tai Chi Master, Mike Chow, and the wushu Master, Audrey Au. They saluted as we sat.

Mike was a huge Chinese who'd gained Immortality about seven hundred years ago. He'd taught Meredith, then suggested that she take over as Energy Master because she was so much better than he was.

Audrey was a tiny Chinese lady who looked far too delicate to have anything to do with any of the Arts.

Wushu was the demonstration Art, rather like rhythmic gymnastics: gorgeous to look at but not generally useful as a fighting style. This sort of Art, the elegant presentation type, was what many practitioners meant when they said 'wushu'.

It was understandable that these two had survived the demon attacks; neither of them were terribly useful in battle and had probably stayed with the junior students. Liu had been with Simone, so he hadn't been attacked.

The three of them were all we had left.

'First,' Liu said, 'Disciples. Casualties: ten seniors. What to do?'

'What about the juniors?' I said.

'The seniors and the Immortals gave their lives for them,' John said matter-of-factly. 'And succeeded. We lost only the first two.'

'Which seniors did we lose?' I said.

Liu handed me a list and I scanned through it. Ten of the best. All but one were Chinese. They were all over the age of thirty; a couple of them were in their sixties. John had discussed them with me before: he thought that some of them were well on the way to attaining the Tao. We had planned a small ceremony in the next few weeks to officially promote eight of them to Master, as they were already doing the duties of junior Masters. They were all like family and I felt a pang as I perused the list. I would really miss them.

'Did any of them get there?' I said softly.

John didn't say anything.

'Maybe next time,' I said, hoping for some sort of reaction.

John's and Liu's expressions didn't shift.

'Are you allowed to say anything at all about it?' I said.

Liu leaned back. 'Ten seniors. What to do?'

'Families?' I said.

'Three had families, grown-up children. The other seven didn't. None of them have immediate family back in China, or Europe in Jim's case, just the extended clans.'

'Inter them on the Mountain, John,' I said. 'It's the least we can do for them. Send ancestral tablets to their clans in China. Can you cremate them on the Mountain?'

'Yes,' John said. 'You will arrange it, Chow Sifu. I will have Jade send a couple of dragons to assist you. If you have trouble, contact me any time.'

'I'll need the right people to do the tablets,' Mike said.

'General Pak will be in touch. There are plenty of clergy in the Northern Heavens — refugees from temples destroyed during the Mountain Attack. They will come to the Mountain and perform the rituals.'

'My Lord,' Mike said, lowered his head and disappeared.

I sighed. I glanced back at the list of seniors and noticed there were a couple more pages stapled to it. I flipped the paper and froze with horror.

The next two pages were lists of numbers, English and *Greek* numbers. And a couple of names. One of the names was 'Sonia'. I dropped the paper on the desk and put my head in my hands.

'How many demon staff did we lose?' I said into my hands.

'The four security guards — the two on the ground floor and the two at the entrance to the car park — are all that remain. The only reason the security guards weren't destroyed is because the demons ignored them when they came into the building and went right past them,' John said, his voice very calm. 'All of them, Emma. The attacking demons seemed to have a grudge against ours, and singled them out for special attention. The defenders concentrated on protecting the humans, and the demons helped them. Many of them fought valiantly.'

'But Sonia was human,' I whispered.

'I think they knew, love.'

I had to look away. I wiped my eyes.

'My Lord,' Liu said, and hesitated. He looked down at his hands. His expression under his bushy white brows was miserable.

'We can't spare you, old friend,' John said gently.

'She's all alone down there,' Liu whispered.

'Meredith?' I said.

Liu nodded.

'Let him go, John. Please.'

'We can't spare him, Emma. We only have three left.'

'How long will she be down there?' I said.

'Where?' Leo said. 'I wish you people would stop talking in riddles.'

I smiled at Leo. 'Do you have any idea what happens to Immortals when their physical forms are killed?'

'They go to Hell, stay there for a while, then turn up again, good as new,' Leo said. 'That's it, isn't it?'

'That's right,' I said. 'Straight to Level Ten, the bottom level, stay there for a while doing who knows what, then pop back up here.'

'What happens to them down there?' he said.

'None of the Immortals will talk about it,' I said loudly without looking at the three Immortals who sat, unmoving, at the table with us.

'All of the Celestial Masters are in Hell?' Leo said. 'Is that just for China?'

'I have no idea, and it's a waste of time asking,' I said.

'What about ordinary people?' Leo said. His face cleared. 'Oh, that's why you said "next time".'

Once again nobody said anything.

'Once it is all handled, you may go, my friend,' John said to Liu. 'Until then, you are needed here. She will understand.'

'How long will it take?' I said.

Liu and John shared a look. 'About three months,' John said.

'Intercede,' the stone in my ring said. 'You need them.'

John made a soft sound but didn't say anything.

'You can do that?' I said.

Neither John nor Liu spoke. Their faces were rigid.

'You're not supposed to talk about it, are you,' I said.

'There have always been people who wanted me thrown from Heaven, Emma,' John said softly.

'I see,' I said.

'How come you know all this, Emma?' Leo said.

'Research.'

'Far too much for your own good,' John said. 'Only about twenty-five per cent of what's out there is correct anyway.'

'I can tell what's right,' I said. 'It's obvious.'

'I think you should start doing a PhD to keep yourself busy, before you *do* get me thrown from Heaven,' John said with grim humour.

'I have well and truly enough to do right now as it is,' I said.

John straightened and changed the subject. 'We only have three Celestial Masters left. We also have three of the original human Masters, all of whom are really too frail to take up much of the workload. There's only one thing we can do.'

I dropped my head. 'Close up shop.'

'No,' Leo whispered. 'You can't.'

'We'll send them all home, Leo,' I said. 'There's not much else we can do.'

'I'll rent the ballroom of one of the hotels in Admiralty, have a farewell dinner, make the announcement,' John said, his voice full of pain. 'The seniors who want to remain with us can stay at the Folly. Many of them have no other family, no other interests, and nowhere else to go. Emma and the remaining Celestials can look after them after I'm gone. All the juniors should go home to their families.'

'It's the only thing we can do,' I said, my heart breaking. The juniors would be devastated when they heard.

'Once the juniors are home, the seniors are organised, and the demon is taken out, you have my permission,' John said to Liu.

'My Lord,' Liu whispered, his voice hoarse.

'Hold it a minute,' I said. 'You can't rent a ballroom — we don't have Gold. We'll have to do it at Hennessy Road. And we don't have space for everybody in one room.'

'What's the problem?' Leo said.

'Language,' I said. 'They'll be able to understand Lord Xuan, but nobody else.'

'Oh.'

'You're quite correct,' John said.

'Gather them into the training rooms at Hennessy Road, make the announcement by telepathy,' I said. 'It's the only way.'

'We lost Jade and Gold as well?' Leo said.

'We lost Gold,' I said. 'Have you heard from him? Is he in Hell?'

'We haven't heard from him,' the stone said, completely emotionless. 'He has disappeared. He is not in Hell, he is not on Earth, he is not on the Celestial. He does not answer when he is called.'

'Oh *God*,' I whispered.

Leo moaned gently and rubbed his hands over his face.

'We lost all the stones,' John said without looking up. 'All of them. The attackers had some way of disabling them. At this stage it is not clear whether the same thing has happened to them.'

The stone made a soft hissing sound, but didn't say anything.

'What about the dragons?' I said.

'Most of the dragons escaped death because of their speed,' John said. 'They fought valiantly. Many of them were injured, though, and have been moved to the East to recover. We have about a dozen dragons left, including Jade, who couldn't fight.'

'Is Jade okay?' Leo said.

'Jade's apparently sitting on a clutch of eggs and didn't tell anybody,' I said.

'Terrific timing,' Leo growled. 'She didn't even look pregnant.'

'Typical dragon behaviour. Never tell anybody anything.' I sighed and rested my chin on my hand. 'Geez. This is really bad.'

John leaned back, his face tight but his eyes burning. 'Anything else?'

'Yes,' I said. 'Why couldn't you sense them?'

Leo glanced at John.

'Nobody could sense them,' Liu said. 'They were specifically engineered to appear human right the way through. There was absolutely no demon essence that was visible to any sort of inspection.'

'Sounds like the fire elementals, except more so,' I said.

'Precisely,' John said.

'How did you recognise them once you knew then?' I said. 'If there's no demon essence about them?'

'They are not completely human, and the difference is easy to spot once you are looking for it,' John said. 'In the past we only looked for existence of the black demon essence, and if it wasn't there we could safely assume it was human. Now we can't; we must look at its human nature as well.'

'We need to see Helen again,' I said. 'Were you awake, stone?'

'Yes,' the stone said. 'I can show you.'

'First, I must report,' John said. 'The residents of the Celestial must be notified about the new demons. Only the Heavens know how far they have infiltrated. I've summoned the Tiger, he'll be here shortly. Then we can examine Helen.'

'Were you awake when Kitty came to get her from school?' I said.

'Yes,' the stone said.

'Good, we'll look at Kitty too. Oh,' I said, suddenly remembering, 'was that April?'

'No,' the stone said. 'And it wasn't a Mother either.'

'Well then, what the hell was it?' I said. 'It sure as hell looked like a Mother.'

'Something completely new,' the stone said. 'You'll need to devise a name for them, I think.'

The Tiger appeared at the other end of the room and fell to one knee, saluting. 'Xuan Tian Shang Di.'

'Emma,' John said, 'what the Tiger and I are about to discuss is not for mortal ears. Please.'

'Come and see yourself in the newspaper, Emma,' Leo said, rising. 'There's a huge story about you on page three of both the English and Chinese papers.'

'My Lord,' Liu said, saluting, and disappeared.

'Dismissed, Au,' John said. 'Go and supervise the clean-up crews.'

'My Lord,' Audrey said, and disappeared as well.

'I'm in the paper?' I said, shooting to my feet. 'Holy shit, nobody saw me, did they?'

'They didn't just see you, they took photos, and called the Agriculture and Fisheries Department to come and get you,' Leo said. 'Apparently you're a really big cobra. Caused a lot of panic around Kowloon Tong station. They spent the entire afternoon trying to catch you. You should see the photos — the Ag and Fish guys look terrified.'

I sagged with relief. 'Oh, they saw the *snake*. I thought they saw *me*.'

'That would cause mass panic as well,' Leo said dryly, putting his arm on my back to guide me out. 'Come and have a look. You're a celebrity. You were even on the television, but we weren't quick enough to tape it for you.'

'Are you okay, Leo?' I whispered as he closed the door behind us on John and the Tiger. 'You're not too freaked?'

'About you being a snake?' Leo said. 'Or about this demon thing?'

'Everything.'

'Simone is okay,' Leo said.

I understood.

I parked the car at a meter near the vacant lot. I walked up to the fence and studied it. I looked around. Nobody nearby.

'Try walking right through,' the stone said. 'Don't go over. Concentrate. Make yourself permeable. I will supervise. When I give the word, gently push your hand through the fence.'

I concentrated on making myself, as the stone had said, *permeable*.

'Try,' the stone whispered. 'Just your hand.'

I retained my concentration and put my hand on the fence. I could feel the fence, but I could easily push my hand through the wire.

It was agony. The pain was indescribable. I did my best to retain my concentration and slowly pulled my hand back out.

'You are not there yet,' the stone said. 'Well done. Many others would have lost their concentration at the pain and lost their hand in the fence.'

'You just nearly cost me my hand,' I said. 'There are no energy healers left at the Academy, just me, and I don't think I'd be capable of fixing something as major as that.'

'You are quite correct, Lady Emma. Please accept my apologies,' the stone said. 'I will, in future, be more careful.'

'Good,' I said, took three steps back and jumped over the fence, somersaulting at the top and floating down the other side to land lightly on my feet. My snake track was visible in the soft dirt and I followed it to the back of the lot. The King's phone was on the ground in the tall grass. I jammed it into my pocket.

'You were hoping I wouldn't remember it, weren't you?' I said as I walked back to the fence. A Chinese couple strolled past on the other side of the street but didn't see me. I waited for them to go.

I do not like to think of what would happen to you if you were to use that phone, the stone said silently into my ear. *The King obviously has plans for you, and they may not be pleasant or honourable. I hate to think what he could do to you if you went to him.*

'That is totally unimportant,' I whispered. 'What is important is that Simone is safe. And it's looking more and more like I may have to use it.'

Please be warned, Emma, you should only use it as a last resort, the stone said. *For you, death may be a preferable option to Hell.*

That stopped me. 'Same thing, isn't it?'

The stone didn't say anything.

I took three steps back and jumped over the fence again. I returned to my car.

'What happens to me if I go to Hell is of no importance whatsoever,' I said. 'If I go, Simone will be safe, and the King will free me when Xuan Wu returns. That's what matters.'

The stone remained silent. I pulled myself into the car to go home. I checked the clock. Dinnertime.

'Does he know I came to get the phone?' I said.

'Yes,' the stone said. 'He's as worried as I am.'

I sighed and turned the key. I pulled away from the kerb and headed home.

CHAPTER THIRTY-ONE

Na Zha wanted to see the new demons as well. The Tiger came too, and brought Michael.

Na Zha was obviously intimidated by John's presence. He'd toned down his appearance and appeared as a Chinese of about seventeen, wearing a plain T-shirt and a pair of cargo shorts.

Leo took Simone out to a playground slightly higher on the Peak, and the rest of us sat around the dining table together.

I put the ring on the table and the room expanded and contracted. We were in the living room. Simone and I were playing a board game on the coffee table with Helen.

'Were you awake when Kitty collected Helen from the school?' I said.

The scene shifted and we were on the long outdoor corridor outside the classrooms at the school.

'This where you go to school?' the Tiger said.

'Yep,' Michael said.

Na Zha made some derisive noises but didn't say anything.

Kitty was there, holding Helen's hand. Michael and I were standing in front of them, studying Helen.

John approached Kitty and touched her hand. 'Human. All the way through. He hasn't done anything at all to her.'

'On the plane she bossed One Two Two around,' I said. 'It sounded like he actually took orders from her.'

'She doesn't know any other way of talking to people except to give orders,' John said, crouching to study little Helen. 'It's probably more like a partnership of equals. I'd say that they detest each other, but stay together because it's a beneficial union for both of them.'

'Wonder if he screws her,' the Tiger said, and I thumped him on the arm. 'What?'

'Is that all you ever think about, Ah Bai?' John said with resignation as he touched Helen's head.

'Good coming from you,' the Tiger said.

'Cut it out, you two,' I said. 'Helen. Well?'

'Human,' John said. 'Slightly larger than a normal human inside, because she is half fox spirit, but that is all. Have a look.'

The others all touched Helen's head then stepped back.

'Would you like to go back to the apartment?' the stone said. It had appeared behind us again in its European human form.

'So that's what you look like,' Michael said.

'No, I'm square and green,' the stone said, and the scene shifted back to Simone, myself and Helen playing Monopoly in the living room.

'Take it forward to the demon and the Snake Mother,' John said, lightly touching Helen's head. 'We've already seen inside Helen. *No! Wait!*'

The scene had started to shift and it snapped back.

'This is not the same little girl,' John said. 'This is a demon copy.'

The other Immortals moved forward to study Helen.

John's eyes burned. 'I had this creature in my house for half a day. It walked right in through my seals. And I was absolutely unaware.'

'You never touched her, or came close to her,' I said.

'We must show this to Simone when she returns, so that she can recognise them as well,' John said.

'This is getting really heavy,' the Tiger said softly.

'Is that why Kitty made such a performance at the school?' I said. 'To make us have Helen over so they could check if we could sense that she was a copy?'

'Obviously,' John said. 'The stone turtle was probably a diversion, to make us think that it was the point of the exercise.'

'We signed a death sentence for her mother when we paid her a visit,' I said. 'I wonder where Helen is now.'

'It's obvious where she is now,' John said. 'I am appalled by this demon's behaviour towards children. I have never seen its like before. It must be destroyed. I've half a mind to call the King and talk to him about it, negotiate something.'

'The King offered to swap me for Wong,' I said softly. 'How about I use the phone and call him? With Wong out of the picture you won't have to worry about Simone.'

John gazed at me, his face expressionless. 'You said that you would only use the phone if I went down, or if Simone was in real danger.'

'Yes, I did. But we were under attack when I said it.'

His face didn't shift. 'I hold you to your word, as a woman of honour, Emma Donahoe.'

'You could release me from my word,' I said.

He was silent.

'Okay,' I said, turning away. 'April.'

The scene shifted again. We were inside the training room. I was facing the Mother.

'Backtrack to when she was April,' I said.

I was facing April. 'Let me see.' I touched her head. 'As far as I can see, this is my human friend.'

John came next to me and touched April's head. He concentrated. 'Fascinating. Ah Bai, Michael, Ah Na Zha, come and look at this.'

The other three came, and John moved so that they could touch April. All of them concentrated intensely.

'I see her as human,' Michael said.

'So do I,' the Tiger said.

'Nothing demonic about her,' Na Zha said, sounding bewildered. 'And she changed into a *Mother*?'

'Show us,' John said.

Wong appeared, kissed her; April went rigid, then changed.

'Holy shit,' I said softly. 'The taste of the blood makes her change.' I suddenly found it extremely difficult to breathe and I grabbed John's arm. 'Oh my God.'

John wrapped his arm around me and gave me a squeeze.

'But you said it's not April, stone,' I said.

'I have seen your friend before and this is not her,' the stone said. 'This is not the same person that you stopped on the street in Causeway Bay.'

'The stone is quite correct, Emma,' John said. 'Two entirely different creatures.' He gave me another squeeze.

'Let's see the one on the street then,' I said. 'Wait, let me look at this one first.'

'We should all look at this interesting creature,' John said, and moved forward to touch the April Mother. Everybody crowded around and studied it. Then they shared a look and backed away.

'I thought they could only come in one at a time,' I said.

'That is correct,' John said.

'Well?'

'It appears human. As far as the seals were concerned, only one demon came in. This is extremely disturbing.' John nodded without turning.

The scene shifted. We were with April on the street. There was such a crowd of people on the pavement that we had trouble finding places to stand.

The Immortals and Michael moved to touch April. I did too. We crowded around her.

'This is a normal human being,' Na Zha said. 'This is all mixed up. Copies, and demons, and humans, it's all a big mess. Shit.'

'Take us out,' John said.

We sat around the table and studied each other in silence.

'So. He has access to a half fox child, Helen, and he's made a demon copy of her that is almost undetectable,' I said, recapping to get the facts straight in my head. 'He hasn't done anything to Kitty Kwok. My friend April: he has her baby. And he's made a copy of her that turns into a Mother when it tastes blood.' I took a deep breath. 'The same way I turn into a snake when *I* taste blood.'

'You're gonna be ordered in, Xuan Tian,' Na Zha said with grim certainty. 'If the Demon King's not doing anything about it, the Celestial's gonna want somebody to make a move, and you've got the army to take the bastard down. It's obvious where this is headed, and we can't let it go for much longer. Look at these things. Demons and humans mixed together. It's just not right.'

'No,' John said with finality. 'I will not leave Simone.'

'He won't send his Elite Guard in after what happened on the Mountain,' Na Zha said. 'That was the Demon King's army we faced on the Mountain, and the Guard were cut to pieces. It'll be you and the Thirty-Six.'

'What'll you do if he orders you in, Ah Wu?' the Tiger said softly.

John didn't say anything. He studied his hands. His eyes blazed.

'Disobeying an order like that *will* get you thrown,' the Tiger said.

'If the Celestial can provide someone who can guard Simone and Emma I will consider it,' John said. 'I will not leave them undefended.'

'You know exactly what he'll say, Ah Wu,' the Tiger said.

'*The soft and weak overcomes the hard and strong*,' John said. 'That's all very well to say, but this is my daughter and my Lady that we're talking about here.'

'Whoa,' Na Zha said.

'Holy shit,' the Tiger said. 'Have *you* been spending altogether too much goddamn time human. I cannot believe you just said that.'

'I will not leave them undefended,' John said. 'Dismissed. Ah Bai, report. Ah Na Zha, I'd appreciate your cooperation in not travelling too far.'

I shot to my feet. 'No! Wait.'

Everybody hesitated. I pushed my chair back and moved away from the table. 'Na Zha, Tiger, please come here.'

Neither of them moved.

'Please come and look at me.'

They remained unmoving.

'Tell them, John.'

'Do it,' John said wearily. 'She won't rest until she's sure that she's not the same thing.'

'I've seen inside you before, Emma, and you are not the same thing,' the Tiger said gently. 'You are something completely different.'

I returned to the table and leaned on it. 'Are you absolutely sure?'

'Yes.'

'The Dragon saw a heart of pure monstrous darkness in me,' I said.

'Then in that respect you are a perfectly normal human female,' the Tiger said. He saluted John. 'My Lord. By your leave.' He disappeared.

'Dude,' Na Zha said, and disappeared.

'What did he call me?' John said, turning to Michael and me.

'Equivalent to "most honoured old and dear friend",' Michael said.

'I think you are stretching the truth slightly, Michael,' John said. 'But right now we don't have time to worry about it. Let's get Leo and Simone back, and show the demon to Simone. I would also like to ask you, Emma, to reconsider your position on leaving Simone in school. There is only one capable Celestial remaining to defend her if necessary.'

'I'll talk to Simone about it anyway,' I said. 'I'm beginning to wonder myself. This is getting very bad.'

We made the announcement to the students first thing the next morning. They waited for me in the training room, sober and sad. First years, second years, third years — as many as I could fit in one room.

'Are you okay, ma'am?' Monique said.

I waved her down. 'I'm fine. You know what happened?'

They all nodded, very serious.

'Okay. Please take a seat on the mats, the Dark Lord has something to say to you about this.'

I checked my watch; he would be starting. I fell to sit cross-legged as well.

Just waiting for one more group to be ready. Okay.

The students all stiffened as John spoke into their heads.

You all know that we lost a great many of the Masters in the last attack. We also lost ten of the best seniors, eight of whom were ready to be promoted. Frankly, we have nobody left to teach you, save myself, Emma, Leo and the three remaining Celestials. Six of us can't teach six hundred students.

Sofie sobbed once quietly.

We have to close the school, Disciples. This is as difficult for me as it is for you. The Arts are more than my life; they are my existence, my essence, my reason for being.

Monique handed Sofie a tissue and the girls hugged each other.

We will arrange for all of you to be sent home. I know that some of the seniors have nowhere else to go, so can stay if they wish —

There was silence for a while.

Okay, okay, calm down, not all at once. Those seniors who have nowhere else to go can definitely stay. We will provide for you; don't be concerned about that. This isn't about funds; this is about your safety. Without the Celestials we cannot guarantee it.

There was complete silence.

But rest assured that after the Celestials have returned, and this demon has been removed from the picture, the Academy will restart. Emma can handle it — I have complete faith in her. The Masters will return, and you will too.

'How long?' Joe whispered.

Somebody here in my senior class just asked me how long. I am not supposed to tell you this, but I will anyway. It is August now. It will take three to four months for the Celestials to return; do not ask where they are or what they are doing. So by the end of this year, or early next year, we will be restarting. Take a break. Have a holiday with your families. Perhaps the more senior Disciples can return to your homes and teach. We will have you back when the situation has improved —

Okay, okay, seniors can stay if they have to ... Sakamoto, if you don't shut up I will send you home ... Good.

There was complete silence.

I was just asked how long I have.

I dropped my head into my hands. Somebody came and put their arm around me. I looked up; it was Kathy, one of the American juniors. She smiled weakly at me. A few other students gathered around to comfort me.

As soon as you are all safe at home I will see the Lady. After that I will probably have three or four months myself, no more.

'Oh my God, I didn't know that,' I whispered. 'He's due already. No.'

Kathy gave me a squeeze and one of the other students patted my shoulder.

Sorry, Emma. I should have told you. But the needs of the students always come first, you know that, and they have the right to know.

Monique and Sofie clutched each other and wept silently together.

The seniors will arrange the transportation. It is best that you leave as soon as possible — it simply isn't safe for you here. Go home. We will bring you back when it is safe for you to return.

That is all. Dismissed.

I gently shook Kathy off, squeezed her hand, and rose. I didn't look behind me as I went out and called the lift. The entire Academy was eerily silent.

I took the lift to the top floor, went into my office

and sat behind my desk. I moved a few papers around and absently checked my email. I felt completely empty.

Then it was as if a circus arrived outside my door. There was a huge commotion in the hall; people shouting. I raced to the door and threw it open; the entire lobby was full of clamouring students.

'There she is!' somebody shouted.

A chorus of voices. 'Lady Emma! Lady Emma!'

'Whoa, whoa, calm down, everybody,' I said as loudly as I could. 'What the hell is going on?'

Leo came out of the lift, followed by another dozen students who'd crammed in with him. He came to me and shrugged, smiling slightly.

'What the hell is going on, Leo?'

The stairwell door opened and John came out. He'd been in the training room directly below us with the seniors and had come up the stairs rather than the lift. He stopped when he saw all the students then came to me too.

The minute the students saw John they all went quiet, fell to one knee, saluted, and pulled themselves silently to their feet.

The three of us turned to face the students. They were crammed in the hallway in front of us, overflowing into the lift lobby.

The lift doors opened and another dozen students tried to squeeze in.

'Get to the lift and stop it, Leo, before somebody gets hurt,' I said.

Leo pushed through the students, pulled his wallet out of his hip pocket and jammed it into the lift doors, forcing them to remain open so that the lift couldn't leave.

'Do not for a minute think that any of you are staying,' I said loudly, and the shouting started all over again.

Silence!

That worked.

One at a time, alphabetical order, in my office. Whose surname starts with A?

Five students raised their hands.

Okay, in my office. Bs are next. Everybody whose surname does not start with B, return to your room. I will call the Cs, but I will do it by surname for the Chinese. Out. Now.

Somebody pulled Leo's wallet out of the lift and returned it to him, then the students silently took the stairs back down with the regimented discipline that we would normally have expected from them.

'Whoever's first, in the office, come on,' I said, and young Cynthia Anderson came forward.

John, Leo, Cynthia and I went into John's office.

'This is administrative, you don't need me in here. How about I send them in for you?' Leo said.

'Good idea,' I said, and John nodded. We sat around John's desk with Cynthia, a very fair redhead from New York. 'Well?'

'My Lord, Lord Xuan, Lady Emma.' Cynthia took a deep breath. 'If I could, I'd like to stay — take a job here in Hong Kong, if I can, and learn off the seniors who are staying. Only once or twice a week, just to keep my skills up. I really don't want to go home. I want to stay here.'

'How many seniors are staying, John?' I said.

'All of them,' John said. 'Two-thirds of them are staying now. The other third,' he said with a sigh, 'will go home for a couple of weeks, then come back. They want to keep their skills up, and they want to stay here with us.'

'Me too!' Cynthia said. 'Even if it's only twice a week. Even if it's learning from a third year. I want to stay!'

'We'll think about it,' I said. 'Your safety is paramount, you know that.'

'My safety is entirely unimportant,' Cynthia said. 'I don't care if I have to walk over hot coals, I want to stay here with you. Damn it, Lady Emma ...' Her voice broke and she pulled herself together. 'My Lady. The Academy, the Mountain, the Folly, this is my home. The other students, you, Lord Xuan, Master Leo, you are my family. I'll risk it all to stay here.'

'As I said, we'll think about it. Dismissed, Cynthia,' John said, and leaned back to share a look with me. 'Send the next one in.'

It became apparent before we even reached the Cs that they all wanted the same thing. We didn't have much choice. Even if we did send them home, they'd be on the first flight back to find work, find a place to live, and sneak into the Academy to learn from the seniors.

Both of us were pleased, even though we were concerned for their safety. But we didn't need to say it out loud. Words weren't necessary.

CHAPTER THIRTY-TWO

After we'd given the juniors permission to stay and sent them back to the Folly, we had a meeting with the seniors to work out what to do. We had ten of the most advanced of them: all over thirty, strong, reliable and intelligent. We had lost most of the human Masters in the Mountain Attack; now we had lost all of the Celestial Masters in the latest one. These guys were all we had left. John would not have promoted them because they lacked the talent, but we had no choice.

I had felt uncomfortable when I learned that I was better than any of them and was made Master after only just over a year. John said that I had more talent than all of them put together. He said the same thing about Leo. Leo was tremendously embarrassed as well. And the worst part was that all of the seniors agreed with him.

'Okay, people, here's the situation,' I said over the conference table on the seventh floor. 'The juniors refuse point blank to go, and they want to learn off you guys.'

'No. None of us are good enough,' Sakamoto said.

'We don't have a choice. If we send them home, they'll be on the next plane back and sneaking into the Academy to learn off you anyway.'

'It will take the Dark Lord years to undo the damage if we teach them,' Cheung said. 'We are simply not capable.'

'The Celestials will be back in three to four months,' John said. 'Just hold things together until then. Don't teach them anything new, just revise what they've done.'

The seniors were silent.

'Any questions?' John said.

'No, sir,' they chorused, obviously unhappy.

'Emma will do the rosters with you later. Maybe go out now and talk about who'll do what, to save her time. Dismissed.'

The seniors saluted and filed silently out. John and I remained.

'You need to see the Lady already,' I said softly.

John just looked at his hands.

'Damn. When is good?'

He glanced up at me. 'I think I can go another two, three weeks before I need to see her.'

I had my diary open in front of me. I flipped forward. 'Mid-August.' I sighed. 'Oh well, we knew it anyway.'

He rubbed his hands over his face. 'We thought I'd last until August next year.'

'Will Simone be ready?'

He studied his hands. 'After I have seen the Lady, I will pay a little visit on One Two Two.'

I dropped my head onto my arms where they rested on the table. 'No.'

'Once it is out of the picture you will be fine. You can handle nearly anything thrown at you. Simone is close. When One Two Two is gone, and we have cleaned out its nest, I think you two will be okay.' He looked back up at me. 'We'll go home and have a family meeting and tell everybody the plan.'

'I don't want to tell Simone. It will devastate her.'

'She's known the situation for a year now, Emma.'

'It will be completely different when we tell her to her face.'

'I know.'

Simone, Michael and Leo were already in the dining room when we went in. Leo and Michael saluted. Simone's eyes were huge.

John and I sat down together. Neither of us said anything; we didn't know where to start.

'I think I'd better just show you,' John eventually said. 'Simone, come and sit in my lap.'

Simone hopped off her chair and crawled into her father's lap. He turned her around so that she faced him.

'Look inside, sweetheart.'

She put her hand on his forehead and concentrated. Then she dropped her hand, leaned forward to touch her forehead to his, and sobbed quietly. She wrapped her little arms around his neck and held him close, and he buried his face in her hair with his eyes closed.

'He needs to see the Lady in the next three weeks. After that any further energy feeding will be ineffective,' I said quietly.

Leo shot to his feet. 'She's *not ready*! I *knew* you were in trouble. I've been feeling *lousy*!'

'No,' Michael said. 'Oh, geez. No.'

'Go and sit next to Leo, darling,' John said, and Simone returned to her chair.

I passed her the box of tissues and she pulled a few out and wiped her eyes, then blew her nose loudly. 'Sit down, Leo,' she said. 'I think there's more.'

Leo's face went rigid and he sat.

'After I have seen the Lady, we will visit a certain

Demon Prince,' John said. 'A Black Turtle, a Black Lion and a White Tiger, if he is free to come along.'

'No, Daddy,' Simone whispered. 'If you change into the Turtle you can't change back.'

'I want to go too,' Michael said vehemently.

'Three of us. That is all.'

'My Lord,' Leo said. He hesitated. 'Thank you.'

'I don't want you to go, Leo,' Simone said, still sniffling. 'You'll *die*.'

Leo smiled gently and took Simone's hand. 'You know I won't last long anyway, sweetheart.' Simone grabbed some more tissues with her other hand. Leo turned to John, still holding Simone's little hand in his enormous dark one. 'Where will we go to see the Lady?'

'How far away can you go now? Back to Kota Kinabalu?' I asked.

'I can't go any further than here,' John said. 'We'll do it on the top floor of Hennessy Road. We will be attacked when we do. Emma: you, Simone and Leo will remain here at the Peak. The seals will protect you, and I trust the two of you to defend Simone. Michael will go to the Western Palace. I expect the main assault to be at Hennessy Road. I will call the Phoenix and Na Zha, and perhaps a couple of other friends, to defend the building. We will clear the students out and put them in the Folly, defended there.'

'This is a very bad idea, my Lord,' Leo said. 'I think if all of them are at that sort of risk, then perhaps we should just go in now.'

'*No!*' Simone shouted.

'I don't have the strength,' John said. 'I am much too drained to go in right now. I will not be able to do it until after the feed.'

The doorbell rang, and both John and Michael shot to their feet.

'He is supposed to be in Hell,' John growled. 'I will take his head for this. Leo, Emma, with me. Michael, stay here with Simone.'

He turned and went out, Leo and I following him.

Ah Yat held the door open. Martin was on the other side of the huge metal gate.

'Let me in. I know the situation — I can help you protect Simone,' Martin said. 'I give you my word: I will harm none of you.'

'Go to hell,' John said.

'My Lord. Lord Xuan. *Father*,' Martin said, and John winced. 'She's my sister and I want to see her safe. I can arrange safety for her while Kwan Yin helps you. Let me in. I swear, this is an honest offer.'

I moved forward to open the gate.

'No, Emma,' John said, but I ignored him. I let Martin in, and he smiled and saluted me.

'I will kill you one day,' Leo said in a menacing rumble.

'I don't blame you,' Martin said gently. 'If it means anything to you, I wasn't pretending.'

Leo glared silently at him.

'Living room. Let's talk about it,' I said.

Martin sat on one of the couches and we all stood around him. 'It's like this,' he said, leaning his elbows on his knees. 'Number One knows that once you've been fed this time, it's the end. So you're probably planning to take True Form and see One Two Two straight after.'

Nobody said anything.

'But you can't travel any distance right now. So when she does feed you, you'll do it here, and attract the largest horde of demons the Celestial has ever seen.'

'Tell me something I don't know,' John said.

'Number One has provided me with a safe house. Your Lady and my sister can go there while you do this. They will be safe.'

'Why?' I said.

Martin spread his hands and looked up at John. 'Obvious. He wants you to win. He wants One Two Two out of the way as much as you do. And if you don't have to worry about the Lady and the child, your chances are that much better.'

'I do not require a demon's assistance,' John said, glowering.

'The demon will not be assisting you. It will be me providing safety for the Lady and the child. He's given his word, Ah Ba.' John winced again. 'They will be safe.'

'I will consider,' John said, turning away.

'No! Wait!' I said, and Martin glanced up at me. 'Contact me the first week of August. You can take Simone, but I'm staying here.'

'You can't trust him, Emma,' Leo said softly.

'Neither of you are going,' John said.

I glared at John. 'Simone will be safe. You want me to use the phone?'

'Shit,' John said, spun on his heel and stalked out.

'I'll be in touch,' Martin said, smiling gently. He disappeared.

The next morning I went into the training room and quietly closed the door behind me. I moved into position in the middle of the mats, then began to work through a wu-style Tai Chi set. The rest of the apartment was silent. Michael was at the Western Palace; Leo was out; John was resting; and Simone was watching television.

I felt something under my foot and kicked it away. It made a clicking noise in my head as I hit it. I froze.

I very carefully put the chi back, then moved silently and slowly to find whatever I had kicked.

It was a tiny pebble on the floor, only about half a centimetre across. I leaned over it, and nearly fell over from the shock of recognition. It was Gold, in True Form. I touched him carefully, then picked him up.

'Gold. Gold. Can you hear me?'

Nothing. Not even a click.

I carefully carried Gold out and went to find John. He wasn't in his office, so I went to his room and rapped on the door.

Hm? Come on in, Emma.

I went in. John had been sleeping, his long hair almost completely out of its tie. He didn't move, he just smiled at me from the bed. I went to the bed, crouched, and put Gold in front of his face so he could see the stone.

He leaped up, grabbed Gold out of my hand and ran out of the room, his long hair flying behind him. 'Come on, I may need you too,' he called as he raced away.

I followed him down the hall and into the kitchen. He pushed Ah Yat aside and stood in front of the stove, fiddling with the knobs. The minute he had the big wok burner on, he dropped Gold into it.

'Will that help him?' I said.

John crossed his arms over his bare chest. He'd just been wearing a pair of plain black shorts to sleep because of the heat, even with the air conditioner on. 'I hope so.' He pulled his hair roughly out of the way and retied it.

'Can a stone like him die?'

John lowered himself to watch Gold in the flames. 'Normally, no. But he's been almost completely drained of all energy; nearly destroyed. Damn!' He made a sudden, sharp movement towards the flame. 'I don't have anybody who can drop him into a volcano.'

'Can the Phoenix help?' I said. 'If he needs to stay in fire?'

'She's on the Celestial in Court, Emma. Not available.'

'Amy,' I said.

'Good idea,' John said, and his eyes unfocused. 'Go and open the living room window for her. She's not too good on direct travel yet.'

I went to the living room and opened the window. It seemed like an eternity before Amy appeared, whipping through the air in her black dragon form. She came through the window, landed lightly on the carpet, and transformed. She fell to one knee and saluted me.

'Did the Dark Lord tell you what happened?' I said, gesturing for her to follow me into the kitchen.

'Something to do with Gold,' she said. 'I'm so glad he's not dead. I thought he was dead.'

'He nearly is,' John said as we went into the kitchen together.

Amy stopped dead and blushed furiously when she saw John.

'What?' he said.

'She's not used to seeing a god in his underwear,' I said with a grin. We moved forward to the flame. 'He's in the fire, Amy.'

'Will he be okay?' she whispered.

'We'll leave him in the flames for another ten minutes or so, and then you will need to fly as fast as you can and drop him into an active volcano,' John said, studying Gold closely. 'Do you think you can do that?'

'Where's the nearest one?' she said.

We all shared a look. 'I'll go and look it up,' I said. 'I'll be right back.'

I came back with a printout of the website I'd found. 'Do you need to have flowing lava, or is just the crater enough?'

'Lava,' John said.

'Hawaii then. I'm not sure about the closer ones, they may not have any lava. Hawaii definitely does, and there's more than one of them. It's our best shot.'

'Got it,' Amy said. 'Come on, Gold, you can make it.'

'Amy?'

Amy crouched, moving her face as close to the flame as she could. 'I'm here, Gold. We'll make it.'

'Amy,' Gold's voice sighed. 'What happened?'

'Don't worry about that,' John said. 'We'll just let you toast in the fire for a while, and then Amy will take you to Hawaii and drop you into the volcano there.'

'That would be good,' Gold said weakly. 'That really sounds very good.'

'You'll have about fifteen minutes once I've turned off the flame,' John said to Amy without looking away from Gold. 'You will need to fly very, very quickly. Don't attempt to take him directly — you would destroy him. Don't go underwater; that would be too cold for him.'

'I can do it,' Amy said softly without turning away from Gold.

'Amy?' Gold whispered.

'I'm here.'

His voice softened. 'Don't leave me.'

'I'm not going anywhere.'

'Find a couple of oven mitts,' John said.

I scrabbled through the cupboards until Ah Yat shoved a pair of mitts into my hand. I accepted them with a smile. She was the only one who knew where anything was in the kitchen.

'Gold, if I take you out now, do you think you could make it to Hawaii with Amy?' John said.

Gold didn't make a sound.

'Gold. No,' Amy said, almost moving to touch him in the fire.

'I think I can do it,' Gold whispered.

'Okay,' John said. 'Emma, is the window still open?'

'Yep.'

'Amy, put the mitts on and change.'

Amy transformed, the mitts looking very strange on her black dragon form.

'Okay,' John said. 'I'll turn off the flame, you grab Gold, and go. Go as fast as you can.'

Amy nodded.

John turned off the burner. Amy grabbed Gold and ran for it. She flew through the living room, out the window, and disappeared quickly.

'They'll make it,' I said softly.

'I know they will,' John said.

'How long will he be gone?'

'If she can get him into the volcano before he expires, then he should be back in a couple of days.'

'That soon?'

'Yep.' John smiled. 'I don't think I can go back to sleep now. Too much excitement.'

'Well, if you're not going back to sleep then put some clothes on,' I said. 'I was doing a set in the training room. How about some long sword?'

'Sounds good to me,' he said as he headed down the hall back to his room. He retied his hair again, the muscles moving under the smooth skin of his back.

'I changed my mind,' I said loudly.

He stopped and turned. 'Hm?'

'Don't bother putting any clothes on. I think I like you like that.'

He smiled and shrugged. 'Okay. Whatever. Long sword.'

I followed him into the training room. '"Whatever"? You've been around Michael too much.'

'Whatever. Long sword.'

CHAPTER THIRTY-THREE

The next Saturday the Tiger met us at the outdoor arena and all of us leaned on the fence to watch Michael take Star over the jumps.

'You've taught him well,' John said.

'Natural talent,' the Tiger said. 'One of the best. His mother can ride too.' He glanced at me. 'You still don't want one for yourself? A new crop of Arabs is coming through. I could give you one, keep you occupied after Ah Wu's gone.'

'I think I'll have enough to worry about,' I said without looking away from Michael. 'When the Celestials come back I'll have a lot to do.'

There was a clatter behind us and we turned. Some riders were passing us on the concrete path and their horses had spooked at the Tiger. The riders battled for control as the horses danced sideways, trying to get away.

The Tiger concentrated and the horses immediately calmed and walked past placidly. We turned back to the arena.

Star refused one of the jumps and Michael went forward over his head, crashing into the sand. Star pulled back, but Michael still had the reins, and he hopped up, brushed himself off, and waved to us. He vaulted back onto Star and turned him to take the jump again.

The Tiger concentrated on Michael. Michael waved his hand over his shoulder, then turned the horse and took him easily over the jump.

'He is extremely insubordinate sometimes,' the Tiger said with amusement.

'Can I have a pony?' Simone said. 'Can we try again?'

'That's a good idea,' I said. 'John? She doesn't have school right now, a pony would keep her busy.'

'I'll bring a few to choose from next time I come,' the Tiger said.

'After,' John said.

'Okay,' the Tiger said.

We were all silent for a while.

Michael finished. He dropped the reins and Star lowered his head, blowing heavily. Michael rode him back to us at a walk.

'Take him up and get the *mafoo* to hose him down and give him a roll in the sand,' the Tiger said. 'Then have a shower and meet us up at the terrace.'

'My Lord,' Michael said.

'You're not hurt?' I said.

'Nah, just a few bruises. Nothing serious. Already healed them.'

'Meet us up at the terrace. Battle plans,' John said.

Michael nodded and turned the horse to the gate. We went to the restaurant at the top of the country club. Leo waited for us in the shade. We sat around the table he had reserved, Simone with us. Everybody was a part of this.

We waited until the waiter had taken our orders and moved away.

'When is the Lady coming?' the Tiger said.

'August twenty-first,' John said. 'Two weeks from today. It will be Saturday, so the streets will be busy; that should hold them back slightly.'

'Who's going where?' I said.

'Me and the Lady, top floor, Hennessy Road; Na Zha on the roof. Students at the Folly, guarded by the Tiger and the Phoenix and half the Academy dragons.'

The Tiger moved to protest but John cut him off. 'Emma, Simone, Leo, on the Peak. Gold with you, Emma. The Dragon on the roof, guarding, with the other half of the Academy dragons. We'll make them split their attack three ways.'

'You don't have enough to defend yourself,' the Tiger said. 'Add some dragons at Hennessy Road.'

John dropped his voice. 'It would not necessarily be a bad thing if One Two Two were to take the advantage and come for my head. I could end it there.'

There was complete silence.

'No, Daddy,' Simone whispered.

'If he doesn't come for me then, I'll go and take him anyway, sweetheart.'

'No.' Simone cast around, then decided and climbed into Leo's lap, facing him. She began to shake and he pulled a packet of tissues out of his pocket and kissed the top of her head. He held her close and she buried her face into his huge chest.

'Simone is going with Martin,' I said.

Simone turned in Leo's lap and took a tissue from him. 'I want to go with Martin, Daddy.'

'We can't trust him,' Leo said, wrapping his arms protectively around Simone.

'Yes, we can,' John said. 'In this case, we can. We know that Simone will be safe.' He sighed with feeling. 'It's probably for the best. You should go too, Emma.'

'I would like to be with you,' I whispered. 'I want to be on the top of Hennessy Road. With you.'

'No, Emma, you'd be in danger,' Simone said. 'You should come with me and Martin. 'Cause I'll need you after Daddy and Leo have gone. You have to stay safe.'

I sighed. She was right.

'They will launch an all-out attack the minute the Lady and I link. If we survive the attack then we will probably be able to finish the process,' John said. 'It will take about a week. We will come home if we survive the initial attack and finish at the Peak. Martin can bring Simone home, and Michael can return, when the matter is decided, one way or another.'

Michael arrived, his blond hair dark from the shower. He threw himself to sit at the table next to his father. 'Did I miss anything important?'

'Xuan Wu, Na Zha, the Lady in Hennessy Road,' I said. 'Tiger, Phoenix, students, Folly. Me, Leo, Peak, Gold and the Dragon guarding. Simone is going with Martin. You are going to the West. We're splitting the dragons between the Folly and the Peak.'

'Why so few at Hennessy Road?' Michael said. 'You need more than that.'

The Tiger grunted but didn't say anything.

'Lord Xuan wants to lure the demon in so that he can transform and take it out,' I said.

'Oh, geez,' Michael said, his voice full of misery.

'If we survive this then we'll make plans to go in and take it out anyway,' Leo said over the top of Simone's head, and she clutched his arms. 'Michael, any idea where his headquarters are?'

'No idea,' Michael said.

'We'll send somebody in, taking a harmless human form, and check out the law offices during the week while the feed is happening,' I said. 'There are four altogether. One of them is probably a front.'

'We will find that little ...' The Tiger swallowed what he was about to say.

'Simone,' John said gently. She didn't move in Leo's massive arms. 'Simone, you have me for two more weeks. Please, think about what you would like to do. For the next two weeks, it'll be you and me, anything you want. And I want you to always remember that I have promised to return for you. I will be back. I promise.'

'Emma and Leo too. And Michael. All together,' Simone said, clutching Leo's arms.

'All the family together,' John said gently.

Simone dropped her little head, her tawny hair falling around her face. 'Okay,' she whispered.

The waiter arrived with the food but nobody was in much of a mood for eating.

Three days later Martin turned up at Hennessy Road. The guard demons called me to see if they should let him in. I told them to send him up.

He came into my office wearing a plain tan pair of trousers and his usual dark green polo shirt. He smiled gently and sat on the other side of the desk.

'Okay,' I said. 'It's happening on August twenty-first. The Lady and Xuan Wu will come here to this building, and they'll start the feed about noon. We're expecting to be attacked immediately.'

'I'll take Simone that morning,' Martin said.

'Where are you taking her?'

'Number One has an underground facility in the old tunnels on the Island. She'll be in there; there's no opening to the outside. She'll be safe.'

'The old war tunnels? The ones they used to escape from the Japanese?'

He nodded. 'Those ones.'

'Where on the Island?'

'Kennedy Town. Sai Wan. Inside the mountain above Belcher's Street.'

'And she'll be absolutely safe?'

'Absolutely. I will be with her. She will be safe. They will have no idea where she is.'

I sighed with relief. Whatever happened, Simone would be safe. I had an inspiration. 'Somebody should go with her to care for her if we're all taken down.'

'You, Emma. You are the best to stay with her, and you would be safe too.'

I leaned forward over the desk and spoke intensely. 'Martin, did you know that I've made a pact with the King of the Demons?'

'You made a pact with the King?' he said with disbelief.

'If I go to him, and stay with him, he can guarantee Simone's safety.'

'So you want to be where you can know what happens. If my father is taken down, and One Two Two has his head, you'll call the King. That way, you can be sure Simone will be completely safe.'

I studied him. His face was expressionless. He wasn't as stupid as his recent actions had made him appear.

'Will you promise to look after her if we're all killed, or if I have to go to the King, Martin?'

He smiled, then gracefully rose to his feet and placed his hand on the table. 'I swear that I will dedicate the rest of my life to ensuring my sister's safety and happiness.'

He sat back down and pulled his chair in, then leaned his arms on the desk. 'I'll be at the Peak on the day. About nine in the morning. If all goes well, I'll return her by dinnertime. If not, I'll just see what happens. She will still own the apartment on the Peak. We can stay there together. If you are all gone I will stay with her, regardless of the outcome, I swear.'

I was tremendously relieved. 'You have no idea how much this means to me, Martin. Thank you.'

'My Lady,' he said, bowed his head slightly and disappeared.

We spent the next two weeks doing exactly what we would normally do. Simone didn't want to do anything special at all. She didn't even spend more time than usual with her father. She clung to her normal life with both hands. She even talked about returning to school in September.

On August twentieth, the night before the feed, we all sat together after dinner in the dining room. Nobody had eaten very much.

The other three Winds, Na Zha and the Lady had joined us; the dining room was nearly full. Normally a meal like this would be full of fun and banter, with the Tiger teasing the Dragon mercilessly and Simone laughing hysterically. But this time we were all subdued.

'Martin will be here at nine tomorrow,' I said, checking the schedule clipped to my diary. 'When are you taking Michael, Tiger?'

'Right after this,' the Tiger said. 'I'm taking his mother too; we can't be sure that little bastard won't come after those who aren't involved. Everybody will be kept safe. I'll be back tomorrow morning — I'll make it nine o'clock as well. That son of yours had better be as good as his word.'

'He is,' John said.

'You should call in the Thirty-Six,' the Tiger said.

'You know I can't call them in; this is personal,' John said. 'There is also a chance that the North will be attacked, or the Mountain attacked, as well. They will be on standby just in case there is an attack at the Celestial level.'

'One Two Two is after us, he won't attack the Celestial Plane,' I said.

'The King may take the opportunity of me being distracted,' John said. 'If the Armies aren't on standby he may attack. He only promised not to come after us. He didn't say anything about the Celestial Plane.'

'Oh my God,' Leo said softly.

I shot to my feet. 'I didn't know that! What the hell are you doing staying with us? You should be protecting your homes, and your families, and your realms, just in case!'

'As long as the Thirty-Six are on alert we will not be attacked,' the Phoenix said. 'Sit down, Emma. We know what we are doing.'

I fell into my chair with a bump. 'Will he attack once Xuan Wu is gone?'

'I doubt it,' John said. 'The Celestial Armies are very strong. I doubt he will attack at all. The probability is very small, as long as the Armies are on standby.'

'You'd better be right,' I whispered.

'Tomorrow morning,' John said briskly, 'Martin will take Simone. I will move down to Wan Chai with the Lady. We will lock down the students, and prepare. At noon, we will begin the feed, and take it as it comes from there. Leo, take Dark Heavens; Emma, use the Serpent. I will not require a weapon. We will meet here 9 a.m. tomorrow. Dismissed.'

The other three Winds and Na Zha saluted and disappeared.

'You and Simone need your rest,' Kwan Yin said. 'I will help you. I will stay here with you until I go with Ah Wu tomorrow.' She reached out and took my hand. 'You will be fine, Emma.'

'Are you sure?' I whispered, looking for reassurance in her eyes.

She smiled her sad smile and didn't say anything.

* * *

Simone, Leo and I were already awake and waiting in the dining room when John and the Lady came out.

'Why aren't you wearing your armour?' John said.

'I won't need it until you start the feed,' I said. 'Besides, I feel really stupid wearing it.'

'It took the armourers a long time to make that fit you, Emma,' John said. 'You know it has special abilities. Wear it.'

I didn't say anything. I hated that armour. It was heavy, even though it fitted me perfectly and was exceptionally comfortable to wear. I was the first European woman the armourers had fitted; Immortals like Meredith could conjure their own. It had taken the forge staff six weeks to get over the fact that European women were much curvier than Chinese; they refused to believe that my breasts and hips were actually that much larger around than my waist. In the end John had to take a photo of me and send it up to the Mountain before they'd believe the measurements.

'Please wear it for me, Emma,' John said gently.

My throat thickened and I nodded into my tea.

'Have you eaten anything?' John said.

Both Simone and I shook our heads. Leo glowered into his coffee.

'You will need to eat something, ladies, Leo. We are going into battle today and you will need your energy.'

'Eat,' Kwan Yin said.

Suddenly I was starving. 'Ah Yat!'

Ah Yat poked her head around the dining room door.

'Toast and peanut butter for me, cereal for Simone, please.'

'And apple juice,' Simone said.

'Eggs, ham,' Leo said.

Ah Yat smiled, nodded, and disappeared behind the door.

'Thanks,' I said.

The doorbell rang. 'It's Martin,' Simone said.

'Finish your breakfast before you go with him, sweetheart,' John said.

Simone nodded. Ah Yat came in with the breakfast things. I went out to get Martin. He waited outside the gate.

'She's just started eating,' I said as I opened the gate for him. 'Wait until she's finished, and then take her.'

'I'll wait in here then,' Martin said, gesturing towards the living room.

'No, come with me. It's okay.' I took his hand and led him into the dining room.

The minute Martin entered, Leo grabbed his breakfast and coffee and slinked into the kitchen without a word.

Martin and Simone shared a smile, a hug and a messy kiss before he sat next to her. I buttered my toast. John glowered.

'My Lord, my Lady,' Martin said to John and Kwan Yin.

Ah Yat poked her head around the door. 'Can I get you anything, Ming *Daiyan*?'

'Ceylon, please, Ah Yat,' he said. 'How close are you? You should be there soon.'

'Nearly there,' Ah Yat said, bobbed her head, and disappeared.

'You know Ah Yat?' Simone said.

'I tamed her,' Martin said. 'Just before ...' His voice tapered off.

John's expression darkened but he didn't say anything.

'Where are we going, *ge ge*?' Simone said. John grunted at the table.

'I am taking you to a cave that is very safe, *mei mei*,' Martin said gently.

'A cave?' Simone's eyes were wide, her spoon poised halfway to her mouth.

'Eat, Simone,' John said.

Simone nodded and ate.

We sat in uncomfortable silence until Ah Yat brought Martin's tea.

'You should eat something too, John,' I said.

'Eat,' Kwan Yin said. 'She is correct.'

John concentrated. Ah Yat brought him some congee. He picked up his spoon and stirred the rice, then put his spoon down again.

'Eat. That's an order,' I said firmly.

He shrugged, picked up the spoon and mechanically ate. Martin made a quiet sound of amusement and John glared at him.

Simone put her spoon down. 'Finished.' She hesitated. 'Martin, Aunty Kwan, could you go out, please? I want to say goodbye to Daddy.'

Martin left, taking his tea with him. Kwan Yin rose and followed him.

John dropped his spoon and leaned back.

I choked on my toast. I took a huge gulp of tea. 'I'll go too, and let you say goodbye to Daddy by yourself.'

'No, Emma, I want you to stay,' Simone said. 'Because I'm going to hold Daddy's hand, and you can kiss him goodbye.'

I tried very hard to swallow. My throat was so thick I couldn't manage words.

Simone went to John and climbed into his lap. She threw her arms around his neck and held him tight. 'Come back, please, Daddy. Don't die today.'

'I can't die, Simone,' he said. 'I will just be gone for a while, whatever happens. The important thing is that you are safe.'

She held him tight and he buried his face in her hair,

squeezing his eyes shut. They remained unmoving for a while.

'I love you, Daddy,' Simone whispered.

'I love you, Simone,' John said, his voice thick. He nuzzled her hair. 'I will return for you, I promise.'

'And Emma,' Simone said softly.

John glanced up at me and smiled sadly. 'And Emma.'

John held his arm out and I knelt beside him. I buried my face in his chest next to Simone and he held me close. We remained still, holding each other, for a long time.

'Kiss Emma goodbye,' Simone whispered. 'I'm not looking.'

'We don't need to, sweetheart,' I said. 'This is enough.'

John didn't say anything. Words weren't necessary.

John remained in the dining room while I took Simone to Martin. She went into the kitchen to see Leo first, and was in there for a while. Then she came out, gave me a final hug, and she and Martin were gone.

I returned to the dining room and drank some more tea. John ate his congee. We didn't say anything.

The Tiger turned up and sat down without a word. Ah Yat brought him a pot of Chinese tea and he drank it silently while we ate. Leo came in and finished his coffee.

Ten minutes later the rest of the Immortals arrived. Ah Yat made tea for them. Nobody said a word.

CHAPTER THIRTY-FOUR

At ten o'clock we all took our places. John and the Lady went together to Hennessy Road in the car, with Na Zha sitting in the back in case they were attacked before they even started.

The Tiger and the Phoenix both quickly embraced me then disappeared to guard the students at the Folly.

Gold went with them to organise the students, then returned. 'All is ready.'

Leo helped me into my armour, looping the leather through the buckles and making sure it was fitted correctly. We checked through our weapons. Ah Yat gave us sports bottles full of water without being asked and then disappeared.

Ready, the Dragon said from the roof. *I have about six other dragons with me. Nothing will get past us.*

A while later John's voice appeared in my head. *We will start the feed in twenty minutes. Dragon, inform Gold if you sense them coming. Gold.*

'My Lord,' Gold whispered.

'Where is a good place to wait for them?' I said. 'In the training room?'

'Anywhere,' Gold said. 'They can only come in one at a time, unless they blow the seals.'

'I'd like to stay in the living room. That way I know what's happening,' I said. 'If they come through the front door, or through the glass, we can stop them.'

'Training room, Emma,' Leo said softly. 'Please.'

'Okay,' I said, just as softly.

'Go. I'll stay in the living room and keep you posted,' Gold said.

'You don't have armour,' I said to Leo as we prepared ourselves in the training room.

'Never wanted it,' he said. 'Too heavy. I'm big enough as it is; with armour on I can hardly move.'

I nodded. That made sense.

'I love you dearly, Leo,' I whispered. I sidled to him and put my arm around his waist. He threw his enormous arm around my shoulder and we held each other without lowering our weapons or turning away from the door.

'You're like a sister to me,' he whispered back. 'I think a long time ago I told you he'd never love anybody the way he loved her. I was right.'

'Yeah. What I have with him is completely different. But I do have something in common with her, I think.'

'What?'

'She bossed him around even worse than I do. He's the world's biggest softie. You'd expect the Dark Emperor of the North, the God of Martial Arts, to be harsh and scary. Instead, he's all marshmallow inside.'

'That's why we love him,' Leo said softly, and gave me a gentle squeeze around the shoulders.

'I think you're right,' I whispered. I moved away from him and checked my watch.

'Don't put yourself at risk,' Leo said. 'Don't take any chances. Simone needs you. Whatever you do, you must survive this.'

'I intend to,' I said, and hefted my sword.

Leo's voice softened and he spoke without looking away from the door. 'And I would be honoured if you would permit me to give my life defending you. If you allowed me to do this, I would die a very happy man.'

'I'm the one that's honoured, Leo,' I said.

The chime pinged on my watch and we readied ourselves.

Nothing happened. Complete silence.

'Gold?' I called.

HOLY SHIT! the Dragon roared in my head, so loud it made me wince. *Phoenix, SWAP! We have metals! The dragons are being cut to pieces!*

Water here, the Phoenix said more calmly. *They are attacking our weaknesses. I am on my way. Ah Qing, come and take out the waters. Ah Bai is being attacked by fires. What the hell is going on?*

He has made elemental hybrids and is attacking the Winds at their weaknesses, Gold said into my head from the living room. *Qing Long, the Wood Dragon, is weak against metal, so we have been attacked by metals here. All the dragons are weak against metal. They have no defence, they are being destroyed. Zhu Que, the Fire Phoenix, has been attacked by waters at the Folly. As has Bai Hu, the Metal Tiger. He has been attacked by fires. All attacked at their weaknesses. The Winds are quickly swapping so that they are either strong against or not affected by the elementals.*

I have not been attacked at all, John said into my head with wonder. *Emma, they are coming after you and the students, not me.*

'Still too much of a coward,' I said. 'Wants to swap me or a student; too scared to face Xuan Wu.'

Leo didn't move or say anything.

Gold's voice appeared in my head. *The Phoenix is here. She and her fire elementals are taking out the fake metal elementals. Damn! Some of the demons may enter through the windows, and the fire creatures cannot follow them in without igniting the building. The metals are large and sharp and —*

There was a crash of splintering glass and a loud whirring sound, like a propeller.

Leo and I both took a couple of steps back and waited.

There was the sound of a buzz saw hitting concrete — a shrieking metallic noise that made me cringe. Oh my God, the elemental had attacked Gold.

The sound stopped.

'Gold?' I called.

I'm okay, Gold said. *Look at me, I'm a daddy. Shit!*

Gold appeared in the doorway to the training room. He turned and backed so that he was standing next to Leo in front of me now. He had shrunk to about two-thirds his normal size; he was about the same height as me now. He must have lost about twenty centimetres in height, but he was in his standard battle form: his human shape made of stone.

'They've blown the seals,' he said. 'Move out of the way, Leo, so that Emma can hit them with energy — see if that affects them. Weapons don't hurt them, and they slice pieces off me, but I think energy can do it. I think that's how I destroyed the one in the living room, but after what happened I can't use any more energy. Having the child has drained me completely.'

'Where's your baby?' I said.

'In me,' Gold said. 'If I'm destroyed, it will stay behind. Look after it for me, will you?'

I didn't have a chance to answer him. A metal elemental appeared at the door.

The top of it touched the doorframe. It was like a very good computer-generated image of a robot: polished metal surfaces, mirror-like, smooth and rounded. Its limbs moved fluidly, taking many forms as it decided which weapon attachment to use on us. Eventually it settled on spinning blades.

'Hit it, Emma,' Gold said.

I hit the elemental with chi from my sword and it exploded.

'Okay,' Gold said. 'There are about forty of them —'

'*Forty*?' I cried. 'That was about level forty equivalent. I can't take more than about five of them with energy before I'll blow myself up!'

'Use the weapon to throw the energy,' Gold said.

'That *is* with the weapon throwing the energy.'

Another elemental appeared at the doorway. As soon as it entered the room I threw energy from the sword and blew it up.

'Where's the goddamn Phoenix? She's fire, it's strong against metal.'

'She is dealing with the other hundred fifty odd elementals outside the living room windows,' Gold said. 'The forty I mentioned are already in the living room, but the seals are still holding them.'

Another elemental appeared. I threw chi at it; it exploded.

'That one was even bigger!' I wailed. 'I can't take any more out with chi. We'll have to move to hand-to-hand.'

'We can't,' Gold said. 'Weapons are useless against them. Pass the chi to me, Emma, I'll absorb it.'

'Don't be ridiculous, I need you alive.'

I had a sudden inspiration. I didn't have time to speak; another elemental appeared in the doorway. Black chi would send the energy away, if it worked. Please work.

I dropped my sword, generated black chi in my hands, and threw it directly at the demon. The chi ricocheted off the elemental's shiny metal surface and hit Leo square in the chest, knocking him off his feet.

I prepared another ball of black chi and threw it at the demon. The demon absorbed it.

There was a sickening wet sucking sound from Leo, but I couldn't turn away from the demon to see him. It sounded like somebody dislocating the bones on a beef carcass. I'd killed him.

The demon approached me, its bladed hands spinning. I readied myself, and generated ordinary gold energy on my hands. I was very close to the edge with energy. It was quite likely that this bolt would kill me. The demon's spinning blades were very close to my head.

The demon stopped dead and the blades disappeared. I hesitated, waiting to see what it would do.

It held its arms out on either side of me and generated two halves of a cage, one from each arm. It closed them together around me with a metallic clang, nearly taking my feet off as it swept the cage halves along the floor.

I was trapped in a spherical silver cage. I called my sword to me, but it didn't come.

A long metal spike flashed out of the demon cage and stabbed me in the left thigh. I shrieked with pain, grabbed it and tried to pull it free of my leg, but it wouldn't shift.

It burned straight into my leg and my leg went numb. Either poison or sedative; probably a sedative. Wong wanted me harmless before he took me.

I concentrated and filled my hands with energy, ready to blast the demon through direct contact. This would probably kill me, but the alternative was worse than death. I concentrated in the split second I knew I had before it took me.

'Don't do anything, Emma!' Gold yelled. 'Help is on its way!'

Na Zha appeared on the other side of the demon in True Form — a young man of about twenty in traditional pale blue robes, a headpiece on his topknot, long hair flowing. *Allow me,* he said, and threw his razor-sharp ring weapon, glowing with energy, at the demon, slicing straight through it. The weapon returned to him. The demon dissipated.

Na Zha disappeared. *I will take out the rest. See to Leo and Gold.*

'Are you okay, ma'am?' Gold said. 'That leg looks bad.'

'I'll live.' Somehow I managed to stay on my feet. 'I don't think it injected too much into me. What about you?'

'We're fine,' Gold said. 'But I think you've killed poor Leo. Was that black chi?'

'Yes,' I said, and limped to Leo's side. I stopped dead when I saw him. 'Holy shit.'

'You got it in one,' Gold said. 'Is he alive?'

Leo was an enormous black lion lying like death on the floor. I lowered myself stiffly to sit next to him. I didn't have time to worry about the sedative, and it didn't seem to be affecting me too badly. I lifted one of Leo's forelegs and felt along the underside of the limb. There was a pulse, and I sagged with relief. 'He's alive.'

'Take care, Emma,' Gold said. 'When he comes around he may be one hundred per cent beast and mad as hell.'

The lion's dark brown eyes opened and cast around, looking, not focusing. Leo's eyes.

'Leo,' I whispered. 'Leo, are you okay?'

'What happened to me?' the lion whispered in Leo's voice. 'I can't move.'

We are victorious, John said into my ear. *I'm coming home.*

Leo dropped his head to the floor and sighed. 'Good.' He went limp.

'Your leg is bleeding,' Gold said. 'Emma, you're very pale. Are you sure you're all right?'

The training mats crashed into me from the side, but I didn't really feel them.

'Emma. Emma.'

'Hn?'

'She's coming around.'

My eyelids were incredibly heavy. It was hard to breathe and my leg hurt like hell.

'Simone?'

'She's not back yet, love. She's still with Martin. But I talked to her and she says she's safe.'

I was still in the training room. John and Ms Kwan were above me, both holding my hands. I struggled to pull myself upright and they helped me. I looked around. My armour was gone; somebody had removed it for me. There was a bandage tied around my left leg, over the jeans: a field dressing. Blood had seeped through it but the bleeding had obviously stopped.

Leo was next to me, still a black lion, still unconscious.

'How do you feel?' John said.

I released his and Ms Kwan's hands. 'I'm okay. I just need to work the drugs off.' I concentrated to heal my leg and nearly passed out. I pulled my awareness back.

'Don't attempt to heal yourself, Emma,' Ms Kwan said. 'You cannot while you are affected like this. Let the wound heal by itself.'

'How long have I been out?' I said.

'About half an hour,' John said. He passed me the bottle of water that Ah Yat had left for me and I took a huge drink.

I pulled myself around to sit next to Leo. Every time I moved, my left leg hurt like hell; the thigh was beginning to swell. I ignored it as I put Leo's head in my lap and buried my hands in his thick black mane.

'You did this?' John said.

'It was an accident.'

John put his hand on Leo's head. 'Definitely more than a coincidence; I told him that.'

Leo stirred. 'Mr Chen?'

'I'm here, Leo,' John said.

Leo's voice was warm with relief. 'My Lord. Is Simone okay?'

'Simone's fine. She's still with her brother.'

Leo pulled himself onto his front legs, then tried to stand upright on his hind legs. He fell heavily. 'What happened to me?'

'Leo,' I said gently, taking his enormous black head in my hands. 'Leo, slowly turn and look in the mirrors behind you.'

Leo pulled himself onto his front legs again and clumsily turned to see himself. He studied his reflection. 'How the hell did this happen?' He flicked his tail. 'Whoa.'

'I threw black chi at the demon and it reflected onto you,' I said, my hand still on his shoulder. 'I am so sorry, Leo.' I dropped my head and my voice thickened. I felt ill that I had done this. 'I'm sorry.'

Leo pulled himself to his feet, tried to take a few hesitant steps, and fell over again. 'This four leg business is the pits. It'll take me ages to work out how to walk.' He stopped and his mouth opened, revealing his enormous gleaming fangs. 'But my speech is okay now.' He inched back to me and dropped his huge shaggy head into my lap.

I gasped as his head hit my leg.

Leo saw the bandage. 'You're injured. What happened to you?'

'The demon stabbed me,' I said. 'Geez. One Two

Two is such a coward. It wanted to sedate me before it took me.'

'Tranquilliser dart on the wild animal,' Leo said wryly. He shook his head and his mane swung around him. 'Two wild animals.'

'I'm okay,' I said, shifting under his head so that the leg didn't hurt as much. 'What about you? How do you feel?'

He gazed up at me. 'I'm fine, Emma. We're all alive, and that's what's important. I'd better get this walking business sorted soon, 'cause as soon as Simone's home she's gonna want a ride.'

I put my hands on either side of his head, burying my fingers into his plush black mane. 'You really okay?'

'Yeah.'

'We can turn him back,' John said. 'There has to be a way.'

Leo turned his head in my lap to see John. 'I'm sure there is. We'll find it. Not important. I can go and visit One Two Two like this anyway.' He stretched out one paw and turned it over, admiring it. 'Lookit them claws. I think I could have some serious fun with them on a certain Demon Prince. I just need to practise this walking stuff and then I'm up to go.' He sighed. 'Suddenly I'm starving. Can you get Ah Yat to bring me a big rare steak? No,' he said, and paused, 'make that a *raw* steak.' He turned back to me. 'Get me a steak, and then you two work out what you want to do. Now that we've survived this, we need to plan the next move. Come on in and tell me, or I'll get these four legs working and visit you.'

'Leo,' I said, my hands still on his head, 'you are the most remarkable man it has ever been my privilege to meet.'

'Just get me a steak,' Leo growled, the lion vocal chords making his voice a throaty rasp. He shook his head free. 'Go.'

I felt a stab of pain in my leg as I pulled myself upright. Ms Kwan helped me.

'Oh, one other thing,' Leo said. He shifted so that he was lying on his belly like a cat.

'What, my friend?' John said.

'A bowl of coffee.'

On the way back to the dining room we passed Gold. He sat in the living room holding his new child and gazing at it with wonder. Both John and I stopped and went to him. Ms Kwan left us and went into the dining room.

The living room was a disaster area. All of the windows were broken and shattered glass covered the floor. Some of the priceless Tang and Ming china had been smashed, and a couple of rosewood side tables had been totally destroyed. John's collection of antique English books was scattered on the floor. Ah Yat was busily sweeping up the glass on the carpet.

Gold's child appeared as a small stone, pink-flecked grey granite, about the size of a child's fist.

'Are you okay, my Lady?' Gold said. 'You're wounded.'

'I'm fine,' I said, limping to sit with difficulty on the couch. The leg was beginning to stiffen as well as swell. 'The demon stabbed me in the leg to sedate me.'

'Wake my parent, my Lady,' Gold said. 'It will want to see.'

I tapped on my ring. It had slept through the whole attack.

'Next time wake me up! I could have been of use to you!' the stone demanded loudly. 'Damn! You're injured!'

'I'm okay,' I said.

Gold's baby squeaked, a tiny sound, then went silent.

'By the Grandmother,' the stone in my ring whispered.

'Gold ... I am ... By the Grandmother.' Its voice became even softer. 'It is so beautiful.'

'I have the sudden urge to take female human form,' Gold said with a small smile.

'You can if you want,' I said.

The gentle smile lit up his face. 'No need. It's all the same to us.' He rolled the stone in his hands and it squeaked again, a quiet sound of contentment. 'Besides, I don't think Amy would be too impressed if I did.'

'How much care does it need?' I said. 'Does it need feeding, or cleaning, or anything like that?'

'Nope,' Gold said with a shrug. 'Nothing like that. Basically all it needs is lessons from its parent on being a good stone.'

'You'll be a great parent, Gold,' the stone in my ring said.

'Thanks, Dad.' Gold held the stone out to me. 'Take it. Let my parent see it.'

I held the stone gently in both hands. Its surface was rough and unpolished, quite unlike Gold's smooth quartz. It was warm and seemed to be pulsing gently in my hands.

'It's beautiful,' the stone in my ring said with awe. 'I wonder what mineral it will take.'

'It could be jade, like you, Dad,' Gold said. 'Or gold, like me. Either way, it's precious.'

'Precious,' the stone in my ring said. Its voice became more brisk. 'Emma, you need to send them somewhere safe.'

I held the stone out for John to take.

Gold and the stone in my ring both yelled '*No*!' at the same time, and Gold shot to his feet.

John didn't move. 'I should not touch something so young and fragile.'

I took the stone back and Gold sagged with relief. 'Return it to me, please, my Lady. You nearly gave me a heart attack.'

I passed it back to him and he held it with reverence.

'Jade has nested on the top of Tai Mo Shan,' John said. 'The tallest mountain in Kowloon. She has found a hollow in the hillside there, far from any hiking trails. It is quite remote for Hong Kong. You and your child will join her, and all of you will return when the situation is resolved, one way or the other. Go.'

Gold didn't move. 'I won't leave you.'

'That is an order, Gold. Go. Emma will send for you when this is resolved.'

'My Lord,' Gold said, and hesitated. His voice softened. 'Please let me stay here for a while. I want to make sure you are all safe. My child is here with me, we are protected.' He smiled and shrugged. 'Besides, I need to rest, and there are nice soft beds here.'

'Do you want to go back to your flat at the Folly?' I said.

'I'd rather just hang around here and make sure everything's all right,' Gold said. He fell to his knees before us and saluted without looking up, still holding the baby. He left his hands in front of his face, beseeching. 'Let me stay.'

John and I reached agreement without saying a word to each other.

'Go and rest in the student room, Gold,' I said. 'Come out when you're feeling better. You're probably exhausted.'

Gold grinned up at me. 'You have no idea.' He saluted John and then me again, pulled himself clumsily to his feet, and shoved his child into his chest. He turned and went down the hall towards the student rooms.

'Why couldn't you touch the baby?' I said.

John didn't say anything, he just rose to go into the dining room.

'Xuan Tian Shang Di, you stop and tell me why you couldn't touch that baby,' I said fiercely. I rose with difficulty to follow him.

'He's too yin, Emma,' the stone in my ring said.

I understood with a shock. 'That's why there are no plants and no pets. No goldfish, no hamsters, nothing. Simone asked for a hamster and you wouldn't let her have one.' John had stopped halfway to the dining room, but didn't turn back to me. 'You're so yin you kill them. You probably don't even need to touch them. You just kill them.'

'Simone had a hamster for her fourth birthday,' John said, opening the door to the dining room and gesturing for me to enter. 'The Tiger ate it. She refused to speak to him for a week. Not a good idea for us to keep small furry creatures in the house; the Tiger can't control himself. Adult creatures are safe, it is just babies that I must be careful with right now. Of course not my own, only other people's. When I have the Serpent back, it will not be a problem.'

I shook my head as I went into the dining room. 'I really am consorting with monsters. My parents were right.'

'Of course they were,' John said.

CHAPTER THIRTY-FIVE

The victory meeting was a cheerless and gloomy affair. The Dragon, the Phoenix, the Tiger and Kwan Yin were already seated at the table when we went in.

'You're limping,' the Phoenix said. 'What happened?'

'A metal hybrid stabbed her, tried to sedate her to take her,' John said as he pulled a chair out for me.

The Phoenix rose and gracefully helped me into my chair. When I was seated she didn't release my hand; she held it and concentrated, looking at the injury.

'Sit with me after the meeting and I'll heal it for you,' she said. 'But you shouldn't do anything too strenuous for the next few days.'

She released my hand and sat in the chair next to me. I nodded my appreciation and she smiled.

'What's the plan?' the Dragon said.

'The Lady and I will spend a week linked,' John said. 'While we are performing the feed, Emma will find the location of One Two Two's headquarters. We require assistance; preferably an Immortal who is powerful enough to see through walls.'

'I'll come along, Ah Wu,' the Tiger said. 'My Number One is handling things right now. I have a score to settle with this little piece of shit.'

'Mind your mouth,' John said.

'Sorry, all,' the Tiger said without a hint of remorse. 'I've heard the Dark Lady say worse anyway. It has four law offices, correct?'

The Dragon snorted with disdain. 'Of course the thing is a lawyer.'

'It's the leader of all the underworld activity in Hong Kong,' I said. 'It needs the expertise with the law. Of course it is.'

'Not all lawyers are underhand. I have met some as honourable as any,' the Phoenix said. 'How is the Golden Boy? I heard that he had been sundered.'

'If you mean he had a baby, yes, he did,' I said. 'He's resting right now. Later he'll go into hiding with Jade and her clutch.'

'Jade has a clutch?' the Phoenix said, then glanced quickly at the Dragon. 'I did not know this.'

The Dragon ignored her completely and she turned back to me. 'What will you do when you find the demon's location?'

'Myself and the Tiger will find it and hunt it down,' John said. 'We will destroy it, and everything it has created.'

'I am looking forward to doing battle alongside my Lord the Xuan Wu in True Form,' the Tiger said, his voice a low menacing growl. 'It's been a hell of a long time.'

'I feel the same way, old friend,' John said.

There was a soft scraping sound at the dining room door. John rose; we both knew who it was.

He opened the door and Leo entered unsteadily, his hind end wandering out of control every few steps. 'I hope you're including me in this.'

'Yeah, Leo's a beast, I saw that,' the Tiger said loudly. 'How the hell did this happen, Ah Wu? I've never seen anything like this before. The Lion was *human*.'

Neither John nor I said anything.

Leo made his way to the chair next to John's. 'I don't think I can do it on my own yet,' he said. 'Anybody care to help me?'

'You're too big to sit on one of Ah Wu's dining chairs, you'd break it,' the Phoenix said, and the chair next to Leo transformed into a large rosewood chest.

The Phoenix used PK to raise him like a kitten being lifted by the scruff of the neck, his legs curled in front of his vertical body. She lowered his back end gently onto the chest and his front end onto the table.

'Thanks,' he said.

'My pleasure,' the Phoenix said.

'How did this happen?' the Dragon said. 'Humans don't change like that.'

'I do,' I whispered.

'Yeah, that's right,' the Tiger said. 'Must be something to do with continuous prolonged exposure to the extremely peculiar Xuan Wu creature.'

'Or black chi,' I said miserably.

All of them stiffened at that. They studied me intensely. I even felt more than one of them turn their Inner Eye on me.

'That is my Lady and your Regent that you are prying into,' John said forcefully, and the examination stopped.

'Black chi?' the Tiger said, slightly too loudly. 'You, Emma? Black chi? Really? Whoa.'

'Demon,' the Dragon said.

'Oh, will you give it a fucking *break*, Ah Qing,' the Tiger said, leaning back and slapping his hand on the table. 'I looked inside her, and she told me herself, truthfully, that she is *not* a demon.'

'Show us, dear,' the Phoenix said gently. 'Just a very small amount, don't over-stress yourself.'

I held my hands out and generated a ball of black chi about the size of a tennis ball.

'Move it in front of me, I want to see it,' the Tiger said.

I moved the chi so that it was about ten centimetres from his nose. He gingerly held out a hand and touched it. 'Yep, that's the same stuff, all right. Maybe you're right, Ah Qing.'

'My Lady is no demon,' John said. 'And I suspect that I could generate a similar thing if circumstances warranted. Also, I have investigated, and the effect that this chi produces is entirely different to that produced by the King.'

'There's a King that does stuff like that?' Leo said as I reabsorbed the chi. 'Which King?'

'King of the Demons, Leo,' I whispered.

'Leo, I want you to come with me,' the Lady said. She had been silent throughout the entire exchange. 'I would like to look at you. I may be able to remedy the situation.'

She gracefully rose, raised her hand, and Leo disappeared. 'I will examine him in your practice room, Ah Wu,' she said. 'I may be able to reverse the process. I will return when I am sure one way or the other. I do not think you require me in these arrangements.'

'Mercy,' John said softly, and she disappeared as well.

'This black chi turns people into beasts?' the Tiger said.

'He was the first human I've hit it with,' I said, 'and it was an accident. It bounced off one of those fake metal elementals.' The Tiger nodded, understanding. 'Sometimes it doesn't do anything at all; sometimes it changes the demon to another type of demon; and once it ...' I stopped, unable to finish.

'It what?' the Phoenix said. 'What?'

'It changed a demon into a human being,' John said.

There was complete silence.

'Why didn't you tell us about this, Ah Wu?' the Dragon said softly. 'This is most important.'

'No, it isn't,' I said, 'because I'll never use it again. The results are too destructive and unpredictable. Heaven knows what it'll do next time. Never again.'

'What if it's life or death?' the Tiger said.

'Then death,' I said. 'That stuff is too dangerous.'

'What if it's life or death for *Simone*?' the Dragon said.

I was silent. He was right. I wondered what would happen if I used it on myself.

'Let's return to the topic at hand,' John said. 'After the Lady and I have done the feed for seven days, the Tiger and I will go in. Dragon, Phoenix, will you remain with the students and my Lady while we do it?'

'I'm going with you,' I said.

'You are staying with Simone,' John said. 'Don't be ridiculous.'

I sighed with feeling and decided to drop it. 'Can't you take some Horsemen or something?'

'No need,' the Tiger said. 'In True Form, together, nothing will stand against us.'

'He is correct, Emma,' the Phoenix said gently. 'The Bai Hu and the Xuan Wu are the two greatest demon destroyers on any Plane. Together they are unstoppable.'

'Take the Third Prince,' I said.

'Good idea, if he's up for it,' John said.

The Tiger nodded agreement. 'He should enjoy some straight-out rampant destruction. Just what he likes.'

'We will meet back here in seven days,' John said. 'Dismissed.'

The Dragon disappeared.

'Let me heal you first, Emma, then I will return and check my chicks,' the Phoenix said.

'Are they okay?' I said as she took my hands and her fiery presence moved through me. She was like a liquid flame coursing through my energy meridians, but I felt no heat. Her essence moved to my leg and I felt the warmth on the injury.

'The Demon King obviously did not wish to take advantage,' the Phoenix said. 'The Celestial Plane was not attacked. Tell me if the heat is too great.'

'My Lord,' the Tiger said, shaking his hands in front of his face. 'I want to wait and see if the Lady can remedy the Lion. If she can't, I can give him some quick lessons on being a cat. I can have him walking, running and fighting in that form, and you will have a valuable ally in the battle.'

'Ah Bai,' John said. 'Bring Michael back. We may need his help to guard when Simone returns.'

The warmth in my leg stopped and the Phoenix removed her consciousness from me. I shivered; I suddenly felt cold.

'It will pass,' she said. 'You adjusted to my fire essence remarkably well. Very impressive.'

'Yang. Serpent,' John said.

'Yes,' the Phoenix said. 'Most serpents are quite yang. Can you transform at will, Emma?'

'No,' I said.

'Stand up,' she said. 'Let's see how it looks.'

I rose. The leg was still slightly stiff but the wound had definitely healed. I pulled the bandage off, wrapping it around my hand. There was a large hole in my jeans where the metal had pierced them. I opened the hole and inspected my leg; there was an angry red mark where I had been stabbed, but it was healed. I lifted my leg and swung it: still stiff and difficult to move, but nothing worse than the aftermath of a hard workout with the sword.

'Thanks, Zhu Que.'

'My pleasure,' she said with a small smile. 'Rest it for a couple of days. The wound was very deep. By your leave.'

'Go and check your babies,' I said.

Her smiled widened, she saluted me, and disappeared.

Emma, come, the Lady said in my head. John and the Tiger nodded to me and I went out. The door of the training room was closed. *Come in,* the Lady said before I'd tapped on it.

Kwan Yin sat cross-legged in the middle of the mats in True Form, her beautiful serene face radiant. The long white robes cascaded around her. Her enormous shining pile of hair nearly touched the ceiling. I watched her with awe. Her hands were held out over Leo's prone form, a pure white light surrounding both of them. Leo was human again. He appeared to be unconscious, stretched out naked on his side on the floor in front of her.

Do not approach, she said, her glowing oval face not moving. *I am not quite finished. I suggest you go find some clothes for him for when he returns.*

I turned and went out, closing the door softly behind me.

'It worked,' I whispered, hoping the Tiger's acute hearing would pick it up.

Good, the Tiger said into my head. *He will be much more useful with a weapon anyway.*

I let myself into Leo's room and laughed quietly as I went through his drawers. He'd kept some of the pink underwear, hidden at the bottom. I hadn't known that. I grabbed some boxers and a robe for him.

Come in, Ms Kwan said when I reached the door to the training room.

She was sitting exactly the same way, but had returned to her normal human form. Leo sat cross-legged opposite her, his face full of calm serenity.

I hesitated, then went in anyway.

He heard me and glanced up. He smiled. 'I feel doubly naked when there's no fur.'

I tossed him the robe and he pulled it around himself and rose. I passed him the boxers and he tugged them on.

Kwan Yin gracefully stood.

After Leo had tied the belt of the robe, he fell to one knee and saluted her. She placed her hand on his head.

'Will he be able to do it at will?' I said.

She hesitated, gazing at him, her hand still on his head. 'With a great deal of concentration and training, in the right circumstances he will.'

'I won't get a chance to try then,' Leo said, returning to his feet and fixing the robe. 'One more week, and then I'm off demon hunting.'

'You may be able to learn it in a week,' I said.

'I'll be practising with the sword,' he said. 'That will be much more useful than claws anyway.' He turned to go out of the room, took a couple of steps, and tottered. I rushed to hold him up, and he leaned on me.

He straightened. 'Let me go. I'm not weak, it's just a matter of regaining my balance.' He took a couple more steps, realised that he had it, and moved more confidently. 'Tell Mr Chen I'll meet him back in the dining room when I've put some clothes on.'

'Emma,' the Lady said, and I turned back as Leo went out. A glowing white aura surrounded her. 'It does not matter what you are. The fact that you can make this energy is inconsequential. Do not let the foolish Dragon sway you. You will never harm your family. Never.'

'But what am I?' I said.

The aura blinked out. 'It does not matter what you are. Because it is who you love that is the most important.'

She was right. She was always right.

I went to her, fell to one knee and saluted her as Leo had. She placed her hand on my head and I felt her power move through me: a feeling of total peaceful serenity. 'You will never harm them,' she whispered. 'Go and prepare. Ask Ah Wu to teach you energy calming techniques, because very soon you will need them.'

'Not for a week,' I said. 'But thank you, that's a good idea.' I pulled myself to my feet.

'I am no longer needed here,' she said. 'Remember, though, Emma, you can call me any time you need me.'

The doorbell rang: Simone was back. I raced out of the training room with delight. John and the Tiger were already in the hallway, and John opened the door.

Simone threw herself at her father and squealed. He raised her so that she nearly touched the ceiling, then held her close.

Martin smiled through the doorway and disappeared.

John moved Simone to one hip and closed the gate and then the door.

'Hello, Uncle Bai!' Simone said loudly. She saw me. 'Everybody's okay? Everybody's fine?' She saw the wreck of the living room. 'Is everybody okay?'

'Everybody's fine, sweetheart,' I said. 'And Gold had a baby.'

'A *baby*?' Simone cast around excitedly. 'Where? Where?' She stopped. 'Where's *Leo*?' She concentrated, looking for him. 'You're in your room, Leo, come on out. I know you're there!'

Leo came out, fully dressed, and Simone wriggled a request to her father. He let her down and she raced to me, gave me a quick hug and a kiss, and then ran to Leo, who hoisted her into his arms. She wrapped her little arms around his neck with glee. 'Everybody's *okay*!' she shouted into his grinning face.

'Gold's sleeping, he's very tired after having the baby,' I said. 'It just looks like a rock anyway.'

'Uncle Bai, give me a ride!' Simone shouted, jiggling in Leo's arms with delight. 'And then Daddy can do some sword with me! I hope Ah Yat's made something good for dinner!'

'If Leo lets you down I'll give you a ride,' the Tiger said. 'But you know you're really getting too big for this.'

Leo gently lowered Simone and she grabbed the Tiger's hand and dragged him into the living room. Ah Yat had finished cleaning up the glass and was taping clear plastic over the window frames. The Tiger transformed and Simone crawled onto his back. She was so big now that her feet nearly touched the floor.

I checked my watch. Three twenty. Only just over three hours since the attack. It seemed like forever.

'Should we get together and discuss what we'll do while the feed happens?' Leo said.

I shrugged. 'I suppose.'

John gestured towards the dining room and he, Leo and I went in and sat together. My diary was on the dining table in front of me, where I had left it that morning. I flipped it open and pulled out the card for Simon Wong's law firm.

'Will they be able to recognise the Tiger when he walks into the law offices?' I said.

'He should be able to hide his nature and appear as an ordinary human,' John said. 'He'll probably take the form of a woman.'

Leo snorted with amusement.

I nodded, studying the card. Wong had four offices: one in Central, one in Sham Shui Po, one in Tsim Sha Tsui, and one in Kowloon City. I glanced up at John. 'The Tiger doesn't need to go. I know where Wong is.'

There was a tap on the door and Michael entered. He saluted John and me, then sat next to Leo.

'How do you know?' Leo said. 'You don't have that look.'

'It's on the card,' I said, flipping it around. 'It says he has an office on the top floor of Kowloon City Plaza. The top floor's the car park. There are no offices there, that's all shops.'

Michael's face filled with comprehension. 'That's what he did with the girls in Kowloon City.'

'What?' I said.

'Kowloon City?' John said.

'Yeah,' Michael said. 'He has some sort of office in Kowloon City. That's where they took the girls. He's had that place for a long time. Like, nearly forty years or something. The guys used to joke that he'd been around for so long he had to be a demon.'

The Tiger came in and sat next to me. 'What did I miss?'

'Is Simone okay?' I said.

'Your demon has her. She's okay.'

'He's in Kowloon City,' I said. 'The pizza delivery guy.'

'What?' Michael said.

'We were attacked by a demon posing as a pizza delivery boy,' John said. 'A couple of years ago, when Emma had just started here. The real delivery boy was found later, cut into small pieces, in a dumpster in Kowloon City.'

'The copy of me too,' I said. 'It all fits together. He's somewhere in Kowloon City. Top of Kowloon City Plaza.'

'Too exposed,' John said. 'Too much in the open.'

'Kowloon City, Kowloon City.' I had it. 'Kowloon Walled City!'

'That's gone now,' Michael said. 'They tore it down and put a park there.'

'It would have been the perfect place for him to have his headquarters though,' I said. 'Narrow, twisting alleys between rotting ten-storey tenements. A part of Mainland China, but neither side would take responsibility and police it. Completely lawless. It would have been perfect.'

'But it's a park now,' Michael said, insistent. 'They tore it all down.'

'And Kowloon City Plaza is right next to the park. What if he's underneath? He's had forty years, John. Could he be underneath?'

'On my way,' the Tiger said, and disappeared.

We waited silently for him to return.

The Tiger reappeared. 'For some reason I can't see underneath,' he said. 'You'll have to send a stone. Do you have any handy?'

John concentrated. There was a tap on the door and Gold came in.

'Oh no you don't,' I said loudly. 'This new parent is not going anywhere.'

Gold pulled his baby from his chest and put it on the table.

'The stone in my ring can go,' I said to Gold. 'Don't you go anywhere.'

'She's right, Gold, I hadn't thought of that,' John said. 'Go back and rest.'

I tapped the stone in my ring.

'Yes, Emma?' it said.

'Stone,' John said, 'you are ordered to Kowloon City Park. Scout. We suspect that the demon may have tunnels underneath the park.'

'My Lord,' the stone said, and disappeared out of my ring.

'Go back and rest, Gold,' I said.

'Can I wait and see my parent safely back?' Gold said, picking up his child and returning it to his chest.

'Quite a few weird things have been happening lately. I want to be sure.'

'There's nothing there that will hurt it,' the Tiger said. 'It'll be okay.'

I gestured towards the chair next to me. 'Wait with us if you want.'

We sat silently at the table and waited for the stone to return. It took quite a while and I began to become concerned. I could see from Gold's face that he was worried as well.

The stone appeared in its human form between me and Gold. It sagged to lean on the table with one hand; its face was pale and it was trembling. I had never seen it so emotional.

'Are you okay, Dad?' Gold said, quickly rising to help his parent.

The stone appeared unable to speak, and Gold gently guided it to sit next to me, then sat beside it, holding its hand.

'There is a large network of tunnels under Kowloon City Park,' the stone said, its voice hoarse. 'I am probably the only one able to see inside. Nobody else would be able to do it.'

'Why?' the Tiger said. 'I thought it was just me.'

'The walls of the tunnels have been coated with the essence of powerful stone creatures,' the stone said, its face and voice expressionless.

'No,' Gold whispered, gripping the stone's hand. 'No.'

The stone dropped its head. 'The demon has painted the walls,' it said, then took a deep breath, '*with the guts of my children*!'

'Go,' I said. 'Both of you. Thanks, stone. Gold, take him out, look after him.'

The stone ran its other hand over its face and smiled at me with misery. 'I'm not finished, Emma. There are well over fifty extremely large demons in those tunnels.

Most of the demons are between level eighty and ninety; some are bigger than ninety.'

'Holy shit,' the Tiger and Michael said in unison.

'The demons are *turtle* and *snake* hybrids,' the stone said with anguish.

John shot to his feet. He stalked to the door of the dining room and opened it.

'You don't have time to do sword katas right now, John,' I said with compassion. 'Come back and sit down, and we'll work out what to do about it.'

John hesitated, holding the door, without looking at me. Then he shrugged, closed the door, turned and returned to sit at the table. He dropped his forehead into one of his hands and didn't move.

'What?' Leo said.

'They were turtle and snake hybrids, Leo.' I gestured towards John. 'Heaven knows how many of his children were destroyed to create them.'

'You would know if your children were missing, my Lord, wouldn't you?' Leo said, his face filling with the grim realisation of what had happened.

'I am a reptile, Leo,' John said into his hand without looking up.

'Go,' I said to the stones.

'Some of the things that demon has done are beyond comprehension,' the stone said, hoarse with emotion. 'Humans. Demons. Shen ...' Its voice trailed off and it shook its head.

'Come on, Dad,' Gold said, putting his arm around the stone's shoulders. 'Let's go and work out how many of our family we've lost.' He guided the stone gently out.

'Gold,' John said loudly as they opened the door.

Gold turned. 'My Lord?'

'You are relieved of duty until further notice,' John said. 'You may take True Form as often as you want until I order otherwise. Understood?'

'My Lord,' Gold said, then turned and went out, holding his parent's arm.

'Take your time, stone,' I called after them.

Neither of them replied.

'He's waiting for you, John,' I whispered. 'I wonder what else he has ready for you.' I suddenly remembered, and inhaled sharply. 'No.'

'Leo, Michael, leave us,' John said.

'No, you don't,' Leo said loudly. 'I'm staying. I'm a sworn Retainer. I'm part of this. I'm coming with you, I'm fighting this bastard, and there's nothing you can do about it.' He glared at Michael. 'Out.'

'Let them stay,' I said. 'It won't hurt for them to know. You can trust both of them.'

'How many of your children know about this, Ah Bai?' John said.

'Nobody knows. I'm surprised you told Emma,' the Tiger said. He smiled wryly. 'Actually, no, I'm not.' He turned back to Michael. 'Emma's guessing that the demon has a little surprise planned for us. With the right sort of ...' he hesitated, 'cage, we can be imprisoned.'

Both Leo and Michael went completely still, staring at the Tiger. Then they glanced at John.

'Yes, me too,' John said.

'What sort of cage, Dad?' Michael said.

The Tiger hesitated.

'Tell them,' John said. 'It makes no difference, we can trust them. Both of them would die before divulging this information, you know that.'

'It needs to be constructed entirely out of Celestial jade,' the Tiger said. 'Jade that has been on the Celestial Plane for at least five hundred years. A single unbroken piece of jade should be carved to make the cage. We must be in True Form to be taken. If we are caged by such a thing, we can be held indefinitely.'

'Has this happened before?' Leo said softly.

'The Turtle has been imprisoned in the past,' John said. He smiled wryly and shrugged. 'A human sorcerer did it to me, and presented me to the Emperor, hoping to curry favour. He didn't even know what I was; he thought I was just a mystical turtle. A demon gave him the cage and told him where I was.'

'Stupid damn Turtle,' the Tiger growled. 'Too busy dragging your tail in the mud to see the human sneaking up behind you. *I'd* never take True Form that small.'

'We have been through this many times before,' John said. 'What's done is done.'

'Stupid damn Turtle,' the Tiger said under his breath.

'You think One Two Two has one of these waiting for you?' Michael said.

'Of course he does,' John said. 'So I must conserve my energy until we go in. If my energy is good, I can take a very large True Form that will not fit into the cage.'

'What about your head?' I said.

'I think he'll be happy with either,' John said, smiling sadly. 'If he can take the captured True Form to his father, the King will be even more pleased.'

I leaned forward over the table to speak intensely to them. '*Are you sure that both of you can take them?*'

John and the Tiger shared a look. They weren't sure.

'With Na Zha?' I said.

Neither of them spoke.

'Anybody else you can call up?'

'I'll see what I can do,' the Tiger said. 'Er Lang, maybe. Zhao Gongming, perhaps.'

'Marshall Zhao won't go in with you, Bai Hu, don't be ridiculous,' John said.

'I know your history with him, and I agree with John,' I said. 'Anybody else?'

'I'll think about it, see who I can round up,' the Tiger said. 'Maybe the other Winds might want to come along, but I doubt it. They should stay here and guard Emma, Simone and the Disciples.' He saluted John. 'By your leave.'

'Bai Hu,' John said. The Tiger disappeared.

'Let me use the phone, John,' I whispered.

John's face went rigid. He shot to his feet and stalked out. The door to the training room opened and closed.

'What's this phone, Emma?' Leo said. 'That's the second or third time you've mentioned that phone, what is it?'

Michael stayed silent. He hadn't been close enough to hear what we'd said when we met with the King in London; he didn't know either.

'You might as well know,' I said. 'I made a pact with the King of the Demons. While we were in London.'

'A pact?' Michael said.

I nodded. 'He wants me. If I go to him, and stay with him and don't try to escape, he guarantees Simone's safety for the rest of her life.'

Both of them stiffened.

I pulled the phone out of my pocket and held it up to show them. 'I can call him any time. I'm surprised you didn't notice it — I take it with me everywhere.' I shrugged and tried to smile. 'The King has promised that if I go to him, he will release me when Mr Chen returns. But Mr Chen is convinced that the King would try to win me over, and if he failed he would just throw me to the Mothers.'

'But the Mothers,' Michael said, looking at Leo. 'What they did to Leo . . .' His voice trailed off.

'What they did to me was nothing,' Leo said, his voice slurring more than usual. 'You'll need to come with us when we go in, Emma, so that if Mr Chen goes

464

down or is caged, you can call the King to make sure that Simone is safe.'

'I know, Leo, but I think Mr Chen is in denial about it. When the time comes, expect some major fireworks.' I shrugged. 'Why don't you go and spend some time with Simone? Take her up to the playground until dinnertime, both of you. Lord Xuan won't be in any state to do anything useful for a while, and my leg is killing me.'

'What about demons?' Michael said.

'Both of you should be enough to guard, and Simone can nearly look after herself,' I said. 'The demons are waiting for us under Kowloon City. You should be okay.'

They both rose. As Leo passed me to go out, he stopped, rested his hand on my shoulder and kissed the top of my head. I put my hand over his. He released me and they went out.

CHAPTER THIRTY-SIX

I stumbled back to my room, opened the door and stopped dead. The stone, in human form, lay on its back on my double bed, asleep. It had changed into a pair of ridiculous baggy green shorts and a plain white T-shirt. Its snow-white hair was tousled from sleep and its elegant face was peaceful. I had never seen it look so human.

To hell with it. I pulled off my jeans, left them on the floor, and climbed in beside it. I stopped: something was between us. It was Gold, in True Form, with his child next to him. I moved them gently to make room, turned onto my side facing away from them, and closed my eyes.

The stone shot up to sit.

'Don't go anywhere,' I said without moving. 'It's okay. I know there probably wasn't space for all of you in the student room. You're here every night in the bed with me anyway. This is your room too, really. Go back to sleep.'

'Another coup,' Gold said softly.

'For both of us,' the stone said, just as softly.

It lay back down then turned so that it was facing me and put its arm around me. I spooned my back into it, and it held me close. Gold and the child moved up the bed to make room, resting against the back of my head.

'I should take female form,' the stone said. 'This is inappropriate.'

'Don't be ridiculous,' I said. 'That makes no difference at all.'

'Lord Xuan would have kittens if he knew,' Gold said.

'Of course he knows,' I said through a huge yawn. 'Is he still doing sword katas?'

'Yes,' Gold said, sounding sleepy.

I didn't remember anything else.

I woke an hour later, alone in my bed. The stone had returned to the ring, and Gold and his child were gone. My leg protested as I turned to rise. It had stiffened badly while I was resting.

'How many children did you lose?' I said.

'We're not sure, but at this stage it appears that I have lost about fifty or sixty,' it replied as I went into my bathroom.

'That piece of demon scum is going to *die*.' I pulled off my clothes and turned on the shower.

'You forgot to leave me outside the bathroom,' the stone said.

'No, I didn't.' I stepped into the shower, closing the screen behind me, and held the stone under the wash of hot water. Then I reached for the soap with my left hand, moving it out from under the stream.

'Thanks, Emma,' the stone said softly. 'The water feels good. I really needed that.'

'I know,' I said. 'That's why I did it. Have you told the Grandmother?'

'Not yet. But when she finds out you can expect some major earth tremors in Central Australia.'

'I'd really like to meet her one day,' I said.

'One day I must take you,' the stone said. 'I think you and she will get along very well.'

I moved the soap into my right hand and held the stone under the water again.

I went into the dining room; nobody was there. I slipped through the door into the kitchen. Ah Yat was busy with vegetables for dinner. She quickly pulled down a mug for my tea without me asking.

'Where is everybody?' I said.

'The Dark Lord is in the training room,' Ah Yat said, returning to the vegetables. 'Princess Simone is still at the playground with Master Michael and Master Leo.'

'Where's Gold?'

'Sleeping, ma'am,' Ah Yat said.

'Let him sleep,' the stone said.

I pottered around, feeling useless, for about half an hour. I asked Ah Yat to check on Simone occasionally. She was fine; she'd been through the shops at the Peak Tower and was playing in the little play area on the roof of the Peak Galleria.

I went into John's office and began to tidy his mess. I sorted through the documents; some of them were tasks that weren't finished. I tried to control my emotions as I put all the loose ends to one side to go through with him.

The training room door opened and closed, and I poked my head out into the hallway. John had emerged, exhausted.

'Are you okay?' he said when he saw me.

'I'm a bit stiff but I'll be fine. You?'

'I'll live. Stone?' John said.

'My Lord,' the stone said.

'Go and have a shower,' I said. 'Then we need to sort through the paperwork. We should do it before dinner, have it fixed now. We won't have time when the Lady returns; you'll be locked up with her for the rest of the week.'

468

He nodded sadly, and turned away to go to his room.

'Emma, sit,' John said when he returned to the office, his long hair still damp from the shower. 'We need to talk.'

I didn't ask, I just sat. He flopped into his big chair across the desk from me.

'Emma,' he said, leaning on the desk and looking me right in the eyes, 'we don't have much longer. I want you to do something for me after I have gone.'

'Anything, John.'

'I want you to promise me something.'

I hesitated. 'What?'

He looked down at his hands and spoke softly. 'If you have to go to the King, I want you to promise me something.'

I leaned on the desk as well. 'I'll never fall for that bastard, John, you can trust me. Don't worry. I know he's charming, but I can see right through it.'

'I know that,' he said, not looking up. He smiled gently at his hands. 'I want you to promise that if you do have to go to him, you will pretend. So that he won't give you to the Mothers. Make him think he has won you over.' He raised his head to gaze at me. 'Pretend. Until I return. Make him think he's won. And when I return, you can hold him to his word to release you.'

I sat there, completely stunned, staring at him.

'Promise me, Emma,' he said. 'Anything is preferable to you being given to them. Anything. Give me your word.'

I struggled to speak.

'Please do this thing for me, my Lady. I do not wish to see you harmed. He will not hurt you. You will be safe. Simone will be safe. That is all that is important.'

I didn't say anything. I couldn't do it.

Suddenly John's head snapped up. He shot to his feet, vaulted over the desk, and raced out into the hall. I ran to follow him. He went into the living room, where Leo waited for us.

Leo fell to his knees. His face was full of anguish.

I had a sudden, horrible, sinking sensation. *Simone wasn't with him.*

'Where is she?' I yelled. I crouched in front of Leo, grabbed his arm, and shouted into his face. '*Where the hell is she?*'

'She is with Ming Gui,' Leo said, his voice hoarse. 'While we were at the playground, he appeared. He said hello, she ran to him, he took her hand and they both disappeared.' He dropped his head. 'I didn't think fast enough. I should have grabbed her.' He sagged over his knees. 'I have failed. Again.'

'Martin won't hurt her, John, she'll be fine,' I said, pulling myself to my feet with relief.

John wasn't convinced. 'What if he's taken her to Number One? To swap her for my head?'

'Would Number One do that? He's renowned for being honourable.'

John moved to sit on one of the couches. 'I don't know.' His eyes turned inward. 'She says she's okay; they've gone out for something to eat.' He snapped back to Leo. 'Michael?'

'Michael followed them, my Lord.'

'Michael travelled?'

Leo nodded, still on his knees.

'He has had no training. He could quite easily kill himself.' John concentrated. 'Found him. But he lost track of Simone. Wait.' He was silent, focusing. 'He wanted to return directly but I've told him to come the long way. It will take him a while, he's on Kowloon side.' He concentrated again. 'Simone says she's okay.'

'Ask her where they are, John, and we'll go and get her back.'

John's face went rigid. 'She won't tell me. She says she's fine, she's having fun.'

My blood went cold. She was just being a perfectly normal six-year-old girl who loved her big brother. 'Can one of the staff track her down?'

'Not if she doesn't want them to.' John's eyes unfocused again. 'She's telling me to leave her alone. If she is harmed in any way by your actions, Leo, I will have your head for this.'

'I'll present it to you myself,' Leo whispered.

'There's nothing we can do. We'll just have to wait,' John said.

Leo rose and moved to sit next to me, putting his arm around me. I wrapped my arm around his waist and we held each other.

'I have a really, really bad feeling about this,' I whispered.

The doorbell rang.

'Everybody get weapons *now*,' John said. 'It's a huge demon.'

'One Two Two?' I said. 'Why here, now?'

'It's not One Two Two,' John said grimly. 'It's Number One.'

'What's he doing here?' I said as I rose to get my weapon. Leo waved me back and went into the training room to collect them.

John went to the front door, grabbed Dark Heavens from its clips, then threw the door open.

Number One stood on the other side of the gate, smiling without humour. 'I think you need to hear what I have to say.'

'Come in.' John opened the gate and Number One entered. He went into the living room and sat on one of the couches.

'Your son has been duped.'

'What?' John said, standing over him.

'One Two Two is immensely powerful. I don't know what it's done to itself, but it can do astonishing things. It took my form, promised your son it would not harm the child, and said that if Ming Gui took her to a place it knows, she would be safe and protected and they could spend some more time together.'

I took a huge deep breath. 'Martin's taking Simone to *One Two Two*?'

I heard a clatter behind me. Leo stood in the doorway, the weapons in a pile at his feet. His face was grey.

'I thought Ming Gui would be useful,' Number One said, studying his hands. 'He has been much more trouble than he is worth.' He glanced up at John. 'Are you sure that this one is yours, Turtle? Everybody knows that your kind produce nests of mixed parentage, that you just walk away from.'

John stiffened and his eyes blazed. Then he sagged. 'I can't contact either of them.' He fell to sit on the other couch and put his head in his hands. 'No.'

The demon rose. 'I'd better go and clean out my nest,' he said. 'You should have taken me up on my offer.'

'Wait!' I said before he disappeared. 'Where's Simone? Where are they?'

The demon shrugged. 'Don't ask me. Could be anywhere.' He smiled. 'I suggest you give my dad a call, Emma. The only way the child will stay safe now is if you go and screw the hell out of him.' He nodded to John. 'Turtle. It's been nice knowing you. You should have given me your head.' He disappeared.

John grabbed Dark Heavens from the couch next to him, threw himself up and went into the training room without saying a word. Leo turned like a puppet and headed down the hallway, also towards the training room. I followed them. John waited for Leo with Dark Heavens in his hand.

'Kneel,' John said.

Leo fell to his knees without a word.

'Leave us,' John said.

'No,' I said. 'Anything you do to Leo, you'll have to do in front of me.'

'Very well then,' John said, and hefted the sword. He moved to stand over Leo.

Leo smiled slightly and lowered his head.

'Wait,' I said. 'If we trade your head for Simone, I'll need Leo to assist me guarding. And I may have to use the phone. If I use the phone, then Leo will be all she has left.' I gestured impatiently. 'We don't have time for this. Let's just go and get her out!'

John hesitated.

'Do it,' Leo said without looking up.

'You would forfeit your life?' John said.

'I have failed. Again. I should pay.'

'And you will,' John said. His voice was very mild. 'First, you will pay by living. Then you will pay by helping us to get her back. And then, if we do get her back and you survive it, you will pay by guarding her until the day you die. A natural death. That's an order.'

Leo collapsed over his knees and moaned, a wordless sound of agony.

'You have failed me, Leo,' John said mildly. 'And your punishment will be: that you live.'

'No,' Leo whispered into the floor.

'Get up, collect your weapons and prepare,' John said. 'Both of you.'

'I still don't have your promise, Emma,' John said as Leo drove us to Kowloon City. John sat in the front seat, I was in the back.

'Where's Michael?' I said. 'Do you have any other Celestials to help out?'

'I sent Michael home. He and Gold will guard the apartment so you have a safe place to return to. The Tiger, the Phoenix, the Dragon and the Third Prince will meet us at Kowloon City Park. I want your word, Emma.'

I tapped the stone.

'I was awake. I know what's happening,' the stone said.

'Do you know where the entrance to the tunnels is?' I said.

'In the *yamen* building,' the stone said. 'I couldn't find exactly where. Gold will have to help me look. We will both need to move around the room to find it.'

'Your word, Emma,' John said. 'Promise me.'

I was silent.

'Please, Emma, don't make me beg you. I will if I have to. *Ngoh kow* —'

'Don't you dare beg me — you're a Celestial Emperor!' I snapped. I ran my hands through my hair with exasperation. 'I don't want to give you my word on this, John, you know I don't.'

'I want you safe when I return, love.'

'What's he asking, Emma?' Leo said softly.

'He wants me to pretend to fall for the Demon King if I have to use the phone. So that I won't be thrown to the Mothers.'

Leo was silent, watching the road.

'Promise me, Emma.'

'Only if I have no other recourse. Only if that's the only way to avoid the Mothers. Only as a last resort,' I said.

'Your word,' John said.

'Do it, Emma,' Leo said without looking away from the road. 'This is about as close as he can get to a last request. Both of us will be able to die with our minds at ease, knowing that you won't be hurt.'

'We will find Simone and get her out of there,' I said grimly. 'And then we will all go home and spend a few more weeks together.'

'I will not come out the other side of this, and you know it,' John said. 'Either the demon will capture me and take my head, or I will take True Form and tear it into very small pieces. There is no other way out of this. So I ask you, Emma Donahoe, as a woman of your word. Promise me.'

'No,' I whispered.

'Promise him, Emma,' Leo said.

'Do it, dear,' the stone said. 'It would reassure me as well. I don't want to see you thrown to the Mothers. All three of us are asking you here.'

'Promise me,' John said. 'You will only use the phone if I go down or if Simone is in real danger. And if you must use the phone, you will pretend to give in to the King's advances. Promise me.'

'Only if I must,' I said. I took a deep breath. 'I promise.'

'I thank you, my Lady,' John said, and turned back to the road. 'Now let's go and destroy this demon and get our little girl back.'

'This is all my fault,' Leo whispered.

'You have failed us, Leo,' John said. 'If you wish to redeem yourself, then do your best to stay alive.'

'My Lord.'

Leo stopped the car in a yellow-lined no-parking zone directly in front of the Kowloon City Park gates. We slammed the car doors shut, pulled our weapons out of the trunk, and moved as one through the gates of the Park. John took Dark Heavens; he was too weak to carry Seven Stars. I had my Serpent sword. Leo carried Michael's white sword.

It was nearly six o'clock and there were still many people strolling around. The park was Chinese-style gardens with paved paths meandering between them, and pavilions alongside the paths. A large pond formed the centrepiece. We attracted quite a few concerned glances as we stormed along the path holding the blades.

The Tiger, the Phoenix, the Dragon and Na Zha appeared from behind a pavilion and joined us. They all appeared as perfectly normal Chinese; they'd even made themselves very plain. The Phoenix was a middle-aged Chinese lady; the Dragon and Tiger were men of similar age. Na Zha looked like a regular Chinese teenager.

'There is an entrance under the *yamen* building,' I said.

'Let's go,' the Tiger said, and we headed through the gardens towards the building.

John stopped dead. 'Wait.' He concentrated. 'Stone.'

'My Lord?' the stone said.

'Will you be able to talk to us once we're under here?'

'I will be able to communicate with the Lady,' the stone said. 'Other than that, I will be silenced.'

'Not even Gold?' John said.

'No,' the stone said. 'Only the one who bears me.'

'Okay,' John said, glancing around. 'Mark this place. About one hundred metres below us, directly below me, Simone is being held. Can you guide us back to this location once we're under?'

'Yes,' the stone said. 'Done.'

'Can you see through, John?' I said.

'No,' he said. 'I can just sense her presence. She is there.'

'Can you talk to her?'

'No,' he said. 'From what I can see, however, she is unharmed.'

'Can you sense Martin?' I said.

'No.' He hefted his blade and continued along the path, pushing past a family who were strolling very slowly through the park. 'Let's go.' The family saw the blades, exclaimed loudly and took off, walking quickly.

'Damn,' I said. 'They'll probably call the police and report a gang war.'

'Here's the *yamen* building,' Na Zha said. 'The police won't find anything.'

The *yamen* building was the old administration building for Kowloon Walled City. It was red brick, with a traditional green tiled roof and a pair of cannons flanking the doorway. Inside, it was bare concrete. We all stopped and looked around.

'This is difficult,' the Phoenix said, concentrating. 'Because of the blockage to our vision, we cannot see the entrance at all.'

'Stone?' I said.

Gold appeared and saluted us. He took his stone form and floated around the room, checking. The stone drifted out of my ring, grew to a similar size to Gold, and moved along the opposite perimeter of the room from Gold. It shrank and returned to my ring, and Gold returned to human form, gesturing to indicate the floor.

'The entrance is here. I don't know how to open it. It appears to be some sort of trapdoor.'

John nodded. 'Don't worry, we will find a way in. You are dismissed. Well done.'

'Get the bastard who did this to my siblings,' Gold said, and fell to one knee before us, saluting. 'Lord Xuan. It's been a blast.'

'I hope you're free when I return, because there's a job for you if you are,' John said.

'Double my salary and I may consider it,' Gold said. 'I have a family to support now.'

'Done,' John said, and Gold disappeared.

'But we don't pay him anything,' I said, crouching to examine the floor.

'That's precisely the point,' John said, crouching next to me.

The other Immortals moved to join us.

'Stand back,' Na Zha said. 'I'll just blast it open.'

He didn't need to. The building's external doors slammed shut by themselves and the trapdoor flew open. We all stepped back. About a dozen young men climbed up some stairs into the room. They looked like gang members with their dyed hair and tattoos. They carried small guns and grinned.

'Damn!' John said softly.

The Dragon concentrated and they all collapsed as if they were dead.

'That was unnecessary, Ah Qing,' the Phoenix said. 'You will be reprimanded for that.'

'They were only humans,' the Dragon said, and gestured for us to follow him down the stairs.

I checked one of the young men. The Dragon was right: they were human. And he'd killed every single one of them with his Internal Eye.

The stairs went a long way down but the corridor didn't darken. The walls were lined with white enamel panels, similar to the walls of some of the more up-market exits to the MTR stations, but there was no visible lighting.

'Touch the wall for me, Emma,' the stone said softly.

I put my hand on the wall as I walked down.

'Touch me to it.'

I turned my hand over and slid the stone against the wall.

'The Grandmother will be nearly as pissed as I am,' the stone said. 'I have half a mind to take human form and join you.'

'Stay there,' John said. 'He may not be aware of what you are.'

The stone was silent.

The Tiger took True Form and loped ahead of us. The Phoenix and Dragon stayed in human form; their True Forms would be too big to fit on the narrow stairway. John didn't transform either.

'Will you take True Form, my Lord?' Leo said as he followed us down the stairs.

John was silent, still moving quickly. It was a long way down.

'Oh my God,' I said softly.

'What, Emma?' Leo said.

I stopped. 'Wait, John,' I said. 'Tell me how bad it is.'

'At the bottom,' John said. 'There are no demons there.'

'At the bottom you will tell me exactly how bad it is, John Chen Wu,' I said grimly, rushing to keep up.

When we reached the bottom, I looked back. We were a good five storeys down, and the stairs hadn't turned so we'd travelled about two hundred metres in as well. The trapdoor was a tiny square of light a long way behind us.

'Can you sense Simone?' I said.

John concentrated. 'Yes. She is behind us, about three hundred metres away.'

'And about fifty metres down,' the stone said. 'You will need to descend further.'

'Now that we are inside, can you still see the layout?' the Phoenix said.

'In a way,' the stone said. 'Some of it. I may be able to guide you.'

'Good,' John said.

There was an opening at the bottom of the stairs, and we went in. The smell was indescribable. This was obviously where the men had their rest room. There was a television, a table set up for mah jong, a filthy couch and a microwave. Cigarette butts coated the floor and the walls were greasy with smoke. Beer cans were strewn everywhere.

I moved as close to John as I could. 'You will tell me how bad this is right now, or I swear I'll use the phone anyway,' I said.

John glanced at the Tiger.

'Tell her,' the Tiger said, his tail twitching.

John gave in. 'It is very bad. I don't know how much will remain once I take True Form. If there are demons present, the Turtle will destroy them. After that, I don't know.'

'What do you mean, "remain"?' Leo said.

'Sometimes I'm glad none of my wives are as smart as this one,' the Tiger said.

I explained for Leo. 'If he changes while he's this drained, the True Form will probably be all animal. John Chen won't exist. That's why he'll be gone for so long. Like he said, if there are demons around, the Turtle will destroy them, that's its nature. But if there are no demons present, the Turtle could very well just take off.'

Leo glanced at John. John's face didn't shift but his eyes blazed.

'You should have told us this, my Lord,' Leo said softly.

'I thought I would be coming in after a week with the Lady,' John said. 'If I had spent that week with her, I would have been able to retain control long enough to see the demon destroyed. Now ...' His face didn't shift. 'I am very drained. It is best if I do not release the Turtle until we face One Two Two. Let's go.'

The door opened onto a wider corridor, but it didn't go down. It did make a U-turn to go in the right direction though. We didn't hesitate, we followed it. It was lined with the same white enamel panels and seemed to stretch forever.

'Any corridors or turns or stairs up ahead?' I said.

Nobody said anything.

'Can anybody see anything at all?'

There was complete silence as we marched down the hallway.

'Hold,' the stone said. 'I think I can sense some demons ahead on the left.'

Nobody stopped.

'Stop,' I said. 'The stone says there are demons up ahead on the left.'

'You will need to relay for me now, Emma. I'm silenced,' the stone said.

The Immortals stopped and concentrated.

'Hard to tell,' the Phoenix said.

'A large number of very big ones, about ten metres along this corridor on the left,' Na Zha said. 'I'll take them. You go past.'

'You sure?' I said.

Na Zha transformed into his True Form. His pale blue robes flowed around him and his long hair was down to his waist. He held his whip in his left hand and his ring weapon in his right.

'Just go past,' he said. 'Let me take them.' He shook out his shoulders. 'I've been looking forward to having fun with some real opposition for a while. This should be good.'

'Meet up with us later,' John said. 'Enjoy.'

About fifty metres down the hallway, on the left side, was a door. The corridor turned a corner at the door and continued to the right. Na Zha stopped at the door and nodded to us as we went past. When we were about twenty metres away he opened the door and laughed loudly.

We didn't look back. We raced down the hallway. It turned a sharp left at the end. We went around.

A slime waited for us. It was a fluorescent lurid shade of green and hung off the ceiling in a mucousy stringing curtain.

'What the hell is that?' Leo said behind me.

'Slime,' I said. 'Very rare and highly toxic. Only energy can take it out. Impossible to tell how big it is until you've hit it. Energy workers have to be very careful with these; sometimes they're big enough to kill you with the chi backlash, but you don't know until you've tried.'

'Then it's obviously meant for you,' Leo said.

'Obviously,' I said. 'It's probably big enough to kill me.'

'That's beside the point,' the Phoenix said. She quickly transformed to True Form and blew a shaft of searing flame directly at the demon from her beak. It shrivelled, blackened and fell off the ceiling. The Phoenix turned back into her preferred human form, with flowing long red hair and a red robe.

'Don't step in it,' she said as she lifted her robes to walk carefully over the smouldering mass on the floor.

We all followed her, the Tiger leaping easily over the blackened slime. The corridor ended about ten metres away at another door. As one the Immortals stiffened and spun. The Dragon grabbed me and pulled me behind him.

'What?' I said.

'Back,' John said.

'What?' Leo said.

'Ah Na Zha was taken down,' the Dragon said softly. 'I am not sure what these things are that destroyed him, but they are on their way.'

We backed to the door. It was tiled with white enamel and didn't have a handle. I gave it an experimental push. It didn't move.

The Dragon and the Phoenix transformed and moved into position in front of us.

'Go,' the Dragon said, and the door flew open behind me. 'Go and find Simone. Zhu Que and I will handle them. Tiger, Turtle, take them.'

I heard them coming down the hallway, but never saw them. The Dragon pushed me through the doorway with his tail, then pushed Leo and John after me. The Tiger came last. The door closed in our faces.

We were at the top of a flight of stairs that went down about fifty metres to a door at the bottom.

'Simone is at the bottom of the stairs, about twenty metres further along,' the stone said. 'You are nearly there.'

'Nearly there,' I said. 'Bottom of the stairs, about twenty metres further along.'

John didn't say anything as we raced down the stairs. Then he and the Tiger stopped and concentrated.

'There are more on the other side of this door, waiting for us,' John said. Then he went rigid. 'The Dragon and Phoenix are gone — the demons destroyed them — but they managed to take the last couple of turtles with them.'

'Can you three handle them?' the Tiger said.

John concentrated. 'Yes. There are about fifteen level sixty snakes on the other side of this door.'

'I'll scout ahead and find the demon, you get Simone,' the Tiger said. His body shimmered, then he snapped back. 'Can't travel in here; interesting.' He shook his shaggy head. 'Ouch.' He grinned up at me. 'I'll just have to destroy these demons with you.'

'Let me go through the door first,' Leo said. 'I'll see how many I can take out before I go down. You can take the rest.'

'Go through together,' the stone said. 'Emma, with energy. Turtle, Lion, Tiger, physical. Go in swinging. You will have more of a chance.'

'Stop, Leo,' I said. 'The stone says go in swinging together. Me with energy, you three with physical.'

'Yes,' John said. 'I'll open the door, Leo stand back, Emma hit them first with energy.'

'Can I shoot chi into the ground?' I said. 'Are we on the ground?'

'Good idea,' the stone said. 'Yes.'

'Into the ground,' I said, and John nodded, understanding.

We readied ourselves. The Tiger used PK to open the door, then he and Leo stepped back.

All I saw was a writhing black mass on the other side of the door; they were silent, not hissing. They must have been at least thirty centimetres across.

Using my sword, I shot a bolt of chi into the floor and it went right through the middle of the snakes, blowing them up. It popped out of the floor about three metres away at the other end of the room, and I managed to make it swerve through a few more as it returned to me. I'd taken out about five of them. I sent the chi into the earth; if I retrieved that much it would kill me.

John and Leo raced through the door, swords swinging. The Tiger leapt. I followed them in and threw another bolt into the floor, destroying another three demons. Eight down. Seven to go.

The room was about three metres to a side, plain concrete. Just us and the snakes.

John had no difficulty with the demons he faced. He backed into a corner and only one at a time could battle him, they were so enormous. Dark Heavens destroyed them easily as it sliced through them; just its touch seemed to be enough to make them dissipate.

Leo had trouble with the demon he was attacking, so I took it out with a bolt of chi, then threw the result into the floor at another one.

The Tiger was a white blur. He leaped at them, tore their throats out, and worried them as they fell.

The demons moved back from me, obviously concerned by the energy. John, Leo and the Tiger continued to battle.

I sent another bolt of chi through the snakes, then more into the ground.

John ripped Dark Heavens through the demon he was facing and it fell.

All gone.

We all stood, panting, trying to regain our breath. Leo stumbled to me and leaned against the wall next to me. John came and stood with us, the Tiger backed to us.

'Anybody injured?' John said.

'Poisonous,' the Tiger said, panting. 'Fangs. Leo?'

'Yeah,' Leo said.

The Tiger transformed into human form and went to Leo. Leo slid down the wall to sit on the floor, his face ashen. The Tiger took his hands, lowered his head and concentrated. Leo's face screwed up with agony and he gasped.

'Hold,' John said, putting his hand on Leo's forehead. 'The pain will pass.'

Leo was completely still, his face stiff with control.

'Breathe,' John whispered.

Leo took a deep gasping breath and arched his back, then went limp. The Tiger concentrated again, and his hands filled with the golden glow of chi. The energy grew like a nimbus around his hands, then moved onto Leo, creating an aura around him. He appeared to be surrounded by golden fire for a split second, then it was absorbed into him.

Leo exhaled a huge deep breath, snapped open his eyes and smiled. 'Thanks.'

'It wasn't as bad as I thought,' the Tiger said. 'The fang just grazed you. You were very lucky.'

Leo raised his left forearm and examined the long red mark where the fang had sliced across. 'Gone.' He pulled himself to his feet. 'Any more between us and Simone?'

John and the Tiger faced the door at the end of the room and concentrated.

'No idea,' John said. 'Stone?'

'What you just faced was nothing compared to what is on the other side of that door,' the stone said grimly. 'Twice as many. Much bigger. Turtles.' Its voice softened. 'They are guarding Simone. She is on the other side of that room, in a holding room.'

Everybody looked blankly at me, so I relayed the message.

'Emma, Leo,' John said, 'you two will go straight through, grab Simone and take her out. Take her straight home, both of you. The Tiger and I will finish our business here. Just make sure Simone is safe.'

I didn't say anything, I just studied the door.

'Emma?' John said.

I nodded. 'Okay. I suppose this is goodbye.'

'No, it isn't,' John said. 'Because I will return for you. I promise. Now.' He hefted his sword. 'Let's get Simone out of this.' He didn't look away from the door. 'Leo, I am giving you a direct order. You do not have permission to give your life. Simone will need both of you. I order you to stay alive.'

'My Lord,' Leo said, expressionless. 'It's the least I deserve.'

'Tiger, on the count of three, open the door,' John said. 'One, two —'

The door flew open by itself and Martin threw himself through, holding Simone, unconscious, in his arms. His eyes blazed. 'Go!' he shouted when he saw us. 'Get out of here!'

John ran to them and turned to bring up the rear. 'You heard him, run!'

We all turned and raced for the door. Leo hit it first and went down. The Tiger crashed into it as well. The rest of us managed to stop before we reached it.

I put my hand out. There was an invisible barrier

where the door should have been. The door appeared to be open, but we couldn't go through.

'Move,' John said. He raised Dark Heavens, filled it with brilliant white shen energy and tried to break the barrier with it. The sword glanced off.

John pulled the energy back out. We all faced back into the room. The door on the other side was open, but the demons weren't coming in yet.

The Tiger shook his shaggy head and pulled himself to his feet. 'Never seen that before.'

'Leo?' I said.

Leo grunted, then pulled himself up to sit, shaking his head as well. The Tiger moved next to him. 'How many paws am I holding up?'

'Two,' Leo said.

'Close enough,' the Tiger said.

Leo clumsily pulled himself to his feet and staggered to the white katana to retrieve it.

I went to Martin. Simone lay limp in his arms.

'Is she okay?' I said.

'Yes,' Martin said. 'I broke out of my cell and found her. But —' He glanced at the other room, then gently put Simone onto the floor next to the door. 'Give me your sword, and stand back with Simone. Let us deal with them.'

I glanced at John. 'Do as he says,' John said.

I passed the Silver Serpent to Martin and he studied it. 'It's been a long time.' He hefted it and faced the centre of the room with the other men.

'You two stay back,' John said. 'Emma, lean on the doorway. If the barrier is taken down, grab Simone and run. Leo, stay with them, stand your ground. Go with them if the barrier falls.'

They all stiffened and faced the open door.

'Here they come,' Martin said softly.

CHAPTER THIRTY-SEVEN

John was ugly in Turtle form, but these were monsters. Their shells were twisted with protuberances and indentations; some of them dragged feet that seemed to be only half flipper. Each was about a metre and a half from nose to tail; not physically large, but at least level eighty demons. Enormous.

John raised Dark Heavens, then opened his mouth and released a sound I had never heard before. It was a combination of rage, anguish and grief, and seemed to gather all of the pain that he had suffered since the demon had killed Michelle.

Then his voice was drowned out by the Tiger's roar and the three of them threw themselves at the demons. I clutched Simone.

'Don't look,' Leo said without turning to me. 'Some of these are more animal than demon.' He ducked and a spray of blood shot over our heads and splattered on the wall above us.

'Has John taken True Form?' I said, trying to peer around him to see.

'No.' Leo ducked again, then raised the sword and sliced the head off an injured turtle that had come for us. It dissipated into black feathery streamers.

Martin moved in front of Leo, blocking any more demons from coming for us. He had filled the Serpent with shen and it sang, but it didn't seem to make any difference to the demons. He sliced through the turtles with the singing sword anyway.

John stood in the middle of the room and destroyed them in grim silence. He was faster than the demons, and they were incredibly fast. He was almost invisible. The Tiger battled next to him; they guarded each other's back.

A turtle threw itself at us and Martin blocked it. It landed with all four feet right in the middle of his chest, knocking him over. Leo leaped forward to take off its head, but it was too fast. It lunged its head on its long flexible neck, opened its mouth and snapped it shut on Martin's throat. Martin gave a strangled cry and went limp.

Leo didn't hesitate; he took the turtle's head off, then scooped up the Serpent and held it behind himself without looking back. I grabbed it, and he moved forward again, guarding.

Martin disappeared. Dead.

Another turtle rushed us and Leo readied himself. This one leaped for his throat, knocking him over, and he fell onto his back. I sliced its head off before it could take out his throat.

Leo rolled the turtle away. 'You always were faster than me.' He tried to rise but couldn't. He struggled to pull himself to his feet, then gave up. 'I think I'm in trouble.' He crawled to the wall and leaned on it next to Simone, who was still unconscious.

I hefted my sword. I stood in front of Simone.

John and the Tiger still battled back to back, taking the demons out around them. The Tiger's flank was stained with blood, soaking through his fur, and one ear hung lopsidedly. The side of John's shirt was dark with blood and there was blood on his face.

I couldn't do anything. These demons were far too big to take out with energy. The backlash would kill me.

Another turtle approached us and I took its head off before it could attack me.

Only a couple of turtles remained, fighting John and the Tiger. The Tiger lunged, took out the neck of a turtle, and it fell. The Tiger fell as well; his bloodied side heaving. He disappeared.

John ran his sword through the top of the last turtle's head. All gone. Most of them had dissipated, but some had died like animals, their dark blood spreading over the floor. Even in death they were grotesque caricatures of the natural animals; wrong in the wrong places.

John staggered to us and flopped down next to Leo. 'Has the barrier gone down?'

I felt behind me. 'No.'

'Reinforcements are on the way, we don't have much time,' John said. 'Give me a minute to catch my breath and rebuild my energy, and then I should be able to break it down and the two of you can get Simone out of here.'

'We could just take Simone home, John, the three of us,' I said softly. 'We could just go home and have some more time together.'

John shifted where he sat, and grimaced. 'My side is cut open. I wouldn't make it. I'll use the last of my energy to unseal the door. Once I've done it, I will change. You go. Once the barrier is down and the Turtle is released, take them, Leo. Take them and go.'

'I'm not going anywhere either,' Leo said. 'My spine is broken. I can't feel my legs, I can't move them. My Lord, quickly. They're coming. You don't have enough energy to break the barrier, you know it. Drain me —'

'No!' I whispered.

'He has to,' Leo said to me. 'It's the only way you're gonna get out of here.'

'I can't, Leo,' John said. 'You're Worthy. If I drain you, you can never gain Immortality.'

Leo snorted. 'My spine is broken and I'll stay that way, I know I will. All eternity being a cripple pining after something I can't have? Please. Do it. Quickly. My last request, Lord Xuan: drain me. Allow me to become part of you. Hurry!'

'Do it, John, it's what I'd want,' I said. 'Quickly.'

John hesitated.

'Please,' Leo said, begging. 'Take my energy. I know I'm big. Take my soul. With what I have you can get Simone and Emma out.'

'Do it for him, John.'

John shook his head fiercely. 'I wish there was another way.' He placed his hand on Leo's forehead and Leo smiled up at him. A white aura of glowing shen energy surrounded Leo and he began to fade. He became transparent. John was taking all of him.

There was a blinding flash of light and Kwan Yin appeared in True Form next to Leo. John jerked his head back and stared at her, incredulous.

'The Black Lion is mine,' she said. She reached out and touched Leo's head. Leo's eyes widened and his face filled with wonder. Then his expression changed to a fierce grimace of anger. '*No!*'

He cast around at us, desperate. He became totally transparent. He was gone.

Kwan Yin disappeared.

'Oh, dear Lord, John. She's going to Raise him, isn't she?'

'She has taken him to be Judged,' John said.

'But if he's Raised he'll stay as he is. For all eternity.'

'As a human Raised Immortal, yes. I know.'

'He'll fight it every inch of the way.'

491

'I know.'

'Can we help him?'

John looked down and hesitated, then spoke without raising his head. 'No. There is nothing we can do for him right now.'

'Oh my God. Poor Leo,' I whispered.

'We do not have time to worry about Leo. The best thing we can do is take his gift and fulfil his will. I will break this barrier, and you and Simone can go out.'

'I hope you're right, Xuan Wu,' I said. 'But what about the energy?'

'I received nearly all of his energy, and most of hers,' he said. 'She nearly drained herself.' He rose. 'Are you okay?'

'I'm fine.'

John glanced at Simone. 'She is heavily sedated. I can't even say goodbye.'

'Stone, if you can hear me, take a recording,' I said. The stone didn't change its shape or say anything. 'Do we have time?'

'No,' John said. 'I will break the barrier, then you will go.'

'Will you still transform after breaking the barrier?'

'Yes.' John studied the door on the other side of the room. 'They're here. We have to move.' He turned back to me. 'Hold Simone. Ready yourself to run once the barrier is down. Don't look back.'

I gathered Simone and rose. John rose with difficulty, grimacing. He reached out and stroked Simone's cheek, then his face went rigid and he seized her out of my arms, ran to the wall and pinned her against it with his body.

There was a thumping bang and John was thrown away from the wall towards me, spreadeagled. He skidded to a halt next to me. His face and the front of his black shirt were covered with blood.

492

Something grabbed me, turned me around and pushed me into the wall. He had used PK to turn me away so I couldn't see him.

Stay there, he said urgently. *Don't look at me, the injuries are major. She was programmed to explode at my touch.*

I suddenly understood what had happened. John had shielded me from the blast with his body. He must have been horribly injured.

He still held me. Leo was gone. John was dying. Simone was dead. My insides hurt like I was about to burst, but I couldn't move or make a sound.

'That was the copy of Simone,' John said. His voice sounded completely normal. He released me. 'I couldn't see what it really was until I touched it.'

I heard him moving but didn't turn around. 'It's okay,' he said. I glanced at him, expecting his face to be a bloody shredded mass of flesh, but he was fine. 'I've healed myself. I must be whole, because we need to go in there and get Simone out.'

Leo was gone. John wouldn't make it. Simone was still held by the demon. We'd lost. We'd lost everything.

Hold, John said silently, but I didn't really hear him. *I concede. Wait.*

I slid down the wall to sit on the floor. I was very close to losing it. That monster had Simone. I tried to breathe but my throat was thick and my heart was pounding. I couldn't see for the tears in my eyes. I was going to lose both of them. I was going to lose all of them. No. *No!*

'Emma. Concentrate. Move your chi into your central dan tian,' John said.

I did as he directed, trying to breathe as I did.

'Good. Now move it up the major meridian to the top cauldron.'

I concentrated.

493

'Don't open the gate. Leave the chi there. Do you have it?'

'Yes,' I said, concentrating, my breath rasping through my dry throat.

'Now. Slowly. Move it all into your Inner Eye. Concentrate. Carefully. If you lose it then immediately drop it and recentre it. You have time. The demons are waiting for us now, they're not coming in.'

The world glowed around me.

'Don't open the Eye. Leave the chi there. Concentrate.'

I nodded silently.

'Now. Very carefully, move the chi back down and recentre it.'

I moved the chi and suddenly felt completely relaxed and in control. I was calm and focused and absolutely serene.

'Thanks,' I said.

'I should have taught you that a long time ago,' he said. 'I think in the near future, unfortunately, you will be using that skill quite a lot. Emma.' His voice sharpened and I glanced up at him. 'You can only do that twice at one time. The effect will last for six to twelve hours. At the end of that time, the stress will return, and it will be worse. If you do it twice, it will be four times worse when it returns. If you do it more than twice in a row, you could easily kill yourself.'

'I understand.' As I rose I pulled the Demon King's phone out of my pocket.

'I have not gone down, and Simone is not yet in real danger,' John said. 'You cannot use that yet. Put it away, I don't think you will need it.' He studied the door. 'We will just go in and get her.'

I hesitated, then shrugged, put the phone away and retrieved my sword. The stupid damn Turtle was right. I had given him my word. Simone was alive and we were getting her out. Right now.

'Why didn't you tell us she was a copy, stone?' I said.

'I've been shouting at you for the last twenty minutes!' the stone snapped, its voice desperate. 'I even tried to stab you again, but that hybrid child was binding me even though she was unconscious!'

John collected his sword without saying a word.

I was suddenly full of ice-cold fury. The monster that held my Simone had used a copy child — *April's* child — as a weapon, and *killed* her.

'That little piece of scum is going to *die*,' I growled.

'No, it isn't,' John said as he moved towards the door. 'We will trade my head for Simone's safety. That is the only way, love.' He spoke silently again, and this time I heard what he said and felt a shock of dismay.

I concede. I am willing to trade my head for my Lady's and daughter's freedom and safety.

Come on through, Simon Wong said.

The other side of the door was a corridor, empty and featureless. It went for about twenty metres, then there was another door at the end.

'This is not what I sensed,' John said. 'This is different. I cannot sense any large demons now. It was an illusion.'

'They're waiting for you at the end,' the stone said. Its voice changed. 'My Lord Xuan. It's been a great deal of pleasure.'

'Look after her,' John said.

'My Lord.'

Wong waited for us with a couple of minor demons and Kitty Kwok. Simone sat quietly in a chair between them. When she saw us she jumped to get away from them, but Kitty grabbed her by the arm and threw her back into the chair.

The room was like a large, modern library: shelves with books, a bank of computers, pale blue carpet tiles on the floor, but no windows. They sat at a meeting table together, with books strewn around them.

Wong rose and came around the table to face us. Kitty Kwok stood behind Simone and held her shoulder.

Wong leaned back on the table and crossed his arms over his chest, quite relaxed. 'Don't try taking True Form and coming for me. You wouldn't make it in time.'

Don't do anything to attack it, Emma, John said. *It's immensely powerful. You don't need to use the phone; I don't think either of you are in danger. We'll just give him what he wants.*

'No,' I moaned, my heart breaking, but John ignored me.

He stretched his arms in front of him at eye level and slid Dark Heavens back into its scabbard, acknowledging defeat. 'One Two Two,' he said without emotion as he lowered the sword, 'whatever you want, you can have it. Just don't harm the child or the Lady. You want my head? It's yours.'

'Have they hurt you, Simone?' I said.

'I'm okay,' Simone said, her little voice strained. 'They haven't done anything to me.'

Wong moved his hands so that they were on the table either side of him and leaned back. 'I just want your head, Turtle. That's all.'

'I won't give it to you until I'm sure that my daughter is safe,' John said.

Wong gestured with his head. Kitty roughly pulled Simone out of the chair and walked her around the table until she was on the same side as us.

'Is that her?' I said softly.

John was silent.

'My, but you are very drained, aren't you, Turtle,' Wong said. 'It's astonishing you can hold the shape at all.'

'If I lose the shape my head will be gone,' John said.

'Hello, Emma,' Wong said. 'You're a prize in your own right, you know.'

I didn't say anything.

'Okay,' Wong said, crossing his arms over his chest again. 'Let's do this, before the Turtle loses it completely. You.' He nodded towards John. 'Kneel, drop your weapon. You.' He nodded towards me and smiled. 'Take his weapon, take his head and bring it to me. Then you'll get the girl.'

'*No!*' Simone wailed, a long drawn-out sound of misery.

'I want to be a hundred per cent sure that it's her, and I want safe passage out of here,' I said.

'Even if he guarantees it, his word's no good, Emma,' John said. 'How about this: we go to the roof of Kowloon City Plaza. I'll give you my head, you go. But I want you to do it; you take the head, not Emma. End of transaction.'

'Inside the *yamen* building,' Wong said. 'The girls can go out from there.'

'Done,' John said. 'I'll have to walk out. I'm too big to carry.'

'Oh, we'll come with you,' Wong said. 'An afternoon stroll with the family.'

John turned and gestured. 'After you.'

Wong grinned and concentrated. An enormous hunting knife appeared in his hand. He grabbed Simone, jerked her towards him and put the knife to her throat. 'By all means.' He removed his hand and the knife remained at her throat. 'Kill me and she dies anyway.'

'I've done a deal, I won't go back on it,' John said. 'I am a creature of honour.'

Wong jerked Simone closer. 'Come on, little girl,' he said through his teeth. 'Let's go see the creature of honour lose his head.'

* * *

'I don't want you to die, Daddy,' Simone said as we went back down the tunnels.

'I can't die, sweetheart,' John said. 'Even if he cuts off my head, I'll just turn into the Turtle and be gone for a while. I'll be back.'

'And we'll all have a lot of fun in the meantime,' Wong said. 'All of Hell will come out to play.'

'You sure that's Simone?' I said.

'Emma, I'm so drained that I can hardly see anything,' John said. 'I can't be sure, but I'm not willing to take the risk.'

'Say something silently,' I said to Simone.

'I can't,' Simone said. 'He can somehow block me.'

I opened my Inner Eye and turned it on her.

'It's *me*, Emma,' she said.

'Is it?' John said softly.

I asked the stone.

It's her.

I hesitated.

Yes, of course I'm sure! It's really her. I had the copy picked immediately. I would know if it wasn't her!

'What's the word, Simone?' I said.

'I say "cool" too much,' Simone said.

'Yes,' I said. 'It's her.'

'Shut up. All of you. All I want is the head.'

We went up the stairs and through the floor into the *yamen* building. A hot humid breeze blew in from the open doors. The park and the glowing clouds of the Hong Kong night sky were visible through the doorway.

So close.

'Where's Leo?' Simone said.

'Emma will explain after you're out of here,' John said.

'He's dead, isn't he,' Simone said.

'No, sweetheart, he's not dead,' I said. 'I'll explain it all later.'

'Now,' Wong said. 'Let's get this head.' He gestured to John, still holding Simone with his other hand. 'Kneel and put your sword on the ground.'

John stood watching Wong expressionlessly. Then he fell to his knees and lowered his head, his hair falling like a dark curtain around his face. He pulled his sword from its scabbard and placed it on the floor in front of him.

Wong gestured to me, still holding Simone. 'Bring me the sword.'

I moved to John and crouched next to him. Then I had a sudden inspiration. I grabbed his head, turned it towards me and planted my mouth on his.

John pushed me away and I fell. I threw myself up and tried to go back to him, but I couldn't move. John didn't have enough energy left to bind me, so it had to be Wong.

Simone shrieked, and then sobbed. Wong had sliced her with the knife, not deep enough to kill, but deep enough to hurt her. Blood ran down the side of her throat. Without shifting the blade of the knife, Wong lifted his other hand to her throat and collected her blood on his index finger. He shoved it into his mouth. He pulled his finger out and smiled at me, the blood still on his teeth.

'The little ones are always so much sweeter, don't you think? You'd better hurry up and get me that sword, because she does taste very, very sweet.'

He released me and I completely lost it. The Snake came out.

Wong didn't move.

I generated an enormous ball of chi and shot it straight at Wong's head.

He held one hand up, smiled, and absorbed it completely.

I changed back and sagged to my knees. I'd nearly killed myself. I was almost completely drained. I cursed myself for an idiot.

'You okay, Emma?' John said quietly.

'I'll live.' I pulled myself back to my feet.

Simone sobbed quietly. 'Don't die, Daddy.'

'Do it, Emma,' John said. 'Give him the blade. I can't hold the shape for much longer. Quickly. Do it. I'm gone anyway. Give him what he wants. Don't worry, Simone, I'll be back.'

I moved back to John.

'Don't try to feed me,' he said. 'It would be a waste of time; I wouldn't have enough to take him down anyway. Just let him have my head.'

I crouched next to him. 'I love you,' I whispered.

'I will return for you, Emma. I promise,' he said, without looking up. 'I would prefer you and Simone don't see this. Take her and go.'

I picked up the sword and took a deep breath. 'Pass Simone to me and I give you my word. You can have the sword. I won't stop you. Let us go, and you can have his head.'

Wong let Simone go and she ran to me. I pulled her behind me.

John lowered his head and closed his eyes, his face serene. 'Do it.'

I moved carefully to Wong and gave him the blade, preparing for him to attack.

'No, Emma,' Simone said softly.

Wong took the sword and smiled viciously at me. He didn't move to attack me, so I backed away until Simone was behind me. I held her there and backed towards the door.

'Yes,' Wong said. He turned the blade over in his hands, admiring it, then grinned at John. He moved beside John, and John stiffened but remained on his knees. Wong readied the blade. 'About fucking time,' he said through the grin.

'I love you,' I said, choking out the words.

'Words aren't necessary,' John said without looking up. 'Go. Hurry.'

I grabbed Simone's hand, spun and raced for the door. I heard the clean whisper of slicing steel behind me. Simone and I fell through the door into the darkness.

CHAPTER THIRTY-EIGHT

'She moved,' a voice said.

I tried to pull myself upright but was completely incapacitated. Again. I had to stop doing this to myself. I tried to open my eyes, and managed it. Okay; not completely incapacitated. I felt for John's or Simone's hand holding mine, but they didn't seem to be there. First time for everything.

'Quickly, restrain her. We haven't finished.'

Strong hands moved to bind my wrists and ankles. Hold on; that was wrong. What the hell was happening? I tried to struggle but the bonds were tight. I stopped struggling and attempted to focus.

There was an enormous gleaming silver face right in front of mine. I felt a shock of panic and tried to escape. I couldn't. I was about to struggle, then I saw it properly. It wasn't a face at all. It was a huge hospital examination light, like the ones used in operating theatres.

I looked around. Dark shapes ... I couldn't quite make them out. Green. Lights. Okay. I took a few deep breaths. Concentrate. Hospital. I tried to remember what had happened.

Oh my God — John. I must have cried out because

suddenly there was a grinning face jammed right in mine.

'Hello, sweetie,' Simon Wong said. He turned to my left. 'Are we nearly finished?'

I turned to see who he was talking to. It was a small humanoid demon in True Form, checking an IV bag. Kitty Kwok was behind it, looking smug.

'Still a while to go,' Kitty said. 'We should knock her out again.'

'Let me watch her first,' Wong said. He moved his face very close to mine and nuzzled into my cheek. 'Mm. Sweet.' He bit me on the cheek, and I clenched my teeth to stop the sound from coming out. He dug his teeth in harder. I used the energy meridians to block the pain. There, eat that, demon. I couldn't feel anything.

'She's used energy to block the pain, my Lord,' the smaller demon said.

'Damn,' Wong said softly into my face. He licked the blood off my cheek, then pulled away.

I moved my awareness back into my face and checked the damage from the inside. He'd torn a gash in my face. I quickly healed it using chi, but something didn't feel right. There was a blockage. The chi wasn't moving the way it should.

'She shouldn't be able to still do that,' Wong said. 'How much more?'

'Still a while to go, I said, Simon,' Kitty said impatiently. 'She's only absorbed about a litre.'

'Well, make it go faster!' Wong said.

'Can't, we'll kill her,' Kitty said. 'This is already five times faster than any other we've done before. Obviously the preparation we did when she was working for me was effective.'

'How long will this take?' Wong said.

There was silence. Then Kitty said, 'About two hours.'

'And we'll have her when we're done?'

'Should be,' Kitty said.

'What do you mean *should be?*'

'You know she's the first adult to survive it. The others died. If she survives it, we should have her.'

'Damn, Kitty, you should never have let her go in the first place,' Wong said.

'It was really sudden. I wasn't able to stop her,' Kitty said. 'She just turned around and moved in with the Dark Lord without any warning whatsoever. There at work one day, providing samples and being fed like a good little thrall, then not working for me the next. Always was an impulsive little bitch.'

'Do you think she knew?' he said.

'What we were doing to her?' Kitty hesitated. 'If she knew, I think she'd kill herself. I honestly think she loves that bastard more than her life.'

What were they doing to me?

I looked around. Then I realised with an ice-cold shock. The IV was *black*.

Okay. Deep breaths. I was bound, I couldn't move. If they moved away, I could try escaping, but with them right on top of me like that it was a waste of time. I moved my consciousness into my arm where they were feeding me with the demon stuff. I felt what was going into me and gagged.

My head was grabbed and raised just as I vomited. I couldn't help it. I hoped I'd hit one of them but apparently they were ready for me. I retched for a while, then stopped. They dropped my head. I desperately wanted to rinse my mouth.

'Yum,' Wong said.

'You are completely disgusting, Simon,' Kitty said.

I took deep breaths and weighed my options. I had another couple of hours before they gained control, Kitty had said. I checked my energy level and nearly panicked again. No wonder it had felt so strange when I healed my face. My chi was disappearing. It was like my dan tian was filling with the black stuff, replacing the chi. About a third was gone.

I felt my shen. It was perfectly normal. I felt my ching. Same.

I quickly considered trying to use shen, but dismissed it. Maybe if there was no other option, I'd try. Ching; I knew what would happen if I tried to work ching, with essence. It would be like an implosion. I would die quickly, cleanly and without leaving a trace.

I thought at the stone. It wasn't there. No, wait: a very small voice, right on the edge of consciousness. *Can you hear me, Emma? Make a sound if you can hear me.*

I made a very small squeak, hoping it could hear me.

Do that again if you can hear me.

I squeaked again, and Kitty glanced at me.

'Are we hurting you, dear?' Wong said into my ear. 'I do hope we are. Does it burn as it goes in?'

I am here, Emma, the stone said. I concentrated on its voice, focusing, and managed to bring it to me more loudly. *You have only been unconscious for about half an hour*, it said. *I don't like the look of what they are doing to you though.*

I asked it a question silently.

Simone is fine. They haven't done anything to her. They want control of you first, that way she will cooperate. They have her heavily sedated but unharmed. I think they want to do something similar to her.

I tried to control my fury. Then I felt a shot of anguish.

Yes. He's gone. He was gone anyway, dear. Either way, he would be in True Form by now.

I thought another question at it.

Yes. He is in True Form. He is gone, but remember, he will return. Simone is alive. You need to work out what you'll do. I will do what I can to help.

Another question.

What happened? It was all a ruse. That wasn't the yamen *building at all. The Dark Lord was too drained to tell. It was the real Simone, and that's all he cared about. Even Simone was too distressed to look closely at the surroundings. The demon took the Dark Lord's head, then they somehow knocked you out and brought you here. You are still under Kowloon City Park.*

I tried not to let my face betray my despair. After all of that we had lost, and Simone was in this demon's hands. I frantically considered my options. First, get free. Then find Simone. Then get her out of there. Or find the phone and use it. Either way, I had to make sure that Simone was safe.

'My, but look at her thinking. This is *such* fun to watch,' Wong said.

'We should sedate her again,' Kitty said.

'How much longer will it take if she's conscious?' Wong said.

'About half an hour longer,' Kitty said. 'Two and a half more hours and she's ours.'

'Then let's watch,' Wong said, his voice full of satisfaction. 'I want to see her try something. Come on, Emma, try something. Can you break the bonds? They're rated at a hundred kilos, dear, I really don't think you can.'

That was what he thought. I could do it, but not with him there. It would be a waste of time trying to escape while he was there.

I wondered if they had the short attention span of typical Hong Kong people. It was worth a try.

I willed myself into a very deep trance for exactly thirty-four minutes.

* * *

I snapped back but remained perfectly still. I tried opening my Inner Eye to see how many demons were around me, but it was gone. I couldn't use it any more.

I checked my chi. More than a third gone.

I could try to remove the black stuff internally, burn it out with my own chi, but that was a thing to try only if they weren't watching.

I had an inspiration. I asked the stone.

Just the humanoid. Kitty and Simon became bored and went off to have sex. He finds this incredibly arousing.

I nearly chuckled. Then I realised that I would probably be next. I checked myself, and breathed a very quiet sigh of relief.

That's right. Not yet. But he certainly does have plans for you. He wants you cooperative though; he's too frightened to try taking you before you're fully converted. Even bound, he won't try you.

What?

That's the word they used: converted. And the humanoid is about level thirty. He doesn't have many high-level demons left — you destroyed most of them.

Gotcha.

I used every ounce of speed I had. I ripped my hands free of the bonds, shot upright, spun and took its head off with both hands: snap.

I looked around. Operating theatre.

I ripped the IV out of my arm and nearly gagged again when I smelled its contents.

I jumped off the bed. Only one way to go: out.

I crept to the door, opened it and poked my head out. I asked the stone.

Next on the right. Nobody else is around. Kitty and Wong are still busy. He can go for hours if he wants. Simone: I'm not completely sure. Let's go and find her.

I crept out into the hallway and listened. I really wished my Inner Eye was working. Not a sound.

I moved stealthily up the hall to the next room, opened the door and entered. Dark.

The stone glowed for me, a small pale green light. I used it to light the table holding my stuff. I grabbed the phone and shoved it in my pocket.

I asked the stone.

Your diagnosis is correct. I don't know if you can burn the demon essence out with your chi. It doesn't seem to be harming you, or giving them control. Your unusual nature is limiting its effectiveness. But if they manage to fill you more than half full, I fear that they will succeed.

I went back to the door. I opened it a crack and looked through. Nothing. The hall had plain beige walls and a linoleum-tiled floor, like a hospital.

There are demons at the entrance to the hallway, about level fifteen or twenty. Two of them.

Easy. I crept down the hall towards the door at the end. It was double doors, like a hospital.

No. Not a hospital. You are still underground.

I had an inspiration.

Sorry, Emma, I can't call anybody. I'm underground, remember.

I threw open the doors. There was a demon on each side. I used my speed again; I hit the right one with a spinning roundhouse kick that destroyed it completely, then dropped my kicking foot and lashed out with the other foot. Both gone.

I had black stuff on my legs, but it wasn't seeping through my jeans onto my skin. I should be okay. I gasped. The black stuff made a very quiet sucking sound and disappeared into me. I looked at my hands.

The black stuff from the first demon was gone too. I checked my dan *tian*. Holy shit.

By the Grandmother herself but you are in very serious trouble, Lady Emma Donahoe.

I couldn't help but agree. But first: Simone.

Left.

How far?

I have no idea. Probably a few metres.

I wanted to hug the wall but it would be a waste of time. If anyone came they would see me anyway. There were doors on either side of the hallway.

Do not go into any of those rooms, Emma, the stone said. *You do not want to see what is inside them.*

At the end of the corridor there was no door; it just opened into a larger area. It was about three metres across and disappeared to the right. I crept to the end and poked my nose around the corner. The larger area opened out to the right for about five metres. It was devoid of any furniture, with beige walls and a tiled linoleum floor, like a hospital. I wondered why it seemed so different to a hospital when it had so many similarities; and then realised. No windows. Underground. There was a glass wall with a large glass door at the end on the right. The wall directly across from me had three doors at regular intervals. I asked the stone.

Let me look. The middle one. There is an anteroom with a level forty demon in it. Then something similar to a hospital ward, with Simone in it.

I shot across and threw open the door. The demon wasn't expecting me. I went for its head but it blocked me, twisted my arm down and grabbed my throat.

I tried to head-butt it but it had me. I lifted myself on my pinned arm and neck and lashed out with my feet. Both my feet thumped into its abdomen and the force of the blow broke its grip. I somersaulted backwards and landed on my feet, but I was hit with the black stuff anyway as it exploded.

I looked down at myself. Another quiet sucking sound. The demon stuff disappeared, absorbed into me. Damn. I checked my dan *tian*. Holy shit. Nearly half full.

I tried to imagine Simon Wong giving me an order and felt only disdain. Good. I hoped this control business wasn't as bad as they thought it was. I didn't want to try it though.

I opened the door on the other side of the room. Simone was sleeping peacefully on the hospital bed, her face full of angelic innocence. She still wore her little blue dress from that morning, when she had gone into safety with Martin. I grabbed her and pulled her up and crushed her into me. My eyes stung with tears that I really couldn't afford.

Then I shrieked with agony and dropped her. She fell like a rag doll. I sobbed with the pain. My arms went black; then they rippled and returned to normal.

I bent over the bed and leaned on it, gasping for breath between the sobs. 'No. No. No.'

I took deep breaths and tried to control it. Okay. I gingerly reached out and touched Simone on her hand. I jerked away again; the touch was like acid.

I tried her dress. That didn't hurt.

I carefully put my hands around her middle under her arms, where the dress was, ready to lift her and get her out of there.

It was subconscious at first, but after a few seconds the burning was so intense I had to drop her.

'Shit. Shit. Shit!' I whispered. 'What the hell am I going to do?'

She was limp. I spoke gently into her ear, trying to wake her. Nothing.

She is heavily sedated. I don't think anything you can do will bring her round.

I suddenly felt very calm. 'You realise what this means.'

The stone was silent.

I felt absolutely serene. 'If I can't touch her, then I can't touch him. I'll never be able to touch either of them.'

The stone didn't speak.

'I've lost my only reason for living,' I said.

No, Emma. Simone needs you.

'What Simone needs right now is to be safe. I must get her out of here. You know what they'll do to her. I can't let them have her.'

The stone was silent.

'What are my chances of getting her out of here when I can't even touch her?'

The stone didn't say a word.

I pulled the ring off my finger and very carefully put it into the pocket of Simone's dress. The contact of the fabric was enough to start my skin burning. 'Will you explain for me?'

The stone didn't answer, and then I understood. I put my finger carefully into her pocket so that I could touch it and hear what it had to say.

I'd prefer to stay with you, Lady Emma.

'Well, how about that. After all this time of driving me nuts, now you want to stay with me.' I pulled the King's phone out of my pocket, keeping my other hand on the ring. 'As far as I can see, I'm out of options. If you can see any other way of ensuring Simone's safety, I'd love to hear it.'

The stone was silent for a long time, then it said, *My Lady.*

'Thanks for everything.'

It's been fun, Emma. I hope to see you again when the Dark Lord returns.

'I sincerely doubt that I will want to be around when he comes back, stone,' I said. 'When he sees what they've done to me it'll kill him. I think I'd prefer to be dead. I may just stay in Hell.'

The stone was silent.

'Look after her,' I whispered. 'Try not to annoy her *too* much.'

I quickly zipped up Simone's pocket, then jerked my hands away from the pain of the contact. I pressed the button on the phone and lifted it to my ear.

'Goodbye, Simone,' I said. 'I love you.'

The phone clicked. 'Yes, dear?'

'You have me. I'm yours.'

CHAPTER THIRTY-NINE

I was in a large, elaborate old-fashioned Chinese-style hall with a vastly high ceiling. The pillars and beams were decorated with intricate paintings and good-luck motifs. There were no windows.

The King stood in front of me. He looked like an enormous Snake Mother, but blood-red instead of black. He quickly changed to human form: a good-looking Chinese man of about twenty-five, with a cheeky, boyish face. He wore a scruffy pair of jeans and a T-shirt, both the deep maroon of dried blood. His short ponytail was the same colour.

'Welcome to Hell, Lady Emma,' he said, then held out his hand and waited.

I took out one of my black jade earrings. It was a jade disk, shaped like a Chinese coin: round with a square hole in the middle. The hole was decorated with a large diamond.

I passed the earring to him. He took it in one hand and held the other hand over it. The diamond, still with the post attached, drifted out of the jade disk into his upper hand. He returned the diamond to me and pocketed the black jade coin.

I put the diamond back into my ear.

He held out his hands again. Something small, round and white appeared in one palm, and a glass of water appeared in the other.

He came to me, hands still out. 'Valium. Two milligrams. I suggest you take it.'

I studied the little pill suspiciously.

'I give you my word it is what I say it is, Emma. You have been through a lot. More will happen before you can stop and catch your breath. You will need therapy after what you've been through, and I will arrange it.' He smiled slightly. 'Take the pill, Emma. It's a very small dose. It will calm you without making you drowsy. You need it.'

'No, I don't,' I said. 'And I'm still feeling the effects of what One Two Two did to me. Enough drugs.'

The pill and water disappeared. 'Let me know if you feel too stressed then. I don't want you breaking down — there's a lot we need to do.'

I stopped and considered, then decided. 'If that's the case then wait. Give me a moment.'

He nodded.

I closed my eyes. I took all of my remaining energy and moved it into my central dan tian. I focused, and moved it up through the meridians. I took it into my upper dan tian, into my Inner Eye, then moved it back again. I gathered it and exhaled deeply. I was perfectly calm and in control. I only had about half my chi left. The rest was black stuff.

'Well done,' he said.

I opened my eyes. 'Does this mean that I'm half demon now?'

'That's one way of putting it,' he said with amusement. 'What they have done to you is fascinating. I've never seen this done before. Try using the demon essence much the same way you would use the human chi. You may find it useful.' His face softened. 'I really like you much better this way.'

'You have me,' I said, ignoring him. 'What are you going to do with me?'

'Absolutely nothing.' He turned and gestured for me to follow him. 'Come with me.'

I didn't have much choice. I followed him to the end of the hall. There was a dais raised at least three metres above the floor, with elaborate zigzagging steps.

'Is Simone okay?' I said as he led me up the stairs.

'Simone is at home on the Peak crying her eyes out,' the King said. 'Forgive me, my Lady, but it is not my will right now to let you talk to her. But she is perfectly safe and shall remain so.'

'Who's with her?'

'Michael. Ah Yat. Gold. Monica will arrive soon. All of her family are around her.'

'No.' I swallowed. 'All of her family have left her.'

'Well, you are here now, my Lady, and we shall see what happens next,' the King said. 'I'm expecting a very interesting visit soon, because of an oath I made. You should come and watch; this will prove most diverting.'

A huge Chinese-style throne, at least two metres long, was set upon the dais. It was made of elaborately carved rosewood, the back picked out in gold. But the carving wasn't the usual dragons; it was Snake Mothers. A couple of demons stood behind it; one with a horse's head, one with a bull's head. Both of them bowed slightly to me as I approached.

'Please sit and enjoy the show, my Lady,' the King said. 'Nobody will harm you, I promise.'

I shrugged. What the hell. I kicked off my shoes and pulled my feet up to sit cross-legged on the gold silk cushions next to him on the throne. He glanced admiringly at me, his handsome face lighting up with a kind smile.

'You are an exceptional woman, to do what you have done.' He faced the hall. 'Please watch carefully, my Lady, because I am relying on you.'

'To do what?'

'All will become apparent,' he said. 'Watch.'

The doors flew open. Simon Wong strode in, holding John's head by the hair.

I collapsed over my knees but didn't make a sound.

'Steady, Emma,' the King said softly. 'Remember, it is just a shell.' He made a soft sound of amusement. 'The shell of the Turtle.'

'You are such a bastard,' I said quietly. I swallowed hard. I didn't want them to see me lose it. I took some deep breaths.

'Don't look at it, dear,' he said. 'He's done some rather nasty things to it. My, but he is a piece of work.'

'I will kill that piece of shit one day,' I whispered into my knees.

'You will never get the chance, dear,' he said. 'Now stay quiet and watch. Without looking at the Turtle's head.' He stopped and his voice filled with humour. 'Your English is a remarkable language, you know. You have a word for everything. Even for what he has done to this head. A single, precise syllable, with so many layers of meaning.'

I pulled myself upright. I had to retain my dignity. I didn't look at the head, as much as I wanted one last glimpse of John's face. I knew that it wouldn't be him. And I knew exactly what the King was talking about.

Hundreds of demons appeared in the hall and stood silently watching Wong. They were all in True Form and all different types: humanoids, dogs, worms, bugs, slime, everything. There were some that I didn't even recognise and some that were just creeping horrors.

'I have the head of the Dark Lord,' Wong said loudly, holding the head up and turning around so that all could see it.

He dropped it and kicked it to the base of the dais.

I nearly went for him but the King grabbed my arm. 'Don't waste your time, dear.'

Wong walked to the bottom of the steps. 'Your Most Loathsome Majesty.'

'Hi, Simon,' the King said.

'You vowed that whoever brought you the head of the Dark Lord while he was in this weakened state would be promoted to Number One.'

'That is quite correct, Number One,' the King said.

Wong grinned viciously with satisfaction. He walked carefully up the stairs and stood in front of the King. 'I want to see.'

The King gestured with one hand and a male demon appeared on the dais before us. He appeared to be a Chinese man in his mid-fifties with an intelligent face marred by cruel eyes. Number One. He wore a standard Western-style shirt and tie. His shirtsleeves were rolled up. He fell to one knee and saluted the King. 'You summoned me, Your Most Loathsome Majesty?'

'Made a run for it, did you, Number One?' Wong said. 'Wondered why I didn't see your ugly face in the crowd.'

'There is no running from me, One,' the King said.

'I wasn't running, Dad,' Number One said. 'I was in my quarters, killing all my wives and children.'

'Damn,' Wong said under his breath.

'Oh, so sorry, I didn't realise,' the King said warmly. 'Want to go back and finish?'

'Nah, Dad,' Number One said. 'All done.'

'Good. You have been replaced. Choose. Demotion or destruction,' the King said.

'Seppuku,' the demon said without rising.

'Oh my,' Wong said. 'This is turning out to be a very fine day indeed.'

'Not in front of the Lady, One,' the King said. 'I do not wish to distress her.'

'You don't know me well at all, King. I want to see this. I know this one. Tell you what,' I leaned forward to speak to the demon kneeling before me, 'how about I act as second for you?'

Wong stiffened but the King clapped his hands with delight. 'Truly remarkable!'

'I want to see him die *slowly*,' Wong said, his voice almost a whine. 'I want to see him *suffer*.'

'It is One's choice,' the King said. 'Just shut up and be a good boy, Simon. You'll get your turn.'

Wong scowled but didn't say anything.

The King concentrated and a small knife appeared in his hand. It had no handle, just the metal sticking out of the blade. 'Take the knife, One, and let's get this over with.'

Number One pulled himself gracefully to his feet and stepped forward to accept the blade. He bowed slightly as he took it carefully using both hands. Then he bowed to me. 'I am most honoured. My heart is filled with joy. I am given the opportunity to depart with dignity, seconded by you.'

'Hmph,' Wong said. 'Seconded by a *chick*. Can't see any honour in that.'

'You see no honour in anything, Simon,' the King said. 'You wouldn't know honour if it kicked you in the balls.' He concentrated again. A katana appeared in his hand.

The Japanese sword had a jet-black handle wrapped in black ray skin and a black lacquer scabbard. Gold silk cords bound it at the end and in the middle. It was completely devoid of any decoration; even the guard of the hilt, the *tsuba*, was plain.

Wong and Number One both took a sudden, deep breath. Every demon in the hall froze and watched silently.

The King rose, holding the blade in front of him. 'Stand up, Emma, let's do this right.'

I rose and we faced each other on the dais. 'Holy shit,' I said quietly, 'that's the Murasame, the Destroyer, isn't it?'

'You are quite correct, my Lady,' the King said. 'I won this from the Turtle himself about two hundred years ago.'

'You are giving the Murasame to the Lady of your most mortal enemy?' Number One said with disbelief.

'Just proving a point, One,' the King said. 'I can give her another blade if you like.'

Number One was silent for a while, then, 'I am really most profoundly honoured, my Lord.'

'Good.' The King held the blade out to me and I took it. 'Emma.' I looked up. The King gazed right into my eyes. 'The Murasame is the only blade that will destroy me.'

I looked down at the sword, then up at the King. I nodded without speaking and turned to Number One. 'Where do you want to do this?'

'What the hell are you doing, you stupid cunt?' Wong shouted. 'Take the bastard out! This is your chance!'

'You really are quite a piece of work, Simon,' the King said mildly. 'I must say I am most tremendously glad that your Mother is dead.'

I looked Wong in the eye. 'Unlike you, I keep my word. I will make you suffer horribly for what you have done, Simon, that I promise.'

'There aren't enough gold coins in the whole world for you, my Lady,' the King said softly behind me.

Number One stood holding the short blade.

'Where do you want to do this?' I said.

'Here. Now.' Number One faced the gathered demons and knelt in a *seiza* position. He placed the

519

blade on a lacquer tray that appeared in front of him. 'Wait until the second cut. I will nod.' His voice softened as he wrenched off his tie and tore open his shirt to reveal his bare abdomen. 'I am profoundly honoured. My Lord, my Lady, I thank you both.'

'It's been fun, One,' the King said. He turned to sit on the throne. 'Come and sit with me, Simon, let's watch the show. I wonder if Emma knows how to do it right?'

'I know how to do it right,' I whispered.

'I'm sure you do,' Number One replied, just as softly. 'Thanks, Emma. I don't deserve this from you.'

'Just do it.'

He leaned forward and picked up the blade. He closed his eyes and his face became a mask of concentration.

I stood behind and to one side, unsheathed the dark blade, and held it ready. The jet-black blade of the Murasame was so cold that condensation appeared on it. It was a blade of pure yin. I wasn't surprised that John had once owned it. I wondered how he had lost it to the King.

Number One plunged the small blade into his abdomen and sliced himself across from left to right, his face not shifting at all as he pulled it viciously upwards at the end of the cut. He jerked the blade free, his face not moving. He plunged the blade into the middle of the lower part of his abdomen and sliced it upwards. His entrails started to slide out of the almost bloodless wound.

He pulled the blade free and opened his eyes to see the crowd. He smiled and nodded slightly without looking away from the massed demons.

I swiftly swung the Murasame to take off his head, carefully leaving a flap of skin on his throat so that the head would not be completely severed. Beheading was for criminals. Men of honour did not have their heads taken completely off.

The head fell forward and, to my surprise, blood gushed from his neck. He really was a very senior demon.

The body collapsed forward and there was a concerted sigh from the gathered demons. The body didn't dissolve.

'Give me something to clean the blade,' I said, then saw it. 'No need.'

'The Destroyer absorbs the blood of its victims,' the King said. 'It really is a very bloodthirsty blade indeed.'

I put the sword away, turned and held it out to the King.

'I tell you what, Emma,' the King said with a small smile, 'how about you keep it? A gift from me.' He gestured with one hand. 'The blade is yours. Use it well.'

'Use it on him!' Wong hissed.

'One day I will use it on you,' I said. I moved to stand near them.

The King eyed the body with amusement. 'Well, what do you know — he did have guts.' He waved one hand. 'Clean up.'

The horse-headed demon nodded and disappeared, taking the disembowelled body with it.

'What are you going to do with me now?' I said.

'I'm giving you to Simon.'

'The hell you are!' I shouted. 'I vowed to stay with *you*! You can't do this to me!'

'Do you want her, Simon?' the King said mildly.

'Hell, yeah,' Wong said.

'What if I made you vow not to harm her?'

'I promise I won't harm her,' Wong said, eyeing me hungrily.

'His word's no good, you know that, King,' I said desperately. '*You can't do this to me*!'

'I want a blood oath, Simon.'

Wong stiffened and his eyes widened.

'Shit,' I said quietly.

'Will you swear not to harm her? In your own blood?' He smiled at me. 'If he breaks the oath he'll be destroyed. Rather good, eh?'

'I vowed to stay with *you*.'

'Emma, dear, there is method to my madness. Just stay quiet and watch, please,' the King said kindly.

I couldn't believe this. 'Shit!'

'What good is she if I can't hurt her?' Wong said petulantly. 'I can't even use her in the lab if I can't hurt her.'

'No suffering, physical or mental. You may have her, but she must remain unharmed and well cared for. I won't expect her to be happy, being where she is, but I will expect her to come out at the end unscathed. Physically sound and mentally intact.'

Wong glanced sideways at me, thinking.

'No, you can't even do that to her,' the King said. 'She is to stay exactly as she is.'

'Why the hell are you doing this?' I whispered. 'What's in it for you?'

'Wait and see,' the King said. 'Well, Simon?'

'Better than nothing, I suppose,' Wong said. 'Okay. I'll take her. No idea what I'll do with her though.'

Raw fury filled me. I was *not* going with this bastard. '*You can't do this to me*!' The Snake came out. The sword hit the dais with a clatter.

Wong leaped back but the King didn't move. I pulled myself up and hesitated, working out which one I should strike first.

'Wonderful!' the King said with genuine delight. 'I was hoping I'd see this!' He clapped his hands. 'Perfect!'

I struck at him. He was faster than me. He grabbed me around the throat, threw my head to the floor and held it down with his foot. I struggled; my black coils writhed around us. He had me in a death grip. The pressure was killing me.

I changed back and he raised his foot from the back of my neck.

'Hop up, Emma. I don't think I've hurt you. Thanks for that. I was really hoping I'd see the Serpent. Stunning.'

I picked myself up and brushed myself off. Fortunately I'd missed the puddle of blood in front of the throne.

The King looked me in the eyes with a smile. 'You'd make the most tremendous Mother, you know that? The offspring you'd produce would be really exceptional.'

'I'd almost prefer that to going with this bastard,' I growled. I retrieved the Murasame from the floor and looked at it, then changed my mind. I turned and sat on the throne. I rested the blade across my knees.

'Don't worry, Emma, you'll be fine. He won't hurt you,' the King said. 'Just remember: I have ensured that you will not be harmed. I know what I am doing. *Remember*. My vow still holds: as long as you stay with him, Simone Chen will be perfectly safe.'

He turned to Wong. 'I won't use Emma's blade to draw the blood; just the touch of it would probably destroy you outright.' He concentrated and a stiletto appeared in his hand. 'Come here, love, and let's do this.'

Wong sidled forward and held out his wrist.

'Stick him deep,' I said softly.

'With pleasure,' the King said, and plunged the blade into Wong's wrist, then slashed it viciously across.

Wong howled and blood gushed from his wrist. He went silent and stared at it with wonder. 'Blood.'

'Yes, my pet, you are Number One now,' the King said. He gestured towards a table that appeared at the end of the throne. 'There's the brush, there's the scroll, sign your name like a good little boy.'

Wong went to the scroll and read it. He picked up the brush, loaded it with blood from his dripping wrist, and signed. One horizontal stroke: he was Number One.

'Read it out loud,' the King said.

'I swear the Dark Lady, Emma Donahoe, will come to no harm, physical or mental, as long as she stays with me,' Wong said dully. He glowered at the King. 'Enough?'

'I think that will do,' the King said. 'Do go and clean up, there's a good boy. You are quite disgusting to look at. Then you can come back and collect your prize.'

Wong saluted the King and disappeared.

The King looked down at the floor. 'Quite a lot of cleaning up to do.' He smiled at me. 'You've caused quite a mess. Look.' He gestured. 'The blood of my old Number One and my new Number One mingle.' He looked me in the eye. 'They will share similar fates.' He sat on the throne next to me.

'They'd better,' I growled. 'But I don't want any honour for Wong when he goes. I want him to die like a dog.'

'So do I, my sweet, so do I,' the King said softly. He turned to the massed demons in the hall. 'Piss off. Show's over.'

The demons disappeared.

He turned back to me. 'Tea?'

'*Sow mei*,' I said.

'Very good,' he said, and lightly clapped his hands.

'Simone will be one hundred per cent safe?' I said.

'On my honour, and you know I have some,' the King said, 'she will be safe.'

'Send the head back to Jade and Gold,' I said. 'We need the body whole so that Simone can claim the inheritance.'

'Already done, my Lady.'

'Where's Leo?' I said.

'Court Ten,' the King said.

'He went straight there?'

'Yes.'

'No,' I whispered.

'He is arguing most ferociously not to be Raised.'

'No.'

The tea materialised on a small table between us on the throne and he poured. 'You realise, Emma, the more he argues, the less effective his arguments will be.'

'I know,' I whispered. 'If he strode in demanding to be Raised he'd have no chance at all.'

'He is much too honest for his own good,' the King said, raising his teacup.

'He always was.'

'You can go and say hello if you like,' the King said kindly.

'I'd prefer he didn't know that I'm here,' I said.

'Perfectly understandable. Ah, here comes my new Number One son, to take his prize.' The King put down the tea and handed me another mobile phone. 'If he gives you any shit, just give me a call. I'll come and land on him. You are to be kept in ease and comfort. If you aren't held in perfect luxury, let me know.'

I took the phone without a word.

He looked intensely at me. 'Emma. Remember. I have kept you safe. I have kept Simone safe. I have protected both of you. Remember that I have done this thing for you. I'm counting on you.' He leaned back and smiled. 'Come around and have lunch with me some time.'

'If I do, will you give me updates on Simone, Leo and John?'

'Of course,' he said with a gentle smile. 'I will give you anything that your heart desires, short of your freedom.'

Wong reappeared before us. 'Come on then, bitch,' he said and howled with pain.

'You will treat the Lady with respect,' the King said casually. 'You will provide her with comfortable apartments. You will treat her well. I will know exactly what you are doing, little Simon.' He shifted slightly on the gold silk cushions. 'Do not let her witness any of your more unsavoury activities. I will be watching you.'

Wong glowered at the King then gestured towards me. 'My Lady.'

'Remember, Number One,' the King said. 'If you harm her at all, you will be destroyed. And if you go anywhere near the daughter of the Dark Lord, you will answer to me.' He turned to me and his blood-coloured eyes blazed. 'Remember.'

We materialised in the living room of a luxurious Hong Kong penthouse. The view over the Island through the windows was spectacular. The apartment was decorated in modern tan and beige, with expensive dark wood panelling on the walls and plush woollen carpet. The furniture was European-style: slim, low-line and expensive.

'You can have this one,' Wong said. 'Anything you need, let me know.'

'Anywhere in here with room for me to train? Practise?'

'I will arrange it,' he said. 'Need to keep you fit and in good shape, otherwise my dad will rip my scales off.'

'I want a computer with broadband and a webcam.'

'You may have the broadband, but I'll be holding meetings here and I don't want you telling anybody what's going on. So you won't be able to email out, and

I can't let you have the webcam. Sorry,' he said without meaning it at all.

'I want a full set of the classics: *Creation of the Gods*, *Journey to the West*, *Journey to the North*, *Red Chamber*, *Heroes of the Marsh*, all of them. Both languages.'

'I'll see what I can do.'

'How do I call you if I need you?'

'Tell one of the thralls.'

'Okay, then. Piss off.'

He bowed slightly with a vicious grin. 'Nothing I'd rather do more.' He disappeared.

I looked through the apartment and opened every single door. None of them led out of it. I was imprisoned.

The apartment appeared to be on top of one of the exclusive blocks above Harbour Centre in Tsim Sha Tsui, overlooking Hong Kong Harbour. Ocean Terminal's open-air rooftop car park was visible through the living room windows. Simone often went to the huge toy shop in Ocean Terminal, and enjoyed parking on the roof of the terminal: the view was spectacular. I might even be able to see her there occasionally, if I was very lucky and kept a sharp eye out for the car.

The energy calming still worked. I didn't lose it at the thought of Simone. The effect was fading though.

I could see the clock tower of the old Kowloon train station, next to the Star Ferry. Half past twelve, midnight. Just over twelve hours since the attack on the Peak apartment. It felt like a week had passed.

The suite had four bedrooms. I chose the master bedroom. It had a king-size bed and the bathroom was enormous, with a spa. I would have him convert a couple of the other bedrooms to a training room for me.

There were two smiling demon maids in the kitchen. I didn't say a word to them.

The dining room had a Western-style rectangular rosewood table, large enough to seat ten. Meetings.

The fourth bedroom would make a perfect study. I would have him remove the bed and put in a desk for me. There were things I needed to do.

I returned to the bedroom I had chosen, sat on the bed, dropped the sword beside me, and put my head in my hands.

I pulled myself back up and went to the window. I opened the thick tan-coloured curtains and looked out.

Some of the buildings on the Peak still had their lights on.

John's building was close to the top. Our building. Our apartment was on the top floor. The curtains were open in Simone's bedroom and the light was on, but the other three bedrooms — mine, Leo's and John's — were dark.

I thought I saw a small silhouette against the window, then the curtains were drawn closed and the light was gone.

I went to the bedroom door and locked it. Then I fell onto the bed on my stomach, curled up and let go.

I was incapacitated for about thirty-six hours. When I recovered, I had a shower. The wardrobe was full of clothes that fitted me perfectly. I went out of my room and discovered that the apartment had already been changed for me.

The training room was even better than the one on the Peak, but he hadn't provided me with any weapons. I leaned the Murasame against the wall across from the mirrors. I would have him provide a stand for it. I wondered if it had a matching *wakizashi*. The complete *daisho* set of both destructive blades would be rather cool.

I stopped. I was being totally cold-blooded again. Understandable, now, perhaps. Now that I was what I was.

I eyed the blade. I had vowed not to try to escape. And I wouldn't: to keep Simone safe. But when the Dark Lord returned, I would have my escape. The Murasame would provide it.

And then I realised with an ice-cold shock: I had promised Simone. I couldn't escape. He would come back, and he would see me like this. No.

I tried something. I went into the centre of the room and performed a yang-style Tai Chi set. When I had the chi flowing, I moved it into the central dan tian and attempted to use it to burn out the demon stuff.

When I came around I felt like I'd been hit in the head by a small building. Okay, that didn't work.

But I could still manipulate the remaining chi, and that was good enough for now. I would work something out.

I ordered the maids to make me some food and ate it silently and alone in the dining room.

Then I went into the study. All of the classics I had asked for graced the bookshelf.

I sat at the computer and opened the word processor. I had memories to record so that I would never forget. One day Simone would be able to read the whole story. Well, maybe not the whole story. Some parts would be just for me.

CHAPTER FORTY

I woke up and cast around, then remembered. I threw myself out of the enormous bed and wandered into the bathroom.

I yawned in the mirror. Then I just about broke my jaw shrieking. I leapt back.

The face in the mirror had *no skin*.

I took a deep breath, then carefully slithered forward for another look.

I realised that I'd *slithered*. I collapsed and curled up on the floor. I pulled my black coils in and gasped. I tried not to look at my hands but I couldn't help it.

No skin. *No skin*. I watched with silent horror as the blood moved over my skinless arms.

Okay. Deep breaths. I was still me, wasn't I?

I pictured Simone in my mind, and imagined being ordered to hurt her.

I collapsed again. The thought of that wonderful little girl, and how much I missed her, tore my heart out.

Okay. Deep breaths, again. I was still me.

Holy shit. I had a True Form. I looked inside myself. The black stuff had moved through me during the previous two days; it wasn't just in my dan tian now, it was everywhere. Thank you *so damn much*, Simon

Wong. I quietly pondered *exactly* what I wanted to do to that bastard when I didn't have to worry about Simone's safety any more.

Right. Looking inside: where's Emma? I studied myself. I didn't look like a hybrid, which was interesting. I didn't look like a Mother on the inside either. I looked like something extremely old and powerful.

Something floated to the surface of my memory. The creator of the human race, in deep mythological history, had been half serpent, half human. The Great Mother. The Dark Woman, Nu Wa. I was something like that. Very interesting. Damn, I wished I still had the stone with me. It would have known what Nu Wa looked like, and would have been able to tell me if I was something like her.

I grinned to myself, still curled up on the floor. Look at the Snake Mother being cold-blooded.

Okay. I pulled myself upright. I wouldn't look in the mirror again, thank you very much. I slithered back to the bedroom.

I went to the window and looked out, trying to calm myself. There was a quiet knock on the door.

'Who is it?' I said, my voice hissing.

'It's me, ma'am,' the demon servant said. 'Your breakfast is ready.'

I suddenly became extremely aware of exactly what Mothers ate. Well, well. You learned a new thing every day.

'Later,' I said. 'Leave me.'

I saw her move away with my Inner Eye, then froze.

My Inner Eye was working in this form. I checked my chi; but it wasn't the chi that was running the Eye. It was the black stuff.

I took another deep breath. Okay, ignoring for a moment the source of this power, I used it to have a look around. Holy shit. I wasn't on top of Ocean

Terminal at all. The windows were an illusion. I was underneath Kowloon City.

What I really needed to do, though, was find my own form, my human form. My *real* True Form.

I ordered my body to take human shape and was knocked flat.

When I came around I quickly checked my hands. Back to normal. Back to me.

I raced into the bathroom and breathed a sigh of relief. Okay. I'd even managed to conjure the same clothes I'd been wearing.

While I washed and readied myself I thought about what I would do. I should try to take this Mother form at will, it could prove useful. Particularly if I could work with the black stuff. Then I decided against it. It was just too damn ugly. And weird.

I opened the door and went to find breakfast. I tried not to think of John's reaction if he were to see me.

I tried not to think of Simone at all.

I sat at the dining table and ordered the maids in from the kitchen.

They appeared to be tiny round Chinese women in their mid-forties, less than one and a half metres tall, wearing traditional servants' black and white. They crept in and smiled nervously.

'Sit,' I said, gesturing to the chairs across the table from me.

They shared a look and didn't move.

'Sit,' I said. 'That's an order.'

They looked uncomfortable but sat.

'Ceylon tea, brown toast, peanut butter,' I said.

They nodded and rose, and I raised my hand to stop them. 'Not yet. I want to talk to you first. Do either of you have names?'

They both shook their heads.

'Can you speak?'

'Yes, ma'am,' they whispered, bobbing their heads.

'When were you hatched?'

They both opened their mouths at the same time, then the one on the left continued, the one on the right stayed silent.

'I was hatched about three months ago,' the left one said.

'Six weeks,' the one on the right said.

'Geez,' I said. 'You're only babies.'

They remained silent, watching the table.

'I suppose he didn't have any thralls left after they all turned to us,' I said. 'You're new ones, replacements. Okay.' I smiled and made my voice more brisk. I gestured to the one on the left. 'You're One.' The one on the right. 'You're Two. I'll name you in Putonghua, I learned some with Simone's teacher.' I gestured towards One. 'Yi Hao.' Number Two. 'Er Hao.'

They both bobbed their heads. 'Ma'am.'

'I'm completely vegetarian. Chinese vegetarian food. Ceylon tea, or *sow mei* or *tikuanyin* Chinese tea. No soda. Mineral water only.'

'Ma'am.'

'How do you go out?' I said.

They shared a look.

'Not allowed to tell me?'

They shook their heads.

'It's okay, I can't get out.'

I had a sudden inspiration. After what had been done it me it was possible that I *could* get out. I should have a try at teleportation. Waste of time though; I'd vowed to stay.

'What have you been told about me?' I said.

They shared another look. Yi Hao, the older one, decided to answer for both of them. 'You are a famed destroyer of demons,' she whispered. 'You hate all demons with a vengeance. If we survive more than a day in this house we are lucky. You wield the Blade of Destruction; we have seen it. If we anger you ...' She pulled herself together. 'You will destroy us without a second thought.'

'All of that is quite correct,' I said with a smile, and watched them squirm.

Hold on, that wasn't like me at all, tormenting helpless creatures for amusement. What was wrong with me?

Wonderful. I really was half demon. Okay; let's try to control this demon nature and make sure that Emma stays in control.

'I won't harm you, little ones,' I said gently. 'I have tamed demons, and I have had demon servants for years. I have never harmed a single one of them. You are quite safe with me.'

Neither of them relaxed. They didn't believe me. Not surprising, after working for Wong for any length of time.

'Go and get me my tea and toast,' I said. 'And a copy of the *South China Morning Post*. And don't eat all the peanut butter,' I added with a grin. 'I know you demons love it.'

Neither of them moved.

'Dismissed,' I said gently.

Both of them rose, carefully pushed their chairs in, bowed slightly and disappeared into the kitchen.

I furiously beat myself up inside. I had just tortured these two poor infants for my own amusement. I would watch my behaviour carefully and keep this dark stuff under very strict control. I was staying one hundred per cent goddamn pure *me*.

Er Hao brought my toast and the paper. I flipped it open. I'd been out of the loop for a few days but nothing much had happened. The government, as usual, was in trouble about something; people were complaining about poor service and shoddy craftsmanship in the letters to the editor; and sports was mainly English soccer.

The body of a Chinese woman in her early thirties had been found hacked to pieces in a dumpster in Kowloon City, the second murder in six months.

I knew it was April. I just knew. Now that they had me, and April's child had served her purpose, they didn't need April any more.

The days blurred past. I practised with the Murasame; it had some interesting abilities. I tried different things with the demon stuff; I had some interesting abilities as well. I wrote my story. I read the classics. Wong never came.

I was absolutely miserable. I missed my family so much it ripped my heart out. The loneliness was soul-destroying. I lost weight. I just wasn't hungry most of the time, despite the fact that the two demons were excellent cooks.

I dealt with it. I stayed busy. I watched the top of the car park, hoping to catch a glimpse of a black Mercedes with a little girl in it. Even though it was an illusion, the image was real.

I spent many long, sleepless nights watching the lights of the Peak apartment. Only Simone's bedroom light was ever turned on. I knew when she went to sleep; it was very late for her sometimes as well.

I even missed the stupid arrogant stone.

About a week later I was doing a set with the Murasame when a young woman appeared on the other side of the training room. I recognised her immediately: a Mother, about level seventy or eighty. A big one.

I lowered my sword. 'Can I help you?'

'You are the Dark Lady?' she said without introduction.

'Yes.'

She took True Form and poised on her coils.

I readied myself.

She raced towards me and I bound her by taking half her chi out. She froze.

'Yield and I will let you go,' I said. 'Give me your word and you can go.'

She didn't speak, she just hissed at me, trying to free herself from my binding.

'I've been wanting to practise some techniques on a demon,' I said. 'If you don't yield now, I will practise on you.'

'Try me,' she said, but she sounded like a yowling cat.

I'd wanted to try this for a while. I concentrated, and drained about half of the black demon essence out of her. I didn't put it into my dan tian; I didn't want to absorb any more of the stuff. I loaded the Murasame with it instead. It was easier than draining chi. Her face went blank with astonishment.

I launched the demon stuff back at her.

She folded up, growing smaller and smaller, then eventually turned into a shining black bead that fell onto the floor, rolling slightly on the mats.

'So that's how he did it,' I said softly. I went to the demon and picked her up; she had definitely turned into the bead.

'Yi Hao!' I yelled, and the demon servant appeared in the doorway. She froze when she saw the bead in my hand. 'Yi Hao, I want you to get me an airtight jar about thirty centimetres tall, half that across, with a good metal seal on the top. Hurry.'

She bobbed quickly and disappeared.

It took her about five minutes. When she returned I put the demon in the jar and sealed it. 'Thanks.'

'What was that, my Lady?' the demon said.

'That was a level seventy Mother that came for me,' I said.

She inhaled sharply. 'You did that to her?'

'Yep,' I said. 'She's dormant. I can bring her out any time.'

Yi Hao stared at me with awe.

I put the jar in the corner. Looked like I'd started a collection. I wondered how many more would come after me.

'Don't touch the jar, sweetheart,' I said. 'You could let the Mother out and it could hurt you.'

Yi Hao stared incredulously at me.

'What?' I said.

She shook her head and smiled. 'You called me sweetheart. As if I was your child.'

I went to her and patted her shoulder. 'You are a child. And you are mine.' I put my arm around her shoulders and gave her a squeeze. 'Go and make me some *sow mei* tea. I'll have it in the living room. And tell Er Hao not to touch the jar — I don't want either of you getting hurt.'

Yi Hao's eyes were full of tears. 'Yes, ma'am,' she said with a huge grin, and hurried out.

That was much more like me. It felt good.

I drank the tea in the living room and opened *Dream of the Red Chamber*. This was the hardest of all the classics to read; the story meandered without much purpose and there were far too many characters to keep track of without writing notes. But the main storyline soon became frighteningly obvious.

The family of a young wastrel, Pao-yu, arranged for two beautiful girls to come and live with them as potential brides for him. One was Precious Virtue, the other was Black Jade, and the two girls loved each other like sisters.

Black Jade was sickly with consumption, so the family decided not to let him marry them both. They arranged for him to marry Precious Virtue alone. But they told the young man that he was marrying Black Jade, the one he truly loved.

In the Chinese tradition, the bride's face is covered with a veil until she enters the wedding bedchamber. When Pao-yu pulled aside the veil and saw he had married the wrong girl, he left the family forever, only appearing years later in passing as a monk.

Black Jade died of her illness and grief.

No wonder everybody had been so concerned about the amount of black jade I was presented with. I felt the earring in my ear. I still had one black jade coin left.

One afternoon a few days later I heard voices in the living room. I went out.

Wong and Kitty were there with a few demons, standing around talking, holding large glasses of red wine. At least I hoped it was red wine. Demon cocktail party.

'And here she is,' Wong said loudly, gesturing towards me. 'My house guest. May I present the Dark Lady herself, Lady Emma Donahoe, chosen of the Emperor of the Northern Heavens.' He grinned and lowered his voice. 'Have a look inside, guys. You *have* to see this.'

They all bowed and smiled slightly. Then they studied me. Kitty watched them impatiently.

'*Wah*,' one of them said. She looked like a slim, elegant, middle-aged Chinese woman wearing a grey silk pantsuit. 'You did that?'

'Yep,' Wong said with satisfaction. 'Unfortunately

the King made me promise not to hurt her, so I can't complete the process.'

'Can we talk in front of her?' a rotund young Chinese man said.

'Not a good idea, I think,' Wong said. 'She can't get out to tell anybody, but we can't make her suffer at all. It'll destroy me.'

The others watched him impassively.

'I know exactly what every single one of you is thinking,' Wong said, completely unfazed. 'And remember, without me, you get nowhere.'

They turned as one and studied me again.

'Why?' the woman said.

'Oath in blood,' Wong said.

The round male demon turned to him quickly. 'Blood?'

Wong spread his hands. 'Hey. I'm Number One now.'

'Can you destroy the blood oath on the scroll once you've taken over?' the woman said.

Wong turned and grinned right into my eyes. 'Yes. I. Can.'

My blood ran cold. I spun and went down the hall into the training room.

When I had calmed down I kicked myself. They were holding a meeting out there, sharing their plans, and I was in the training room, totally unable to hear them.

I went back out and down the long hallway. They were no longer in the living room. I had no idea where they were.

I wandered around, and heard them in the dining room. I pressed my ear to the door. I couldn't understand a word they were saying.

I tried to open my Internal Eye to have a look inside but it wasn't working.

Shit. And I had decided that I wasn't going to *do* this.

I went back to my bedroom and locked the door. I moved to the centre of the room, lowered my head and concentrated. I didn't really know what I was doing, but I knew what I wanted to achieve.

I gave up. I couldn't do it. I slithered towards the door. I stopped.

Okay.

I opened the Inner Eye and watched them. They didn't seem to notice my regard.

Wong was meeting with the four other senior demons. All of them were at least level sixty; lords and ladies. There were two female and two male. The slim middle-aged female and the rotund young male were there. There was also a female appearing in her mid-teens wearing a micro-mini, a bikini top and huge boots; and a male that looked in his mid-twenties with a ponytail.

'I just don't *like* it,' the young female said.

'It will work,' the round male said.

'What if he has something up his sleeve?' the young female said.

'He can't have,' the middle-aged female said. 'We hold all the cards.'

'I want a demonstration,' the young female said.

Wong rose and smiled grimly.

'No!' Kitty snapped. 'Not until the time is ready!'

'Let me show them,' Wong said.

'No!' Kitty said again, loudly. 'Don't be a fool, Simon. Don't let any of it be seen until we are one hundred per cent ready!'

'Are you sure you can take him out?' the young round male said.

Wong sat back down, but the smile didn't shift. 'Dead positive. One, two more weeks, I'll be the most powerful thing that Hell has ever seen.'

'You'd better be right,' the male with the ponytail said.

'I'm right,' Wong said. 'And you know I'm right. Otherwise you wouldn't be along for the ride.'

I had to tell the King. I smiled grimly. The sky was falling, and I had to tell the King.

It appeared to be an upmarket café in Hong Kong, but the street outside was eerily quiet. Instead of the constant bustle of traffic and pedestrians, the street was deserted. The café itself was empty except for us. It was creepy.

The King had taken his usual human form. He perused the menu. 'Cheesecake's good.'

'Coffee,' I said. 'Black.'

'That's the way Leo likes it,' the King said, smiling at me over the menu.

I didn't rise to it. It could wait. There were more important things right now.

'One Two Two is planning to make a try for you in the next one or two weeks,' I said.

'So soon?' the King said, unsurprised. 'I didn't know he was ready yet. Thanks.'

An elegant deco coffee plunger and mug appeared in front of me and I poured for myself. The King had a glass of red wine.

'Is that really wine?' I said.

The King glanced at the glass. 'This time, it is. Australian, in honour of the present company. I buy up the best vintages.'

'You've forced the price of good wine through the roof.'

'Cornered the market,' the King said. 'Very lucrative.'

'What are you going to do?'

'Right now? Nothing,' the King said with a small smile. 'I can handle it.'

'He says he'll be the most powerful thing in Hell,' I said.

The King lowered his wine glass and leaned intensely over the table. 'You can call me George, if you like.'

'He says he'll be the most powerful thing in Hell.'

The King leaned back. 'I can handle him.'

'You may not be able to. Look what he did to me. He's made me immensely powerful. If he'd been able to get control of me, I hate to think what I could have done.'

'Don't worry, Emma, I have it all under control,' the King said.

'A level seventy Mother came after me a couple of days ago.'

He smiled slightly. 'Not a threat for you.'

'Did you send her?'

The smile didn't shift. 'Of course not. Mothers have something approaching free will, and they often wager with each other. Looks like that one lost a bet. Call me if one turns up that's too big to handle, but frankly I think you'd be able to take any of them.'

'I'd better return soon. He'll know I'm missing,' I said.

'No, he won't,' the King said. 'There's a shapeshifter in there while you're here with me. And don't you want to hear about them?'

I sighed and dropped my head. 'Of course I do. But first: if he takes you, can he destroy the scroll?'

'Of course,' the King said. 'But it will not come to that.' I heard a rustle and looked up. He'd pulled out a piece of paper. 'Status report: Xuan Wu. Disappeared entirely. Out there somewhere, but we don't know where.'

'Good,' I said. 'Simone?'

'Simone is undergoing therapy, and won't start school for another week or so,' the King said, reading the paper. 'It will be a while before she is able to return to a normal life. But she's resilient, she'll be fine. Rhonda is at the Peak helping out.'

'She'll never forgive me,' I whispered. 'I don't know how many times I told her I'd never leave her.'

'She doesn't believe the stone, Emma. She is in a very deep state of denial. She is quite sure that I am holding you against your will.'

'Damn,' I said softly. I straightened and controlled my voice. 'Leo?'

'That will take a while,' the King said, folding the paper and leaning sideways to put it back into the pocket of his maroon jeans. He sipped the wine. 'The Judges are not amused; they have never seen anything like this before. A Worthy who refuses. First in history. Frankly, I don't think they quite know what to do with him.'

'Let him go,' I said.

'You do know that the Courts are not under my jurisdiction?' the King said. 'I only handle the retribution side. The judgement side of things is handled by the Celestial.'

I dropped my head. 'Yeah. I know.' I looked back at him. 'Can't you do something?'

The King smiled gently. 'Sorry, Emma. But you now know: they are all alive, to a degree. They are all waiting for you. And the Dark Lord has promised that he will return for you.'

'I don't want him to see me like this,' I whispered.

The King leaned over the table and spoke softly and intensely. 'Nothing at all wrong with the way you are right now, dear. You are the most attractive thing I have laid eyes on in centuries. Have you taken any other forms besides the Serpent? I'd love to see you in a Mother form. It's a possibility, you know, considering what he's done to you. Ever thought about it?'

I tried to control my face but he saw through me.

'Do it for me and I'll give you the matching *wakizashi*,' he said.

'I'll do it for you if you let me speak to Simone,' I said.

The King leaned back. 'Ah, it seems that today is a day that neither of us gets what we want.'

'Good.' I lowered my coffee mug and spoke more softly. 'Can I be changed back?'

The King smiled. 'To what?'

I considered it. I had changed immensely in the previous two and a half years. When I had joined John to work for him full-time I was a perfectly ordinary human female. When I had graduated from my MBA at the end of the previous year I was a Master of the Arts who turned into a big black snake when my family was threatened. And now I was a Master of the Arts, a snake, and a half demon Snake Mother who could destroy just about any demon I faced. I dropped my head into my hands. 'I don't know. I don't know what I am.'

He reached across the table and squeezed my arm. 'Yes, you can be changed back. It is possible. Of course, the Serpent would still be there, because that is your nature, but the demon essence could be removed without killing you.'

That stopped me dead. 'The Serpent isn't part of the demon nature?'

'No, of course not,' he said. 'The Serpent is all you.'

'No, that can't be right,' I said, desperate. 'The Serpent came out because of what Kitty Kwok did to me.'

'Nope. One hundred per cent you, dear. If you were to have the demon essence removed, this exquisite Serpent would still be part of you.'

I had been so positive that the Serpent was a result of Kitty's manipulation of me. I shook myself. It didn't matter. As long as the demon essence was removed, I could return to John. I glanced up, full of hope. 'Can you do it?'

His blood-coloured eyes sparkled with amusement. 'Do you want me to?'

I grabbed his hand. 'Yes. If you can.'

He held my hand and studied me closely. 'What would you give me in return?'

I pulled my hand away. 'What do you want?'

'Please. Call me George.' He smiled, relaxed. 'Be mine. Until he returns.' He ran his fingertips over my arm and I shivered. 'I will not force you to break your oath to him. I know that what you have with him is true. I would be content to have you only until then.' He dropped his voice. 'More than just staying with me; *being* with me, as Queen and Consort. And all that it involves. Promise me that, and I will change you back when he returns and you can go to him whole.'

I studied my hands and remembered my promise. 'Let me think about it,' I whispered.

'Take your time, dearest,' he said softly, and I was back in the study of my gold-plated prison cell.

CHAPTER FORTY-ONE

About ten days later I was practising with the Murasame in the training room when there was a tap on the door.

'Come in,' I said.

Yi Hao opened the door carefully and poked her head around. 'The Master wishes to see you, my Lady.'

I put the sword away and put it onto its black rack, wondering. I followed Yi Hao into the living room. Wong waited there for me, alone, standing in the middle of the room with his arms crossed over his chest, glowering.

I stopped and waited for him.

He didn't say anything, he just glowered.

I waited patiently. I could play this game all day if he wanted, but normally he was very impatient with me. This was entirely unlike him.

Suddenly he grinned, uncrossed his arms and put his hands on his hips. 'Want to go out for a spin? I've got something I want to show you.'

I felt a jolt of horror. 'What have you done?'

He held out one arm in a gesture of welcome. 'Come and see.'

I didn't move. 'Have you hurt Simone?'

He grinned more broadly. 'Nope. Come and look what *I* did.' He sounded like a schoolboy who'd just caught a frog.

'If you've hurt any member of my family, I'll take your head,' I said, trying to stay calm.

He shrugged, still grinning. 'I haven't hurt any of them. Come and look. You'll like this. It's really good.'

'*What have you done?*' I shouted.

He moved closer to me. I didn't shift away. His grin turned vicious. 'I'm taking over.' He held his hand out and the blood oath scroll appeared in it.

I ran back to the training room to get the blade, but I was too slow. He bound me before I was out of the living room. I struggled, but he was immensely powerful. He had me.

He walked up to me, very relaxed. He stopped in front of me and touched my cheek gently. He still held the scroll in his other hand. He moved his face right into mine. 'Don't worry, I can't start on you yet,' he whispered. 'There are some others who are a slightly higher priority.' He stepped back. 'But don't worry, sweetheart, you'll get your turn.'

The room around us disappeared. We were on the dais in the Demon King's throne room.

Wong sat on the throne and gestured for me to sit next to him. I could move now; he had unbound me.

I sized him up. He was more powerful than anything I had ever seen. Even if I hit him with chi and blew myself up, I wouldn't be able to destroy him.

Okay. Wait and see. I turned and sat on the throne next to him.

The doors to the hall flew open. Two very senior demons, both with the heads of bulls, dragged in the King. He was in his usual human form, wearing his maroon jeans and T-shirt. When they were halfway into the hall every single demon in Hell materialised around them.

The King righted himself and shook the demons off. He walked with slow dignity to the bottom of the stairs leading to the dais. When he saw me he gave me a huge friendly smile, his whole face lighting up.

'Stay there,' Wong said, and went down the steps to his father.

The two of them faced off, silent and unmoving.

Wong took True Form. He was a huge humanoid with black scales and three eyes. He towered over the King. He had grown since I had last seen his True Form at the charity night; he was nearly five metres tall.

The King also took True Form: blood-red, like a Snake Mother, and three metres tall. Wong towered over him.

Wong growled, a deep sound within his throat. The sound became louder and louder. He raised his taloned arms, the black scales glittering. Dark energy sprang from his hands.

The King silently raised his skinless hands and blood-red energy sprang from them to meet it.

The energy clashed in a ball of black and red.

It didn't take long. The energy ball hit the King and both of them changed. Wong into a blood-red Snake Mother-type demon; the King into a red humanoid, about three metres tall, without scales and with tusks.

Wong was King.

'Hold him!' Wong said.

The bull-headed demons grabbed the King's arms, and he changed back into human form.

Wong took human form as well. The scroll reappeared in his hands. He tore it in half, right down the middle. 'You're next, sweetheart,' he called to me, and some of the Snake Mothers in the hall hissed.

The King didn't attempt to escape. He smiled slightly. Wong led them up the stairs, the King walking calmly between his captors. When they were in front of the throne Wong turned and pushed his face right into his father's.

'You thought I couldn't do it,' he hissed. 'You thought you were stronger than anything. Well, you know what, Dad? You're *stupid*.'

'Not as stupid as you are, Number One,' the King said. 'If you didn't have your little pussy, you wouldn't be anything.'

Wong viciously backhanded the King, but the King ignored it.

'All of this was *my* idea,' Wong said. 'Kitty might have had people with the knowledge and the science, but I'm the one who got us here.' He stepped back and his voice calmed. 'And here we are. I've taken the Dark Lord's head. Which should I take next? Yours, or the Lady's?'

'Do me first,' the King said. 'The Lady has a job to do.'

I glanced at the King, wondering, but he didn't look at me.

'Okay, if you like. Push him down,' Wong said. 'On his knees.'

The King fell to his knees before the demons could push him. He glanced at me and smiled slightly. Wong didn't miss it.

'As soon as I've taken his head, I think I'll take my time with you,' he said to me.

'You really are an incredibly stupid fucking prick, Simon,' the King said softly. 'I cannot believe you are walking into this with all three of your eyes open.'

Wong hesitated, then he grinned. 'Too late, Dad.' He gestured to the demons. 'Hold him.'

He concentrated, and a sword appeared in his hand. It was very plain, with no decoration on either the hilt

549

or the blade. It was Dark Heavens. He held it up in front of him.

'Fitting, eh? You get to go by the Dark Lord's earthly weapon, the one that's already taken the Xuan Wu's head.' He stopped and mused. 'I wonder if I can get that stone thing to pull out the other one. The Star one. That would be lovely.' He turned to me. 'Can you get it?'

'No.'

'No matter.'

Wong quickly stepped forward and sliced through the King's neck. The blade went straight through without harming the King at all.

I tried to stop him, but I was bound again. I couldn't move.

'Stupid,' the King said.

Wong glared blankly at the King. Then he grinned. 'I remember. You told me yourself, you stupid bastard. Only the Murasame can destroy you. What a fucking stroke of luck. You gave it to my house guest. It's at my flat underneath Kowloon City. It's *mine*.'

The King's expression changed. He didn't seem as confident. I didn't struggle, much as I wanted to. Wong had worked it out.

Wong threw Dark Heavens onto the dais with a clatter. He held out his hand again and the Murasame appeared in it.

Wong screamed and dropped the blade, then grasped his hand and held it in front of his face, agonised.

'The Murasame will only serve its master,' the King said. 'No other, unless its master wills it. Right now, only the Lady may wield the blade. Any other who attempts to use it without her permission will be destroyed. Even its touch is agony for any but its owner.' He grinned at me. 'Pretty neat, eh?'

Wong glowered at me. 'If you take his head with the

Murasame, I'll give you your freedom and Simone's safety.'

'Give me your word,' I said.

'What?'

'Give me your word.' I went to the Murasame, picked it up, hefted it and took it to the King. I turned back to Wong. 'Do you promise to free me and keep Simone safe?'

Wong grinned. 'Sure. I promise.'

'Liar.' I raised the sword, swung it and ran it right through Wong's neck.

He didn't stop grinning. It hadn't harmed him at all. I ran the sword through his chest and pulled it out again. I slashed him across, attempting to cut him in half.

'No good, Emma,' Wong said. 'I've been working out.' He leaned closer to me. '*Nothing* can destroy me.'

'We'll see about that,' I said, and put the sword away.

'I must say, Emma,' the King said from his knees, 'you really are incredibly attractive. Such honour and dignity. How about a Mother form for me? Before I go?'

I ignored him.

'Bind him well and throw him into the cell block at the far end of level nine,' Wong said. 'Make sure he can't escape.' He tilted his head and smiled. 'Aren't there a couple of previous Kings in there, rotting away? Our predecessors?'

'Three altogether, all of them insane,' the King said. 'I will be number four.'

'Until I find a way to wield the Destroyer or bring down the Seven Stars,' Wong said. 'Then I'll destroy all four of you. Clean-up time.'

The King smiled at me, still held by the senior demons. 'Remember.' They all disappeared.

'Time for me to take over,' Wong said with satisfaction. 'You'll sit right here next to me as I accept their oaths of allegiance. And then I'll cut your arms off with your own Lord's weapon.'

'I really don't give a shit,' I said softly.

'Let's see how far we can take that,' Wong said. 'Maybe arms and legs both, and I'll keep you under my desk and use you as a footstool. The nigger is here too, isn't he.' He rubbed his hands together. 'This will be a lot of fun.'

Wong turned and sat on the throne. 'As soon as I'm finished here, I'll collect a little girl I've been wanting to play with for ages. And a huge black faggot who I might just make play with her before I have his balls cut off. Oh, I know.' He leaned his elbow on the edge of the throne and smiled. 'He can play with both of you, then you can do the honours.'

I didn't try to escape. I knew it would come for me. It had to come for me. I sat on the throne next to Wong and placed the sword across my knees. It would come.

I sat through oaths of allegiance from three hundred and forty-five senior demons. I counted them. Most of them grinned viciously at me without looking at Wong. The Snake Mothers especially made a point of glowering at me as they swore the oath.

'The ladies want you, Emma,' Wong said. 'Should I give you to them?'

'Oh, yes, please, Simon,' I said. 'I'd love to go and play with them.'

'No, I don't think so,' Wong said kindly. 'I think I'll keep you all to myself.'

Something huge and black materialised in the centre of the hall. It was like an enormous black cloud, but darker and more menacing. The cold seeped from it; the air around it glittered with condensation. The demons raced away from it, a flowing wave of panic.

'Oh *good*,' Wong said with satisfaction. 'I was wondering when it would turn up. This just gets better and better.'

The darkness coalesced into an enormous black turtle, its shell glistening with moisture. It was about five metres long. Its head was pointed and vicious. Its shell was curved and black. Its enormous feet were clawed.

The demons rushed away in panic. Most of the demons disappeared. It was faster than those that were left; it turned and raced right into the middle of them, grabbing them and snapping them in half with its enormous razor-sharp beak, one after the other. They didn't have a chance.

The demons began to scream and there was a crush at the door as they tried to get away.

The Turtle generated a blinding beam of chi and sent it through them, destroying every demon it touched.

Wong rose and sauntered down the stairs to face the creature.

It moved towards him, its mouth open, its huge beak razor-sharp. It wasn't slow; but it wasn't as fast as John was in human form. The remaining demons cowered against the walls.

Wong stopped in front of the creature, totally unconcerned. He concentrated and raised his arms.

The Turtle opened its mouth wider and a blast of pure white shining energy shot out, straight at Wong. Wong disappeared in the brilliance.

The Turtle closed its mouth and the beam of light stopped.

Wong was still there, smiling.

The Turtle moved closer. Wong didn't attempt to move out of the way. A light blue aura grew around his head. He smiled beatifically and the light surrounded him. It was full of crackling bolts of energy. He lowered his head and concentrated, and the energy quickly rushed to his hands, forming a huge ball of something that resembled chi, but a delicate shade of pale blue.

He smiled and raised his head to study the Turtle. He lifted his arms, still holding the huge ball of energy in his hands, closed his eyes and threw his head back. The energy went black. It streamed from him straight at the Turtle's head.

The Turtle raised its head and opened its mouth, a black shadow within the darkness of the energy. Its edges turned blue, then it shredded in the blast.

It dissipated. It was gone.

'No,' I moaned. 'No.' I took a deep, gasping breath. 'Oh God, no.'

'I am the most powerful thing that Hell has ever produced,' Wong said. 'Even the Xuan Wu is no match for me.'

He proceeded up the stairs to me.

'He was weak,' I said loudly. 'When he's back to full strength, he'll come after you and tear you into very small pieces.'

'I really hope so, because his cage is nearly ready,' Wong said as he seated himself on the throne. 'Now. Let's get to work.'

I bided my time. As soon as he brought in Simone and Leo, I would use the Destroyer to free us all.

CHAPTER FORTY-TWO

'Listen up,' Wong said conversationally.

The demons moved forward to hear him.

'There will be some changes. The King was old and stupid. Times have changed. We are mobile, we are active, and we will use the new technology to its fullest.'

None of the demons moved or spoke.

'We will travel to the four corners of the world. We will negotiate with the other Centres. We are going to take control.'

There was complete silence.

'Work is to start immediately on the construction of new hybrids. The old way is gone. There is a new way now. *My* way.'

'Lame,' I said under my breath. 'You've been watching too many Hollywood movies. You need a better scriptwriter.'

The doors flew open at the other end of the hall. There was a huge commotion, but I couldn't see what was causing it. Then demons began to disintegrate. Blinding white flashes of light burst through their ranks and destroyed them.

'Holy shit!' Wong shouted. 'What the hell is *that?*'

The source of the flashes cut a swathe through the demons. The beams of light went upwards and outwards and destroyed everything in their path.

'Stop it!' Wong yelled. 'Whatever that thing is, get in there and stop it!'

Two of the senior demons raced down the stairs, weapons in hand. They were destroyed before they were within three metres of it.

A figure emerged between the remaining demons and stopped at the bottom of the stairs. It was Simone. She was wearing her school uniform. A glowing white aura of shen energy surrounded her as she floated slightly above the floor, her arms out from her sides as if to help her balance. Her hair writhed around her head with the static. Her eyes were blinding white orbs, shining with shen energy.

'Hello, Emma,' she said, her little voice the same as it always was. 'I came to get you.'

'Hi, Simone,' I said. 'I'm perfectly okay and happy here. Please go back home.'

Wong rose to his feet. 'Good,' he said viciously. 'You are mine. Both of you.'

'You want to come home with me, Emma?' Simone said, the brilliance of the shen energy causing shadows around her.

'I'm sorry, sweetheart,' I said, trying to keep the desperation from my voice, 'but I promised the King that I'd stay here until your daddy comes back. So you don't have to worry about me. You can go home.'

'Oh, okay,' Simone said, her eyes still blinding. 'Let's get the King and talk to him. He might let you go.'

'The King is my prisoner,' Wong said. 'I am King.'

Simone seemed to notice Wong for the first time. 'I don't like you.'

'That doesn't really matter, sweetheart,' Wong said,

walking down the stairs. 'Because the way you feel about me makes absolutely no difference at all.'

'Go home *right now*!' I shouted.

Simone raised her hands slightly and hit Wong with a blast of shen, knocking him backwards off his feet.

He clambered to his feet, shook himself, and advanced towards Simone again. 'Not good enough, little girl. I am going to take your head off and put it next to your father's.'

Simone's face went rigid and she inhaled sharply. 'You killed my daddy.'

Wong smiled with malice. 'That's right, sweetheart. I took his head off.'

The white light in Simone's eyes went out. They returned to normal and widened. She dropped to stand on the floor, the aura disappeared, and her hair fell around her face. 'You *killed* my *daddy*!'

'That's right,' Wong said. 'I killed your daddy. I killed your mummy too.'

Simone stiffened, eyes still wide.

'I killed your mummy's brother, and your mummy's mother and father,' Wong said without emotion. 'I killed Charlie. I nearly killed Leo, but I didn't get the chance to finish him. And now I'm going to kill you.'

He concentrated, and the blue light grew around him. He smiled.

'NO!' I yelled and moved to jump between them. 'Simone, RUN!'

I hit a wall halfway down and slid onto the stairs. It was like an invisible barrier. I couldn't approach them.

The Snake came out and struck helplessly at the barrier.

The blue aura grew around Wong, crackling with lightning. His smile broadened, he raised his hands and a huge blast of the black stuff engulfed Simone with a roar like an airplane engine. She disappeared inside the dark energy beam.

The Snake struck again at the barrier, with absolutely no effect. I changed back, grabbed the Murasame and ripped it from its scabbard. I slashed at the barrier with it. I filled it with chi and tried to burn a hole through.

The energy was all around Simone; I couldn't see her. She didn't make a sound. Wong's face was twisted into an ugly grimace of satisfaction.

I put the black stuff into the sword and tried to use it to blast my way through the barrier. Nothing. I threw the sword to one side and pounded my fists on the invisible wall, crying out. Simone. No. 'No!' I sagged down the wall and pounded it helplessly. Simone. I wiped the tears out of my eyes; I couldn't see. I rested my forehead on the barrier. No.

Wong snapped his wrists and the beam of energy stopped. There was complete silence.

Simone stood there completely unharmed, a sweet smile on her little face.

Wong took a step back, unsure now, then raised his hands and began to gather the blue energy again.

'It's okay, Emma, this is my fight,' Simone said with a smile. Her eyes went black. Wong hesitated.

'You killed my daddy,' Simone said absently. 'You killed my mummy.'

She raised her hands.

Something formed above her head. It was difficult to see, because it was so dark. It was a whirlpool of nothingness. Black, empty, cold nothing. The creeping cold coming from it was colder and darker and emptier than anything I had ever felt.

Simone snapped her wrists above her head without looking up. Some of the blackness shot out of the whirlpool and gathered like writhing tendrils around her hands. She watched Wong with her black eyes.

Wong took a step back. 'No.'

'You killed my daddy. You killed my mummy.' Her little voice was as sweet as ever. 'You killed my Charlie. You hurt my Leo.' The black oily mist writhed around her hands and expanded.

Wong was paralysed. 'No.'

'I don't like you.'

He was frozen with terror. 'Yin.'

'Yes,' Simone said, as if from a million miles away. 'My daddy is yin.' She smiled serenely at Wong, her eyes still black. The whirlpool above her head grew and a cyclone of yin detached itself and spun around her head, making her hair fly upwards. It lengthened and darkened into a black writhing mass of shining strands. 'I am yin too, when I want to be.'

The moisture in the air around her froze, forming swirling icy sleet. Simone had gathered pure yin. Pure, dark, cold, absorbing death.

'Are you yang or yin?'

Wong was speechless with horror.

'I suppose it doesn't matter,' Simone said calmly as she approached him, her eyes still black, her hair writhing above her. She smiled sweetly, held out her hands and the yin leapt to him. 'Because you won't be around long enough to tell me.'

The yin spiralled. Wong watched it surround him. His mouth was open but he didn't make a sound. The yin spun like black ribbons around him; where it was close to him, he was sucked into it. Small parts of him separated and flew into the spiralling force. The holes in him grew larger. He raised his face, his mouth wide but silent.

Simone smiled as her black hair whipped around her head.

The yin spiralled up around him and circled his head. His eyes rolled up. His head dissolved. The rest followed. He was completely sucked into the yin. He was gone.

Simone held out her hands and the yin leapt back to them. She raised her arms, her face became a mask of rapture, and the whirlpool above her head absorbed the yin. It spiralled out of her hands, upwards into the vortex. The vortex shrank and disappeared.

Her eyes snapped back to normal and her hair lightened and fell to frame her face.

The barrier disappeared and I fell forwards. I pulled myself to my feet.

'Now,' she said, 'let's find the King and get you out of here.'

'I'm here,' the King said behind me. 'Hello, Simone.'

Simone's eyes went black again.

'No!' I shouted. 'Don't hurt him, Simone!'

'He took you away from me,' Simone said.

'He had to,' I said softly. 'It was the only way he could get both you and the bad demon here, so that you could destroy it.'

'Well done, my Lady,' the King said. 'I was right about you all the time.'

'Why did he do that?' Simone said.

'Because you were the only one strong enough to kill the bad demon,' I said. 'Even stronger than your daddy, right now. And the only way to get you here was to have me here first, so that you'd come and find me.'

'I want to take you home,' Simone said. 'If he doesn't let you go, I'm going to yin him.'

'He's not holding me here, Simone,' I said. 'I promised to stay, to keep you safe. I'm here by my own free will.'

She dropped her little head and her tawny hair fell forward around her face. 'I want you at home with me, Emma,' she whispered. 'You're all I've got left.'

'You are released from your oath, my Lady,' the King said. 'You can go home with her if you choose. The choice is yours.'

'I'm free to go?' I said.

'Yes, but please consider, Emma,' the King said. 'If you go with her, all deals are off. I won't make any attempt to keep her safe any more. And if the Dark Lord touches you while you are like this, you will be destroyed.' He smiled and shrugged. 'Stay here with me instead. When he returns, I will make you whole and the two of you can be everything you want for each other.'

'I want you at home with me, Emma,' Simone said, her voice small. 'I need you.'

I approached Simone and crouched in front of her, not touching her. 'Look inside me, Simone, very carefully.'

I felt her Inner Eye and stiffened with the agony. It snapped off before I screamed from the pain.

Simone's face screwed up and she turned to the King, furious. She pointed at me, glaring. 'Did you do this?'

'No, I swear, Princess,' the King said. 'I had nothing to do with it.'

Simone turned back to me and her little face softened. 'I don't care, Emma, I want you at home with me. Please come home.' She reached out to touch me but I pulled away.

'Stay here, Emma,' the King said. 'If you go with her, you will never have a chance to be whole.'

'I'll find a way to change her back,' Simone said fiercely.

The King just smiled indulgently at her.

I rose. I hesitated, watching the King.

'There isn't much of a decision to make, Emma,' he said gently.

'You are quite correct,' I said. 'If I were to stay with you instead of being with Simone when she needs me, then neither Xuan Wu nor I would ever forgive me. We would never put our needs before hers. There's no decision to make at all.'

I pulled the remaining black jade earring out of my ear and passed it to him. He held one hand above it and the diamond post floated out of the black jade coin. He returned the diamond to me without a word.

'How will you get me home, sweetheart?' I said.

'Hold my hand,' Simone said. 'I'll take you home.'

'I can't hold your hand, Simone. You know what I am.'

'They've done something to you, Emma, and we're going to take you home and fix it.' She held out her hand. 'It's okay. You know we can touch things without hurting them when we want to.'

I trusted her. I reached out and took her hand. I felt my shape dissolve, but held her hand anyway. Simone's eyes widened. She dropped my hand and I returned to normal.

'You looked like a Snake Mother, Emma.'

'I know, sweetheart,' I said. 'If you want to leave me here I would understand.'

'Bye, King,' Simone said. 'Don't come and visit us. You're not welcome.'

'I'm sure I'm not, Highness,' the King said with a wry smile. He took my hands, pulled me close and kissed me on the cheek. 'I would forsake my kingdom for you, you know,' he whispered into my ear.

I pulled away and he didn't attempt to hold me.

'I have something for you,' he said. 'A gift.'

He held out his hand and a braided lock of long, black hair appeared in it.

I suddenly found it very difficult to breathe.

'Take it,' he said. 'Remember.'

I took the hair out of his hand. It was smooth and silken. I raised it to my face. It smelled of the sea.

'Thank you,' I whispered.

'You are most welcome,' he said. 'Remember: any time.' He shrugged. 'Come and visit, I'd love to see you.

Until he returns, that is. After that you probably won't be able to come for coffee.'

'Where's Leo?' Simone said loudly. 'I want him to come too. I know he's here somewhere.'

'Leo is in the holding cells of Court Ten,' the King said. 'I have no control over the workings of the Courts, Princess. They are incredibly busy right now; they have more Immortals there than any time in recent history. The Celestial himself is managing this particular case. I suggest you take it up with him.'

'The Celestial?' Simone said.

'He means the Jade Emperor, Simone,' I said.

'Oh,' Simone said, very softly. She straightened. 'Okay, I'll go and talk to him.'

'You do that,' the King said.

He picked up the sword that Wong had dropped. He moved a few paces, collected the scabbard and put the sword away. He held it out to Simone. 'This is yours, I believe, Princess.'

Simone didn't move.

The King pushed the sword towards her. 'This is Dark Heavens. And until your father returns, my dear, it belongs to you.'

Simone silently moved forward and accepted the blade.

The King gestured towards me. 'The Murasame is yours. Use it well. I won't attempt to touch it, but you can call it when you are home and it will come to you. You are its master.'

'Come on, Emma,' Simone said, and held out her hand.

I didn't take her hand. 'One thing before I go, King.'

'Hmm?' His gorgeous face lit up.

'Do you know what I am?'

The King looked at me blankly, then roared with laughter. He fell over his knees laughing. He pulled himself up, still chuckling. He wiped his eyes. 'Oh, my.' He studied me, a huge grin on his face. 'Oh, dear.' He shook his head. 'The answer to your question, my Lady, is: yes. I do know what you are.' He chuckled again. 'The irony is superb. Goodbye.'

Simone and I were back in the living room of the Peak apartment.

Three green and gold baby dragons gambolled on the floor, rolling Gold's child between them, all of them squealing with delight. Jade, Gold and Amy watched them indulgently from the couches. The windows were fixed and the furniture had been restored.

When they saw Simone and me, they rushed over and embraced me tearfully. Then they all started talking together, asking me what had happened, then turned to Simone, checking that she was okay.

Michael and Rhonda came in, and Monica and Ah Yat too, when they heard the noise. Michael rushed to Simone, lifted her and pulled her close for a hug, making her squeal. Then he gently lowered her and threw his arms around me. Rhonda hugged and kissed us as well.

'Don't you ever go off by yourself like that again,' Rhonda scolded Simone, then grabbed her and held her tight.

Something moved in the corner of my eye. The ring had been sitting on the hall table next to the front door. It floated into the air, then the stone took human form. He came to me and embraced me. He pulled back and held my face in both hands. 'It's good to have you back, dear,' he said, his pale blue eyes shining under his white hair. He dropped his hands onto my shoulders. 'Now, hold your hand out. I want to go home.'

I put my hand out and he folded up, back into the ring, which slid itself onto my finger.

That feels so much better, it said. *It's good to be home. Who was buying your clothes? You look like a street sleeper.*

I didn't have a chance to say something scathing. The doorbell rang and everybody froze.

'It's two small demons,' Michael said softly. 'Everybody back.'

I knew who it was. 'It's okay,' I said, and went to open the door.

Yi Hao and Er Hao stood uncomfortably on the other side of the gate.

'Come on in, ladies,' I said. 'Come and meet the family, and then I'd better find something for you to do.'

The two demon servants came in, obviously intimidated by the large number of people in the living room. Yi Hao held a small box wrapped with red and gold paper.

'It's okay, nobody will hurt you,' I said, and closed the door behind them. 'These two little demons looked after me.'

'This is for you, ma'am,' Yi Hao said, holding the gift out to me. 'I don't know what it is; he said to give it to you.'

I took the gift to examine it.

'What is it?' Michael said.

'I have no idea,' I said. 'Simone, what's inside it?'

'A CD,' Simone said. 'And a phone.'

'What on earth for?' I said. 'Simone, is it safe to open?'

'Can't you see inside it yourself, Emma?' Michael said softly.

'It's safe to open,' Simone said.

I knelt next to the coffee table and opened the box. The little dragons raced up, wide-eyed with curiosity. The baby stone lifted itself and hovered above them, watching as well.

565

Inside the box was, as Simone had said, a CD and a phone. The CD was a writable one, obviously containing files. There was a note on top.

Call me. Come and have lunch, I'd love to see you. Here's your story. Please send me a copy when it's all finished. Have you thought about publishing it? It's a great read. I loved your description of me.

George R.

I put the lid on the box and pushed it to one side, then turned to sit on the sofa.

'I suppose I'd better tell you where I've been for the last three weeks.'

We sat around the dining table: Jade, Gold, Michael, Simone, me. It was five of us now, and would be for a very long time.

'Can you see him?' I said.

'Yes,' Gold said. Jade nodded. They didn't elaborate.

'Tell us,' Simone said.

Jade and Gold shared a look.

'Something's wrong,' Simone whispered. 'Is he okay?'

Jade sighed. It was Gold who spoke. 'Underneath the icecap of the North Pole, where the water is freezing and dark, swims a great black Turtle, its shell half a *li* across.'

Simone grabbed my hand before I could pull it away.

I changed, knocking the chair over behind me with my tail.

Michael, Jade and Gold all shot to their feet. Jade moved into a guard stance, but Gold and Michael both generated enormous balls of chi and hurled them straight at my head.

I closed my eyes and waited. Nothing happened. I opened my eyes.

'They did something to Emma, everybody,' Simone said, her voice small. She had risen to stand next to me and was still holding my hand, her other arm protectively in front of me. 'Don't try to hurt her. It's really her. Okay?'

Michael turned his Inner Eye on me and gasped with the pain.

'Whoa,' he said. 'You're half *demon*.'

'Who did this to you, my Lady?' Gold said.

'One Two Two,' I said, my voice hissing. 'It's still me, I swear. Simone's touch forces me to take ...' I hesitated, then took a deep breath. 'True Form.'

'We'll need to tell your students,' Gold said. 'And the staff of the Mountain. So that nobody attacks you.'

I shook Simone's hand free so that I changed back. I picked up my chair and flopped into it. I put my elbows on the table and my head in my hands. 'No. Please. I don't want them to know.'

'Don't tell anybody,' Simone said. 'We can fix it.'

'My Lady,' Gold said.

'Geez, this really sucks, Emma,' Michael said.

'What's done is done,' I said. 'Tell me about the Turtle. Under the icecap of the North Pole.'

Gold looked down. 'The Turtle has no memory of what it is. It has no intelligence. It is ...' He looked straight into my eyes, his own filled with anguish. 'It is a beast. It has no consciousness, no sentience, no awareness. All it knows ...' He breathed a deep sigh. 'All it knows is that it has lost all that is dear to it. It searches through the darkness and cries.'

'No,' Simone said softly.

'At least now he's whole,' I said.

Jade and Gold looked at each other again.

'He did rejoin?' I said. 'He *did* become whole?'

'No,' Jade said, barely audible. 'The Serpent is swimming in the stormy freezing waters of the Antarctic, half a world away.'

Simone moved to grab my hand again but I managed to avoid her.

'He has lost everything,' Jade whispered. 'Only the Heavens know when he will return.'

Gold looked back at me and his voice became firmer. 'Remember, my Lady. He has promised. He will find you. He will Raise you. He will marry you. And you will go to live on his Mountain with him.'

'Oh my God,' I said softly.

'What, Emma?' Simone said.

Jade and Gold looked at each other again.

'He didn't think at all when he made that promise to me,' I said. 'He is so stupid sometimes.' I glared at Jade and Gold. 'Why didn't you tell us?'

They both looked down.

'What?' Simone said again.

'He'll have to *find* me,' I said softly.

'But you're not lost,' Simone said. Then she understood. 'No.'

'It wasn't just an oath, Simone. It was a curse,' I whispered.

'I'm going to be very cross with him when he comes back,' Simone said.

'Wait in line.' I leaned back. 'Well, whatever happens, he'll Raise me and marry me. I don't care about the meantime. I'll just wait.'

'I'll wait with you,' Simone said. 'We'll find a way to fix you up, we'll go and find Leo, and then we'll wait together. We have each other, and we'll be fine, whatever happens.'

She hopped off her chair and climbed into my lap. I wrapped my arms around her.

I changed again. I lowered myself onto my coils, wrapping my tail around so that she could sit on me. She sat on my black scaly body and we held each other close. 'I love you, Emma,' she whispered, leaning her head on me. 'Everything will be okay.'

I buried my face in her hair and held her tight. 'I know.'

I wandered through the darkened office. Neon lights from the Wan Chai street lit up the ceiling. Complete silence. I paused for a moment, enjoying the solitude. Not another living thing; I could sense the security guards on the ground floor, far, far below, but that was all.

I'd stayed late to review the reports for the latest recruitment drive. Gold had done well. Some of these kids would go far.

I sighed. Time to go home. I went to the corner of the building. I couldn't help myself; it was a ritual I indulged in every evening before I went home.

The door was closed. I opened it and went into his office.

The desk was immaculate; I'd tidied the paperwork after he'd gone, to tie up the loose ends he'd left. He wouldn't recognise it when he returned.

I went to the chair, stood behind it and ran my hand over the back, looking out the window. For a moment it was as if he was there with me, searching for me, and then the feeling left me.

Time to go home. The family would be waiting for me. I turned and went out, closing his office door behind me.

The Turtle surged blindly through the thick water.
Its shell scraped the ice with a vibration felt for miles.
It searched through the darkness.
It cried.
There was no answer.

The Serpent tossed its head above the waves. The sky
was roiling and low.
The water was dark and freezing.
It cried.
There was no answer.

GLOSSARY

A NOTE ON LANGUAGE

The Chinese language is divided by a number of different dialects and this has been reflected throughout my story. The main dialect spoken in Hong Kong is Cantonese, and many of the terms I've used are in Cantonese. The main method for transcribing Cantonese into English is the Yale system, which I have hardly used at all in this book, preferring to use a simpler phonetic method for spelling the Cantonese. Apologies to purists, but I've chosen ease of readability over phonetic correctness.

The dialect mainly spoken on the Mainland of China is Putonghua (also called Mandarin Chinese), which was originally the dialect used in the north of China but has spread to become the standard tongue. Putonghua has a strict and useful set of transcription rules called pinyin, which I've used throughout for Putonghua terms. As a rough guide to pronunciation, the 'Q' in pinyin is pronounced 'ch', the 'X' is 'sh' and the 'Zh' is a softer 'ch' than the 'Q' sound. Xuan Wu is therefore pronounced 'Shwan Wu'.

I've spelt chi with the 'ch' throughout the book, even though in pinyin it is qi, purely to aid in readability.

Qing Long and Zhu Que I have spelt in pinyin to assist anybody who'd like to look into these interesting deities further.

Aberdeen Typhoon Shelter: A harbour on the south side of Hong Kong Island that is home to a large number of small and large fishing boats. Some of the boats are permanently moored there and are residences.

Admiralty: The first station after the MTR train has come through the tunnel onto Hong Kong Island from Kowloon, and a major traffic interchange.

Amah: Domestic helper.

Ancestral tablet: A tablet inscribed with the name of the deceased, which is kept in a temple or at the residence of the person's descendants and occasionally provided with incense and offerings to appease the spirit.

Anime (Japanese): Animation; can vary from cute children's shows to violent horror stories for adults, and everything in between.

Bai Hu (Putonghua): The White Tiger of the West.

Bo: Weapon — staff.

Bodhisattva: A being who has attained Buddhist Nirvana and has returned to earth to help others achieve Enlightenment.

Bo lei: A very dark and pungent Chinese tea, often drunk with yum cha to help digest the sometimes heavy and rich food served there.

Bu keqi (Putonghua) pronounced, roughly, 'bu kerchi': 'You're welcome.'

Buddhism: The system of beliefs that life is an endless journey through reincarnation until a state of perfect detachment or Nirvana is reached.

Cantonese: The dialect of Chinese spoken mainly in the south of China and used extensively in Hong Kong. Although in written form it is nearly identical to Putonghua, when spoken it is almost unintelligible to Putonghua speakers.

Causeway Bay: Large shopping and office district on Hong Kong Island. Most of the Island's residents seem to head there on Sunday for shopping.

Central: The main business district in Hong Kong, on the waterfront on Hong Kong Island.

Central Committee: Main governing body of Mainland China.

Cha siu bow: Dim sum served at yum cha; a steamed bread bun containing barbecued pork and gravy in the centre.

Chek Lap Kok: Hong Kong's new airport on a large swathe of reclaimed land north of Lantau Island.

Cheongsam (Cantonese): Traditional Chinese dress, with a mandarin collar, usually closed with toggles and loops, and with splits up the sides.

Cheung Chau: Small dumbbell-shaped island off the coast of Hong Kong Island, about an hour away by ferry.

Chi: Energy. The literal meaning is 'gas' or 'breath' but in martial arts terms it describes the energy (or breath) of life that exists in all living things.

Chi gong (Cantonese): Literally, 'energy work'. A series of movements expressly designed for manipulation of chi.

Chinese New Year: The Chinese calendar is lunar, and New Year falls at a different time each Western calendar. Chinese New Year usually falls in either January or February.

Ching: A type of life energy, ching is the energy of sex and reproduction, the Essence of Life. Every person is born with a limited amount of ching and as this energy is drained they grow old and die.

Chiu Chow: A southeastern province of China.

Choy sum (Cantonese): A leafy green Chinese vegetable vaguely resembling English spinach.

City Hall: Hall on the waterfront in Central on Hong Kong Island containing theatres and a large restaurant.

Confucianism: A set of rules for social behaviour designed to ensure that all of society runs smoothly.

Congee: A gruel made by boiling rice with savoury ingredients such as pork or thousand-year egg. Usually eaten for breakfast but can be eaten as a meal or snack any time of the day.

Connaught Road: Main thoroughfare through the middle of Central District in Hong Kong, running parallel to the waterfront and with five lanes each side.

Cross-Harbour Tunnel: Tunnel that carries both cars and MTR trains from Hong Kong Island to Kowloon under the Harbour.

Cultural Revolution: A turbulent period of recent Chinese history (1966–75) during which gangs of young people called Red Guards overthrew 'old ways of thinking' and destroyed many ancient cultural icons.

Dai pai dong (Cantonese): Small open-air restaurant.

Daisho: A set of katana, wakizashi, and sometimes a tanto (small dagger), all matching bladed weapons used by samurai in ancient times.

Dan tian: Energy centre, a source of energy within the body. The central dan tian is roughly located in the solar plexus.

Daujie (Cantonese): 'Thank you', used exclusively when a gift is given.

Dim sum (Cantonese): Small dumplings in bamboo steamers served at yum cha. Usually each dumpling is less than three centimetres across and four are found in each steamer. There are a number of different types, and standard types of dim sum are served at every yum cha.

Discovery Bay: Residential enclave on Lantau Island, quite some distance from the rush of Hong Kong Island and only reachable by ferry.

Dojo (Japanese): Martial arts training school.

Eight Immortals: A group of iconic Immortals from Taoist mythology, each one representing a human condition. Stories of their exploits are part of popular Chinese culture.

Er Lang: The Second Heavenly General, second-in-charge of the running of Heavenly affairs. Usually depicted as a young man with three eyes and accompanied by his faithful dog.

Fortune sticks: A set of bamboo sticks in a bamboo holder. The questioner kneels in front of the altar and shakes the holder until one stick rises above the rest and falls out. This stick has a number that is translated into the fortune by temple staff.

Fung shui (or feng shui): The Chinese system of geomancy that links the environment to the fate of those living in it. A house with good internal and external fung shui assures its residents of good luck in their life.

Gay-lo (Cantonese slang): gay, homosexual.

Ge ge (Putonghua): Big brother.

Guangdong: The province of China directly across the border from Hong Kong.

Guangzhou: The capital city of Guangdong Province, about an hour away by road from Hong Kong. A large bustling commercial city rivalling Hong Kong in size and activity.

Gundam (Japanese): Large humanoid robot armour popular in Japanese cartoons.

Gung hei fat choy (Cantonese): Happy New Year.

Gwun Gong (or Guan Gong): A southern Chinese Taoist deity; a local General who attained Immortality and is venerated for his strengths of loyalty and justice and his ability to destroy demons.

H'suantian Shangdi (Cantonese): Xuan Tian Shang Di in the Wade-Giles method of writing Cantonese words.

Har gow: Dim sum served at yum cha; a steamed dumpling with a thin skin of rice flour dough containing prawns.

Hei sun (Cantonese): Arise.

Ho ak (Cantonese): Okay.

Ho fan (Cantonese): Flat white noodles made from rice; can be either boiled in soup or stir-fried.

Hong Kong Jockey Club: a private Hong Kong institution that runs and handles all of the horseracing and legal gambling in Hong Kong. There can be billions of Hong Kong dollars in bets on a single race meeting.

Hutong (Putonghua): Traditional square Chinese house, built around a central courtyard.

ICAC: Independent Commission Against Corruption; an independent government agency focused on tracking down corruption in Hong Kong.

Jade Emperor: The supreme ruler of the Taoist Celestial Government.

Journey to the West: A classic of Chinese literature written during the Ming Dynasty by Wu Cheng'En. The story of the Monkey King's journey to India with a Buddhist priest to collect scriptures and return them to China.

Kata (Japanese): A martial arts 'set'; a series of moves to practise the use of a weapon or hand-to-hand skills.

Katana: Japanese sword.

KCR: A separate above-ground train network that connects with the MTR and travels to the border with Mainland China. Used to travel to towns in the New Territories.

Kitchen God: A domestic deity who watches over the activities of the family and reports annually to the Jade Emperor.

Koi (Japanese): Coloured ornamental carp.

Kowloon: Peninsula opposite the Harbour from Hong Kong Island, a densely packed area of highrise buildings. Actually on the Chinese Mainland, but separated by a strict border dividing Hong Kong from China.

Kowloon City: District in Kowloon just before the entrance to the Cross-Harbour Tunnel.

Kwan Yin: Buddhist icon; a woman who attained Nirvana and became a Buddha but returned to Earth to help others achieve Nirvana as well. Often represented as a goddess of Mercy.

Lai see (Cantonese): A red paper envelope used to give cash as a gift for birthdays and at New Year. It's believed that for every dollar given ten will return during the year.

Lai see dao loy (Cantonese): 'Lai see, please!'

Lantau Island: One of Hong Kong's outlying islands, larger than Hong Kong Island but not as densely inhabited.

Li: Chinese unit of measure, approximately half a kilometre.

Lo Wu: The area of Hong Kong that contains the border crossing. Lo Wu is an area that covers both sides of the border; it is in both Hong Kong and China.

Lo Wu Shopping Centre: A large shopping centre directly across the Hong Kong/Chinese border on the Chinese side. A shopping destination for Hong Kong residents in search of a bargain.

Love hotel: Hotel with rooms that are rented by the hour by young people who live with their parents (and therefore have no privacy) or businessmen meeting their mistresses for sex.

M'goi sai (Cantonese): 'Thank you very much.'

M'sai (Cantonese): Literally, 'no need', but it generally means 'you're welcome'.

Macau: One-time Portuguese colony to the west of Hong Kong in the Pearl River Delta, about an hour away by jet hydrofoil; now another Special Administrative Region of China. Macau's port is not as deep and sheltered as Hong Kong's so it has never been the busy trade port that Hong Kong is.

Mafoo (Cantonese): Groom.

Mah jong: Chinese game played with tiles. The Chinese play it differently from the polite game played by many Westerners; it is played for money and can often be a cut-throat competition between skilled players, rather like poker.

Manga: Japanese illustrated novel or comic book.

Mei mei (Putonghua): Little sister.

MTR: Fast, cheap, efficient and spotlessly clean subway train system in Hong Kong. Mostly standing room, and during rush hour so packed that it is often impossible to get onto a carriage.

Na Zha: Famous mythical Immortal who was so powerful as a child that he killed one of the dragon sons of the Dragon King. He gained Immortality by unselfishly travelling into Hell to release his parents who had been held in punishment for his crime. A spirit of Youthfulness.

New Territories: A large area of land between Kowloon and Mainland China that was granted to extend Hong Kong. Less crowded than Hong Kong and Kowloon, the New Territories are green and hilly with highrise New Towns scattered through them.

Nunchucks: Short wooden sticks held together with chains; a martial arts weapon.

Opium Wars: (1839–60) A series of clashes between the then British Empire and the Imperial Chinese Government over Britain's right to trade opium to China. It led to a number of humiliating defeats and surrenders by China as they were massively outclassed by modern Western military technology.

Pa Kua (Cantonese): The Eight Symbols, a central part of Taoist mysticism. Four of these Eight Symbols flank the circle in the centre of the Korean flag.

Pak Tai: One of Xuan Wu's many names; this one is used in Southern China.

Peak Tower: Tourist sightseeing spot at the top of the Peak Tram. Nestled between the two highest peaks on the Island and therefore not the highest point in Hong Kong, but providing a good view for tourist photographs.

Peak Tram: Tram that has been running for many years between Central and the Peak. Now mostly a tourist attraction because of the steepness of the ride and the view.

Peak, the: Prestigious residential area of Hong Kong, on top of the highest point of the centre of Hong Kong Island. The view over the Harbour and highrises is spectacular, and the property prices there are some of the highest in the world.

Pokfulam: Area of Hong Kong west of the main business districts, facing the open ocean rather than the harbour. Contains large residential apartment blocks and a very large hillside cemetery.

Putonghua: Also called Mandarin, the dialect of Chinese spoken throughout China as a standard language. Individual provinces have their own dialects but Putonghua is spoken as a common tongue.

Qing Long (Putonghua) pronounced, roughly, Ching Long: The Azure Dragon of the East.

Ramen (Japanese): Instant two-minute noodles.

Repulse Bay: A small swimming beach surrounded by an expensive residential enclave of high- and low-rise apartment blocks on the south side of Hong Kong Island.

Salute, Chinese: The left hand is closed into a fist and the right hand is wrapped around it. Then the two hands are held in front of the chest and sometimes shaken.

Sashimi (Japanese): Raw fish.

Seiza: Japanese kneeling position.

Sensei (Japanese): Master.

Seppuku: Japanese ritual suicide by disembowelment: hari-kiri.

Sha Tin: A New Territories 'New Town', consisting of a large shopping centre surrounded by a massive number of highrise developments on the banks of the Shing Mun River.

Shaolin: Famous temple, monastery and school of martial arts, as well as a style of martial arts.

Shen: Shen has two meanings, in the same sense that the English word spirit has two meanings ('ghost' and 'energy'). Shen can mean an Immortal being, something like a god in Chinese mythology. It is also the spirit that dwells within a person, the energy of their soul.

Shenzhen: The city at the border between Hong Kong and China, a 'special economic zone' where capitalism has been allowed to flourish. Most of the goods manufactured in China for export to the West are made in Shenzhen.

Sheung Wan: The western end of the Hong Kong Island MTR line; most people get off the train before reaching this station.

Shoji (Japanese): Screen of paper stretched over a wooden frame.

Shui (Cantonese): 'Water'.

Shui gow: Chinese dumplings made of pork and prawn meat inside a dough wrapping, boiled in soup stock.

Shroff Office: A counter in a car park where you pay the parking fee before returning to your car.

Sifu (Cantonese): Master.

Siu mai: Dim sum served at yum cha; a steamed dumpling with a skin of wheat flour containing prawn and pork.

Sow mei (Cantonese): A type of Chinese tea, with a greenish colour and a light, fragrant flavour.

Stanley Market: A famous market on the south side of Hong Kong island, specialising in tourist items.

Star Ferry: Small oval green and white ferries that run a cheap service between Hong Kong Island and Kowloon.

Sticky rice: Dim sum served at yum cha; glutinous rice filled with savouries such as pork and thousand-year egg, wrapped in a green leaf and steamed.

Tae kwon do: Korean martial art.

Tai chi: A martial art that consists of a slow series of movements, used mainly as a form of exercise and chi manipulation to enhance health and extend life. Usable as a lethal martial art by advanced practitioners. There are several different styles of tai chi, including Chen, Yang and Wu, named after the people who invented them.

Tai chi chuan: Full correct name for tai chi.

Tai Koo Shing: large enclosed shopping mall on the north side of Hong Kong.

Tao Teh Ching: A collection of writings by Lao Tzu on the elemental nature of Taoist philosophy.

Tao, the: 'The Way'. A perfect state of consciousness equivalent to the Buddhist Nirvana, in which a person becomes completely attuned with the universe and achieves Immortality. Also the shortened name of a collection of writings (the Tao Teh Ching) on Taoist philosophy written by Lao Tzu.

Taoism: Similar to Buddhism, but the state of perfection can be reached by a number of different methods, including alchemy and internal energy manipulation as well as meditation and spirituality.

Tatami (Japanese): Rice-fibre matting.

Temple Street: A night market along a street on Kowloon side in Hong Kong. Notorious as a triad gang hangout as well as being one of Hong Kong's more colourful markets.

Ten Levels of Hell: It is believed that a human soul travels through ten levels of Hell, being judged and punished for a particular type of sin at each level. Upon reaching the lowest, or tenth, level, the soul is given an elixir of forgetfulness and returned to Earth to reincarnate and live another life.

Teppan (Japanese): Hotplate used for cooking food at teppanyaki.

Teppanyaki (Japanese): Meal where the food is cooked on the teppan in front of the diners and served when done.

Thousand-year egg: A duck egg that's been preserved in a mixture of lime, ash, tea and salt for one hundred days, making the flesh of the egg black and strong in flavour.

Tikuanyin (Cantonese; or Tikuanyum): Iron Buddha Tea. A dark, strong and flavourful black Chinese tea. Named because, according to legend, the first tea bush of this type was found behind a roadside altar containing an iron statue of Kwan Yin.

Tin Hau (Cantonese): Taoist deity, worshipped by seafarers.

Triad: Hong Kong organised-crime syndicate. Members of the syndicates are also called triads.

Tsim Sha Tsui: Main tourist and entertainment district on Kowloon side, next to the Harbour.

Tsing Ma Bridge: Large suspension bridge connecting Kowloon with Lantau Island, used to connect to the Airport Expressway.

Typhoon: A hurricane that occurs in Asia. Equivalent to a hurricane in the US or a cyclone in Australia.

Wakizashi: Japanese dagger, usually matched with a sword to make a set called a daisho.

Wan Chai: Commercial district on Hong Kong Island, between the offices and designer stores of Central and the shopping area of Causeway Bay. Contains office buildings and restaurants, and is famous for its nightclubs and girlie bars.

Wan sui (Putonghua): 'Ten thousand years'; traditional greeting for the Emperor, wishing him ten thousand times ten thousand years of life.

Wei? (Cantonese): 'Hello?' when answering the phone.

Wing chun: Southern style of Chinese kung fu. Made famous by Bruce Lee, this style is fast, close in ('short') and lethal. It's also a 'soft' style where the defender uses the attacker's weight and strength against him or her, rather than relying on brute force to hit hard.

Wire-fu: Move kung-fu performed on wires so that the actors appear to be flying.

Won ton (Cantonese): Chinese dumplings made mostly of pork with a dough wrapping and boiled in soup stock. Often called 'short soup' in the West.

Won ton mien (Cantonese): 'won ton noodles'; won ton boiled in stock with noodles added to the soup.

Wu shu (Putonghua): A general term to mean all martial arts.

Wudang (Putonghua): A rough translation could be 'true martial arts'. The name of the mountain in Hubei Province; also the name of the martial arts academy and the style of martial arts taught there. Xuan Wu was a Celestial 'sponsor' of the Ming Dynasty and the entire mountain complex of temples and monasteries was built by the government of the time in his honour.

Wudangshan (Putonghua): 'Shan' means 'mountain'; Wudang Mountain.

Xie xie (Putonghua): 'Thank you.'

Xuan Wu (Putonghua) pronounced, roughly, 'Shwan Wu': means 'Dark Martial Arts'; the Black Turtle of the North, Mr Chen.

Yamen: Administration, as in Yamen Building.

Yang: One of the two prime forces of the Universe in Taoist philosophy. Yang is the Light: masculine, bright, hot and hard.

Yang and yin: The two prime forces of the universe, when joined together form the One, the essence of everything. The symbol of yang and yin shows each essence containing a small part of the other.

Yellow Emperor: An ancient mythological figure, the Yellow Emperor is credited with founding civilisation and inventing clothing and agriculture.

Yin: One of the two prime forces of the universe in Taoist philosophy. Yin is Darkness: feminine, dark, cold and soft.

Yuexia Loaren (Putonghua): 'Old Man Under the Moon'; a Taoist deity responsible for matchmaking.

Yum cha (Cantonese): Literally 'drink tea'. Most restaurants hold yum cha between breakfast and mid-afternoon. Tea is served, and waitresses wheel around trolleys containing varieties of dim sum.

Yuzhengong (Putonghua): 'Find the True Spirit'; the name of the palace complex on Wudang Mountain.

Zhu Que (Putonghua) pronounced, roughly, Joo Chway: the Red Phoenix of the South.

Acknowledgements

The journey is far from complete, but the publication of the final book in the Dark Heavens trilogy is something of a milestone, and I'd like to thank those who helped along the way.

Alana and Fiona, who have been reading this story from the first day I started writing it, and have provided help, encouragement, advice, and viral marketing.

My family in Canberra who have told everybody they know all about my books with unrestrained pride.

Anni Haig-Smith my agent, who is accountant, advisor, and sometimes babysitter.

Stephanie Smith who took a gamble on an unpublished author which I hope has paid off as much as she wished it to. All the staff at HarperCollins, who work so very hard to make these books as successful as they could possibly be, and a particular thank you to Darren Holt for making the covers of my books so eye-catching.

My kids, Will and Maddy, who have given up trying to talk to me when I'm tapping away at my computer and just walk away with bemused resignation.

My wonderful husband Jason who is my one-man cheer squad.

Hikari Remora. You guys rock and yes, you do provide me with inspiration, and yes watch for yourselves in future volumes.

All my fans. I'm still a bit bewildered at the concept that I have fans. I've received so many wonderful emails and letters and I appreciate every single one of them. Don't despair, everybody, this is just the beginning of the story and there is very much more to come.

Kylie Chan
June 2007